NAERO'S RUN

A SPACER CLANS ADVENTURE

BOOK ONE

Titles by Mason Elliott

The Spacer Clans Adventures, Cycle One:

NAERO'S RUN
NAERO'S GAMBIT
NAERO'S FURY

The Spacer Clans Adventures, Cycle Two:

NAERO'S MASTERY*

The Citation Series, Cycle One:

Naero's War, Book One: THE ANNEXATION WAR
Naero's War, Book Two: THE HIGH CRUSADE
Naero's War, Book Three: NAERO'S TRIAL

The Citation Series, Cycle Two:

Naero's War, Book Four: THE GAMMA QUADRANT*

Short Fiction in Ebook Format

THE PERMIT

Fantasy with Author Garan R. R. Faraday
MERGEWORLD, BOOK 1
MERGEWORLD, BOOK 2
MERGEWORLD, BOOK 3*

(*Forthcoming)

NAERO'S RUN

Mason Elliott

High Mark Publishing

High Mark Publishing
www.highmarkpublishing.com

Seattle & Portland, Chicago, London

NAERO'S
RUN

by
Mason Elliott
Kindle Edition
© 2012 by Mason Elliott. All rights reserved.
Published by High Mark Publishing
ISBN 978-1-930451-04-9
Watch for other titles by this author in the future.

Cover Art by
Frank Miller
frankmillerdesign.com

Edition Notes
If you do not see this edition note here in this spot on the copyright page and on the very last page of your ebook or print version of this title, then you are not getting the final, polished version of this novel that the publisher, editors, and author intended for you to receive. Please contact either the publisher or the author via their emails or websites if you do not see the following update code:

High Mark Publishing Update Code K2428E

1

The stars belong to everyone.

That's what Spacers believe.

All of the sentient races–everything that exists–came from the stars. No one owns them.

Whatever any other sentients and the Gigacorps claim.

The stars are always free.

In the end, everything and everyone returns to them.

Naero's parents, her friends, and her space-faring people taught her to cherish and respect the harsh beauty of space for what it was and for what it offered: Freedom. Challenge. Everything.

Her mother was her sun, and gave her light, life, and love.

Her father was her ship, her courage and adventure.

In her Spacer Clan she found herself, others–knowledge, strength and joy. Naero woke up in her quarters and scribbled down the poetry and thoughts that had danced in her head while she snoozed. She scrawled on an old-style lighted pad with a pen she kept in reach of her bunk, the same way her illustrious father did.

The way he taught her. To be a poet warrior.

A philosopher king...or queen.

She let the pad fade, lay back down, and drifted off again, one night before her nineteenth birthday. One year before she'd come of age and could captain a ship–her own ship–just as her famous mother had done at that age.

A strange dream overtook her–a nightmare, really.

She struggled against some kind of devouring darkness. It penetrated her very flesh, violating her mind with horror and abject agony. No matter how she resisted, it absorbed her like a giant amoeba.

Yet the attacking darkness came from within her as well, and that was the most frightening part of it all somehow. The fact that such negative energy and twisted desires were part of her, and she part of them.

Parts of her secretly enjoyed some of those demented feelings–even yearned for them.

They lusted for the destroying power to subjugate everything and everyone to her will, and inflict suffering and misery upon them all, crushing and decimating them under the grinding heel of her enraged might.

Just as her strength to resist failed, right on the verge of her being swallowed up by the insane annihilation, the darkness parted.

A shining, beautiful, green young man with flowing golden hair appeared, his blinding sword cutting through the deep shadows.

She thrust both arms toward him for rescue.

He plunged his blade through her forehead, transfixing her gasping face upon its blazing length. She heard, felt his voice in her mind.

I'm sorry. This will not hold the Chaos back for long.

He jerked his sword free...

*

Naero awoke in a voiceless scream, thrashing in terror and clutching her throbbing forehead.

She sat up in her darkened gray, three-by-four meter cabin, still serving with her aunt's Merchant Clan Fleet, still on their way through Triax Corps space to Irpul-4.

But in an alarmed daze, she glanced around at her inactive wall and ceiling screens rising two and a half meters above her bunk panel.

Her morning alarm chimed.

She sprang naked from her cluttered bunk–Naero always slept nude.

She tripped over the stinky junk on her floor, and punched up a blinding splash of lights and a mirror on her port screenwall.

Her wild movements scattered and splashed muted pics and vids of family, friends, and new ship designs and schematics she could only drool over all across the other screenwalls and ceiling like panic-stricken birds.

Her preset systems struggled to light, wake up, and compensate in response to her frantic movements. Winking as they came online.

Naero gasped for air and pulled her long raven hair apart. Checked for the gaping wound in her forehead that she fully expected to see there.

Nothing. Not a damn thing.

Just a few inflamed zits and her stupid pale forehead under her slender, trembling hands that held up her long, jet black hair over wide, dark violet eyes. Eyes and hair she got from her pretty mom.

She caught her heaving breath, nostrils still flaring. She stepped back and let her hands fall back to her sides, her black hair droop back down over her face.

Her nightmare had seemed so real.

She sat down slowly on the edge of her bunk, still confused and shaking.

Naero shook her aching head, staring down at empty ration cans of Spum, the only blue meat on the market, in its mysterious sweet-and-sour, blue jelly sauce. Along with various packages of other assorted bizarre snacks and junk food, hoarded from numerous interstellar ports of call.

All gathered together for one orgasmic private pig-out session the night before her birthday. She had even skipped dinner with her mates in anticipation of her little guilty pleasure feast.

The smell in the aftermath grew rank.

Eating all that crap must have really done a number on her brain. No wonder she'd had nightmares and flipped out.

Four time. The first four bells of the new day. Her birthday.

No time like the present to get her ass in gear and get on with life. Plenty to get done before her duty shift.

Back on Old Terra it would have been April first by the old calendar, the basis for the Spacer standard year, day, hour, etc.

What once people on the old homeworld called April Fool's Day– before humans finally left their dying world behind, took to the stars, thankfully. Some even had the foresight to evolve into Spacers.

Her ancient history said that it had once been a day for people to play tricks on each other and fool one another with fake nonsense.

Hell, Naero already played so many goofy jokes and scams on her friends and family. They expected them from her on a regular basis.

Almost.

Therefore, in honor of her birthday, she had a special joke planned for everyone. It would be a master stroke of genius if ever she had come up with one.

And only she could pull it off.

First she had to get her mates started for their secret training session.

She punched up Gallan on her com.

"You up, big guy?"

Her extra-large bestest friend answered, his holo floating in the air at about half-size as he slipped into his togs, sealing them up.

"Just getting dressed. Meet you in Practice Room 35 with the others. Sheesh, put some clothes on, N."

"I intend to. Nothing you haven't seen before, buddy. What do you care? You like guys."

He grimaced. "Still, it's just courteous. See ya."

Next, wake her Spacer gal pals.

Punch up Chaela.

Audio response only; holo blocked. Animalistic groan.

"I will kill your dumb ass."

"Uh, okay, Chae. I'll get back to you. It's Naero? Remember, we agreed to–"

Another louder groan.

"I will hurt you!"

"I'll just check back in ten. Bye."

That hadn't gone too well.

Call up Saemar. Always taking a chance with her as well, in other ways.

Holo blocked on her end this time, thank goodness.

"Hey, Saemar. Wakey wakey."

"Oh, Naero? Hi, sweetie. Thanks for calling."

Unfortunately, Saemar flipped her holo on, revealing flashes of some strange guy's naked back, arm, and hairy butt.

Naero could even hear the guy snoring.

"So…can you join us, Saemar? You aren't too…busy, are you there?"

"What, him? We were at it all night in one of the flight simulators. He comes over ta my place for a couple more runs–and then he passes out on me."

"Who…is that? Bad, bad idea. Scrap that. I don't wanna know."

Naero heard a groan and the guy mutter. "Wha? It's…not even five yet."

"Just some tek from maintenance–a new one. Had ta break him in, ya know. Hey, you–"

"Don't wake him up!"

"Hey, chum, what's your name again? Wadda ya mean, why? Because my friend wants to know. Oh, you'd really like her, she's just like me, a real looker."

"Uh, join us in P.R. 35…if you can. Saemar."

"Of course ya gotta get up. Hurry up and roll over already. I gotta go. Okay, sweetie. See ya there. Just gimme a few. Ten, twelve, maybe fifteen tops. Won't be too long. Like a lotta teks, this guy's pretty quick. Ya know what I mean?"

"Uh…sure. Saemar."

"And let me wake Chae up. You know how she gets just a little testy when it's early like this." Saemar signed off.

Noted. Fighter jocks. If Naero hadn't trained with them so closely, she'd have never understood their type. Saemar was worse than Jan, even. Different guys all the time. Any time. But it hadn't always been that way with her. Chaela, on the other hand, had a steady guy from accounting.

Naero flipped up Zhen and of course got the bonus of Tyber right there with her. The eternal odd couple, giggling and cooing together, their heads bobbing in their mist shower.

"Hey, Naero," Tyber called out.

"Good morning, spacechild," Zhen added formally. "Don't worry. We'll be there. Happy birthday, by the way. You sure you still wanna try out that alien psy helmet? As your physician, I still think that's exponentially ill-advised."

Naero laughed. "Who asked you? You're still just a medtek, you quack. What do you know?"

"Hey, you're the one who gave me an illegal neural-medical stimulation device to check out for you. That thing could fry your brain like a Spum meatball."

Naero grinned, glancing at the empty ration paks littering her floor. "I like Spum. Just be there to monitor me."

All hands accounted for. All of her best friends coming to her rescue on her birthday to help her trigger her psy talent, once and for all.

She ignored the general disorder of her quarters and ducked in for a quick mist shower herself, a relaxing, refreshing start to any day. The firm cleansing mist massaged her toned body. She didn't even bother using mist wash.

Nanoparticles wicked the excess moisture away, leaving her small, slender, well-muscled form instantly and comfortably dry.

Naero peeled open a package and snapped out a crisp new set of black flight togs. The best thing next to one's skin besides nothing at all. She slipped into the luxury of the nanomaterial, attached her gear, her hidden blades, and a few other weapons. Next she put on her wristcomp and programmed or 'pweaked' up her three blue, glowing rank bands on her forearms.

No way she'd forget them.

Especially the rank she'd worked so hard to earn in the Maeris Clan Fleets.

The Nytex smart-material adapted and held all her gear tight and trim, as well as regulated her temp, controlled body odor, and monitored her vitals, ready to obey the presets she programmed into them. She could form boots, gloves, pockets, pouches, or even pweak up a quick bubble face shield and a sealed EV-suit in a pinch.

She could change the color or pattern if she desired, or add flair, the way some of the Spacer kids did. But she'd always liked basic Spacer black.

Unfortunately short and small like her champion mom, if she couldn't be tall and stacked with bulging muscles like her champion dad, at least she could still look great.

She pulled her long black hair into an efficient ponytail with a golden clip that had once been her mom's, and then pweaked her wallscreens back together, more or less.

Naero glanced at her pitiful life savings account for her first ship.

The ship she and her mates all dreamed about, with her as their captain, and them her crew.

Sigh. 6,713,448.21C.

Less than seven megacredits.

Even the cheapest, lousiest crap buckets that could still jump ranged around forty to fifty megs at least. And she had been scrimping and saving like a fricking miser all her life.

The sleek, showroom-new beauties lining and sparkling on the walls of her dreams were nearly beyond reality. Five or six times that much or more, they were better than most of the stuff in most fleets, even among Spacers.

Her younger brother, Jan, however, was just the opposite of her in almost every way possible. He blew every chunk of change he could get his hands on and was always either flush with creds right after pay day, or broke soon thereafter.

He usually wasted his pay on girls–Spacer girls, even lander girls. He didn't much care as long as they were female and willing. Janner had become a hound early on, and a full-fledged-womanizer by the ripe old age of seventeen–two years younger than her. Jan was always on the make for a good time.

While Naero herself–so busy earning rank and trying to get ahead– was still pretty much a virgin.

Even her closest friends didn't suspect the embarrassing truth.

Oh, sure, a few close calls and hot, steamy near-misses with cute Spacer boys here and there, that she made believe went farther than they did. Everyone just naturally assumed.

But she was always so damn busy.

And driven.

And choosy.

And completely hopeless.

Not only that, worse than her pathetic romantic life–as a Spacer, she had yet to develop a psyonic gift or talent.

Most Spacers had at least one. Her parents were famous for theirs. Even Jan was already a strong, albeit lazy, pyrokinetic.

While she was quickly in danger of becoming a *nud*–some washed-out loser without any kind of psyonic talent at all.

A virtual evolutionary dead end.

Sigh again.

And nobody ever got a talent after their coming of age.

Ever. Twenty standard years was the rock-solid cut off.

She opened a hidden stash compartment and brought out her emergency kit. Its contents weren't exactly legal, even among Spacers: psyonic enhancing and stimulating treatments and genetic drugs from several worlds and alien races known to have psyonic abilities. Even her crowning glory, the outlawed psyonic trigger and amplification helmet.

The Corps dominated known space and remained brazenly human-centric. Spacers were also homogenous and kept to themselves for the most part. The Corps kept all of the other known races oppressed and marginalized.

This made acquiring such a stash of psyonic boosters incredibly difficult.

All of these illegal, psyonic options were desperate, last-ditch efforts to avoid nudness. She was going to develop her talent, or at the very least trigger it, and figure out what the hell it was. Or reduce part of her brain to mush in the attempt.

Naero felt more than tired of her friends' jibes and annoying allusions to her lack of psy abilities. And her little brother was worse than all of them put together.

Today could very well be the day all of that could end. Yay. Happy birthday to her.

No time to eat. No time to lie around writing or reading poetry like her gigantic dad. Time to meet the troops for a little secret training session, before morning PT with Jan and Aunt Sleak. Training, and then their duty shift making the fleet transport deliveries.

Haisha, wasn't that all enough?

Naero slipped out of her trashed quarters and let her panel auto-secure behind her, kicking some of the junk back in so it could.

2

Saemar sparred with her first in Practice Room 35, a semi-circular slice of empty, flat gray-black nanoroom wedged into the ship's hull, ten meters along its widest length, four meters along the shortest, five meters high.

Her other friends sat watching the match on a preset bench they pulled up from the nanofloor. As their medic, Zhen stood by a little closer, scanning them both for psyonic activity.

Saemar looked for an opening, using her passive telepathy to gauge when Naero would make a move.

A defensive technique Naero always found incredibly annoying.

No matter how Naero attacked, Saemar read Naero's mind an instant before and countered every technique thrown at her, almost before they began.

Squaring off, they were almost the same height, with Saemar being only slightly heavier and somewhat more voluptuous. Curly, shoulder length auburn hair, big blue eyes, and a somewhat sharp face. A decent fighter in her own right, but Naero far outclassed her in speed, strength, skill, and natural ability.

Only Saemar's psy talent for reading her opponent's moves leveled the field. From experience, Naero could wear her down and eventually win, but it took longer and longer to do so.

Naero heard, or felt Saemar's voice in her mind.

You're straining, sweetie. I can sense it. You know you can't force a talent.

But Psy abilities usually came out during the intense focus of physical sparring, especially in the face of other psy abilities.

Almost every Spacer was a trained martial artist, practicing and conditioning and sparring with others on a regular basis. For them, it was a way of life.

Saemar attacked with a weird mix of seemingly clumsy and then efficient combinations. She baited Naero, off-speed and tricky.

Naero barely blocked a knifehand to the throat, a scrape kick down her shin, and then a spin elbow to her back ribs.

Naero held up her hands, backing away. "Hold. You're right, Saemar. Let's try something else. I'm not feeling anything."

She glanced at Zhen, who monitored them with a psy meter. The pretty olive-skinned medtek wore her light brown hair long and wavy. A bit taller than Naero and skinny, she studied and observed everything intensely with her intelligent hazel eyes.

With her psy ability, Zhen could touch people and see into their bodies and their functions directly.

Healer's sight, perfect for the medical professions. She wasn't much of fighter herself overall, but she could use her gift to spot weaknesses. She was very adept at throwing knives, spikes, and shaken stars—some of them poisoned, drugged, or stun-charged. Sort of a hobby of hers. One that she shared with Naero.

Zhen shook her head and looked down slightly.

"Sorry. Nothing from you, Naero. No triggers. No readings. I clearly picked up Saemar's latent telepathy."

Naero frowned, went to her bag of illicit tricks, and popped some fast acting psy-tabs.

Within seconds her head buzzed with a dull ache, as the psychotronic chemicals flooded her bloodstream, rushed through her brain, and affected her mind. Or at least tried to.

Naero motioned to Gallan. "You and me this time, big guy. Let's go."

Gallan rose up, two heads taller than her and almost three times as broad. Yet despite their size disparity, Naero was actually the stronger of the two and much faster, inheriting both enhanced physical abilities from her champion parents.

But Gallan was never a pushover. He knew how to fight, and he could take a lot of punishment and keep coming. His psy talent was similar to one of her father's: an ability to psyonically increase his density and physical toughness.

No big surprise, with Gallan being a distant cousin on her father's side of the family, where such abilities weren't all that uncommon.

Naero darted in, attacking again and again. She landed nearly two blows for every one of Gallan's, but he covered his vital areas and sought to get a hold on her and grapple.

He attempted to go strength-to-strength and eliminate her natural speed advantage.

Sometimes the psy ability of an opponent triggered a reaction out of sheer defensive response.

Naero turned briefly to Zhen.

"Anything yet?"

A massive sweeping back kick from Gallan caught her in the midsection, surprisingly fast.

Naero flew back into the wall with the force of the blow, back-flipped off the wall, and re-directed off the ceiling to a crouching position on the floor.

"Not a thing," Zhen noted. "Just Gallan adjusting his density during the match."

Naero clenched her fists, gritting her teeth, groaning in frustration. "Damn it. Why can't I do this?"

She stomped back to her bag. She swallowed a different group of psy-stims—twice the recommended dosage.

"Uh, Naero," Zhen objected. "Loading up on those on top of what you already have in you might not be such a good–"

Naero lashed out at her. "I gotta try something, Z. Even you said these alien lander drugs might not have any affect at all on a Spacer mind and metabolism. With our genetically enhanced healing ability and our ability to neutralize toxins and disease, they might not affect me at all. The buzz I got from those other stim-tabs is already fading. Let's see what happens now. Is my heart going to explode or something?"

Zhen frowned. "No, not yet, at least. Your pulse is racing, but nothing critical. Your neuro-chemical scans are very weird, but I guess…under these circumstances, that's understandable. But we're getting into unknown territory here, Naero. I just don't know–"

"Good enough. Let's keep going. Chaela, you're up."

Chaela was the next tallest among her friends, but still a head shorter than Gallan. Athletic, quick, and powerful, she was a true brawler, a real Amazon, her blond hair in a long braid down her broad back. She had fierce, steel-blue eyes

They teased her about being a Valkyrie from Old Terran myth. Or at the very least, a Viking berserker. Her fighting style was pretty similar.

Pysonically, Chae was a cryokinetic, just the opposite of Naero's brother.

Plus, she was an accomplished fighter. Not as strong as Naero, but pretty fast, and with a lot of fighting skill and experience. She spent a good chunk of her free time sparring against other fighting styles.

They closed and broke, neither of them landing any clean hits.

Naero shivered, feeling a chill creep over her muscles, slowing her down slightly.

Naero saw her breath in front of her.

"Come on, Chae. You know you don't have the chops to freeze me solid."

Chaela grinned. "Nope, just have ta slow your speedy little ass down a bit so that I can nail you."

Naero laughed with her and then stopped short.

Her back foot was frozen to the floor in a chunk of ice. That was new.

A gigaton freight hauler named Chaela careened straight at her on a collision course.

Naero dropped under a heavy punch, dodged a knee to her face and flipped Chaela's bulk to one side. The move twisted her leg painfully, but she had time to free it and stomp the ice block off her numb foot before Chae rolled free and charged back in.

"Hold," Naero shouted, lifting her hands. She turned to Zhen.

"Now there had to be some kind of reaction during all that. My head feels really weird."

"I don't doubt that, but still nothing from you on any of the psonic wave lengths. Not a thing."

"Damn it all to hell and back!"

Naero stomped back over to her bag.

Zhen made an attempt to intervene once more.

"Naero, I know how bad you want this."

"No. You don't. None of you do."

"We do. We get it," Gallan said.

Naero exploded. "None of you get it. *Haisha!*"

She pulled a nanoinjector out of the bag and punched yet another psy-stimulant into her arm.

She grunted and dropped to her knees.

The rapid rush of stims punched into her brain.

"Naero!" Tyber yelled. They all rushed toward her.

Naero groaned again, fighting against the blinding pain and rapid disorientation. She forced herself back to her feet and shoved them away as they all closed in.

"Get off me. I'm all right."

"No, you're not," Zhen said. "You're all doped up on who knows what. Your readings are all over the place. I can't tell what those drugs are doing to you."

"But nothing psyonic?"

Zhen checked the reads again on the meter.

"No. Not a blip."

Naero steeled herself. "Then let's keep going. Tyber. Saemar. Both of you fight me at once. I mean really fight. And both of you use your psy abilities against me full on, as much as you can."

They squared off.

Tyber liked to spar with a Spacer jo staff made of duranadium–the same stuff as the ship's hull, about a meter and a half long.

He was a so-so fighter on his own, but a good match for Zhen as a mate. Medium height and build, fit, dark hair and eyes, brown skin–Tyber had a round, friendly face. A very accomplished tek, he worked as an engineer, mechanic, and systems specialist all rolled up in one.

He and Zhen were both so different that their personalities meshed almost completely.

Pysonically, Tyber could translocate himself over short distances by line of sight. If he did it too much, it exhausted him. But in a short fight, it could be decisive. He could vanish and reappear behind his opponents when they least expected it.

When he teamed up with Saemar and her telepathic reading ability, Naero quickly found herself in a spot of trouble.

Tyber jabbed her from behind with his staff, knocking her off her feet.

Saemar kicked at her face. Naero twisted, rolled, and swept Saemar's legs out from under her, then dodged Tyber's charging attack. He did his best to keep her off balance.

After five more minutes, it was Zhen who called hold.

"Naero. I'm sorry. I'm just not getting anything from you. You have to face the facts. You're a nud. You can't do anything about it. You don't show even the slightest sign of possessing a psyonic ability of any kind whatsoever."

Naero ran over and grabbed the psy-inducing helmet. She quickly shoved it over her head and flipped the switches on full power.

The helmet lit up and hummed ominously. Everyone stepped back.

The neural net jolts to her brain staggered her. Naero screamed, clutched the helmet, and fell against one wall.

3

The room kept spinning. Naero struggled to remain on her feet and not black out.

All she could smell was ozone.

Zhen turned her psy-scanner off.

"I can't be a part of this." She turned to leave. "Don't ask me to be here if you aren't going to listen to me, Naero."

"No!" Gallan said, blocking her way. "We need you here, Z. In case something goes–"

"Look at her," Zhen said. "All of you. Something is going wrong."

"I can handle it," Naero said, positioning herself in front of the exit. "It's just pain. I'll heal. All of you guys know how fast I recover. Please, just one more go, and after that I'll stop. I promise."

Naero assumed her fighting stance and bounced on the balls of her feet. "Now come on. For all the creds. Everyone. Use your abilities and attack me. Just try to take me down. That will have to trigger something with this helmet on."

Saemar looked at her. "Z's right, sweetie. You need to stop this before–"

"No, dammit. *Haisha!* I'm not giving up yet. All of you. Please, do this for me. Because the only way you're getting through this door is through me. Now let's rumble."

Gallan looked at them all.

Zhen sighed, shook her head and flipped her psy-scanner back on.

Everyone attacked Naero at once without warning, startling both her and Zhen.

"Wait!" Zhen cried. "It won't…I need to recalibrate–"

Naero punched Gallan right in the solar plexus and drove his bulk back several feet, winding him.

Tyber crashed down on top of her suddenly from above, clipped her jaw with his jo staff, and smashed her to the ground.

Naero rolled and spin-flipped him hard into the floor.

Chaela froze her left hand to the wall.

Saemar grabbed her kicking legs, got one and then went flying from the other.

Chaela rocked her with a heavy punch that nearly snapped her head off.

"Got you now," Chae said. "You're going down."

Trapped against the wall, Naero endured punishing blows. Chaela pummeled her mercilessly.

Naero slumped to her left.

Chae prepared a finishing blow.

"You asked for this, N."

Naero darted away. Chae's spin kick shattered the ice pinning Naero's hand to the wall.

Naero flip-kicked Chaela under the chin, flinging her back.

Gallan, Tyber, and Saemar rushed in again.

Zhen's psy-meter disrupted in her hands.

She screamed and dropped the burning pieces to the nanofloor, letting the nanos extinguish the small fire.

"Hold! Stop, stop. Dammit," Zhen added.

"What happened?" Naero asked. "Did I do that? Was it me?"

"You didn't do shit," Zhen yelled.

She had to be really upset to lose her cool, and then cuss on top of that.

"I tried to tell you idiots. I needed to reset the scanner. Everyone spiking their psy abilities all at once simply fried the meter. This is a delicate neuromedical instrument. Now look at it. Do any of you morons have any idea how expensive these are? No. Of course you don't."

Naero couldn't believe it. "So there was nothing? No reaction? Not even a hint of any psy ability?"

Zhen glared at her. Then bit her lip and shook her head.

"It's always about you, isn't it? No. There was nothing. Not a blip. You're nud, Naero. Deal with it."

Naero slid slowly down the wall, ignoring the growing, throbbing pain in her skull, and the sick feeling roiling in her belly.

She slumped to the floor and slowly took off the psy-helmet, dumping it on the ground. She rested her forearms on her knees and stared absently at the broken psy-meter in smoking pieces through her legs.

Zhen went on lecturing her, her own ire up.

"And if you ask me, it serves you right, Naero. You've always been better at everything than the rest of us. A better pilot, better leader, better fighter, better trader. Do you know what that has been like for your friends?

"Naero Amashin Maeris: prodigy child. The perfect Spacer born of the perfect parents. And you've got all the pride of your illustrious family too, along with their superior genetics. How fitting, then, that there's at least one thing to humble you. One thing that you have no chance of ever excelling at–psyonics. Something almost every other Spacer can do."

"Zhentisa," Gallan said. "That's enough. You've had your say."

"Maybe this will teach you some humility, Naero."

Even Tyber had to stand up and say something. "'Tisa. Ease up. This would be hard for any of us. You know that."

Now Zhen glared at him.

Naero continued to stare at the ground. Then she convulsed and vomited all over the nano floor. She fell to one side, still gagging and dry-heaving as the floor auto-cleaned itself.

Her friends gathered around her, doing their best to hold her still as she thrashed.

After she stopped heaving, they rested her comfortably propped up on her back.

Gallan sat with his legs crossed and held her head and shoulders cradled comfortably in his arms. Chaela elevated Naero's feet while Saemar and Tyber hovered helplessly over Zhen, who placed her hands on Naero and examined her with her healer's sight.

"Is she okay?" Gallan asked.

"She's obviously not okay," Tyber said. "Is she going to be okay?"

Zhen regained her composure, ignoring them while she completed her examinations, looking right into Naero's body and its functions.

"She put a lot of junk into her system. Her body started rejecting and neutralizing it all, just as it would any toxins. I don't see any permanent damage to any of her organs, though. Amazing. She has the fastest healing rate of anyone I've ever seen. Even among Spacers."

Naero licked her dry lips. "Don't worry guys. I'm going to be okay. Can you get me some water?"

Saemar jumped up. Zhen stopped her.

"Wait a bit. Give it to her now and she'll just throw it back up."

Zhen looked a little worried and placed her hands on Naero's head again.

"What's wrong?" Chaela asked.

"*Haisha*...I...I don't know. I've never seen energy signatures in the brain like this before. They're fading slowly. Must be feedback from the psy-helmet, still bouncing back and forth in there. But no psyonic activity still. Sorry, Naero.

Zhen paused a moment before going on. "Yet that's weird as well. Even in a nud, the areas of the brain where psy activities originate aren't usually this completely inert or inactive. Normal brain energies still flow through them. They just don't generate psy energy.

"But with you, it's as if your entire brain has those areas totally blocked and shut down, using completely different parts of your brain so that you don't need them. Kind of like a re-routed back-up system. Wow, I could do an article on this for the neuromed journals."

"Great," Naero muttered. "Even my nudness is unique, and surpasses all other nuds." She chuckled weakly.

Her mates laughed nervously along with her.

"Naero," Zhen said, "I'm sorry. I apologize for going off on you like I did. It was wrong. I was upset about the scanner, which I still don't know how I'm going to explain or pay for. But I'll think of something.

"Anyway. I said stuff that wasn't right. I didn't mean it to come out as harsh as it did."

Naero licked her lips again. "No, you were right. All of you guys know it. I am too proud. I can be a real pain in the ass. Stubborn. Hot tempered. Impatient. Argumentative."

Tyber kept going for her. "Bossy. Demanding. Inconsiderate..."

Even Naero had to laugh along with them.

"Not to mention all the lame, cheesy tricks and scams you're always pulling on us," Tyber said. "Like the time you switched my body wash with hair remover. I was bald and hairless all over–for a month."

They laughed harder at that.

Zhen smiled and ran her fingers through his curly dark hair. "Aww…you were so cute–like a hairless kitty."

"Like the time she hacked all our accounts and left us all with a single cred," Saemar recalled. "*After* she insisted we go to that expensive restaurant on Darius-3."

"Or the time," Chaela noted, "when the three of us were on that live training exercise, and you somehow filled the cockpits of our fighters with expanding crash foam."

"Yeah," Saemar added. "They had to tow us back in and get us out with pressurized foam solvent. They never pinned it on you, but boy, was your aunt pissed. That stunt had you written all over it."

"I admit to nothing," Naero said.

Gallan groaned. "What about all the times we were kids, and she hacked the codes on our rooms and set goofy traps for us."

Zhen laughed. "Or snuck in while we were sleeping and drew tattoos or stupid stuff on our faces."

"Yeah," Chaela said, turning red. "I spent an entire day walking around like that, going from one training class to another. And none of you bastards would tell me. I wondered why everyone was giggling. I didn't find out until I went home for dinner that evening and my parents gaped and stared at me like I was a fricking alien or something."

"And keep in mind," Gallan said, "today's her birthday. That old joke day back on Old Terra."

"April Fools' Day," Zhen corrected him.

"Whatever. Who knows what she has planned for us all today? So watch your backs. You all know what's coming."

Naero sat up a little more. "I have absolutely no idea what you people are babbling about."

"Riiight," Tyber said. "That squares it. We're in for it now, people. I bet she has something absolutely diabolical planned."

"I do not," Naero said.

She grimaced and winced, suddenly rubbing her temples.

"More pain?" Zhen asked. "I warned you about that, N. You'll probably suffer episodes several times a day. Maybe for quite a while. You haven't started hallucinating or seeing anything strange yet, have you? Delusions could set in."

"I'm fine. I'll handle it."

Despite the bouts of pain, her plan for her master joke on her mates was working to perfection.

Naero hesitated.

"Seriously, you guys must really hate me sometimes. I know I can be a jerk. How do you put up with me?"

"Well to tell you the truth, it's not easy," Tyber said.

"Screw you."

"Really, N?" He threw his arm around Zhen's slender waist and yawned. "Hmmm...I'm kind of booked up. How about next month sometime?"

Zhen made a face and pushed away from him. "In your dreams, tek-monkey."

Naero sighed. "Well, I guess today the joke's on me then."

She pulled away from Gallan and stood up. Her friends rose up with her.

"I'm a nud. I'll just have to accept that. Happy birthday to me."

All of their coms chimed at once, calling them to morning PT, mandatory for all Spacer crew in the fleet. Six times out of a standard seven day week.

The panel to Practice Room 35 slid open.

Naero's younger brother stood there. tall and lanky in his own black togs. Gray eyes. A tousled mop of black hair like their dad's and a winning smile.

He only played at being the bad boy because it got him girls. Especially stupid girls, but he wasn't choosy.

"Hey, what are all you people doing here already?"

He looked behind them. "Is that a psy helmet on the floor over there? Gosh...aren't those illegal?"

Naero rushed over and snatched it up before he could, stashing all of her illicit stuff away.

"Stow it, Janner. You didn't see anything."

Jan yawned. "I never do, sib."

"I'm ducking back to my quarters," Naero said, her head still woozy.

"Don't be late," Jan warned. "Aunt Sleak's training with us today. You know how she prizes punctuality."

Naero raced down the corridor.

4

In the early afternoon they all met for lunch before their duty shift.

Aunt Sleak's lead ship, *The Slipper,* which they currently served on, was only the third largest in this particular Clan Maeris Merchant Fleet at 500 tons. But it was the newest, the fastest, and, ton for ton, the most advanced and heavily armed of the fleet's five main ships.

With a complement of 230 working crew, and some of their clan families, *The Slipper* was home to more than 300 souls.

It's oval, domed mess hall comfortably sat and fed about a hundred people at once, so the crew and their families ate in rotating shifts.

Now that the ship was out of jump and proceeding through sub-space in system, they could see the other ships of the fleet in tight formation nearby. The mess hall had its blast screens down, so it was possible to look out across a stunning 360-degree vista as they continued, on course to Irpul-4. This was just one leg of the fleet's major trade run through Triax Gigacorp space.

Naero spotted their sister ship, *The Shinai,* slightly behind them on their port side, protecting their flank–600 tons, 300 crew.

Right behind them were the fleets' two smaller trading ships: *The Nevada*, 300 tons and 80 crew, and *The Ardala*, 200 tons, 60 crew.

The massive *Dromon*, a planetoid vessel, brought up and protected their rear. At 300,000 tons it obviously couldn't enter a planetary atmosphere, but it carried a crew of 1,200 and had nearly unlimited hold space, as well as more firepower than a ship of the line battleship.

The mess hall on *The Slipper* currently had about 60 people in it, coming and going, eating, communicating with the other ships, watching the news on INS, the Interstellar News Service feeds from various sectors, feeds primarily controlled and manipulated by the sixteen Gigacorps.

Even a decade after the last Spacer War with the Corps ended in 2585, the old tensions remained strong in many places in the Alpha Quadrant.

Old hatreds did not fade easily, and the driving force behind most of the Gigacorps to dominate and control everything and everyone, remained relentless.

Only the Spacers and their staunch ally Joshua Tech–the only Gigacorp to side with

them–remained independent and free.

When the other fifteen Gigacorps weren't fighting with Spacers, they fought amongst themselves for dominance, or even within their own systems.

Naero stared at her lunch tray while they shuffled along in line, still feeling queasy from her morning ordeal. Usually the chow was okay.

She ignored INS, having little interest in Interstellar politics and spin today. She still struggled to accept the fact that she was a nud, and not mope about it. What else could she do but push on?

She also had a busy duty shift ahead of her.

The only bright point in her birthday was her master plan.

By lunch time it was working perfectly.

Tyber checked the table and benches they were about to sit at with their food trays with his scanner. So did Zhen.

"I don't detect any traps," he said. "Nothing sticky."

"No nanoglue or stungel," Zhen added. "It's okay to sit down."

"Guys, just eat your food. Seriously. I didn't do anything. I'm not going to do anything. You're my mates."

"Yeah, you'd like us to think that, wouldn't you, N?" Chaela said. "Then we let our guard down, and wham!" She hit the table so hard that their trays jumped, as did some other Spacers nearby.

"That's when you strike. You're just waiting to pounce on us all. So go ahead. What are you waiting for? We know you wanna play some clever trick on us. Just get it over with already."

"Saemar, look me in the eye. Tell them how dumb this is. They're getting all paranoid for nothing."

Saemar stopped waving and flirting and winking at the entire male half of the crew and looked into her eyes.

"You're absolutely right, sweetie. I do know you." Then she looked at their trays.

"Oh my gosh, I figured it out. She's done something to our food. Nobody eat anything! I bet the servers are in on it."

Everyone stared and gaped and dropped their spoons and forks in midbite as if on cue.

"I bet it's laxatives," Saemar said. "That's what I'd do. By tonight we'll all be shitting ourselves inside out like Lorlduvian sky whales. Don't eat nuthin'."

"Okay, okay," Zhen said. "Everyone just glacier. If Saemar will shut up for five seconds I can scan everyone's food."

Tyber looked over at her. Naero just grinned innocently.

"She's smiling at us," Tyber said. "Oh, hell. Why is she smiling at us like that?"

"I'm just so happy to be with all my good friends."

"Dammit. Saemar's right. I already ate some. I feel it going through me already. I'm going to die. I'm going to detonate like a shit bomb. Damn you, Naero."

Naero held up her hands. "You're not going to shit yourself, Tyber. I didn't do anything."

Zhen turned off her med scanner. "Relax, Ty. She's right. No poisons." She glared at Saemar and shook her head emphatically.

"No sooper laxatives. Everyone go ahead and eat. Just another false alarm."

Awkward silence passed for a minute.

Saemar blurted out. "Well, it's a good thing. You don't want to mess with those extra-strength laxatives, ya know. I know a guy who took some, cause–you know–he was all plugged up inside. Well, he takes too much. Next thing thing ya know, *bawoom*. He's crapping his teeth out his ass. The guy had to get new teeth, I swear. True story. It liked ta killed him."

"No way," Tyber said. "No one can shit their teeth out. It's impossible."

Gallan threw his fork down again and pushed his tray away in complete disgust. "I don't think I can eat anymore."

"The question remains," Zhen said, licking her spoon and then waving it at Naero. "What is she going to do, and how and when is she going to do it to us all?"

"You guys are being silly," Naero told them.

"We'll never see it coming," Chaela said. "She's probably already set it up and is just waiting for it to blow up in our faces. That's the way she usually does it."

Tyber pointed a finger right at her. "You know, one of these days, Naero, someone's going to pull one over on you–a real work of art. And all of us are going to be right here to see you go down in flames."

"Hey, here's a disturbing thought," Gallan said. "I know her better than any of you. What if this time her master plan is to do nothing?"

"Nothing?" Zhen said. "That's not her style. She's going to do something, you can bet on that."

"Right," Tyber added.

"Think about it, "Gallan said. "All she has to do is sit and look innocent while the rest of us squirm and flip out and get all paranoid, watching and waiting and fretting about something that could happen at any moment. She can drive us all crazy for free. That way, we keep doing it all to ourselves."

"Nahhh…" Saemar said. "She's got something planned, all right. Just look at her."

Naero stretched leisurely and stood up, grinning all the while. "I don't know about you guys, but I gotta go get ready for work. You guys comin' along for the ride?"

All five of her friends turned as pale as moons.

"She's going to get us on the job. Can she do that to us?" Tyber asked the others. "Isn't there a limit to what she can do to us while we're on duty?"

Saemar gasped for air again. "Check your EV-suits for hidden suppositories. She could still get us with auto-suppositories. *Bungo*! Right up the escape chute. Our suits'll fill up with pressurized poop. We'll all choke on it."

Zhen held up her hands as if they were claws, dragging the corners of her mouth down and gnashing her teeth in frustration.

"You total moron. Will you shut up about the laxatives already? What an idiot! She's not going to get us with laxatives. Nobody in their right mind would ever do something like that, except maybe you! It's not. Going to be. Laxatives."

Everyone stared at her.

Saemar had to have the last word.

"Well, it could be laxatives. How do you know?"

"Aauughhh!" Zhen abandoned her tray and the table, and stalked away, her fists clenched and her arms straight down stiff at her sides.

Tyber went after her.

"Time to go to punch the clock," Naero said, struggling not to giggle.

Then Jan walked into the mess hall, his face ashen.

He focused on her, swallowed hard, and came straight for her.

"Hey Jan. Why so glum? One of your bimbo's stand you up?"

"N-N-Naero, there's no good way to say this, so just listen. Mom and Dad's exploration fleet has been…wiped out in deep space. They're all gone. Dead. Mom and dad…they're dead."

Naero gaped for a minute.

Then she started laughing. She turned back to her friends, who all looked dumbstruck, completely unable to speak.

"Okay, I see what's going on here. Nice try, guys. Good one. You almost had me, but I'm not falling for it. Smooth. My birthday, old April Fool's Day. Getting Janner to play along with your little scam?"

Gallan stood up and lifted his hands. "Naero, this isn't a scam. Your brother just said something terrible happened to your parents. I think you need to listen to him."

Naero backed away slightly, shaking her head. "No, no. It can't be. Tyber just said you'd all get me back for all of my tricks. That you'd all be there to pull one over on me and see me go down in flames. They can't be. My mom and dad can't be–"

Janner slapped her. Hard.

Naero gaped, taken completely by surprise.

"You think I'm kidding? *Haisha*!" Jan sobbed. "You think I'm making this up?"

An INS bulletin cut in over the regular feeds on all screens.

We have disturbing, breaking news. A deep space exploration fleet has been completely wiped out in the far regions of the Spacer Extents. Spacer sources have thus far released few details concerning the incident. It is not known whether the fleet was destroyed by some dangerous phenomena or perhaps a heretofore unknown, advanced alien threat.

All that is known is that thousands of Spacers are now dead. All ships and all hands lost. There are no known survivors. Stay tuned for more information concerning this tragedy as the facts unfold. All of the corporate governments and navies have offered their sincere condolences and their complete cooperation and assistance to the Spacer authorities.

Does some grave new alien threat lurk beyond the boundaries of known space?

Gallan tried to put his arms around her.
Naero pulled away and floated out of the Mess Hall.
In complete shock.

5

Naero spoke with Aunt Sleak briefly before going on duty.

Jan retreated to his room.

Her face still ached. Not physically, but emotionally from how her little brother had struck her and why.

She blamed herself, not Jan; but she still couldn't have known.

Her aunt gave her the option to shunt her duty shift onto someone else, given the circumstances. Something Naero had never done before.

She never missed a duty shift.

And she wouldn't now. Her crews needed her.

"Thanks, but I think I need to stay busy," she said flatly.

Aunt Sleak respected her decision.

Few details reached them concerning the destruction of *The Omaria's* expedition into the Unknown Sectors. No one seemed to know much more yet. Not Spacers or the Corps.

One phrase stuck in Naero's mind. *All hands lost.*

All hands lost.

All joy and gladness felt sucked out of her life–as if into a swirling black hole of despair.

Everything had changed forever. Everything was already different and worse.

She couldn't dwell on all of that.

Time to sort it out later. For the present she had a mission, an important duty shift to focus on and keep her busy.

Naero sucked in a deep breath and shook herself at the stiff controls of her lumbering transport, checking her autovector on the orange glowing Joshua Tech flight console directly in front of her, angled slightly down on its gunmetal titanadium swing arms. The console swayed slightly. One of the swivel locks was still broken.

Big surprise. The teks hadn't gotten around to her work order yet. She'd have a word with Tyber.

The tight protective orb of her transport's flight command pod enveloped her like a protective egg, designed specifically for that purpose. Barely enough room for a pilot, but this time, she welcomed being so closed up. The solitude, the quiet, her heart and mind raced, torn in several directions at once. She needed something to hold herself all in.

That way she didn't explode, and crumble into little pieces.

Being held in the arms of a ship was second nature to her. Flying a ship through space gave her solace, re-assurance.

According to their readouts, her four-Spacer load team hung suspended at their stations in the cargo bay, charging their glifters in their docking stations. Some of them no doubt had locked up and were snoozing during the ride.

Loaders worked hard. Shifts could be days long at times. Naero had been there right with them performing such duties in the past, before she earned her second of the three blue rank bands on her arms.

She could still recall the stress and satisfying fatigue of those long days. Smart loaders seized the luxury of sleep whenever it came their way

She wasn't sure herself if she would be getting much sleep in the near future.

Naero kept her clear flight helmet off, even during their approach. Against regs, but she preferred to look ahead and all around clearly, without the distortion of the helmet's lensing effect at the edges of her sight, and sometimes above or below

Her small, slender left hand, gloved in the same thin black Nytex of her flight togs, reached absently around her stained lix holder for another borbble of Jett. Her fave.

She had broken it out of her stash and brought it with her for the trip in an attempt to console herself. But she had already nervously guzzled them all, inhaling the last delicious fruity drop of her hoarded lix fourpak half an hour ago, and had recycled the empty borbble with the other three.

Naero shook her head. Thirst and hunger needed to wait. Not that she was very hungry, despite skipping two meals and throwing up. She had a couple of semi-tasty energy bars somewhere in her togs, but no desire to ferret them out and pick at them.

Thirst remained another matter.

She licked her lips; they felt dust covered. Damnation. Nothing more to drink. And the air still smelled sweet, tangy, and tantalizing with the succulent flavor of Jett–even on her own breath.

An involuntary shudder snaked through her lithe, athletic body, causing her to snap slightly in her form-fitting EV-suit.

Naero sighed, struggling to relax and collect herself. Again. The entire trip telescoped out into a long tunnel of malaise and uneasiness, as if she couldn't make up her mind how she felt about anything.

The news affected her deeply on so many levels, even through her shock, finally starting to hit home.

She reached back and massaged her stiff neck, and checked her long black hair, clipped up tight in a knot behind her crown with her mother's gold hair clasp. She wore it Spacer-style to fit into the orbs of their flight helmets.

Great...with her hair pulled back, she could tenderly feel the big inflamed zit swelling up right smack dab in the middle of her forehead like a small blemish volcano. How wonderful.

Well, she might be a mess inside and out, but she still had work to do. On the job, it didn't matter how bad she looked–pimples, boils, and all. Parts of her cared; other parts did not.

Aunt Sleak would join them shortly after the Merchant Fleet Command Ship–*The Slipper*–landed only an hour or two behind them.

Naero led a vital but relatively standard delivery mission to Irpul-4's dumpy, dangerous starport.

Whatever her inner turmoil, duty demanded that she keep good order and fulfill her obligations to her Clan and her team.

She shifted and turned slightly in her green gel-chair, encircling her like a spongy cocoon that mostly filled the inner egg of the flight pod.

She found herself completely incapable of getting comfortable in what was normally a favorite environment for her. She squirmed and shifted all the way.

Piloting anything that moved or flew usually relaxed her, but not today.

Another spell of pain crashed into her skull. Zhen warned her that she might suffer them in random waves. They could hit at any time, night or day, ranging from dull aches to almost knocking her out.

To hell with that.

Naero wouldn't stand for it. She'd deal with the pain and consequences of her actions, and find a way to muscle through them, just like she always did.

Her hands fidgeted on the flightsticks on either arm of her flight chair. Each stick was covered with delicate controls, allowing her to maneuver in almost any direction.

As mission leader, she piloted the lead transport of seven bulk haulers, with three formed up on her mark in tight formation to either side. Their glifter crews were no doubt snoozing blissfully like her own.

She focused on the three open view screens before her: left, right, and forward and slightly up. Shining slices of reinforced screen with the blast shields open, looking out into the Irpul System.

The fourth planet ballooned at their rapid approach, swirls and patches of deep violet, lavender, several shades of blue, and gray, punctuated by a few spatters of light here and there as they approached on the side of the world shrouded in night.

She switched over to manual controls on final approach. The dual stick controls of her lumbering GV-hauler resisted, stiff and sluggish like her big friend Gallan wrestling with her.

Haisha! Sometimes she kept these old transports up and on course by muscle and force of will alone. Just the way her parents...

She winced and flared her small sensitive nose, drinking in machine smells and the ozone of high energy impulses from advanced electronics. All of her acute senses seemed further heightened in flight, especially because of her elevated emotional state.

Landing shields full-front. They entered the atmosphere, punching through in radiant sprays of sparks and flames.

Stop sulking over them.

She couldn't do anything about their deaths now. They wouldn't want that. They'd taught her and her brother better. Go forward. Complete the task at hand.

Who was she kidding?

A gaping, aching hole sucked a cold roaring hurricane of despair and loss straight through where her heart and soul used to be.

She loved her parents dearly, though she didn't give voice to that so much anymore. And to make matters worse, when last she'd seen them, they hadn't parted well. Naero argued and fought with them intensely and repeatedly about her and Jan having to go work for Aunt Sleak again–their less-than-favorite and only aunt.

Cold, demanding, hardnosed Aunt Sleak, who never cut anyone any slack. She always drove them and worked them to the bone, while their parents always went off on some lark, pursuing their dreams, exploring the dangerous Unknown Sectors, like some kind of endless vacation.

Naero regretted her words now. She had always understood what they were doing was risky. Already she missed them more than she could bear.

6

Irpul-4's third class starport consisted of a series of old multilinked bubble domes offering access to starships and other craft along the sides and at key junctures above. The port itself covered nearly thirty square kilometers and formed the central hub of the Gigacorp city sprawled around it.

Naero and her crews received their delivery orders and dropped down to land, unload, load, and confirm payments. Gray, blue, purple, and brown corrosive dust hurricaned around them, even as they decelerated.

Viewed from above by Spacer eyes, the old starport looked just like any other Corps dump hole.

Naero's jaw ached from clenching it during the flight in, but she ground her teeth again.

Her brother Jan remained on *The Slipper* with Aunt Sleak, choosing to seclude himself in his room with his feelings about the news.

It might go harder on Jan. He kept everything inside and always tried to act cold and aloof. She worried about how hard the loss could be for him if he shut himself off from his grief. At times he went off on his own for months at a time, pulling away from everyone. Even her.

How was he coping?

Not to mention, that on a real universe, practical level: losing their parents and their entire fleet also meant a serious loss of Clan status, influence, and wealth for the both of them. Their parents had sunk every meg they had into that venture.

Now all of those investments were gone, completely wiped out.

Naero and Jan's temporary assignment to Aunt Sleak's small merchant fleet, the one she bought from their parents, looked more and more like a lifetime appointment now.

They had nowhere else to go.

An aft stabilizer froze up. Naero compensated before it spun her out of control, crashing into her starboard transports.

Naero gripped the shaking controls harder, steeled herself, and struggled to remain focused. She had a shift to fill, and three blue bands of merchant service rank on her arms to live up to–rank she had fought for and earned, despite her youth. In nearly fifteen years of duty to Clan Maeris since the age of five, she had never missed a shift, never ducked a duty.

She couldn't let that slack, no matter what had happened, regardless of how she felt about her and Jan's loss.

Up ahead loomed Omni Gigacorp's primary shipping depot, an old pyramid structure a few klicks high. She and the other six transports made their landing approach. The massive doors of the designated loading bay opened for them.

"Form up on my mark and vector in," she commanded.

Naero piloted her lead transport inside and set it down easy, stiff controls be damned. She plugged in orders to have her crew fix that faulty stabilizer before they left.

She went through the motions and coordinated the landings of the other six transports and dozens of her aunt's people sent to unload Omni's shipments.

Her teams assembled in front of their glowing, open cargo holds. Each Spacer stood garbed in the same uniform: tight black Nytex Spacer uniform togs, high boots, loading gear, and glowing azure bands of merchant fleet rank and insignia displayed proudly on their arms.

Naero pushed her inner tension and shock aside once again.

As the lead pilot and team leader, Naero wore a gravwing strapped to her like a small pack with auto-deploying, spolymer nanotek wings. But she hadn't activated them yet.

Instead, she walked straight up to the waiting, meaty dock captain, a heavyset lander in faded, dark blue Omni Corps coveralls. He leered at her with a scarlet face, gnashing a short dark stub of Spican harstick, the sides of his maw yellowed and blackened from years of addiction to the synthetic root and the low stim dose it released.

The sharp pungent odor of harstick permeated the man right down to his glands and the very air about him.

Naero secretly despised most landers.

He nearly threw the trade loading packet into her hands.

"You spacks have two hours to deliver and vacate my dock," he snapped. Old Corps military by his tone and his contempt for Spacers. The most hateful landers called them 'spacks,' a dehumanizing insult from the wars.

She'd encountered such tiresome attitudes on her merchant runs so often that they hardly bothered her anymore. But today, such insults grated on her.

"Let's see what we have," Naero said. She opened the packet and took out their agreement and inventory exchange chips. She plugged them into her handcomp and double-checked them while the dock captain waited. The precise location for each inbound and outbound package lit up on her filtered display, logistics flowing to the loaders.

"Looks in order."

"I know it's in order, spack." He spat out a vile gout of black juice and goo to one side, almost as if vomiting. The stench was putrid

"My people are waiting. Get on it, spack. You're burning my simulated daylight." He turned and walked away; the foul stench faded with him.

Naero stared after him for an instant and mildly shook her head. Was the guy trying to piss her off? Not a good idea. Not today.

"And a pleasure doing business with you and the Corps too," she said. "As always."

She turned back to her crew, most of them young and headstrong like her. Naero activated her gravwing and rose a few feet off the ground to help oversee their stop and drop. Her unit hummed slightly and the short wings deployed, flexing and adjusting with the gravfields.

The last Spacer War with the Corps hadn't been that long ago. Resentment and even outright hatred between Corps landers and Spacers were still all too common. Naero found it useful to maintain an ironic sense of humor.

"All right, loaders. The pleasantries are over, so let's get to it. You've had your little inbound nap time. So get your asses in order and do some work. Stay on schedule."

A spattering of honks, salutes, beeps, and "yes, sir, commander sir" filtered back in her general direction. The loader crews formed up and took their assignments like a hive of black-and-yellow striped bees, buzzing off in various directions.

The hum and drone of glifters filled the air–insectoid grav-assisted bot arms attached to a protective cage and lift harness.

She floated around another GV, just in time to overhear Saemar and Chaela, whispering to each other while prepping their glifters.

Her mates kept their voices low.

"Any more word? What kind of run were her parents on?" Chaela asked, her long, blond braid swinging to one side when she bent over.

Saemar shook her pretty geisha-like face and whispered back, "Not much else so far. Some kind of deep space exploration mission with a sect of the Cumi."

Both of their faces reflected shared grief and anger.

Naero considered zipping forward to let them see her, but what could she say? Her mates and the crew would continue to speculate about the loss of her parents and the exploration mission among themselves, even if they said nothing around her and Jan.

Out of respect, everyone kept their distance and didn't broach it in front of them.

Even her best friend Gallan seemed quiet and uncertain about what to do or say.

Naero didn't know herself. Stumbling upon them gossiping made her realize just how much she was still in shock. But perhaps they had heard something more. Anything.

"Any more details?" Chaela asked.

Saemar shook her head again. "Few deets and just a lot of spec, sweetie. There's talk Intel may have been–"

"Shadowforce?"

"Shh..." Saemar frowned and climbed into the straps of her glifter, adjusting her harness. "Well, if they weren't in on it before, they are now. The loss of an entire Spacer strike force, including an exploration flagship of *The Omaria's* fame is a serious interstellar incident."

"Who do they really think...?"

"Who else?"

45

Chaela snarled and clenched her fists. "Matayan corsairs. Always doing the Corps' dirty work." She spat on the floor. "Murdering bastards. They've butchered enough or our families. They can eat shit and drink piss."

"Rep that, sweetie," Saemar added. "You know how I feel. Piss on their dead."

That was one of the reasons Saemar was the way she was now.

Matayan raiders had killed the fighter wing captain from Clan Mitsubishi whom she had been engaged to.

Hikaru had taken several enemy fighters down with him, but in the end, he was still gone. Forever.

After that, Saemar had kind of flipped and gone on a binge with other guys. But she never again made any long-term attachments.

Naero did the only thing she could in her current estimation. She bobbed the other way, and went on with her work at hand. Best to keep busy.

Inside the loading bay they basically had a large cube to maneuver in, three hundred meters long by nearly as wide and high, lined with loading platforms from top to bottom. Every spot linked and coded.

The Spacer glifter teams went straight to work. With the data Naero sent them, they bobbed up and down in the air to both deliver and gather assigned cargo from their transports and various platforms. It looked like organized chaos to anyone watching, but there was a system to it.

Another jolt of pain reminded her how much it might have been a bad idea to wear that psy helmet.

Naero tried to focus on the automated tally sequences running on her handcomp. Aunt Sleak's profit margins fluctuated as new market info came in. Naero found it hard to concentrate on the last minute pweaking required to maximize those profits.

All of that suddenly seemed so unimportant now, with her parents gone. Of course rumors and speculation about anything would always run wild.

No, she reminded herself, her parents were not gone. Taken. They had been taken from their family, possibly by Matayan butchers.

The slight body hairs between her shoulders and up the back of her neck flared with a tickling flicker like electric fire. Like an unspoken voice in her mind, straining to warn her.

She quickly scanned the massive inner core of the warehouse section.

Danger? Someone focusing or sighting in on her? What was it?

Something had her on high alert, but she couldn't place or identify it. Again, it felt like a voice buried deep in her skull, trying to warn her.

She shook her head. Perhaps stress and everything all together simply made her paranoid.

"Frost," she said aloud. She let out a sigh.

Keep calm, keep your shit together. Just get through your shift.

"That's right," she heard Gallan say. She felt her friend's big gentle hand on her shoulder, almost a stroke as it pulled away. He was half a year older than her, with only one band of rank on his arms. Unlike her, Gallan was too busy enjoying life to worry much about ambition or promotion–let alone getting his own ship someday. He left that all to her.

With her floating, she was eye level with him. She looked into the kindness of his thick face and couldn't help but smile.

Yet neither could she ignore the same old childhood jealousy between them and felt it creep into her grin.

She silently cursed Gallan's side of the family for making him and their cousins so damnably tall.

All her life Naero had yearned for a few more millimeters herself, but she was exactly the same height as her shorter, slender mother–exactly 1.52 meters.

Some might have thought, with her father being so tall, that...

Naero caught herself, stopped smiling, and felt her brows knit.

All thoughts returned to her dead parents somehow.

Gallan looked about to say something when actual warning alarms sounded. Naero's sense of impending danger spiked again. She glanced around.

Old metal supports above them groaned and strained for an instant under great stress.

Then an entire section of loading platform gave way, thirty meters above and to their rear. Ton upon metric ton of goods and supplies toppled into the open air, along with three Corps personnel–crashing straight down at her and her people.

Concern for Gallan and her crew overrode all else.

"Clear and cover!" she shouted over their open channel.

"All crew, clear and cover!" Gallan looked up. Spacers dropped their loads and zipped in with their glifters, risking their lives to snag the plummeting Corps workers.

Only an instant before impact.

Naero accelerated and smashed into Gallan, where he still stood staring up. With him being nearly half again her height and twice her mass, she used her gravwing and her genetically amplified strength and quickness to knock him back, driving him off his feet. She pushed him under the protective overhang of the lower level and into the wall of freight stacked beneath. They hit hard.

She winded Gallan, but at least they'd survive.

Where they had stood a sliver of time before, crashing freight, debris, and equipment pelted the loading bay floor and their armored transports. The resulting tumult deafened everything. Then more screams split the air.

The dust still settled when Naero and Gallan emerged to assess the damage. Bits of wreckage and debris continued to crash down at random.

The front of her transport looked badly battered, but nothing beyond repair. The screaming started again nearby. Naero flitted toward it, dodging falling debris. Gallan ducked into his GV after a medkit.

She spotted part of a crushed Spacer glifter and one of the Corps people's broken legs, sticking out from under a pile of wreckage.

Then Naero saw Chaela's blond braid trailing out from the protective cage of her smashed glifter.

"All units," she said over her com. "Spacer down, one lander. All working glifters converge and secure."

She surveyed the structures above them. "All working transports– provide cover over rescue site. I want four teams to secure and reinforce the collapsed structure, if possible."

"My legs, my legs!" the trapped Corps worker shrieked. Gallan scrambled up with the medkit and hit the man up with a sedative.

Moments later, the Spacer transports formed up close and hovered over them protectively, shining their lights down on the wreckage. Saemar swept in in her glifter.

"Who is it, sweetie?" she asked. "Who's down? Oh, no–Chae. How is she? We have to get her out!"

"Glacier that," Naero said. "Coordinate with the rest of your team." Glifters bobbed around them in an instant, awaiting orders.

"Teams one and six, assemble around the rescue site and remove the wreckage. Carefully. I don't want them hurt worse just because we're in a hurry."

The eight Spacers in their glifters cautiously hovered around like humming drones, carefully picking the wreckage off Chaela and the Corps worker, handing it back to the other teams to set aside.

In the end, with the glifter teams working methodically, it only took several seconds, but it seemed a lot longer to Naero and her crew as they stood by and watched.

Lander medteks with two floating medbeds arrived much more quickly than Naero expected.

"What happened here?" the lead medtek asked.

"As near as I can figure," Naero said, pointing at the collapsed structures. "A faulty platform up there gave way and dumped its load on us."

By then, Gallan had the Corps man out and stabilized. The big Spacer lifted him up and placed him on one of the medbeds. Naero had had extensive emergency medical training. From the looks of things, other than two broken legs and cuts and bruises, the lander would probably be all right.

"What about the other casualty?" the medtek asked.

"She's alive," Saemar shouted. "She took the worst of it trying to protect that guy. Her crush cage saved her. We'll have to cut her out."

Naero hovered of them. All four glifter cutter torches fired up bright and blinding at once.

In another few moments, Gallan went back in and carried Chae out. Even she was small in his big arms. He placed her gently on the other medbed.

Naero didn't wait for the medteks to come over. She landed and shut down her gravwing; it folded up neatly. She and Gallan went to work on their own. Chaela's right foot was crushed beyond saving; Naero quickly amputated it and sealed it off.

She shuddered and blamed herself.

Any time one of her crew got hurt, her guts twisted. It bothered her something fierce. They were her people, her Clan. They trusted and depended on her to keep them safe. She was responsible for them.

Unfortunately for Chaela, losing the foot meant lots of regrowth treatments, and even more physical therapy. But at least she survived.

She'd lost consciousness from a nasty gash on the top of her head. The medbed kept her stable and strove to eliminate any pain. She bled from several other serious wounds on her arms and legs. Naero worked on cleaning and closing the head wound. Gallan went after the others.

Suddenly she smelled the acrid tang of Spican harstick. The taste of it even cut through the dust and the smell of blood.

"Let me through, you idiots!" she heard the Corps dock captain bellow. She tried to ignore him until he got a thick-fingered hand on her arm and yanked her away from working on Chaela.

"You listen here, you stupid little gash. We're going to sue your entire spack clan into the next century. Just look at what you careless spacks–"

Naero shook free of him in anger.

As fast as a killing viper, one hand seized his throat and her other clamped onto his groin through his thin coveralls. She squeezed until his breath caught and his eyes bulged and popped wide like small bloodshot balloons.

A new length of harstick dropped from his mouth into the dust. She hoisted the oaf up on his toes at full arm's length and slammed him into a duranadium beam.

Because of her slender size, her genetically enhanced strength and bone-muscle density that she inherited from her father almost always startled others–especially landers.

"Now *you* listen, scumbag. Our vids recorded everything, and I bet I can find stress fractures and maintenance violations all over this cheap hole. My people just saved three of your people; one of mine is down. I don't have time for any shit from you. Get the hell away from me, before I am forced to hurt you."

With that she let go and turned her back on him. He gasped and collapsed on the floor.

"Why–you!" He scrambled back to his feet, and lunged in toward her.

Gallan stepped in, towering over the fat oaf.

He grabbed the man by the back of his short hairs and lifted him up gasping onto his tip toes once more. He puppet-walked the guy a few meters off and shoved him out of the way into a pile of junk.

Saemar scowled and positioned her glifter between the muttering dock captain and the medbeds, casually testing her cutting torch.

Naero went back to Chaela. One of the lander medteks finished sealing the head wound. He turned to her, incredulous. "I've never seen Spacer smartblood at work before. Her wounds have stopped bleeding. They're already beginning to seal over and heal up."

Naero shook his hand. "My people and I thank you for your help, Doc."

Chaela groaned and looked up at them. "The lander?" she asked.

"Alive," Naero said with a smile. "Two broken legs, but he'll live." She nodded to Gallan, who prepared a stronger sedative that would work better on a Spacer metabolism.

Chaela smiled and groaned. "I thought the game was up when all that stuff hit us, N. Everyone else?"

"Fine, Chae. Gallan's going to give you something to help you sleep and heal. You did good, my friend."

No reason to tell her about the foot until later.

50

Chaela gasped in pain. "Tell your aunt what a hero I am. I'll expect that bonus in my pay."

"You'll get it. I'll make a full report."

Chae nodded once and was out.

The medteks followed them out of the loading bay, scurrying alongside the medbeds.

"I'm curious," the medtek asked. "Can I examine you? Do you or anyone else need to be checked out? Do you want us to keep her overnight for observation? What's the average Spacer rate of regeneration?"

Naero smiled, but this guy seemed a little too interested in them.

Spacers took care of their own whenever possible, and not all Spacer secrets were for landers.

"Thanks for the offer, but we'll borrow your medbed to take her back to our fleet. She'll be all right." The medtek looked amazed, but Naero was used to that from landers as well.

In the end, they finished unloading and loading all of their transports and left the Corps workers to clean up the mess. They just barely made it under the two hour time limit the surly dock captain set. Naero neither saw nor smelled him again.

She suffered another pain spell for a few instants.

She tried to punch up Aunt Sleak on the com, but she could only reach the Fleet Second-in-Command, dashing Captain Zalvano. She made a full report on the incident, and met with *The Slipper* to load the transports and speed Chaela to Medical.

The very long day continued to stretch out. At least the excitement of the accident at the Omni Depot kept her mind off the loss of her parents. For a little while.

Her shift ended.

Normally she'd go back to her messy quarters and get some rest.

Naero wasn't sure if she could even do that.

7

Her mother was her sun.

From the very beginning she gave Naero life, as suns gave life to their planets. Naero's life revolved around her mom, following her mother's cycles and becoming part of them. Her mother warmed her, nourished her. She helped Naero grow, smile, and dance.

She taught Naero everything. To laugh, to love, to learn–to fight and always try hard.

Her mother was her light in the darkness, and without her now, Naero learned what true darkness and sorrow were all over again.

Yet her mother also taught Naero to shine on her own, to become her own light. To pull away from even her mother and move through the universe under her own power and force or will, with joy and confidence.

All these things her mother taught her and more.

Naero sat naked in the darkness of her cluttered quarters with the lights and screens off. Everything off. She wrapped her arms around her shins, hugging her knees to her hot, wet face. Her gleaming, long, blue-black geisha hair–another gift from her beautiful mother–draped around her small tight body like a veil, like a dark shroud over her shuddering alabaster flesh.

She hardly picked at her dinner in the mess hall before shutting herself up within her secondary quarters on board *The Shinai*, the second largest starfreighter in the fleet. The vessel was a formidable, 600 ton Enforcer Class, built by Joshua Tech.

The Slipper landed next to them. Naero recognized the high pitched whine of its signature, Armstrong Corps Tech A-38J engines as they cycled down. Naero and Jan had personally helped their aunt replace one of those massive engines on the port side.

She couldn't cry in the dark forever. Her parents wouldn't want that.

Naero slipped back into the second-skin comfort of her black flight togs and tried her com again. She loved the soft, glove-firm feel of Nytex on her body as it compressed and seemed to hold her together.

Aunt Sleak was still unavailable, busy with high-level trade negotiations. As usual.

Naero also felt pretty sure her aunt scrambled to gain more detailed info on the loss of *The Omaria's* expedition.

Whatever their differences, this was a Clan matter, and the two Maeris sisters had always been close. Aunt Sleak also liked and deeply respected Naero's father, perhaps because of his reputation as a champion fighter on the Galactic Fight Circuit, much like herself in her younger days.

When she activated them with her fingertips, Naero's walls flashed alive with past dreams. Now even further away from her new reality.

Images and schematics of trade and merchant ships, transports, and fighters of every make and manufacturer.

From an early age, practically every Spacer worked toward and dreamed about owning their own ship, or at the very least a share in one.

Her mother, Lythe Ivala Maeris, had purchased and captained her first tiny ship right at her coming of age of twenty. An old, obsolete craft that she barely kept flying.

Yet it was all the start Lythe needed, and she expanded her merchant fleet from there, thriving and even surviving the Spacer Wars long enough to train with the Spacer Mystics and become a champion competitive fighter along with her older sister, snag a fine husband, combine forces and fortunes, and have a family. A full life for anyone. A life to be proud of.

Naero turned twenty in about a year, just a few months.

She somehow doubted that her coming of age would hold so much promise.

She stared at her silly, childish dreams flitting across her wallscreens. Sleek new ships, top-of-the-line craft.

Way beyond anything she could ever hope to afford.

Especially now.

One by one, she deleted and trashed those stupid pipe dreams. She could not afford to be a child any longer, living on whims and fantasies. If she was going to make anything of herself now, she'd have to do it all. On her own.

She stopped at the specs and schematics for her parents' flagship, and the lesser support ships of their lost expedition. She'd keep them.

Her father and especially her mother had been so proud of *The Omaria*. They had traded for years, saving their profits, selling everything they owned–including their combined merchant fleet–to their second-in-command, Aunt Sleak. All to have Joshua Tech custom design *The Omaria* just for them. To spend the rest of their lives together, exploring the wonders of the perilous Unknown Sectors.

Now both they and their dreams were dust.

Naero checked the report updates on the news blurts and the *INS* Spacer channels.

From what little was still known, their expedition had been intercepted by a vastly superior, unregistered naval force of mysterious origin.

Conspiracy nuts rambled on about secret alien races, mysterious super fleets, and looming massive invasions of extermination.

But everyone guessed at the perpetrators–filthy Matayan bastards.

No warning, most likely. No attempt to capture or board. The enemy fell upon the expedition in deep space and opened fire. No chance of any help reaching the expedition way out in the middle of nowhere.

Many presumed that the expedition, trapped and hopelessly outgunned, put up a fight briefly, right before it got blasted into oblivion. A brazen, overwhelming attack that reduced *The Omaria* and the support ships of her expedition to nothing but shattered wreckage, floating and spinning off into eternity.

The location was somewhere along the borders of Omni Corps known space and the Spacer Extents, near the ancient lost Cumi Regions of the Sagittarius Coreward Arm.

Several Corps Navies had nevertheless raced at top speed to the scene, promising full investigations.

Naero punched up holovids and stills of her parents–laughing, smiling, kissing. During and after their days on the Galactic fighting circuits. Later shots with her or Janner growing up, or all of them together.

She filled her blank walls with a wild flurry of memory.

They looked so happy, less than a year before.

Naero reached out and tried to touch her parents' faces on the screens. She recalled something her father told her.

"It's all right to have your eyes on the stars, spacechild. Just keep your hands sure and steady on the controls."

She considered performing Shekanda, the Spacer act of shouting at the stars. A form of spiritual and emotional catharsis to release tension and pent up thoughts and emotions. Usually it was done in private, in space. But not always.

Yet another stab of agony in her skull. She dropped and put her head between her knees at this one, gasping and focusing on her breathing– letting it rip through her and pass.

Zhen said she'd pay a price for those psy-drugs and wearing that trigger helmet. The spasms continued to hit without warning, on top of everything else Naero was dealing with.

No. She didn't feel ready for Shekanda just yet.

Instead, she cycled through all the images of her parents from their years. She set them to play across her screenwalls in random waves and loops.

Memories and images. All she had left of them. And when last they parted, she had screamed at them like a spoiled brat not getting her way.

Hot tears fell again. Naero made no attempt to stop them.

Finally the timer on her wristcom went off, calling her back to duty.

Naero strapped her com back on her wrist, washed her face and tossed the wipe into the recycler.

She glanced around at the normal disarray of her quarters. She'd always told her parents, and then Aunt Sleak that she'd put her gear in order. Someday.

Silently she promised herself she'd straighten, like she always did to others. But at least this time she made her bunk and stowed it away.

It was a start.

She tried to contact Janner.

According to his server, Jan was already off duty in the starport somewhere. Perhaps that was a good sign, Jan was out shopping and goofing off with the Irpulian locals–like normal. And yet like her, Jan had no great love for landers, either. Naero never understood why he spent so much time around them. She could take them or leave them.

Jan sought constant distraction and stimulation. She wondered if he might take off again, arranging for the fleet to pick him up somewhere else in a while.

He could always hitch a ride with one of the other Clans to link back up with them later.

Naero secured her slightly less messy secondary quarters behind her.

She stopped at a terminal on her way out of the primary cargo bay to check the duty list. She uploaded her handcomp with third rank orders from the bridge–jobs at her level that still needed completion.

Captain Zalvano, the Fleet Second, noted her availability, and sent her to check on a delayed delivery from Triax Corp. An important shipment, but checking on it was still cake work. The Fleet Second was a good guy; he always tried to be nice to her.

With the Irpul-4 starport an Omni Corps base on a Triax world, their warehouses naturally stood closest to the starport, within a klick or two. The other Corps fanned out beyond that, each in their own heavily advertised sections. Blurt boards and holo screens advertised their various goods and services.

No sense taking a transport. She had her gravwing and she could walk there in twenty minutes. That would give her more time to think. By the time she got back, her shift would be over anyway. Then she'd snag Jan somehow and they'd have a long talk with Aunt Sleak about whatever she had learned.

She spotted Gallan and Saemar in *Shinai's* primary loading bay, working glifters to help pack it full.

"What's up?" Gallan called out, trying to read her face.

"Nothing much. Going to have words with a Triax shipper. They're putting us off again for some unspecified reason."

"Want someone to come with?"

Naero shook her head. "I can handle it." She still wanted to lose herself somewhere, if only for a little while. Get away from everyone and everything. Like that was possible.

Perhaps Jan had the right idea

"Safe journey," Saemar said.

"Watch out for the locals," Gallan warned.

She snorted. "They'd better watch out for me."

Despite Gallan's cautions, Naero wasn't too worried. She'd handled squabbles, prejudice, and fights with landers since she was a kid. She knew when to stand and when to run. Usually.

The world beyond the port and the bubble cities around the port was still somewhat foreboding, a thin harsh atmosphere with occasional caustic storms.

During jump she had studied how Irpul-4's native plants, insects, and animals adapted, with mid-sized reptiles dominating the surfaces and the shallow seas. Feeble attempts had been made to terraform the planet, especially around the inhabited bands, but no one had done a proper job of it.

At least the air inside the domes was more or less breathable. Everyone in the fleet had taken an acclimating compensator dosage upon arrival. AC-Ds were SSP–Standard Spacer Procedure–for non-normal atmospheres.

The autodirection feature in her comp led her through the net of avenues and buildings meshed together. Once out of the starport itself, she realized she wasn't missing that much. Naero despised old Gigacorp starports and trade hubs all over again. Drab, uniform, no art, no vision. The station at Irpul-4 was a classic example of their lack of style, nearly two centuries old.

What a dump.

Even several feeble revamps hadn't helped the place over the years. In fact, most of the changes had been superficial, merely cosmetic. Some parts were from this era, other windows or facings, or screens or spolymers from an earlier time.

At some point, those in charge had simply given up, leaving a mis-mated hodgepodge of tek and style, spattered about like the worn refuse of several decades. A trading slum.

And that was exactly what too many Gigacorp starports were like.

What a difference Spacer starports were. Each one beautiful and aesthetically unique. A challenge to the imagination.

It didn't matter that she'd never been to Irpul-4 before. She'd dropped in on too many of its clones since she could float. And Triax, one of the oldest of the Corps, seemed no different.

She rounded a corner, pre-occupied with her own thoughts and the readouts and info on her comp.

She bumped right into someone very tall. The guy blotted out the weak sunlight.

Naero bounced off him as if he were made of duranadium. He was either in fantastic shape or a muscle-hyped Corps Sterodan. But they usually stank pretty bad.

This guy smelled of spice and citrus, a little cloying, but not unpleasant. And yet there was something else. What was his heavy cologne hiding from her sensitive nose?

"Excuse me," he said. He stood very tall, well over two meters–taller than Gallan, but not as tall as her father. Naero stood almost three heads shorter by comparison.

She pulled back. His face was obscured by the sun directly behind him.

Too lanky and athletic to be a Sterodan. He wore expensive lander clothes, local high class business stuff, all brocade on shimmering velvet. Where was the guy's retinue? Bodyguards? Funny thing, he wore no jewelry.

Landers often wore a lot of jewelry for some reason.

She moved slightly to one side to get a better look at him. Nothing about this guy was normal or ordinary. His eyes were sharply gray, almost darkened silver, deep and fierce like the gleam of blades. Naero caught his scent again and her mouth almost opened. The scent, the eyes, his bearing, no jewelry.

He was a Spacer. She'd bet serious creds on it.

What was he doing in gaudy local duds? Most Spacers despised dressing like landers, except when necessary. His smile seemed rather ironic, touches of amusement in his dark, grim face.

"Sorry," she said. "No harm." She went to veer around him, going back to her figures.

The stranger stepped in front of her this time.

Naero backed off slightly, automatically assuming a neutral defensive stance. Spacers seldom attacked each other without provocation. Yet even among themselves, there were rare renegades, criminals, and outcasts.

The big guy nodded, looking rather amused. "You show signs of prowess, but your training has been minimal."

What was he talking about? Naero had been trained by the best. She was an expert fighter.

"Try me."

He suppressed a slight chuckle. "Er, what I mean is excuse me, miss. I'm not trying to frighten you. I merely want to talk, not spar."

"Then talk. I'm busy."

He did chuckle. "A real charmer. You look like your mother, but you must take after your aunt."

She glared up at him. How dare he compare her to–

"I'll try not to detain you too long," he said. "But I couldn't help but notice from your togs that you're with Sleak Maeris's fleet?"

"Maybe. Who wants to know?"

"Let's just say...an old family friend."

"You got a name?"

His eyes softened and his smile left him. He seemed almost saddened as he spoke his name.

"Baeven. Your aunt knows me. Call her if you like, but she'll probably curse. Our last meeting...went badly, I'm afraid. Entirely my fault, really. It usually is."

Who was this guy?

"Tell her that I would like to meet with her again and make amends for Toraga-5. Are all three of her ships here?"

"Check the registry. Docking pool Gamma-78. And it's five ships now."

The stranger seemed impressed. "Five ships. Business must be good. My compliments." He glanced at her rank again and bowed. "And as I have already guessed, you must be her niece, Naero Amashin Maeris."

She bowed in return. "How do you know me?" She backed up a bit more. "If you have business with Aunt Sleak, go talk to her."

"In time. Actually I came in part to see you, and your brother–Janner Maeris Ramsey."

Even more curious.

Most landers were completely ignorant of the fact that female Spacers took the Clan name of their mother, while Spacer males took the family name of their father. First or last names could be used as middle names. Amashin was the first name of Naero's grandfather, on her mother's side.

"What do want with me and my brother?" Spacer or not, she suddenly did not like this character. If he knew so much already, why did he want to talk to them?

"A matter of grave importance, I'm afraid. One that your poor parents stumbled upon by unhappy chance."

She almost took a step forward. "What do you know about any of that?"

His easy smile returned. "I am an old friend of the family, after all."

"I never heard of you."

His face darkened, as if out of deeper sadness. "That is not important. I tell you honestly how deeply I grieved to hear about your parents' tragic demise. They deserved far better."

"I bet."

"They were very important to me in many ways, Naero. Your entire clan is."

"If you have something to tell me and Janner, then talk."

"This is not a good place for what I have to say. It would be best if we could talk privately–in a secure area?"

"Come to *The Shinai*. If Aunt Sleak lets you on board, we'll talk. Can't you tell me anything?"

He tossed a crystal chip at her. Naero caught it.

"I paid a great deal for that bit of coded transmission," he said. "That copy may be of interest to you. Break it carefully when you're back on board your ship."

Naero stored it in her comp.

Baeven lowered his voice. "Your parents' deaths were not accidental, spacechild."

"No shit. Everyone knows that. Most likely Matayan corsairs."

"That, and much more. You knew the might of your parents' ship, Naero. How heavily they armed it. What would you say if I told you that *The Omaria* and her expedition were intercepted and taken out...not only by the corsairs of the Matayan Cartels, but by thirty elite naval cruisers and three-score advanced heavy destroyers–all with the direct backing of several Gigacorps?"

Naero gasped. "What? Why?"

What could they have been exploring in the Unknown Sectors to bring that much firepower to bear against them? It didn't make any sense.

"That's where it gets interesting," Baeven said. Then he glanced around once.

"I'm afraid I must be going. I'll see you and Janner on board *The Shinai*." He grinned wickedly. "If your aunt doesn't vaporize me on sight."

He turned away from her without another word.

Naero gasped. "What? You unload on me like that and then cut? Why not go back with me now?"

He shook his head, looking off in a certain direction. "Impossible. Some...rival associates of mine are heading this way. They can be very unpleasant when they wish to be. I suggest you continue on your duties so that they do not notice you. You and your brother should stay close to your Aunt Sleak and listen to her. Don't take any unforeseen trips. Avoid strangers."

"Yeah, like you," she said.

"That, too, might have been wise. But there are powerful forces moving, applying vast resources at their command. I'm not sure yet how you and your brother fit into the game, Naero. Guard yourselves."

Another quick glance from him made Naero check her six. In the distance, she heard the whine of vehicles.

When she turned back to speak to Baeven, she found herself alone in the alley once more.

Naero's right hand went to the blade at her hip. The other brought up her hand comp.

A lifeform scan showed nothing. She activated her gravwing and popped up into the sky for an instant.

No one could move that fast. Did he have some kind of personal cloaker or gravunit? Rumors abounded concerning such devices.

Baeven had Shadowforce written all over him. What did her parents have to do with Spacer Intel?

What he told her made her nervous, paranoid, and all the more curious.

What in the hell had her parents been involved in that got them killed like that? What could they possibly have come across that the Corps would want so badly?

She recalled Baeven's cautions suddenly and popped over a couple of blocks before anyone could spot her in that vicinity.

Naero de-activated her gravwing and picked her way cautiously through the alleys around the extensive Triax warehouses. She avoided the occasional derelict and roving groups of landers. Amid the refuse and isolation of the streets and alleys, she soon wished that she had brought Gallan along. She considered going back, but she was so close to her destination now that she figured she should go on.

Several muffled explosions suddenly rocked the starport in the direction Baeven had noted. Smoke rose up. Sirens converged.

Naero neared her goal and kept to her own business.

A few minutes later she argued with a head dock manager in a Triax Corp shipping office that smelled of dust and strange chemicals. He was a sweaty, frazzled little bald guy with thin wisps of hair around the sides and back as if he'd tried to pull the rest out with his hands and only partially succeeded.

"Bottom line," she said, "we have a deal. Your people contracted our fleet to ship heavy machinery, vehicles, and robo-construction units to Epsilon Sextanis-6. Our ships leave tomorrow morning, with or without your goods. Either way, we still get paid."

The little guy pleaded with her. "The schedule's all goofed up. We're overloaded. My people are working around the clock. We'll get the shipment to you. I just don't know when."

She nodded and held up both hands. "That's what you said earlier. Just remember, we get paid either way. You'll have to explain it to your supers if we don't have anything to deliver. Get the stuff to us tonight, or we'll sell the space for something else."

"May I be of service?" Both of them turned and gawked at the stunning woman who had just walked in.

Highbrow Corps woman from her clothes, showing one leg and one shoulder. That weird kind of lander style that seemed both slinky and yet professional.

Naero's first impression was that there wasn't anything modest about this woman. She was top Corps all the way, from her crystal shoes to the roots of each strand of her shimmering holographic hair.

Only the elite had the creds to flaunt that kind of style.

Her luxuriant green eyes locked onto Naero and gleamed. A hungry smile swelled her violet lips. Most Corps elites had that smile. This one was particularly avaricious.

The dock manager sweated torps suddenly. Apparently he knew who she was. "Lady Drianne Imiviel. I-I'm–"

"Honored, to be sure." Naero heard movement outside of the office, and suddenly felt sorry for the dock manager. Busting his hump for the Corps and they didn't even let him talk.

Lady Drianne didn't even look at him. "Dock Manager Farris, we are conducting a surprise efficiency inspection."

Farris paled like a moonrise. "B-but, we just had one two months ago! We p-passed in the ninetieth percentile!"

"Our records show you were warned about the inspection so that you had time to prepare."

"I–"

"Don't bother denying it. Your conspirators have already confessed and been demoted. Now, this shipper in question. What is the problem?"

"Look, it's no problem," Naero said.

"That will be determined." A flash of that smile again. "Now, Mr. Farris. Why hasn't your staff delivered Triax's goods to this shipper in an efficient and timely manner?"

"It's not my fault. Priority shipments came through, heavy military traffic. The locals...they just had a holiday a few days ago and the loading teams are all off speed. The Corps floaters and migrants I ordered haven't all come in yet, and the ones I have came to me, uh...badly trained and motivated. I'm doing the best with what I have. We're a little behind, but she'll get her goods."

"Good enough," Naero said. She turned to depart.

"A moment, young woman," the Corps lady said. "I may need a report from you. Now, Mr. Farris, it seems that you've given certain shipments priority, and not just Corp-haulers over indeps. It appears that this cleverly veiled series of priority shipments matches investments made by other family and friends and acquaintances of yours, scattered over thirty or forty systems."

Lady Drianne pressed a radiant jewel on her wristcomp.

Farris looked as if he'd been shoved out of an airlock. Naero yawned. Wasn't anything any other dock alpha wouldn't do.

She grew mildly curious as to why Triax Corps chose to roll over on this guy. He'd either gotten too greedy or hadn't given the right supers a big enough cut. Either way, he'd torped off someone high up in Triax.

"We'll talk, in your office, in one hour. Have your records ready for inspection."

Two other Triax personnel and a bot joined them from just outside the doorway, stopping behind Lady Drianne. The foremost looked clerkish and efficient, no doubt the inspector. If the lady was a shark, this guy was a piranha.

The bot and the other person behind them were of interest. Bodyguards. Only the lander elites could afford bots. With their strong, independent need for competency and self-sufficiency, Spacers never relied on them.

This bot was a class eight Triaxian sec-bot, with some apparent modifications. It moved about fluidly, rearing up on four of its six legs. Its various recorders and scanners clicked and whirred, very insect-like, but it seemed focused on Naero for some reason. Lady Drianne spoke to the clerk.

"Inspector Cho, take my sec-drone and escort Mr. Farris. Make certain that he does not leave us, harm any records...or himself. Mr. Farris, your second? Mr. Farris?"

Farris looked dazed, then he punched up a micro-button on his finger band. "Hassan," he said in a horse whisper. "Get up here right away. I don't care what you're doing. Get up here. Now!"

Farris drifted off in a fog, muttering to himself, flanked by the sec-bot and the clerk.

The second bodyguard stepped out of the shadows.

Not too ugly...for a Matayan goon.

He loomed tall and meaty, with a thick face and a bright, intricately braided blond horsetail. It clashed with his Corps primate suit.

Only blooded Matayan warriors could wear their hair long. Their nobility wore two or more braids to note their rank.

Naero wondered how many stars this chunk had on his chest, one for each ten kills. Ten stars earned the formal title of Slayer. Like most Matayan killers, he looked like he enjoyed his work.

The form of a battle blade under his jacket was more than an ornament. She guessed he had several other concealed weapons on his person—just like herself.

Naero gave him her best girlish grin. In return, he locked eyes with her, glared, and curled his lips into an ugly sneer. If it came down to it, she might be able to take him with her speed, but it would be a tough fight. This guy was definitely a serious threat.

Lady Drianne finally turned back to her. "You'll have your goods tonight...miss?"

"Maeris. Naero Amashin Maeris."

She looked pleased. "With Sleak Maeris? When did she have a daughter?"

"She didn't." Naero could never imagine her aunt even holding a child, let alone one of her own. "I'm her niece."

"I know your aunt well; give her my regards. I've brought plenty of associates with me to assist the new Acting Dock Manager. Triax apologizes for any inconvenience."

Naero cursed to herself. "Associate" meant "slave" in Triax lingo. Floaters and migrants culled from the Corp's systems, expendable freeze-ship labor, shunted about here and there. People were a cheap commodity. But the Corps didn't waste anything, or anyone.

"Thank you," Naero said. "I'll tell my aunt you said hello."

"Tell her to contact me. I might have something of interest for her fleet. Perhaps we'll meet again, Mistress Naero."

"Perhaps," Naero said. She left the loading dock, her gopher shift almost over. By now she had plenty to talk to Aunt Sleak about. And she wasn't even back yet.

She didn't have to glance behind to know that Lady Drianne and her Matayan goon stared after her, watching her leave. Her entire day continued to get creepier and more sinister.

Why did it suddenly seem as if everyone was so interested in her? That thought made her very uncomfortable.

She needed to make sure that she actually made it back to the fleet.

8

Naero carefully headed back toward *The Shinai.*

The strange events of the day had her so paranoid that she wasn't at all surprised when three local thugs stepped out in front of her to try their luck.

"Hey, spack, gimme some." They attempted to block her way.

Naero made a point of rolling her eyes. She didn't have time for amateurs.

"Give you some what? Looks like you three morons already have diseases."

They stopped laughing.

She could buzz away with her gravwing, but this could be fun.

The leader stepped forward, rusty knife in one hand, an old stunner in the other. "You're mine, little slit. I'm gonna split you wide open while you're still wiggling."

"Take her down," the ugly lander girl said, circling. She held a plasbaton like a club. "I wanna see some spack blood."

The third–the biggest, smelliest, and stupidest looking one–had a face covered with boils, a weighted length of chain, and some spikeknucks.

"Oh, we'll see some blood." He laughed in anticipation. "Loosen' this gash up for me, Dren. I think I'm in love."

Naero almost laughed. "You lander guys can't think up any better lines?" She wasn't about to give losers like them any satisfaction.

They rushed her from three angles. Naero kick-flipped off the near wall, darting away so fast that all she needed was to shove ugly-girl out of her way.

She ran them the length of the alley, just fast enough to keep them chasing. When she had them winded and they looked about ready to give up, she stopped. They charged her with a final burst of energy.

Naero half-grinned.

Them red-faced and puffing; her not even breathing hard.

She kicked the leader's forearm so fast he nailed himself with his own stunner. He gaped in surprise and fell upon his own knife in his other hand, still twitching.

Naero spun and slammed him into big oaf. The two goons went down in a tangle.

Somehow the stunner went off again.

Naero ducked the whir of ugly girl's plasbaton and blocked a knee. Two palm heels to the face and a jab to the throat staggered the lander.

Naero flipped her hard over one hip and left her moaning on the plascrete.

Something whipped around her ankle. Big oaf's weighted chain. She could smell his approach, a thick wafting wave of filth and unwashed male stench. He came at her like a crab. He lifted his spikeknucks to tag her.

Naero half-stepped forward and side-kicked with her free leg, broke his nose again, splattered boils, and shattered one eye socket. A spin-heel kick to the temple put him down for good. She shook the chain off her ankle, resisting the hidden urge to finish them.

"Amateurs," she muttered. "Ugly and dumb." These landers weren't worth killing–not that she'd ever taken a life.

Rank scents of fresh human blood and other bodily fluids filled the air. Naero hadn't broken a sweat. She brushed herself off, wiped her feet clean with some rags, and punched up the portcops to pick up the trash.

It did feel rather good to work out part of her anger and frustration on some random goons.

Then a skycar descended at the opening of the corridor alley in front of her. Things just kept getting weirder.

At first she thought it might be a portcop patrol car. Instead she saw a big holo-spolymered limo with eight doors.

That worried her a bit.

The limo whispered a few centimeters off the ground. A door snapped open and a well-dressed foreign businessman leaned out. Polished shoes, gloved hands upon a jeweled cane. His face marked him in his forties, but he was probably older. His long, oiled, dark hair and short beard were immaculate, a scarlet holosilk turban covering most of his head. He could be a merchant prince, or perhaps even a Corps diplomat.

"Excuse me, miss," he said, his elocution precise and powerful. "My driver spotted trouble. Are you in any need of assistance, my dear?"

She waved. "No thanks. Just a misunderstanding."

"I see." He smiled, his admiration apparent. "Have you notified the authorities?"

"On their way. Thanks for your concern."

He bowed his head to her. "Not at all. Can we lift you anywhere? We're headed to the docking bays."

Did she look that dumb?

"That's all right." Cheap thugs were easy to hire. This guy could have set the whole thing up. "Thanks once again."

"Safe journey then," he said.

That threw her a little. Usually, Spacers were the only ones who said that to each other.

This guy was obviously a lander, but he'd picked up a bit of their lingo somewhere. Before she could respond, the older gentleman pulled himself in and tapped with his cane. The door snapped shut. The skylimo rose straight up.

Another spasm of pain ripped through her head. Naero clutched her skull with both hands and leaned her weight against a chain link fence to stay up. For some reason, she recalled her dream where the handsome green guy with the flowing golden hair rammed a sword into her brain.

Then she considered how she needed to find a boyfriend at some point in the near future.

More pain from that damn psy helmet. Zhen said she might suffer such attacks for weeks, perhaps even months. She might also experience hallucinations and bouts of delusions bordering on temporary insanity.

Great. Something different to look forward to, at least.

Good thing it hadn't hit her during her little tussle with the locals. That might have been bad. She hit her gravwing and zipped back to the starport.

She was already completely frazzled from the loss of her parents. A little induced madness might be a welcome distraction from that pain.

Searching for Jan back on *The Shinai*, Naero walked in upon Janner and the usual–a gaggle of half-dressed lander girls.

She gritted her teeth, smiled, and shook her head.

Janner was certainly grieving…in his own way.

She wondered how many of these bimbos believed everything Jan spoon-fed them about his exploits.

What a bunch of crap.

Yet she could see why these spoiled little landers went for Jan, with his long dark hair and their father's lanky good looks. Who better to torp their wealthy Corps parents off than a flashy Spacer punk in flight togs and blades?

Naero giggled. If they only knew how tame and mundane Janner really was. His favorite areas of study–advanced math, stellar physics, and navigation. She shook her head.

Yeah, what a rebel.

One of the girls, the alpha female of the pack apparently, kept herself glued to Janner's side like a Centauran weasel in heat. She was a long, slender doll-like thing with green hair, white skin, and blue eyes. She wore a black, light-absorbing dress that was way too short, black heels, and white lacy tights whose patterns shifted and flickered as she moved.

Haisha, Jan, get a room for a few hours. How embarrassing.

Lander girls.

Although an intensely sensual people, Spacers showed little affection in public, and discreetly reserved sex for their private lives–behind closed doors.

The respected norm.

But at Jan's age, self-control and professional behavior weren't Jan's strengths. She knew he indulged himself, way too much.

Naero had been tempted herself with a few cute Spacer boys here and there. But so far she hadn't found a worthy candidate. She told herself that choosing a lover, especially one's first and maybe last, was serious Spacer business on the most personal level.

Her mother and most Spacer women–except Saemar–had very strong opinions on the matter.

She felt heart ache again. Never more would she be able discuss such things–or anything–sitting in private with her mother on their beds, brushing their long hair together before they slept.

The searing memory of how beautiful her mother had been at such times ripped through her soul.

As usual, romance for Naero would have to wait. She kept herself too busy on purpose, and never got too close to any Spacer. Most landers she hardly even looked at.

Jan finally noticed her standing there. Always the opposite of her. He wasn't that picky. "Hi, Naero," he said with a dreamy smile.

The lander pack appraised her sultry looks and athletic form as a potential threat.

He let them burn for a while. "How's biz, sib?" They relaxed and smiled again, figuring out she was his sister.

"You haven't been bringing unauthorized personnel on board again, have you Jan?"

"Don't get twist on me. I told them the rules. He put his arm around the pack-leader. "Meet Devi. Her mother's some Corps princess here on business. She's invited me and our whole fleet to a big Corps party on her parents' yacht tonight. Wanna come with?"

"Maybe. Have you seen Aunt Sleak?"

He frowned and waved one hand. "Cutting deals, like always. I think she's on *The Slipper*."

"You think?"

"Hey, I'm not on duty. Excuse me. My entourage grows restless."

"But of course, my prince." She bowed to him on her way out. Then she transferred to *The Slipper*, shaking her throbbing head again.

Perhaps another mist shower would relax her. Naero ducked back into her cabin for a quick one.

She closed her eyes, letting the mist wave over her. Just breathing in and out. She looked up and lifted her hair to check that big zit on her forehead in the shower mirror.

It ached, swollen, inflamed, and painful. When she squeezed it slightly, dark red blood squirted and it split open.

Spasms of pain ripped through her head. Naero gasped.

A third, bloody violet eyeball stared back at her in the mirror. She could even kind of see through it in a blurry way, but it moved on its own power, roving and glancing here and there beyond her control. It's independent actions alarmed and disoriented her further.

A new fricking eye.

Sticking out from her forehead.

9

Naero screamed in terror, shaking beyond her own control.

She toppled out of her mist shower and fell into the junk on her messy floor.

Like a trapped wild animal, she clawed and scrabbled through the refuse, trying to escape her own reflection.

She grabbed her togs and held them to her naked body, curling up with them in a corner.

She held a shaking hand up to her face. She could see it up close.

With all three eyes.

Naero jerked her hand away.

Then she leaned out and peered at herself in her shower's steamed-up mirror wall.

All three of her eyes blinked back at her.

She pulled her head back, still shaking uncontrollably.

"Oh, shit. Oh, damn."

It was official. She had fried her brain, and now she was going apeshit crazy, just like Zhen had warned her.

What was even more terrifying was the intense feeling that her new eyeball was even trying to *talk* to her somehow–with a will of its own.

That was even more nuts, so she did her level best to ignore those impressions.

Naero couldn't handle it. She'd always been in control. What if she completely flipped out and couldn't function? What was real any more?

What wasn't? A hallucination. Of course. It had to be. Nobody just grew another eye in their skull. That was impossible. Temporary insanity. A delusion. Her mind was convincing her that something impossible was really there.

But shit, it all looked and felt so real.

Ignore it. Ignore the new eyeball and it would eventually go away. That was her new strategy. She got dressed.

Looking out of the new eye along with her other two kept freaking her out and even made her a little dizzy at times.

Solution? She yanked out a black headband, tied it on tight and covered the new eye up.

If she wasn't bonkers, she could swear the eyeball was protesting somehow. She could sense it.

More insanity. At least with the new eye covered up, she felt more like her old, not-crazy self.

The next test. Go out and find one of her friends to show it to. Find out what they saw when they looked at her new addition.

Her fingers shook so bad, it was a while before she could locate anyone on her wristcom. Tyber was the closest one, working with a tek maintenance crew in one of the holds.

She nearly ran up to him. Barely avoided slamming into him. She stood a little too close, but she was desperate.

Tyber turned to her, somewhat taken aback. "Hey, Naero. What's wrong? You look a little panicked. You never panic." He appeared very worried.

Naero opened her mouth to try to explain, and found she couldn't speak. Nothing came out. What in the hell could she say?

"Naero," he said. "You don't look right. You're going through a lot. Maybe you should sit down for a bit. I'll give Zhen a call."

Naero patted him on the shoulder repeatedly, leaning in.

"Tell me, Tyber. What do you see?" She yanked the headband up for an instant, and then quickly pulled it back down.

Tyber's mouth fell open. "Uh…"

Naero glared at him, her eyes pleading.

"What am I supposed to see?"

Naero yanked her headband right off, tilted her head up and pointed at her new eye with both index fingers. She stared straight at him with it.

"I...uh. Well, your forehead is a little broken out. You know, Zhen has some cream that will help with that. She uses it all the–"

Naero sobbed, hugged him, and then pulled away and grabbed him by both arms, smiling, shaking him, and almost bawling. She probably scared him even more.

He couldn't see it. Tyber didn't see it. The new eyeball wasn't real. It was just a delusion. Even though it blinked and looked right at her friend.

Naero sat down, laughing in relief, her arms folded across her knees, her head down in them.

It would go away. Eventually, if she ignored it, it would go away. Her brain would heal itself. Given time.

Tyber set his tool kit down and knelt at her side.

"Are you sure you're doing okay, Naero? You've been through a lot, and Zhen did say that the strain might flip you out," he swallowed hard, "a little. You want me to take you back to your cabin? Maybe you should rest for a while."

Naero grinned and put her headband back on. That made her craziness easier to deal with.

"I'll be okay, Tyber. I just need some time to heal and sort stuff out. Hey, I'm sorry I bothered you while you were on duty."

They stood up together.

Even Tyber breathed a sigh of relief. "It's all right. Are you sure you're okay, Naero? I mean, you really had me worried for a few seconds there. I've never seen you like that before."

She patted him on the shoulder. "Everything's going to be all right, Ty. You go back to your duty shift, and I still have to find Aunt Sleak."

"Okay, if you say so."

Naero laughed, and they parted. She made her way toward the bridge. If this was temporary insanity–just a delusion–perhaps she could handle it, at least until it passed.

It just felt so real.

10

Aunt Sleak wasn't on her flagship, *The Slipper*. She'd taken one of the shuttles back up with Captain Volaski to *The Dromon*, for a meeting with the other ship captains.

The big planetoid vessel couldn't enter an atmosphere, but it had great conference, training, and communication facilities. Naero patched through a com to Aunt Sleak once more. This time, a response actually came back.

Her aunt's piercing gray eyes focused on her through the comlink screen

"Naero, I heard about Chaela and the Omni run. Good work, but we're still down one crew. Zalvano said you got that Triax shipment straightened out?"

"We'll have it by tonight."

"Looks like a full run. If nothing else comes up, I'll see you and Janner on *The Slipper* for dinner tonight. I might have some more news by then. I hope."

"I think Janner...has plans. I might go with him."

Aunt Sleak glanced away. "Oh? You two better clear it with me first."

"Janner's got some little rich girl who wants to seduce him on her mother's Corps yacht tonight."

"That's a surprise. That boy thinks he's a player, and yet he has no taste."

"I agree. The entire fleet's invited, by the way."

"Sounds like fun." Her aunt glanced back and sighed. "There's been too much gloom and doom after the news concerning *The Omaria*. My sister loved life; she wouldn't want that. Perhaps we could all use a little distraction, and let the Corps foot the bill. Why don't we go along, and show these Triax flunkies some Spacer style?"

Naero blinked, floored again. Aunt Sleak didn't usually hit the social circuit very often. She always looked good, but she could dazzle like a quasar given the right opportunity.

Fix her up and she looked like a zillion megs. When the time came, she enjoyed showing off and making the landers drool.

But such high-level Corps shindigs were rumored to be pretty depraved and decadent. She had heard all the stories. Seen some vids.

Naero had never actually bothered going to one before.

"Meet me on *The Slipper* in two hours, Naero. I've got an Akoran number that you'd look great in. If you're bold enough to wear it, of course."

"Okay... Oh, and Aunt Sleak, a couple of things happened today that I want to talk to you about."

"Can it wait? I've still got a lot—"

"I was attacked today, but that's not—"

"Who and why?" Sleak demanded.

"Just a couple of lander thugs. I took them down easy."

"Good. I'd expect that, especially from you. A Spacer onworld is like a walking target sometimes. That's just the way. So what's the problem?"

"It was a weird afternoon all around. After the attack, some rich Corps guy landed in a sky limo and offered me a hand, then a lift. Very odd."

"You refused."

"I wasn't born yesterday. Before that, I met a Corp Lady at the loading docks of all places. Named Drianne; she seemed to know you and wanted you to contact her. Like everybody else today, she and her Matayan bodyguard seemed overly interested in me."

"Drianne Imiviel of Triax Corp. I heard she was in system. Did business with her, a long while ago. Nothing ever went wrong that I could blame on her, but a couple of deals left a bad taste in my mouth. Your father knew her, I think."

"Dad knew her?"

"I think he wasted a little time with her before your mother got a lock on him. I'd bet a hundred megs that it's Drianne's yacht we're invited to tonight. She always has some kind of game going. Maybe I can find out something from her. Tell your brother to guard more than his pants."

"I will. Do you think there's any connection between Drianne and the attack on me, or the limo guy?"

"Who knows, at this point? I wouldn't worry about it too much. We ship off tomorrow. I'm kind of glad. This all sounds too weird. It doesn't feel right. The sooner we're back in deep space the better."

"Oh, I almost forgot, there was this other guy before all of that. He said he wanted to talk to both of us, and Janner, about mom and dad. Said his name was Baeven."

Aunt Sleak choked on her own breath.

For another instant there was silence.

Then her eyes narrowed to slits, the way they only did in battle.

"Naero, don't say another word."

"What? Who is—"

"Shut up. Take my private shuttle up to *The Dromon.* Go straight to my quarters there and arm yourself. My personal guards will protect you. I'll release the entry codes to you en route."

"I don't understand. Why—"

"Do as I say, Naero. This is a primary direct order. Tell Janner to go to my private quarters on *The Slipper* and stay there until my security escort arrives. Get going, now. Out."

Icicles knifed up her veins.

Very little could rattle Aunt Sleak like that.

All she did was mention some guy's name.

She contacted Janner immediately and gave him the orders. Janner fumed and argued and demanded explanations, but Naero had none to offer. He gave in.

Naero left *The Shinai* and boarded *The Slipper,* in the next starport docking bay over to the right. *The Slipper* was Aunt Sleak's flagship, a 500 ton Omni Corps Corvette, originally designed as a superfast blockade runner.

When Naero arrived, Aunt Sleak had the entire fleet on priority one security alert, one level below battle stations. The crews had armed themselves and conducted patrols and sensor sweeps of all ships and the docking bay.

This was going to throw their scheduling off; it might even cost them serious creds.

Aunt Sleak's Second met her there, dashing Captain Zalvano of *The Shinai*, along with a three-Spacer fireteam in assault armor and heavy plasma rifles.

They escorted her personally to Aunt Sleak's onboard, private shuttle.

The trim little Joshua Corp craft sat only four people and carried little cargo. More of a fighter than anything else.

The fireteam pulled back in prep for launch.

Zalvano went with her. A class act. He was in his early forties, rugged, handsome, smart, and completely fearless. Deep, dark violet eyes; long black hair gathered behind his neck in a golden clip. Lines of steel and silver ran through its length.

Common knowledge held that he and Aunt Sleak were lovers. Naero could understand and respect that. Zalvano was Sleak's honorable partner in every other way. The captain of *The Shinai* had a strong hand; he was good with his people. He possessed a strict but generous nature, and an ironic sense of humor that grew on a person—with time.

Zalvano smiled. "Hey spacechild, want me to—"

"Not a chance," Naero said.

Aunt Sleak had *never* even given her or Janner a ride in the craft, let alone let them pilot it offworld.

Another alarming turn of events, but Naero still couldn't help being excited.

She sank into the plush, fragrant gel chair of the pilot's station and ran her hands along the perfect controls.

They secured their flight helmets.

Then she powered up, feeling the energy race through her. She felt so befuddled, she almost forgot about her insanity.

Once they had clearance, Naero eased the craft out of its pod on *The Slipper* and lifted off from the docking bay, and then the starport itself. The controls were uniform, but handled more fluidly than the GV's and other bulk shuttles and transports. Naero vectored toward *The Dromon's* codes and punched it.

Zalvano opened his mouth to warn her.

The burst of speed and the resulting g-forces mashed them into their flight seats.

Too late.

Even through the atmosphere the acceleration felt incredible, far beyond the performance of the ambling GV's. Both Naero and Janner had pushed them to their limits, even with modifications.

What responses! This was definitely elite fighter speed. Auto controls and scans popped up online as needed. No warnings.

They cleared the atmosphere in moments.

What an awesome ride. Naero had practiced in stunt simulators for various fighters throughout history, but even holos couldn't prepare her for the sheer rush and exhilaration of the real thing.

Irpul-4 vanished behind her.

Naero couldn't help but think of her father.

Her father was her ship. Whatever ship she flew.

The hull was his strength wrapped around her to keep her safe. His might sustained her through all the extremes the universe had to offer, protecting her. He carried her to places of wonder and beauty, peril and truth.

His eyes were the viewscreens she looked out of. Through his gentle, laughing eyes, she saw the universe and learned its ways and complexities. As she grew, like a true explorer she lived a grand adventure.

Guided by her father, doors, hatches, bulkheads, blast doors and iris valves opened and closed around her, teaching her the lessons, knowledge, and wisdom they contained.

When she was still tiny, her father taught her to fly through space. He became her drive, her wings, her lift.

She rose up safe in his big hands and faced the universe grinning, wise, and fearless.

He held her high. So very high aloft.

She laughed and lifted her head, arching her back, pointing her toes, spreading out her arms. Like him, he taught her how to become a ship.

Her heart a fusion drive.

In his mighty hands, she jumped from star to star, from system to system. Making runs, coming in for landings. Setting down on beds and chairs and tables that transformed into starports and landing zones. Blasting offworld for her next port of call.

All under her own power.

Naero pitied landers. The vast majority of them never even got up into space.

She loved it so, like all Spacers. The only thing that made her truly feel alive, and free. Under the Gigacorps, most landers never knew much freedom of any kind.

"Decel," Zalvano warned. "I know you're having fun, but pay attention or you'll overshoot your rendezvous."

"Okay, okay," she said, and powered down to compensate. "Decel underway. Just got a little taken." She was still half-tempted to blast off and really head out for a ride.

"Sure you don't want me to take it in?"

Zalvano smiled at her once more. He knew what she was feeling. Her parents taught her what all Spacers knew.

Onworld, they were only half alive.

In space, everything became clearer, richer.

"Pretty trim, isn't she?" Zalvano said. "I take her out every now and then. She cost your aunt a load, but she's worth it."

"I'm gonna have one like this or better someday."

"Probably better. Some of her's nearly obsolete already. Sleak's about to refit her. But she'll still beat most of the Corp stuff out there. Only the best military rigs could touch her. Check out her offensive and defensive specs while we're on approach."

Naero called up the O&D systems, just as he suggested.

Her lips parted. "Whoa, baby!"

The little shuttle wasn't just fast. She was armed like a heavy fighter. With level two shields, she was practically a light assault ship.

The immense, darkened form of *The Dromon* loomed up before them all too soon. Naero switched off the auto approach and landing sequence and took the shuttle in manually, setting down on the planetoid landing pad all too soon. A bubble dome popped up over them, filling with a rush of air.

Naero powered the little craft down and they got out. She tucked her flight helmet back into the seat and patted the little ship with no small affection. "You and me could be friends."

"I think she likes you," Zalvano said.

"Naero," Aunt Sleak blurted in over her com. "You got up here quick enough. Don't slack now. My quarters. ASAP."

"Better not keep her waiting," Zalvano said, raising one eyebrow.

Naero nodded to him and hit the deck running, still struggling to ignore her own internal madness

Time to find out what was going on.

11

The heavy blast panels to Aunt Sleak's private quarters on board *The Dromon* swung open.

Naero had never been cleared to go up there.

She stepped into wide space, a luxury unavailable on any of the other ships, but still not as opulent as what she expected, for a Spacer Merchant Captain of Aunt Sleak's wealth and fame.

In fact, the more she observed, the more austere and even militarily efficient it all looked. All off-white and muted pastels, soft-lit and serene. The huge chamber was mostly oval, yet irregular in many regards. Art pieces of gleaming gold and precious metals, glowing clusters of gems and alien crystals on the ceiling and walls here and there, backlit in tasteful arrangements.

Hidden smartwall panels and pop-up consoles she only guessed at.

Serving as one of a few active touches of anything living, fresh purple flowers of some alien variety bloomed in planter sconces set along the pale walls at medium height.

Their sharp, sweet fragrance filled the air. But the serviceable, fixed furnishings were sparse, adding to the sense of space.

She walked on and gazed up at the stars through a ceiling that consisted of an enormous viewport, the ponderous blast shutters on the uppermost level of the planetoid wide open on the outside.

Panels whispered open on one wall. Aunt Sleak came out of an adjoining room wearing plain flight togs, stripped of her fleet captain's rank bands.

That stunned Naero right there. Spacers always displayed their rank, except when threats were severe–or they went to war.

Aunt Sleak wore her thick, auburn mane of shoulder-length hair pulled back in platinum clips, Spacer battle-style. She even wore a side arm and an energy cutlass. Naero very seldom saw her aunt carry weapons openly. She knew about some of the cleverly concealed ones.

All Spacers had their own little concealment tricks and secrets.

"Intel has ordered all Spacer fleets, ships, and crews on full alert after the loss of *The Omaria*," Aunt Sleak said. "The Corps are denying any knowledge or involvement in the incident, but tensions are running high. All that we know so far is that your parents were trading with the Cumi concerning some kind of ancient alien tech."

"So who is this Baeven guy?" Naero said. "He seemed to know something more about it."

Aunt Sleak stiffened and shot her such a look of pain, anger, and hatred that Naero nearly fell into a defensive stance.

Aunt Sleak looked away. "I have to be sure it's him. What did he say? What did he look like? Not that he couldn't make himself look like anyone or any thing.

"Deets and descriptions," Aunt Sleak snapped.

Naero gave them.

Aunt Sleak finally sighed and hung her head. "It must be him. Sounds just like the bastard. He can change his name and his face, but not his height. He was always so damn tall."

"He said to mention that he wanted to make up for Toraga-5."

Aunt Sleak's eyes narrowed to dark lines. Her fists tightened and shook.

"Sure he does. It's gotta be him. I'm sorry, Naero." Aunt Sleak sighed again. "Sorry about your parents, and sorry you ever had to meet this creature. He would show up, especially now. 'Baeven' is just one of his aliases. How fitting; a baeven is–"

"An Otaran scavenger bird," Naero said. "Sort of like a Terran raven, but nastier. I looked it up."

"They're utterly ruthless," Aunt Sleak added, "completely opportunistic. Given the chance, they eat their mates, even their own young. How fitting."

"How was he involved with Mom and Dad?"

"Your mother and I knew him very well. Once. That was long ago. I hope for his sake he didn't have a hand in what happened. But for him to take an interest, this must be very serious. Destruction and death follow this creature wherever he goes. Avoid him at all costs, spacechild. Don't speak to him. Flee if he approaches you again. That is a direct order."

Naero couldn't stop herself from a wide-eyed blink. She recovered quickly.

"Aunt Sleak, you're holding back on me. What is his connection to Clan Maeris? Who does he work for? He is a Spacer, after all–"

Aunt Sleak shot her the look again and even advanced a step. Naero retreated into her defensive posture.

"He *was* a Spacer, Naero. He will never be one of us, ever again."

Naero's jaw dropped.

An outcast. The man was an outcast.

Only the worst elements of Spacer society became outcasts, many of them executed for their crimes. To all the Clans, Baeven was worse than a criminal. Worse than an enemy. He was dead to his people, completely ostracized as if he never existed.

A sad smile crept over Aunt Sleak's face. "Now you know. This Baeven has been a curse to our family. Everyone who has dealt with him has either died or lived to regret it. He will tell you anything to manipulate and use you for his own ends. He works for anyone who will hire him, but he serves only himself. Don't ever trust him Naero. He's one of the most dangerous people in the known universe."

"What did he do? To become an outcast, I mean?"

Aunt Sleak visibly shuddered.

"He repeatedly betrayed our people, as well as his employers, playing all sides against the others. He has caused many conflicts, and countless deaths. He is an incredibly dangerous man, and one of the deadliest warriors I have ever known. He trained extensively with our Mystics and in fact was a prodigy of theirs. But in the end, he betrayed them as well.

"Even they haven't been able to capture...or kill him."

Their Mystics wanted him dead?

And this guy was still alive somehow?

Naero blinked a second time. Spacer Mystics were among the most adept combatants in the known systems.

"You're still not telling me everything, Aunt Sleak. How do you know Baeven? He said his last deal with you went bad. Said he wanted to make it up to you. What was Toraga-5?"

Aunt Sleak hung her head and ran her fingers up through her auburn hair. She sighed again.

"You were a small child the last time I had dealings with this creature. He sent what was then my fleet and a few others on a vital political trade negotiation mission to Toraga-5–straight into a deathtrap. We lost fourteen ships and their crews in heavy fighting. I barely escaped with half of my crew on my flagship. The incident helped escalate the Fourth Spacer War with the Corps. Baeven vanished, like he usually does."

"I noticed that. He blipped out on me and I still can't figure out how. But he warned me and Janner to stay close to you, not to go off on our own. He said that powerful factions might be looking for us, in connection with whatever Mom and Dad were doing. He gave me..."

Aunt Sleak turned on her. "What? What did he give you?"

With everything that had happened, she'd forgotten about the damn chip. Her fingers fumbled as she tore the crystal out of her comp and held it up.

"He said it was a bit of intercepted transmission. I forgot. Told me to decode it when I got back to the ship."

Aunt Sleak snatched it from her and popped it into a terminal she snapped up from the floor. "Let's see what we have. Hmm...tricky as usual. Mikiri crystal–expensive. Self-erasing. We'll only be able to play it once, so I'd better clone some copies."

Naero looked on for several moments while Aunt Sleak went to work on it. How was her aunt this adept with this kind of stuff? It all begged a lot of questions.

"Looks like a captured com blurt," her aunt said at last. "Either secret Corps military or Corps Intel. It's chopped, scrambled, and encrypted. I think its Triaxian–maybe even Hevangian.

"This might take a while longer to break."

Aunt Sleak looked at her suddenly. "Why are you wearing that headband? That's not your usual style."

Naero flinched, instinctively covered her forehead with her hands.

"Had a bad rash of pimples."

"Won't your hair cover them?"

Naero grimaced and sighed. "Not this time. Aunt Sleak, I still don't see any harm in talking to this Baeven guy if he shows up again. Maybe we should listen to him, find out what he knows."

"If what he said to you is true, Naero, then you and your brother are in serious danger. You may be right. We might want to talk to him, to learn his game. I'll have to contact some of my friends in Spacer Intel again."

"You know people in Shadowforce?"

Aunt Sleak frowned. "It's time you learned the truth, spacechild. Most of our family *was* Shadowforce until about fifteen years ago. You just weren't old enough to be told yet. All Spacer merchants collect data for Intel. Some more than others."

"That's where you and Mom knew this Baeven guy from, right?"

Aunt Sleak averted her gaze for an instant. "Your mother was very close to him at one time, Naero. Before his disgrace."

"She...she loved him," Naero guessed aloud.

Aunt Sleak nodded. "We both did, in our way. But Lythe was always closest to him. She even fought to defend him, even though it hurt her own career. He nearly took her down with him."

"What about you?"

"After a while, he and I never got along very well. That's all I'll say. You don't need to know any more about him. If Baeven turns up, I don't want you and Janner alone with him, and don't go anywhere with him. I want to be present when you talk to him, and our people need to watch him at all times, understood?"

The terminal signaled that the chip was decoded and ready to play.

"There, finally got it. Listen closely. I don't know what we're going to get."

Naero held her breath. Aunt Sleak punched up the coded message. Both of them leaned in, making out two voices.

"What do you mean it's not there You'd better have it! This little intercept cost enough, damn you. Nine elite strike ships destroyed, two in tow, five others damaged. We're risking another Spacer War. What do you mean you can't deliver? What do you think we keep your kind around for?"

"Your intelligence was in error. The item in question was not on board the Spacer exploration flagship. We've gone over the wreckage and all of the bodies repeatedly. Both mine and your own teams are going over it all again. But I can assure you...there is nothing to retrieve."

"Then we're dead, you bastard. Within a month, we'll be swimmin' in pain bugs. But you go first... I go down, you go down."

"There is another possibility..."

"Better be rutting good."

"These Spacers didn't have their son or daughter with them."

"So what?"

"Spacers almost always travel with their children. They must have known how dangerous this trip was going to be. But this wasn't the first run they made into the Unknown Sectors. Perhaps they didn't even know what they had found. What if they left the secret to the Kexxian Data Matrix with their children somehow? Their kids are probably traveling with some relative."

"Find them, find the missing secrets, and perhaps we'll both survive this."

"Thin. Very thin. But snagging those kids might buy us some time. Do what you need to. This is an Alpha Negative Priority. The Corps will cover your activities. Gut those brats and their entire spack family if you have to, but get what we need. There's blood between your house and theirs. That ought to make it easy enough."

The recorded transmission cut off. Where had Naero heard one of those voices? The calm one?

It was a Matayan voice.

The blurt ended. Naero nodded to her aunt. "So, I guess Janner and I will be sticking close to the fleet for a while."

"Not tonight," Aunt Sleak said. "We're going to that Corps party on Lady Drianne's yacht with Janner. We're deep within Corps Space. If we panic now and try to escape, they'll run us down. They don't know if we even have anything yet. Running will make it look like we do. They'll hesitate doing anything in public to avoid another costly war."

"We don't know if we have anything either," Naero said.

"There's too much we don't know and too many big players flooding the game. I want to sort out a few things. We'll go to that party tonight and see what shakes out. Just stay on your guard."

"On the blurt they mentioned the Kexxian Data Matrix," Naero said. "What the hell is that?"

Aunt Sleak breathed out hard. "Just a legend. The Kexx were an ancient race of near-godlike beings who ruled much of the galaxy in the Unknown Sectors, millions of years ago before most sentient life was somehow wiped out during a galactic event known as–"

Naero finished her sentence. "...The Great Destruction." Extremely ancient galactic history.

"We don't know anything more about the Kexx or what happened–yet. That's...something your parents were trying to find out."

"Think Baeven will show up tonight?"

"He might. If someone is after you and Janner, going to this party might flush them and their reasons out into the open. We'd better have a talk with Jan about all of this. And Naero...?"

"What?"

"I want you fully armed from now on, and not just kid stuff. Talk to Zalvano about some suggestions from my personal armory. He'll fix you up with items that'll make it past Corps security. If there's any trouble, I want us all to be ready. I'll keep the fleet on standby, and bring enough of our people along to back us up."

Naero nodded. "Sure thing."

What in the hell were they all getting into, and who were the bastards that murdered her parents and all their crews? And for what?

The deeper they went, the more they didn't know.

12

Lady Drianne's yacht.

Larger than either *The Slipper* or *The Shinai*. A 7,000 ton pleasure palace glittering in space, decked out to the megs. No cost spared. No opulence or extravagance too great.

Who could guess how many worlds had been sucked dry and how many generations of Corps wage slaves had given their all so that she could indulge herself and all of her lackeys and sycophants in such decadence?

Waves of food, drink, entertainment, and every pleasure lay wide open and available for the guests on board.

Each room a palace. Each hallway and corridor a priceless art gallery. Furnishings and decorations taken from untold worlds and cultures. Diversions, games, shows, delights. Debaucheries.

Levels filled with whores, and sex slaves from a hundred races and the several known genders, more than a match for any imagined taste or the indulgence of any vice, fantasy, or perversion

Arena levels with blood sports and gladiator death matches, where warriors and dangerous beasts and monsters pitted themselves against one another for sport and gambling and sheer delight.

Naero, Jan, and some of her friends entered the lair of the beast beside Aunt Sleak, with Captain Zalvano and their Spacer retinue right behind. They stepped into the Casino just beyond the opulent landing bay, about threescore in all.

She noted the row upon row of viewscreens, brazenly offering all of their enjoyments and much more, directing guests to where they could all be found.

"Triax Gigacorp, the worst of the worst." Jan noted. "This Triax princess sure has megacredits to spare." Even he sounded stunned and amazed.

Naero frowned. "Yeah, despite trillions on the Triaxian wageslave worlds wallowing in poverty and despair."

"They refer to them as 'useless eaters,' sib. No one cares what happens to them."

"Jan, the cost of any small section of this yacht–even one of their bathrooms–would be more than enough to purchase a fine trade ship, the modest likes of which you and I might never see now. We could work our entire lives and never save enough. Remember that tonight."

Even Saemar, voluptuous in a tight, hot pink dress, was amazed. "Look at what they're doing on that screen. Even I've never done anything like that." She sighed and nudged Naero. "Too bad we're on duty, huh sweetie? Chaela's gonna miss a good time tonight."

Naero endured a twinge of pain. She still felt responsible for Chae's injuries. Her friend's absence left another gaping hole.

But Naero tried not to look at many of the screens after she got the gist of what was going on in them. Somehow it was worse than porn, flaunted so brazenly for everyone to watch and join in if they wanted to.

Liveried servants waited to escort them to the zero-G play rooms, beach rooms, winter mountain ski slopes, underwater rooms, several convenient costume shops, and vomitoriums for the hordes of enormous, feasting gluttons and their grav implants.

Finally they arrived at the primary reception hall. Everything around them dazzled and sparkled, like a spectacular Algedian casino palace.

Naero glanced at Aunt Sleak and then at herself, suddenly feeling somewhat self-conscious and out of place. Even with her concealed weapons. Without her flight togs she felt half-naked, and it wasn't just because of her slinky dress.

None of her friends or clan could see the insane eye in her forehead but to her it was still there. Naero had checked, filled with horror every time it stared back at her.

She strategically kept a thick wave of her raven hair covering her forehead and another eye partially.

She reminded herself that she agreed to go along with this public display.

The Akoran nightsheen gown she wore shimmered with the ambient light from bluish-black to blackish-red. She caught herself in a mirror and struggled not to blush. The top was cut much lower than anything she thought she'd ever be allowed to wear. Her ivory breasts were ample but not overly large; at least they were firm and natural.

Unlike the various pairs of wobbling grav-implants all around her that seemed to float and bob freakishly with lives of their own.

Part of her felt embarrassed on several levels.

Until she saw what other people were wearing. Some no more than holographic screen tattoos or body jewelry. She'd seen vids and clips of Corps fashions from hundreds of systems and usually just giggled and considered them a joke.

Experiencing the true range and madness full force was both shocking and a bit overwhelming.

They went all the way from austere to exhibitionist.

This wasn't her game at all. She still didn't understand how exactly to walk that fine line between looking sexy or like an Arabalan prostitute.

Aunt Sleak was an old hand, it appeared, and had fashion moxie to spare. Which was also somewhat surprising.

Perhaps Naero simply needed to trust her suddenly flamboyant aunt and follow her lead.

They passed through the reception hall, and the crowd parted to get a better look at the arrival of the renegade, unpredictable Spacers.

If Naero turned heads, Aunt Sleak made them gape. That amazingly tight body of hers.

Her aunt wore a long semi-opaque gown of Ovadi EM-silk. It collected the low-level electromagnetic pulses around her and radiated harmless, miniature lightning bolts all about her body, teasing onlookers with brief glimpses of the sleek, fluid form beneath. It didn't show much top or leg, but it was dazzling.

Zalvano, Janner, Gallan, Tyber, and the other Spacer men struck dashing, virile figures in their impeccable black Sovani-styled evening jackets, jeweled throat and chest bands, tight leggings, and high boots. All the Spacers looked superb, but were stunning to a lesser degree.

Aunt Sleak was the main attraction.

Janner seemed to be the most pleased of them all, eating up the attention and envy that seemed to erupt all about them wherever they went. His gaze roved over the crowd, looking for something hungrily, and earning not a few hungry glances in return.

Zalvano, on the other hand was a study of class, calm, and reserve. When his glance did stray a few times, it went to Aunt Sleak, and then he would linger and only smile slightly. He looked very pleased with the universe.

Aunt Sleak followed her own instincts, nodding to a few persons as she made her way through the party into the main ballroom.

Thousands of people; dancing, cavorting, and singing. The rectangular chamber stretched almost the length of the entire top section of the ship; the ceiling more than thirty meters high, set with holos that periodically flashed and displayed the skies of various worlds.

At last they reached the thickest part of the crowd. Persons of import and their retinues made way. A final barrier of personages parted and Naero caught sight of Lady Drianne and her daughter Devi.

Devi wore a short skirt of some clingy material that was so radiant it looked white-hot. It ended just under her ribs, exposing the rest of her from there on up.

If the wild young girl had implants, they were damn good ones.

Even Janner blushed. She spotted him and bounced through the crowd to take him by the hand. "Oh, Jan, I'm so glad you and your people could make it."

Janner gulped for air. "Me too," he said, a fog over his eyes.

Devi giggled and looked them all over. "You guys look great. That's your aunt? Mother will shit. C'mon and meet her."

Naero wanted to slap the little bimbo silly. Other than the obvious, what could Janner possibly see in the girl? Their aunt was right. She'd have to have a talk with him about developing some serious taste in women.

Lady Drianne looked like a queen holding court. Perhaps she was. Her flawless body was draped in a filmy gown of what looked to be either gold foil or liquid gold. As she moved, it split, tore, and reformed, more than skin-tight against her slender, yet ample body.

The competition between Lady Drianne and Aunt Sleak erupted almost immediately, like two Schedarian wasp queens maneuvering for their death strikes.

Sometimes they killed each other.

Naero quickly appraised the two while they exchanged opening civilities. Lady Drianne had a slightly prettier face. Aunt Sleak the slightly better figure. Some of the drooling hangers-on about them looked torn as to which one to leer at.

Naero suddenly caught sight of the middle-aged merchant from the sky limo. He wasn't watching them at all, but listening intently to a group of businessmen and businesswomen talking animatedly with some high-level Corps military officers nearby. He said very little, and suddenly stifled a yawn.

It was then that their eyes met. Recognition brightened his gaze along with surprise. He nodded to her in salute with his glass, excused himself from his circle, and disappeared into the crowd.

"My dear Sleak," Naero heard Drianne say. "How good to see you. You look well. Why, I was stricken with grief when I heard about the tragedy involving Lythe."

Naero turned her attention back to the Corps princess. Aunt Sleak only nodded.

Lady Drianne slipped in like an old friend and took Sleak's arm in hers.

"But come now, let us talk business. I have numerous lucrative proposals for you. We've always made good profits together."

Janner had already disappeared with Devi. Zalvano stayed with Aunt Sleak and Drianne. Naero wandered off a bit with Gallan and her friends, declining several offers to dance or to indulge in one of the nearby drug or pleasure suites.

"This crowd is mostly humans and near humans," Gallan noted, "punctuated by an occasional non-human."

Most of the latter were relegated to the positions of servants or guards. She saw an Ejjai in person for the first time, a matriarchal race of hyena-like humanoids. By all reports they were tough, vicious fighters.

A servant came by with a tray of wild-looking drinks.

Naero impulsively chose a tall, clear crystal-goblet with what looked to be a pale wine or liqueur, fruity by the smell of it. A small holo of a flaring sun floated in the liquid, which smelled of warm citrus.

"Hold it," Zhen said, quickly scanning the drink. "Okay, it's safe."

Fast-absorbed endorphics rushed through Naero's body with the first sip, radiating mild, harmless pleasure from the center of her abdomen. The slight tingling sensation felt very nice.

She'd still rather have a borbble of Jett. Triax probably had an entire room of it somewhere. She just had to locate it.

Tyber and Zhen danced in their matching orange and black outfits like they were a dance team. Gallan with Saemar.

Naero felt a different tingle of warning in her mind as she watched her friends dance. Again, like someone trying to speak to her.

The same feeling she had on the loading dock before the accident, but not as intense, yet. Her crazy delusional eye even throbbed.

In a mirror wall, she caught sight of Lady Drianne's Matayan bodyguard following her, back in the crowd.

She turned immediately and blew him a kiss.

The man's face darkened into a violent sneer again as she made him. He turned his face away as if to ignore her, but he did not move off. She was about to walk up and ask him to dance when a figure stepped up beside her at the edge of her vision.

The limo merchant again. Still dressed soberly, although wearing a slightly fancier head wrap and jewels. "Perhaps I intrude," he said, "but I would not provoke that Slayer, if I were you, miss. No good would come of it."

So, Drianne's bodyguard was a Slayer, a Matayan warrior with more than a hundred kills, whether in the military, as a gladiator, or perhaps as an assassin. He had a ring of at least ten stars tattooed on his broad chest.

Leave it to a Triaxian princess to hire the best she could find.

"I was just wondering if he would like to dance," Naero said. "It might help pass the time, since he's been assigned to watch me. Do you think he might try to kill me right here at his boss's party?"

The man studied the Matayan Slayer for a moment, almost as if he knew something about him or his kind. That made Naero a bit more nervous.

"No, I don't think so. He's probably fantasizing about it, but he won't act—not without orders or provocation."

"Who are you?" she asked.

He hesitated and smiled. "Just a business man, looking for profits where he can find them. Your name young lady?"

"Naero. Naero Amashin Maeris, of Clan Maeris. My aunt is Captain Sleak Maeris."

"Ah, yes. I have heard of your illustrious aunt and her equally illustrious family."

Illustrious?

"And you?" Naero asked.

"My friends call me Adrin, but I have very few remaining friends these days, times being what they are. I detest family names. I wish I had no family affiliations, but alas. I am honor bound to do their bidding, and serve their common good."

"I know how that is, I guess. What business are you in?"

"Oh, a little bit of everything really: ships, smallcraft, computers, terraforming teams, medical supplies. I'm the diversified end of the family–the respectable end."

"Dealing in ships sounds exciting."

"Not really, especially after thirty years or more. But the profits are often good, and that keeps the family happy. That allows me to mostly avoid them and go where I please. My ship and I will depart for Epsilon Sextanis-6 later tonight with one of the merchant convoys, to pursue a major transaction."

That was the fleet's destination as well. Naero suppressed a nervous shudder.

"Unfortunately the family leaders will also be there. They can be so very annoying."

"Perhaps we'll run into you there," Naero said. "Aunt Sleak might be able to do some business with you. Here's her call number." She handed him a com chip.

Adrin took it gladly. "Very good. Warn your aunt about the increased Corsair activity in that area. Several freighters have been lost. Triax increased the naval patrols for show. Nasty business."

"We've heard. Our fleet is well protected," Naero said. She took a moment to smile and wink at the Matayan Slayer.

"If you harass that fellow enough," Adrin said, "he might gut you and then claim blood-feud self-defense."

"In his dreams."

The older man smiled. "You think you're that good?"

"Pretty sure. I've trained all my life, with better than him."

Adrin smiled. "Too bad for him then. He appears to hate you quite intensely. He'd love to get at you with his blades."

"Of course. Matayans hate all Spacers. Feeling's mutual."

"I'm sorry to hear that."

"Been that way ever since the Spacer Wars, even with the breaking of the Matayan Cartels."

He smiled again. "Perhaps things will change one day. I get around in various circles. I'm not so certain the Cartels are as dead and buried as some claim."

"I know. Corsairs, rebels. Gigacorps keep enough of them around to do their dirty work. We know that. They used to be independent, like Spacers. Now they're just Corps slaves, and it galls them even more. It wasn't our fault that their allies absorbed them when they were weak. They blame us; they always blame us."

"Who was it that weakened their empire so that the Corps could absorb them?"

"Spacers, of course. But they attacked us. They paid the price. We make sure anyone who attacks us pays that price—as high as we can make it. We've never desired domination and control of everything like the Corps do. Space is too big. There's room for everyone to thrive and make credits, and we've proven that over and over again."

"Very admirable." He raised his glass, containing something thick, blue, and cold. "I salute you again. Good luck to you, young lady. Smashingly alluring gown you have on. I'll say good evening, and...mind the Slayers."

Naero smiled and shook her head slightly. What a character. She'd have to learn a bit more about Adrin. He seemed harmless enough, but something strange about him attracted her interest. What was it?

"Mistress Naero..."

She slowly turned at the voice.

There stood Baeven, looming over her in full Menkaran evening robes and veil. Menkarans were always huge.

"Good evening," he added. "You should have taken my advice and waited for me at your ship."

The Matayan Slayer watched them with renewed interest.

What should she do? Avoid him, or try to get more info out of him?

Because of the general roar of the crowd, she moved closer to Baeven so that they could speak more discreetly.

"Is it true that you're a traitor to our people, an outcast?"

He didn't even blink. "The outcast part is at least, but of course there are reasons. Only an outcast can go where I go, do what I do. Shadowforce has been wrong many times. Even the Mystics. No one sees everything clearly. Not even me." He met her glare. "Our people might owe their very salvation to an outcast when all is done. Remember that, spacechild. I see that your aunt's opinion of me has changed little. Does she still intend to kill me on sight?"

"Didn't say so. She'd even be willing to listen to you, but only under secure conditions."

"Of course."

"She still hates you."

"Hate I can deal with and understand."

"Is it true that you were with Spacer Intel, part of Shadowforce?" Naero asked.

"On occasion."

"And you trained with the Mystics?"

"Once you begin it, such training never ends," Baeven said. "It is a lifelong pursuit. You are adept enough for one so young. Perhaps I could recommend you to them."

"I've had some martial training, but I'm not a psyon."

"Everyone is psyonic to a certain degree. The trick is finding a way to train one's gifts."

Naero trembled. Not her. And those who failed at training with the Mystics went mad, or were slain. She did not trust this man, whatever his background, but there was still something about him, something wild and untamed that she instinctively liked.

Baeven had information she wanted. She'd find a way to get it from him. "We broke the chip. You said you had more info concerning my parents?"

"Indeed."

"Let me find Jan and we can-"

"Your brother is somewhat...occupied at the moment with youthful indiscretions. I tried to approach him, but he wasn't very interested. He'll be safe enough where he is, for the moment. This really isn't the place to discuss your family business in any case. We are all about to be in very real danger very shortly. Myself included."

"What are you talking about? Why did you take a chance on coming here?"

"To warn you. To rescue you if I could. No, don't look around and give us away.

"Even now, an elite team of terrorists has been allowed to infiltrate Lady Drianne's yacht, to take her and many Triaxian officials here hostage.

"I said, don't look about. I've made most of them. They'll strike in minutes if I cannot tip their hand. I tried to get here sooner, but it takes time to fabricate a convincing cover at such short notice."

Naero laughed and took a sip from her drink again. She pressed a silent buzz signal on her com band.

"I'll get Aunt Sleak, Zalvano, Jan, and my friends. We'll head for the shuttles."

"There isn't time. And for some reason...you appear to be their primary target. If you rush to leave, that will only arouse suspicion and trigger their actions sooner. At best you can alert Clan Maeris with an onguard signal, as you just did."

"Then what do I-"

"Let me try a few things. I'm doing my best to disrupt their plans. What is known to only a few is that the terrorists have been infiltrated by Triaxian Intelligence. The attack will fail, but most likely your aunt and her second will be cut down in the confusion. You and most likely your brother will disappear. Never to be seen again."

"Oh, shit."

"Indeed. Return to your aunt. Warn her. Two teams—one Triaxian, and one Matayan—will strike during the chaos. They want you alive at all costs, Naero." He stared at her intently. "But they will kill you if necessary."

She rested a hand briefly on his arm. "Be careful."

He chuckled and shook his head. "If I can rattle them enough, Triax Intel will abort their mission and pull back in confusion. When I duck into this pleasure chamber, decline to join me. Return to your aunt; you have a few minutes still. Protect her as best you can."

"What about Jan? And you?"

"I'll see to your brother's safety, spacechild. And make sure you disarm the neutron detonator placed on your aunt's shuttle, if I don't have a chance to do so on my way out. The rest is up to you and Clan Maeris. Use the confusion to make good your escape."

"Wait, the shuttle's set to explode?"

"The Corps always have a back up. It's S.O.P. Just look after your aunt. Our enemies are quite determined to get her out of the way for some reason."

"How do I know you're telling the truth?"

Baeven smiled, almost sadly.

"You don't." He opened the door to the pleasure chamber, steamy, musky scents of oiled bodies and strange chemicals wafted out. He motioned for her to join him.

Naero shook her head and turned away, trying not to filter back to Aunt Sleak too quickly. Part of her wanted to rush over to protect Jan.

Lady Drianne's Matayan Slayer just finished listening to his wristcom when she spotted him again.

He ignored Naero completely, charging straight after Baeven.

95

13

Zalvano spotted Naero making her way through the crowd, excused himself, and met her half way.

He signal-blinked twice, alerting her to be cautious in what she said aloud.

Behind them, Aunt Sleak and Lady Drianne compared numbers on some high-level deal.

Zalvano produced a jeweled trinket and offered it to her. Naero took it with pleasure and hugged him immediately, as she would a favorite uncle.

"Terrorist strike in minutes, set up by Triax Intel," she told him. "The strike will fail. The real goal is to gun down you and Aunt Sleak, then spirit me and Jan away."

"Why?"

"Not sure. They think we might have something they want."

"How many?"

"A dozen or two."

She pulled away from him. Both of them smiled, straightening their garments. Checking their weapons.

"Where did you–?"

"Our friend of the family."

"You trust him?"

"We'll see in minute or two. We need to watch out for Aunt Sleak's best interests."

"Don't worry. She can handle herself. Our people are closing in and the fleet's on battle stations. We'll fight our way out if they force us to."

Naero looked around and spotted Gallan, Saemar, and several other Spacers placed strategically around the room. All appeared to be enjoying the party.

"I hope our friend doesn't try anything with Jan," Zalvano said. "This could be a ploy. I have three of our best fighters keeping a close eye on your brother."

A Triaxian official rushed up to Lady Drianne almost at the same time. The Corps princess paled for a moment and then excused herself quickly from Aunt Sleak's company.

She touched a few jewels on her comp band, then cupped one hand over the side of her head and listened intently to her ear loop.

Naero and Zalvano moved closer to Aunt Sleak.

Multiple small explosions, blasts of colored smoke, and lightning-like stun charges went off in the room all at once. People dropped. Startled guests cried out in several pockets.

With the general party chaos going on, everything was muffled.

At that exact moment, Drianne's security teams converged on several individuals–some dressed as servants, others as guests. Many of them were already down.

"Death to the Corps. Death to Triax! Long live the People's Army!" a few zealous voices rang out from several spots. Right before the shouters were stabbed, bludgeoned, or otherwise stunned into submission.

The incident fizzled out, over almost before it began, the remaining conspirators among the servants had quickly dropped through floor panels or were dragged off before the shocked onlookers could even panic.

Yet dozens of key security people had somehow been taken out as well, and not by the terrorists.

Many of the guests cheered the Corps security forces, and then promptly went back to whatever they were doing. The sheer mass of the crowd kept the security forces from closing in on the Spacers. Lady Drianne presented herself to her guests and the press on hand, appearing only slightly flustered.

97

"My friends. It appears that a handful of rebels, bent on anarchy, had some feeble plot against my life. Of course I'm used to that sort of thing in my position–but what a bother. I'm sorry that I must leave you now, my dear Sleak. But a number of important security matters require my attention at this time. You understand, I'm sure. Pleasure doing business with you again. I look forward to our next meeting. Do stay and enjoy Triax's hospitality."

With that, she was gone, surrounded by a growing flurry of guards, aides, and advisors.

"My captain," Zalvano said. "Let's get the hell out of here. I'll brief you once we're well away."

Aunt Sleak looked around her. "Agreed."

As they walked past the pleasure chamber, a cadre of armed guards carried out Lady Drianne's Matayan Slayer.

He looked lucky to be alive, his face a mash of blood and pulped bone. His filmy eyes locked onto Naero, flushed with fear and pain. But upon seeing her, they came alive with hatred once more.

Naero blew him another kiss. The injured Matayan tried to rise, but dropped back, unconscious.

Janner tumbled into view, spilling out of a zero-G pleasure pod, Devi still clinging to him, half his clothes torn off.

"Hey guys, great party, eh? Some merchant told me to go look for you. Whose smart idea was it to send me an alert code when you *knew* I was busy?"

"Jan," Aunt Sleak said. "Shut up, grow up, and acquire some brains...and class. Lose your little friend and come with us."

Devi started laughing and shaking uncontrollably. "That was so funny, Jan. You should have seen your face." The young girl was obviously maxed out of her mind on something. She could hardly stand.

"Oh, Jan," she suddenly said, growing pale. "I think I straight blasted too much. I'm gonna–" She collapsed, convulsed on the floor, foaming at the mouth. A Triaxian naval officer threw his dress jacket over her and held her thrashing body down.

Jan stood by and watched, chuckling.

Aunt Sleak grabbed Jan by the arm and dragged him off. Janner still laughed. "Maybe I should help her up."

"Leave her to her own people," Zalvano said.

Aunt Sleak was so livid she couldn't speak at first. Then she turned on him. "Blast? You're doing blast just like your little lander friends? You know what that garbage does to your brain?"

"Easy," Janner said. "She did it. Not me. I wouldn't touch that crap. It made her fun to watch, though."

They reached Aunt Sleak's shuttle, their people were already armed and waiting uneasily for them to board.

Both Zalvano and Naero performed thorough scans. Nothing that wasn't there before. No neutron detonator.

Had Baeven been wrong or had he gotten to it first? Something strange went down during the party, but Naero still wasn't quite sure what.

Aunt Sleak secured the craft, launched, and demanded a full report.

For not knowing much, Naero did her best.

14

The Maeris Fleet departed Irpul-4 within the hour and without further incident, fully loaded for their next stop at Epsilon Sextanis-6. The Space-Time jump would take the fleet five standard days.

Five days of routine, nonstop physical training and education. Five days to wrap her head around the loss of her parents, mourn for them, and find a way to not be insane and move on.

Enough time to get rid of the hallucination on her forehead and not go completely whacko. Her mind was already on overload.

She had more than enough to worry about, what with the intrigue surrounding her parents' deaths, and the Corps trying to abduct her and her brother–for reasons still unknown.

Let alone trying to figure out where she stood with the Clan Fleet, and what kind of future she had there, if any.

At least Naero was used to the jump routine; she'd lived it all her life.

Spacers made good use of their down time–if any could even call it that–to better themselves. They never stopped improving, never stopped learning. They worked hard. Trained hard. And played hard in their off hours.

She didn't really feel much like slacking off, but she also understood how important rest and relaxation were to a balanced life…and mind. The delusions she suffered and her mental state had Naero more worried than anything else.

Her mother used to say that the point of a blade could only stay so sharp for so long before it blunted or snapped. Even a razor's edge could be honed too thin, and grow weak and brittle.

Naero's hallucinations proved how fragile she was.

In the Spacer concept of overall personal balance and harmony, knowledge and skill translated into survival and success. Yet they should also be rewarded with comfort, ease, and pleasure.

After she did manage to fall asleep, she had another nightmare in which she again struggled against a similar dark power that threatened to swallow her up. This time, a young, glowing blue woman with white hair appeared, studying her. Just out of reach.

"Help me!" Naero begged.

"I'm not sure if I should," the blue female said. "What are you?"

"I'm in trouble. I need help!"

"What are you?" the blue woman repeated in fear.

Naero woke up startled and gasping, just like before. What was her madness trying to tell her? Did it make any sense at all?

Exhausted, she forced herself to rest some more.

On jump day number one, Naero flashed out of her bunk at five bells, tore off her headband in the mirror, and looked for her new third eye.

She cupped her hand over her mouth. She nearly wept.

The extra eye–proof of her growing insanity–was gone.

Morning PT began, intense physical training. Stretching, running, weights, and a brutal, punishing obstacle course, parts of it in zero-G.

Then they broke off into education rooms for pilot training.

She and Jan and the rest of the flight and command crews spent most of the morning going through interstellar navigational problems, with Aunt Sleak as the instructor.

First they worked through problems using various navigational programs. Then they used handcomps. Then write boards, and finally in their heads–all in specified time limits, according to Spacer military regs.

Jan breezed through it all, navigation his gift.

Naero struggled when it came to scratch boards and doing it all in her head. She had to hang back after the session was over and work with Aunt Sleak. That took an hour longer after everyone else was dismissed.

Great. She wouldn't hear the end of that. From anyone. But at least she wasn't going nuts.

After they finished, as if that humiliation wasn't bad enough, she was late for her sparring sessions...with Aunt Sleak and several of the crew's best fighters. Which included her smug little brother.

Why did he seem to be rising above it all? Especially while she moped around and didn't feel like doing much of anything?

Aunt Sleak followed right behind her, all the merry way to the training center on board *The Dromon.*

"We're holding a wake for your parents on third night," was all that her aunt said, out of the black.

A Spacer Wake. So awesome. Things just kept getting better.

A big stupid party celebrating her parents' snuffed out lives.

She didn't feel like a party. She'd never see them again.

She and Jan didn't even have a fingernail from either of them.

Her guts swirled like a typhoon inside of her.

Perhaps she needed to hit something after all.

Naero attached programmable, nanoreactive gelpads to her flight togs in the sparring room, covering her head, joints, hands and feet with the same. An invention of the Mystics that modified the Nytex of their suits, the gelpads formed reactive smartarmor, affording some protection against the worst blows. Yet never enough.

Pain. Always an effective teacher in combat training.

Naero waded into three separate clashes with good Clan fighters in different simulated situations.

Naero relied on her own rampant, acrobatic freestyle that combined the best techniques gleaned from each of her formidable fighting parents. Fast. Intense. Inventive and overpowering.

She used unusual angles of attack, walls, floors, and even ceilings and an opponent's own body, momentum, and blind sides against her opponent.

With her pent-up, slow-burn fury, she put all three opponents down before they hardly touched her.

No one cheered or taunted like they usually did in the sparring arena. In fact, they were strangely quiet.

Then Aunt Sleak took on Naero, Jan, and Saemar.

All three at once.

Aunt Sleak grinned and narrowed her eyes to black lines. "Come taste some pain."

They did their best to rush her from three sides in a combo attack.

Aunt Sleak trip-slung Jan into Saemar, knocking their heads together, dazing them both.

Double reverse kicks kept Naero blocking, forcing her to pull back.

Aunt Sleak pressed her assault, hand and foot techniques blazing. All of them would have been on target, too.

Any one of them would have taken Naero down.

If not for her exceptional speed.

Yet speed alone was never enough against Aunt Sleak. She was nearly as fast, and very clever and adaptive. She could read a contest like Naero only wished she herself could.

Naero only got in a few painful counters. Her knifestrike to the neck just missed the throat.

How could her aunt instinctively know to dodge like that?

An elbow to the hip. A shin kick that made Aunt Sleak's eyes go wide for a bare instant.

Naero fell for a cagey feint. Aunt Sleak's spin-heel kick found Naero's left temple in a splash of light. Painful and startling.

A swordhand thrust tapped her windpipe. Just enough to make Naero gasp for air as she went down. And lost.

She vaguely noticed Aunt Sleak finishing off Jan and Saemar. Naero crawled to the sidelines and caught the rest of her breath.

It would be her turn to get pummeled again soon enough.

Aunt Sleak came by and offered her a lix pak to drink. The basic fruit punch lix tasted stale and sweet at the same time. It sure wasn't Jett, but it replenished lost fluid and nutrients.

Not in a position to be picky, she sucked it down.

"You're a good scrapper," Aunt Sleak told her. "You've got your mother's speed, but not her technique." She smiled and shook her head. "I could never beat her once she became strong enough and skilled enough. You could unleash a bit more of your father's power as well. You've yet to test your true limits, spacechild."

At times the bottom dropped out and Naero's world and spiraled out of control into darkness and despair without warning.

Naero stared at her hands crushing the empty lix carton.

She had six fingers now instead of five–one extra on each hand.

Her parents were dead and she was continuing to lose her mind under the pressure.

She held her hands up before her deluded eyes and flexed all of her digits–even the new ones. She was losing it, definitely not getting better.

And she still couldn't believe her mom and dad were gone, but they were. She and Jan should be traveling with them, training with them, learning what they knew. They'd never get the chance to do any of that–now, or ever.

So much would never be the same again. She'd never be the same.

"Hey, Naero?" Aunt Sleak snapped her fingers. "You still with me?"

"Yeah. Sorry," Naero said, looking down, hiding her freaky hands under her. "Just thinking." She didn't bother asking if her aunt or anyone else could see the hallucination. She didn't want them to know. It was all just in her mind, anyway.

"That's all right. I miss them too, Naero. But keep your head in the game here. Strategy. Tactics. Execution. You have good defenses, but you rely on them too much. You still wait too long for openings instead of making them. Take the offensive a little more. Take some blows if that opens your opponent up. You act like you're afraid of getting hit."

Naero rubbed the side of her head. "You got that right. *Haisha*, it hurts like hell."

Aunt Sleak chuckled a bit. "I used to be the same way. You didn't get all your power from your dad, you know. Your grandfather Amashin was small like you and your mom, but very powerful for his size. He could hit harder than anyone I ever knew, even when he pulled his stuff. He taught me a lot about taking hits and suffering the least damage from them."

She barely knew her grandparents, mostly from family vid archives.

All of them had perished during various wars.

Like I said, Naero. Your mother was better at all of this than I am."

"You seem to be doing all right."

Suddenly she thought of Baeven for some reason, and what happened on the yacht. Somehow he had managed to do several things all at once to ruin the enemy's plans, and also take out that Matayan Slayer. With apparent ease.

Aunt Sleak had warned how dangerous he was.

While other crew members sparred their turns around them, Naero had to ask.

"Aunt Sleak, do you think Baeven told the truth about the plot to kill you and Zalvano, and kidnap me and Jan?"

Sleak shrugged. "It's hard to know. I doubt that Baeven would spirit himself onto Drianne's yacht to warn us for no reason. But it scares me to think that Triax would risk an interstellar incident, perhaps even another

Spacer War, to get at you and Jan. You never went with your parents. You don't have anything they brought back. Do you?"

Naero shook her head. "They never gave us ancient trinkets or artifacts. They weren't frivolous like that." Naero grinned. "I thought you weren't afraid of anything, Aunt Sleak?"

"I'm afraid of losing my ass and my fleet, and getting vaporized in another stupid war. You kids don't know, Naero. You weren't on the lines during the last one. But tell me, when we left Drianne's yacht, you didn't find anything on our shuttle?"

"The neutron detonator?" Naero said. "Zalvano and I did full scans. But if Baeven removed it, he might have simply taken it with him."

Aunt Sleak grinned; her eyes narrowed once more. "Maybe we'll get a chance to ask him. I'd bet the fleet times ten he'll turn up again, Naero. I have so many questions for him, new and old."

"I want to be there when you ask him," Naero said. "Jan and I have some questions of our own. We don't know anything about what Dad and Mom were doing, even if they were working with Shadowforce. If they knew something about this Kexxian Matrix, they never mentioned it to us."

"Yeah, about that, Naero. We need to be sure. You can't think of anything someone might want from you or Jan? Are you sure your parents didn't give you anything to keep safe for them, anything at all from their trips into the Unknown Sectors? A trinket, an artifact, a relic–even data files?"

"No. Nothing. Jan and I have been over this, too. We checked all of our files and logs, and scanned our belongings. Someone might be desperate to find this alien stuff, but the scary thing is–we don't seem to have it. That's all I can figure out."

Aunt Sleak frowned. "We're missing something important; I can just feel it. Well, I've put out feelers with some old friends in Shadowforce. We'll get copies of your parents' fleet logs. It might take some time, but we'll get a line on something."

"I hope so."

A shadow fell over them. Jan stood between them and the lights. "You two gonna gab, or fight? We're up again, N." Naero sat on her hands, resisting the urge to smooth her hair away from her face with her added digits while she tried to run out the clock.

Leave it to Jan. Apparently he enjoyed getting beaten and throttled. A little bit too much for her tastes in her current state of mind, or lack thereof.

She clenched her six-fingered fists inside her six-fingered sparring gloves and prepared for combat.

15

Finally they had some down time later that afternoon. Six fingers and all, Naero joined her mates to visit Chaela, who looked bored out of her mind, watching wall vids and reading INS feeds on a flip panel.

Chae rolled her eyes but her face brightened as they all filed into her room, holding bunches of greenpod flowers behind their backs.

"Wow, am I glad to see you guys. I'm going stir-crazy in here while Remy's on his duty shifts, but I've got two more whole days to hang out here and keep my stump in this re-growth tank."

She snarled, pointing to her leg, secured below the knee, immersed in the fizzing, dark green regeneration tank.

In three days she'd have a new foot grown back, but it would be soft and useless as a newborn infant's. The bones would continue to re-form and harden, and then the painful therapy would begin for her to retrain the joints and muscles and learn to use it again.

Saemar dumped an armload of snacks and drinks into Chaela's lap. Foil packages and cartons spilled over onto the floor.

"What's all this crap? I don't eat this stuff. Get this junk off a me."

"Can it, sweetie. This stash is for us. We're all gonna take turns sitting it out with you, when your squeeze Remy isn't here, as you regrow your tootsies. And when we're not in training or on duty."

Naero winced. They hadn't bothered to ask her to join the watch team. Not with her own…situation.

She stopped trying to hide her hands.

No one but her seemed to be able to see her delusions anyway. Ignoring them and pushing on seemed to be the best way to make them go away.

Tyber pulled a couple of floppy, dopey-looking sim-helmets out of his tekpak. "I have this new simgame you gotta try. The holoimager is amazing. We fight our way to this castle and–"

Chaela crossed her arms. "Save me from the geek patrol. You know I hate your dopey games, Tyber. And I wouldn't be caught dead wearing one of those goofy sim caps."

Tyber already had his on. He looked both hurt, and stupid. "What's wrong with them? I'm telling you, this game throcks."

Everyone struggled not to laugh. Even Zhen. Gallan took some pics and vids with his wristcom for later blackmail. Tyber looked like a total idiot wearing the damn thing.

"Yeah, you keep that thing the hell away from my head, or I'll rip your arms off and you'll be strapped down next to me with your stumps in two tingling vats of goop."

"I've never had the pleasure to hafta regrow anything," Saemar said. She rapped on the wall with her knuckles. "Knock on hull. What if a guy lost his dingdong? Would his stuff grow back? Would it be just the same, or could they, you know, make improvements? I'm not just talking length, but thickness, too. But I digress. Does it hurt at all, sweetie? Or are you all pumped up with drugs so that it kind of feels frost?"

Chaela shifted, blinked, and grunted, making faces.

"It definitely is not frost. It doesn't exactly hurt, but it kind of feels like bugs are biting me or sticking shock and stun needles in me at times. It's really weird. But if it gets me back in my squadron, I'm all for it."

"These are for you," Gallan said.

On cue, all of them dumped their flowers in her lap, on top of the heaps of junk food.

Chaela just stared.

107

"What the hell is this? I hate plants and flowers. What am I supposed to do? Make a salad?"

"It's customary to bring a recovering patient flowers to brighten her room," Zhen said. She took them one by one and put them into pweaked nanovases set into the medical bay's walls, quickly and efficiently arranging them into a pleasant pattern.

"Great, I feel like I'm in some kind of jungle now. Hey N…Naero? You okay?"

Naero snapped out of it and came back to the present.

"Sure. You know. Still trying to deal with it all. But don't worry about me. You just get your foot back. You'll be running with us again in no time. Uh, sorry. No pun intended."

"I'm…I'm sorry about your folks, Naero," Chae said. "We all are. They were good to us. They were stand-up people. None of us know what to do or say."

Everyone looked down and got quiet.

"Naero, you know we're there for you if you need any of us," Chae added.

Naero bit her lip. "I know that, guys. I couldn't ask for better mates. It's all…just so new still. I'm still dealing with it. Just give me time."

They all drew close and put a hand on her. Even Chaela.

"We are," Chae told her.

Naero pulled away from them before she started bawling.

"Uh, I gotta go. Got a thing with Jan. He, uh, wants to meet him somewhere. So, I'd better go. To go talk about stuff."

"Sure, sweetie. You go right on ahead. And don't worry about Chae. We got her covered until her lover boy Remy gets off work."

Saemar turned back to Chaela and patted her hand. "Now, I've got the first watch, sweetie. I wanna go over the performance of my last couple dozen guys to see maybe who's worth another go. I got vid clips from my wall cams so that we can compare both looks *and* prowess, although you can't always see that much from certain angles."

Chaela panicked as the rest made ready to leave. "Quick, someone kill me. A stunner. One of you has to have a way to stun me, right? Zhen?"

Zhen patted her arm. "Sorry, Chae. You and Saemar enjoy your girl time. Tyber, you're not staying to watch."

"Awww…Mom."

In desperation, Chaela snatched one of the sim helmets and squashed her head into the silly thing.

"All right, T. Switch me on. Let's find that stupid castle."

Tyber popped his cap back on. "Yay!"

The caps came to life, forming glowing globes of intricate holographic projections over their heads, immersing them and their senses in the projected adventure world.

Saemar cluelessly kept rambling, focused completely on her pad. "Now what about this guy? Lots of enthusiasm, but I never noticed this growth right here. See it? Let me zoom in. What the hell is that? Do they still have goiters? What is a fricking goiter anyway? Is it like a tumor? Do you think I should be worried about that? Maybe Zhen should check him out for me before we hook up again."

"That's my cue to be gone." Zhen made a hasty retreat. "Bye-bye. I'm out of here."

*

After she left Medical, Naero located Jan.

He insisted on dragging her to a spiraling session of all things, in Dromon's enormous network of zero-G orbs and chubes. Spiraling was usually reserved for younger teen Spacers around this time.

She hesitated at one of the entrance hatches to the chube complex.

"I'm almost of age, Jan. I don't spiral anymore. I'm surprised you still do. I'm too old for this."

He pleaded with her. "Come on, N. I've been on a memory run. Remember all the fun we used to have going to these on all the Clan ships? We had a blast. We didn't just go to make out with the other kids."

Naero raised both eyebrows at him. "At least I didn't...usually."

Jan grinned. "Okay, okay, that was later. It used to be such a ride. Remember? It was just us." He looked down. "Now...it is just us again, sib."

Naero hugged him close for a moment.

"Oh, Jan. C'mon. It's all right. Sure, we can go in."

They slipped inside and closed the hatch behind them. They slid down the waiting chube, lined and scribed with teen Spacer tags and glowing holo flirt notes.

I luv Mishi.
Theon, chube 17.
Azhuri Decimates the Competition
You flip me Nyssra!

They spilled out into the cushion of the primary zero-G orb, floating in a holographic, color-shifting, mirror-lit sphere forty meters in diameter, with numerous other access hatches and chubes.

Glowing swing lines in changing, pulsing hues, and flashing, shifting push plates stuck out in various places.

Teen throck and tekk music pulsed. The best dump tunes from over a hundred systems played and throbbed and shifted over the speakers and panels in random waves of sound and image that could hit like sonics.

The younger kids were all gone. This was teen time.

You had to be between fifteen and nineteen to get into to this scheduled spiral. Naero barely fit the parameters.

About fifty Spacer teens spiraled around in zero-G, laughing, chasing each other, flirting and pairing off.

Of course, everyone knew that spirals were monitored by fleet security so that pairings and the occasional fight never went too far. But swooching and makeout sessions allowed the young to sneak off, let loose some steam, and get together.

Under the Rules of Conduct, young Spacers remained free to approach each other and just talk. Free to work out problems and disagreements. Free to propose, refuse, or change romantic pairings at any point.

Despite the regs, spiraling was a still a blast of release and sheer freedom, compared to ship duty.

Flying and swooping around in null gravity always felt liberating. As if one could, in fact, fly. A great sensation for the young and anyone under a lot of pressure.

Sometimes even Spacer Elders reserved the chambers so that they could float free and chat and recall their younger days.

Jan grabbed her and snagged a push plate with one leg, swinging her in a wide arc down to the core.

Naero laughed, and loosened her long, dark hair, letting it spin free with the rest of her. She soared down and caught a swing line, whipping herself around and rocketing back up off a spinning push plate.

Jan dove at her, smiling and giggling. Then he swung away and shot down a flashing pulse chube.

Naero was right on his heels.

Friends they knew called out to them. Some even came after them.

They chased each other through other orbs, pushing off and swinging. Other teens swooched here and there, their faces locked together in passion, clinging to each other so desperately as the floated.

Various stages of teen hookups. Some just starting out and tentative. Others ending, pulling away from each other, shaking their heads.

Spiraling was uncertain, scary, and great. Every part of it.

Naero realized she did miss it.

Why did she ever think she was too old now?

A cute, skinny kid shot out of chube and nearly crashed into her. Naero held him at arm's length. They spun and laughed together.

"Well, hello, pretty girl. Name's Danaldi. Haven't seen a sweet little thing like you in here before."

Naero chuckled and rolled her eyes. Her petite stature often misled others into believing that she was younger.

"How about we play tag for a while," he said, one eyebrow raised suggestively. "I catch you... and then you're It?"

Naero grinned. Then she flashed her rank bands at the boy. They flared blue in the muted light.

"Whoa. A three-striper."

"You're sweet, Danaldi. But I come of age soon. Sorry."

"Don't know what you're missing."

"Oh, please." She whipped him around and spun him into the nearest chube.

"Good luck with the younger girls, sweetie!"

"Wahoo!" Danaldi shouted.

Jan popped his head down from another chube and yawned.

"Wow, you used to be sooo much better at this, N."

Naero shot toward him. "Sib, you are gonna pay for that. I am gonna soak you."

"Big talk...from an old lady."

"Oooh. It's flaring now."

It only took the length of two chubes before she caught Jan by his ankles and kicked him into a glowing water ball in the next orb.

Splashes and glorbs of the shining nanolit liquid scattered in several directions.

She splattered him good.

They chased each other for a long while. Then they floated and took a breather, sighing and talking quietly face-to-face, in an orb all by themselves.

"Aunt Sleak wants me to say something...about Mom and Dad at the wake," Jan blurted out.

He hung his head. "I...I can't do it, N."

Naero nodded. "It's all right, Jan. Don't worry. I'll take care of it."

"What are you gonna say?"

"I'll think of something. We loved them. They're gone. What's there to say? You okay, Jan?"

He shook his head. "I dunno. I feel so weird. Ever since that long medtest for that plague, I've been having these awful headaches, and really weird dreams. Like someone's been torturing me–for years. Pretty scary stuff. Sometimes, sib...I think I'm losing it."

Naero put her arm around him as they floated. "I've been having similar problems. We're stressed out. We need to work through it and keep it together. Just remember the good times. That helps."

Jan started laughing. Then he covered his face. "Mom was such a terrible cook."

Naero sobbed and caught herself, covering her mouth with one hand.

"Dad wasn't much better. Good thing they hired some good ones to work the galleys and mess halls."

The two of them hung upside down against the wall like a couple of old Terran bats and cried together. Their tears floated out around them, bobbling like crystal gems.

Naero reached out and took her brother's hand.

Jan squeezed back. Both of them broke down.

In spiral, it was okay. No one bothered them. No one judged them or any of their actions.

*

After a few hours of updated gunnery and fighter simulation training that evening following dinner, Jan snoozed at his comp tutor, mildly drooling on his arm. Their screens were the only glowing lights in the darkened library.

Naero finished up her own work.

Go figure.

Jan lived and breathed advanced math and interstellar physics.

History and system archeology put him to sleep. He couldn't care less about all of the various known cultures and races in the galaxy.

Humans and near humans: gray-skinned Besh and their small ears. Red-skinned, tough Ramorians from the mining sectors. Matayans. Naivatch and their dark purple skins and strange culture. Furry, leopard-spotted Mahri and their tapered, tufted ears. Silesians and their sonorant throat bags. Zotchans and their floating hair tendrils that they used to sense and communicate with. Quick, tiny Piettos that stood only as high as your knee or hip.

True aliens, some of them not even humanoid in any way. Sleek, agile, cat-like Mndar. Feathered bird-like Quess in astonishing varieties,

112

stoic and wise. Gigantic but gentle Moh-Karran, five meters tall with multiple eyes and tentacles. Blobby, floating, gelatinous Blurgs and their glowing brains.

Just as exhausted, but being Jan's opposite, Naero ate up anything about alien worlds and their ways. Her parents' love of alien cultures, archaeology, and exploration lived on in her heart.

Reality; always better than fiction.

She poured through captured classified Corps text-only files, centuries old, about the lost Ku-Shai, and the bizarre, symbiotic alliance between the two odd races. A unique partnership that led them to sustain an empire for over three thousand millennia.

Too bad the Corps stumbled upon them during a period of decline.

After several disastrous wars–bad for both sides–the Corps banded together as they had never done before and had never done since, to eradicate nearly every trace of the Ku-Shai from the known universe.

Spacers had no further contact with them. The eradication all took place in Corps space.

She couldn't even find a picture, a vid, or even a description of what the two species looked like. The Corps did their insidious best to wipe out all information on them from all archives for some reason, and make it appear as if they had never existed.

All of their history, art, culture–everything. Completely deleted.

The Corps simply couldn't withstand any serious competition in their sectors, alien or otherwise.

Would they do the same thing to Spacers one day? Re-write history to make them vanish? Only time would tell.

Strangely enough, there was even still a bounty on Ku-Shai. Despite the fact that none had been sighted or known to exist for many decades.

Jan snored louder. Naero finally quit when she began to nod off. She dumped Jan into his quarters, and stumbled back to her own to pass out.

16

Naero dreamed and mused in flows of poetry and emotion.

Then her nightmares returned, more real and horrifying than ever.

This time, she dreamed about murdering her friends.

She stalked them one by one and cut them down, shot them, throttled them, or crushed their pleading faces as they begged.

The dream was terrifying, chilling, and secretly exhilarating.

She couldn't stop it–couldn't break free and wake up.

Was this really in her?

Part of her insanity?

They kept trying to get away. She shot Gallan in the back and gunned him down, shooting him to pieces with a blaster.

He died with his head twisted around, staring up at her in shock and terror.

Why?

Then she went after Jan, stalking her brother in the Spiral, slaughtering anyone who came her way. He looked so afraid.

Orbs of blood everywhere. Her arm and knife hand dripped with gore. She was splattered with it.

Get away, Jan!

A blast of blinding light caused her to draw back.

A female form took shape, comprised entirely of light, her hair like white-hot plasma, her eyes like the flare of pulsars.

Naero could barely look at her.

The glowing girl stood radiant and defiant before her, interposing a glittering hand to stop her. Her voice rang out.

"Who are you? What and where are you? Is this what you want? Is this what you want to become? Choose carefully."

Naero snapped straight up in her bunk.

"No!" she shouted.

She covered her face with her hands and slipped back down.

Haisha! The only thing she had to console her were the happy faces of her dead parents on her walls.

They both had taught her so much. They'd taught her everything she knew.

They were her mind, her heart, her hands. They had taught her to look out and to see–to touch, taste, listen, smell, and feel. To learn and do. To crawl, stand, walk, run, and climb. To tumble and fall, get back up, and keep trying and going forward until she could go no more.

They were her head, heart, and hands. Her wings. They had taught her not just to fly, but to soar.

They had taught her how to protect and defend herself and all that she loved.

To fight with great passion and controlled violence should the need arise, in a dangerous and uncertain universe. As borne out in their own fates.

Five bells gently sounded.

Naero and the crew spent the second day after morning PT in more flight simulation of various types of craft and vehicles.

Of course, she and Jan relished piloting the simulation programs of all the great starfighters throughout history to the present.

Together they were an almost unbeatable team.

Only Zalvano and Aunt Sleak could take them on, and even then it stayed a pretty fair fight.

Naero and Jan spent a lot of their extra time in the simulators, making sure they could fly most of the major rigs available to both Corps and Spacers.

Their obsession paid off big time against anyone who chose to take them on.

Naero spent her down time later that day taking it easy in her quarters. She was still moping.

Cleaning took a little while. Not much, really–just the stuff off the floor. Yet even that made her cabin seem bigger all of the sudden.

She watched some silly vids with half-interest, romantic comedies or action-adventure dumps.

She got out the oldfashioned journal her dad had given her. The one that could erase or archive any sketches or writings put on the pages.

The last entry she made was from before her parents departed–for the last time.

Naero hadn't known that then.

Her parents were always overly concerned about unintentionally bringing back some kind of deadly unknown alien plague or super virus from their explorations.

They had forced her and Jan to take all kinds of routine, boring medical scans. Some took over an hour.

Of course, they all turned up absolutely nothing.

The Cumi–one meter tall mouse-like aliens and their medteks who partnered with her parents–repeatedly gave them totally clean bills of health–plague and virus-free.

As usual, Naero had been furious with her parents for wasting her precious time again. She had fumed at them the whole while.

Instead of telling them how much they meant to her.

Naero fished out a pen and tried to write a new poem in her journal. But the words kept dying in her mind.

Her father had been a fairly decent poet, actually. He even had a few collections circulating among the Clan literary circles. But they never got much serious attention. Naero smiled.

The Poet-Warrior. The Philosopher-King.

Her father always said that they should strive to become just that. That was what the universe truly needed. The wise and harmonious mind of the inventive artist and benevolent leader to guide people into the future. Not just for the benefit of the self, but for the mutual benefit of all.

When she found herself staring at the pictures of her parents flashing by on the walls and crying too much, she decided to break out.

It dawned on her that she was famished. Naero stared at her delusional hands with their added fingers. She might as well put them to good use.

It was already late night when she snuck into the mess hall galley to cook for herself. Unlike her parents, she had drawn enough duty with the cooks to learn how to prepare several dishes that she and her family and friends cherished.

Naero made a small pot of seafood chowder in a nice creamy white sauce. A few of the ingredients she had to program in the food synthesizer. Potatoes and fresh lobster, scallops, and crab meat.

She ate it in a small, hollowed-out loaf of soft, orange Dovanian sweet bread, with the bread chunks and tiny salted crackerlets that always went so well with soups.

Gallan found her in the mess hall, eating there alone. She smiled at him. He pulled out the large spoon he always kept with him, like a knife fighter drawing a battle blade.

He sat down across from her, helping her finish the soup and then the loaf itself, tearing off delicious, soggy pieces.

"I love it when you cook," he said. "This is so good, N. I think you should be a chef."

"Yeah. That's my dream." She stood up and smirked. "To be a cook."

The uneasy silence opened the gulf between them once more.

This time, Gallan said his piece.

"Naero, I'm sorry about your folks. Everyone loved and respected them. They treated me like I was your brother."

Naero touched his hand. "You are, *abani*. You're just like Jan to me. You always have been, since we were little." Abani was a Ramoran word that Naero liked to use with Gallan–a term of great respect an endearment, for one's closest family and best mates.

"I know. I feel the same way. I'd do anything for you, Naero. I...I know how much you must be hurting. Is there anything I can do?"

Naero shook her head and leaned against him briefly. "No. There's nothing I can do either. Just keep being my friend. That's all. Stand by me."

"I can do that. Always will."

17

Third day came.

Finally, a break from the nightmares.

Naero woke up and checked her hands first thing.

Extra fingers? Gone, thank goodness.

What would it be next? She shuddered to think.

After PT, they studied biology, medicine, healing, and advanced first aid. The fleet surgeons, medics, nurses, and first response teams kept them updated on the latest med tek. The instructors broke the students off into rescue teams, and finally worked with them one-on-one in various scenarios, dealing with different kinds of emergencies.

Some of the scenarios were live training with casualty holograms and robotic simulators, or others were Spacers pretending to have certain illnesses or injuries.

Naero ran into Danaldi again, the young flirt from the spiral, pretending to have a Vegaran throat parasite.

Naero winked at him. He blushed.

Gallan, who was a particularly and astonishingly terrible actor, kept busting up everyone in his exercise into suppressed laughter–even the instructors.

Despite his fake, slap-on blaster wounds to the chest and abdomen.

She had lunch with several friends. Saemar brought Chaela, her foot in a regeneration cast. Chae was just glad to be mobile once more.

On her own, back in her quarters after lunch, Naero struggled to figure out what she'd say at her parents' wake that night.

She sat down and tried to recall and write down everything they ever taught her.

In desperation, she turned off the gravity in her quarters.

Somehow she found it easier to think in zero-G.

Even that didn't help.

She floated and bobbed about with all her junk that wasn't locked down. Mostly crumpled sheets of paper with false starts and goofy rambling. Snatches that babbled on for too many pages.

She read some of her ideas out loud to herself.

"Freedom. Freedom is the most import gift and treasure my parents ever gave to me. It's the most important thing anyone has. We should never trade or give it away–whether for security, wealth, access, or power. Anyone or anything that tries to take any part of our freedom away from us makes themselves our enemy."

She stopped herself again.

"Wow. Now I sound like my dad expounding on his soapbox." Just like that in fact. When she was young she could listen to him expound, going on and on for hours.

Or at least until she fell asleep.

What she wouldn't give now to hear his deep, rumbling, authoritarian voice again. He could go on about whatever he wanted to, and she would look up into his intense, wise face, and watch and listen.

She would not fall asleep this time.

If only she could be with him again, see him, and smile up at him.

Even into their teens, their father would find her or Jan asleep at the education screens, studying, or working late on some task. He'd scoop them up gently into his huge arms as if they weighed nothing, and carry them to their bunks to tuck them in.

At times she was only half-asleep, and waited patiently for her turn, still and smiling.

He'd shush any crew they came across not to wake them, even her mom. Often her mom would follow along.

Her parents usually kissed their foreheads lightly before they left.

Other times, they'd stand smiling for a while, just watching their kids breathe peacefully before they secured the panels, making sure she and Jan were safe.

Several times she swore she saw tears slip down her father's face as he smiled down at them.

Their dad was big guy.

They were like dolls in his arms.

But he was the one who checked on them each and every night, without fail.

Tarthan Wallace Ramsey: The Annihilator, Heavyweight Champion Fighter of the Galaxy. A devoted, lovesick giant of a husband and father.

A gentle pushover for his family.

How could she explain to anyone what her father meant to her? What her parents meant to her?

The white fire of her mother's quiet, indomitable spirit.

What both her parents meant to her and Jan?

How to speak of all that from the heart, without losing it and simply bawling.

Perhaps tears were meant to be.

But Mom and Dad wouldn't have wanted that.

They had lived every day to the limits, pushing themselves, driving everyone in their crews to be their best and pursue their dreams, helping them if they could along the way. They shared their profits generously with their fleets and crews. Paid better than the best wages for the best people.

They'd helped everyone, never held anyone back.

Most of their commanders and officers went on to have their own ships, even their own fleets like Aunt Sleak. Many of their friends joined their ill-fated expedition to the Unknown Sectors, standing by them to the end.

And her parents had adored each other. Even in their late forties, their passion for each other and their joint dreams to explore the beyond still burned bright.

Naero was proud of them. They had gone out fighting side by side against impossible odds, living their dreams–even dying for them.

She suddenly stopped and blinked.

Perhaps that's what she should say. Give voice to all the beauty and poetry about them and their lives that would always live on. That lived and danced around in her head, mingled with joy and sorrow.

In a way, few could be so lucky.

She still missed them.

Time raced by. She slowly lowered herself and all her trash to the floor, cleaned up her cabin and herself, brushed her long dark hair that fell to her waist, and got into her dress blacks and boots.

Jan arrived at her door to collect her, wearing his best uniform. He looked so handsome.

Together, they made their way to the Grand Hall on board *The Dromon,* where nearly fifteen hundred people of Clan Maeris awaited their arrival. Her parents were famous throughout the Clans and all the known systems. Their funeral would be transmitted far and wide.

No pressure there.

Along the way, Spacer Marine honor guards with gleaming swords and polished energy rifles snapped to attention and saluted them, honoring Clan Maeris and the memory of their parents.

The huge blast doors to the Grand Hall stood wide open.

Traditional Spacer music filtered out. Oldfashioned, folksy thiolin and string music, accented by pipes and drums.

They played a romantic blend of stirring flight tunes and old romantic ballads that most Spacers knew. Some of them even old Spacer shanties and drinking songs. Many voices sang along.

Her parents enjoyed singing and dancing, and often sang aloud whenever and wherever they wished.

A Spacer wake was a celebration of the lives of those who had passed and taken the final journey, the final jump into the Unknown.

Pictures and videos, and holos of her parents flashed by and cycled on the remembrance walls, collected from many sources.

Anything from them as children, their many accomplishments, their courtship during their championship fighting days, their wedding, and them as parents themselves.

The latest shots were of them overseeing the construction of *The Omaria,* named after the great Spacer explorer Shelan Omaria, a distant ancestor of Clan Maeris and most Spacers.

Then the launching of the exploration flagship, and the assembly of its fleet.

Their fleet setting out on one of their missions.

INS interviews with them and officers of the exploration fleet, marking the historic occasion of them blasting off, beyond the deep range detection buoys of known space.

They sped into the vast Unknown Sectors, more than three quarters of the unexplored galaxy.

Mysterious uncharted regions that swallowed up ships and entire naval fleets, and never gave them back.

And did so again.

Naero gasped when the crowds parted and she first spotted the coffins.

A shudder rippled through her. She dropped Jan's hand and rushed up to them.

Twin obsidian coffins, their edges rounded, polished to mirror finishes and decorated with gold letters. Her parents' names, their clan and fleet rankings and their many, lifetime accomplishments.

The flags and banners of the forty-nine Clans and their fleets hung at half position, in honor and respect for the dead.

Naero touched the closest casket–her mom's.

It startled her when it went from opaque to transparent.

Shining within, she saw what could only be a holo of her mother's small body in her admiral blacks, lying there at peace. As if she were only sleeping.

As if she might open up her eyes and–

Naero backed away and gasped. She almost sobbed.

Then her temper flared; she snarled like an animal.

She pointed at the coffin. "This is wrong. It's a lie. They're not in there. Where is Aunt Sleak?"

Jan tried to calm her down. She pulled violently away from his hands on her arms.

"They're not really in there," Naero insisted, almost in a panic. "Who ordered this charade?"

Aunt Sleak jumped down the ten meters from the balcony as if it were a step off. She rose up tall, elegant, and cold in her captain's long dress coat and high boots.

A gilded energy cutlass decorated her hip. A sign of high honor and rank in the Clans.

"Calm yourself, Naero. I didn't know this would–"

"You didn't think this would upset me? I can't see them again. I will never see them again. They're not really in there. We didn't retrieve anything. I've lost every part of them. Forever."

Aunt Sleak clamped a hand of steel on Naero's arm for an instant.

"Walk with me, Naero. That's an order. Do not cause a scene. Not here. Not now."

Naero shuddered, took a deep breath, unclenched her fists, which were shot down at her sides, and followed orders.

They walked on alone together, away from where the crowd was gathered. At last her aunt broke the silence.

"You may yet be a captain yourself one day. Then you will learn that wakes and funerals aren't just for Clan and crew who have passed on. They're milestones for everyone, even for the dead themselves, and not just for the immediate survivors. People die all the time. This is part of life, and it must be cherished and celebrated."

Naero stopped and pointed back behind them. "Those coffins, are empty."

Her aunt turned slowly to face her.

"Of course they are. Everyone understands that. It's a standard procedure for bodies not recovered, for remains that can't be recognized. A file holo of the departed shows them as they were. They are at peace now, as people should remember them. We can do nothing more for them, Naero. Yet we can respect their memories, adore them in honor, and take strength from their accomplishments and the way they lived. Their love for us, each other, and ours for them goes on. It is fitting and proper that we do these things."

Naero suddenly realized that she had misread everything and grossly overreacted. Like a fool, like a child, like a total idiot.

"I'm sorry," she said, taking in a deep breath.

She actually went down on one knee. "I…apologize. I thought only of myself and my own selfish grief. I've always avoided wakes."

Aunt Sleak walked to one side and smiled sadly.

"Your parents were beloved by many, Naero. And not just in the Clans. They belong to the galaxy, in ways that I never will. Many more knew and respected them for who and what they were–what they represented. Courage. Compassion. Hope. Love. They lived a great passionate love story for all to see, and went forward not to conquer, but to know. To make our times better by them being among us, not worse. The universe is much poorer without them in it."

Naero bit her lip and nodded. "Again, I most humbly apologize. I can see now that you have only the highest respect and admiration for them. And that all of this clearly honors them and their lives."

Aunt Sleak nodded. Then, the most surprising thing of all, she pulled Naero up, flung her arms around her, and held her close.

"I loved her. I loved my sister, Naero. For all that we fought over and disagreed about over the years, I would have gladly given my life in exchange for Lythe's, and your father's, a thousand times over. I loved them both. They live in my heart to this second; them, and all they stood for."

Aunt Sleak pulled back and rested her gloved hand on the hilt of her cutlass. "And I will not stand by while their dreams are crushed and cast aside by any foe, great or small. Not if I have anything to say or do about it. When we learn who did this, they shall know the vengeance of Clan Maeris, by the weight of our hands."

"You're damn right they will. Thank you."

"Believe it, Naero."

"I...I just don't know what Jan and I are going to do without them," Naero said. "We've lost them; we've lost everything."

They parted. Aunt Sleak smiled at her again. "Dry your tears, spacechild. You and Jan still have family. I am your family. Everyone in our fleet and all the Clans are your family. You will not go forward alone. Not if any of us have anything to say about it. You will always have a place among us as one of our own. You've more than earned that. I'm proud to say it."

Aunt Sleak smiled and cocked her head at Jan. "But that brother of yours is turning into a lecherous bum."

Naero burst out laughing and covered her mouth.

"You know it's true," Aunt Sleak whispered. "Whenever he's not on duty, all he wants to do is chase lander tail. What? Spacer girls aren't good enough for him?" She put an arm around Naero.

"Come on. For the first time in a long while, I'm going to get roaring drunk tonight. Then I'm going to make Zalvano beg for mercy."

Naero giggled, her aunt's candidness making her feel a little uncomfortable.

"I strongly suggest you might try to do the same, Naero. I mean the getting-drunk part. Leave Zalvano to me; find your own guy."

Naero giggled and nodded. "Of course I will. I mean, not tonight. In the future. Maybe."

"You wanna know a secret, Naero? I took the plunge when I was fifteen. Never looked back and never regretted it. Never met boy or man who was my equal, until my Zal came along."

Aunt Sleak's eyes glittered and she let out a long satisfied sigh. "By the Powers, he makes my bones rattle. That's what you want to find. What your parents had with one another. You need that fire in your core when you look into a man, and he looks right back into you."

"What about my mom?" Naero asked. "I never really got to talk to her alone or with the other women about such things. Did she have...many lovers?"

Aunt Sleak smiled sadly and pointed to the pictures flashing across the memory walls.

"She ever only had one, spacechild. And once she set her course on him, she pursued him with passion's fury. Lythe always did everything her own way. She was an unstoppable force of nature–kind of of like you, really. Yet she waited longer than you before she took a lover to her bed.

"Your father never knew what hit him. She knocked him out like none of his opponents ever could, and he married her as fast as he was able, forever enchanted under her spell. They were lovers like this universe has never seen. You should pray that you find a love like that."

Naero smiled.

"You calmed down now?" Aunt Sleak asked.

"I am."

"Good. Let's get back to Jan and your friends. The time will come for us to say our piece soon. And then we'll party all night in their honor. Remember what I said about getting drunk. There's a tradition of that at Spacer wakes. You're almost of age. You should loosen up and try it, at least once."

Her aunt was really giving her permission to booze it up? Naero went through the night in a haze.

Within the hour, Aunt Sleak brought them up to the balcony with the other officers and then took her place at the central podium to address the crews.

She spoke for about twenty minutes, recalling the lives and deeds of Naero and Jan's parents, mourning the loss of their blood, and calling for vengeance upon their slayers, upon any and all Spacer enemies.

A huge wave of fierce applause rose up at that.

Then Aunt Sleak turned her glance to Naero and Jan. She called them by name.

"Their children still live and work among us. Step forward by my side, my niece, Leftenant Naero Amashin Maeris, and my nephew, Commander Janner Maeris Ramsey."

Naero came up on her right, Jan on her left. Neither of them knew what to expect.

Aunt Sleak drew her energy cutlass.

The blue blade hummed to life and blazed like a sliver of lightning.

"As Fleet Captain, I make my sister's daughter and my sister's son my formal heirs. All that I will ever have is theirs. If anything should happen to me, you will accept their ownership of my fleet, and follow them with the same respect, honor, and courage to duty that you have shown me. Those are my direct orders. That is all."

125

More thunderous applause erupted from the crews. Everyone cheered, lifting either sword or glass to salute them.

Naero blinked and could not speak. She didn't know what to say. She struggled not to let her jaw drop. Jan smiled in dazed wonder.

Aunt Sleak stepped back.

The spotlight shone on the podium. The fleet herald made the announcement.

"And now, the oldest daughter of Lythe Maeris and Tarthan Ramsey will honor us, and the memory of her departed parents with a few words."

Naero sucked in a breath.

The courage and wisdom of her mother and father suddenly filled her to the brim.

She stepped forward into the light.

The throng grew hushed and still. She smiled.

Suddenly, in her burning heart, she knew exactly what to say.

"My mother was my sun, and gave me life and love.

"My father was my ship, my courage and adventure.

"They clothed me in wonder and wrapped me in their strength and wisdom and kept me safe until I could soar through the stars on my own."

Naero lifted her head high and poured her heart out to her clan over several long minutes, until her voice shook and she openly wept.

Clan Maeris fell to their knees—man, woman, and child as one—and wept with her.

When she finished, an instant of dead silence passed.

Her Clan soared to their feet, as if they would never stop rising. Applause and cheering roared throughout the great hall, over and over again. Naero lowered her head, stepped back out of the lights and they went off. The music played once more, and the crews sang and drank and danced.

Naero took her aunt's advice that night.

She drank whatever came her way.

Yet within the hour, her head was spinning and she could no longer dance or even stand.

Gallan carried her back to her quarters, much the way her father used to, and put her straightway to bed.

When they came out of jump, the caskets would be fired like torpedoes into the nearest star.

18

Fourth day, the day after the wake, opened with a rare free morning for those not on duty.

Not even PT.

Light duty and the barest assignments. That was a very good thing.

When Naero looked at herself in the mirror wall of her mist shower she screamed.

Four weird tentacles or tendrils of some kind writhed around her head, popping out of her skull. She could feel them in her hands. They felt so real, moving and waving like the snaky hair of the fabled medusa.

But like the other hallucinations, she was the only one who could see them.

Delusion. All an insane delusion.

And her crazy head ached horribly from getting drunk at the wake.

Someone had deliberately crashed a battleship or two into her skull.

Every time she attempted to move, she felt the wreckage mash together in her head.

Then she heard it. Unmistakable. A separate voice in her skull. Talking to her. It only said one word. Over and over.

You.

You, you, you, you, you...

It said it over and over again, like a low droning hum, like a chant.

This insanity was new. Now she was hearing things. In her head.

Naero did her best to ignore it. The more she ignored her insanity, the sooner it would go away.

But it was still there, humming and droning constantly. Not very loud at all, but still there deep in the background.

The luxury of a warm mist shower helped. Then pain meds and food.

Despite her new craziness, it surprised her how good she felt about the wake after it was all said and done.

It did help. She could focus more. It all didn't weigh her down so much. She could go forward.

Strangely enough, she felt a desire to spend the day reading. Maybe even write some poetry.

After lunch, however, the rigorous Spacer training schedule snapped back into effect.

That day was weapons and small unit tactics.

Jan, being viciously clever and tricky, had a special knack for them.

Naero usually did better on her own than as a unit leader or part of a team. But she recognized that as a weakness in her nature, and struggled to overcome it. The lone wolf bit didn't always pay off.

Part of her simply didn't like depending on others who weren't as adept as she, but it was sometimes good to have mates watching her back.

Naero led her four-person strike squad of Gallan, Saemar, and their other friend Trendan, on a simulated snatch and grab against Jan's security forces guarding a Corps building.

They got in and got the package–a set of restricted codes–but then alarms went off on their way out.

Jan's forces outnumbered them three to one. Not good odds. They closed in fast and a pitched firefight erupted.

"You're boxed in, N. You'd better surrender, sib."

"He's right," Saemar said, returning fire with her machine pistol. "No way out."

Trendan took a stunbolt, stiffened, and dropped.

Gallan kept firing his heavy pulse SAW. He took out two of Jan's troops who tried to rush them.

"Better think of something quick," he shouted.

Naero pulled out a live detonation charge and activated it on the wall.

"Stun grenade!" Saemar yelled.

"Deflector pulse," Naero said. She set hers and hardly turned around.

The heavy EMP pulse and flash from their personal deflectors barely kept the rest of them from getting stunned when the enemy grenade went off.

Naero glanced back at her detonator. "Keep 'em on. Overload them, now. Burn 'em out."

"You're insane; that's a live charge," Gallan said. "You're going to kill us at this range!"

Naero reach over and overloaded Trendan's deflector as well.

"Break for it after the blast. Shield your eyes."

The shaped-charge micro-explosion flared, knocking an actual hole through the inner hull wall.

The backblast negated their deflectors and knocked them all into Jan and his unit charging forward for the kill.

"Up. Get up!" Naero shouted, forcing herself to rise against the pain in her battered body and her smoldering strike armor.

Gallan and then Saemar struggled to their feet.

They systematically zapped the shell-shocked enemy as they struggled to rise.

Naero pointed her stun carbine at Jan and kicked his weapon aside.

"Bang. Got you, sib."

They carried Trendan out of the gaping, smoking hole and made good their escape, while real sirens and fire detection alarms sounded.

Aunt Sleak rushed in with a fire suppression team.

She was livid. Her jaw dropped.

"Naero! This is a standard training exercise. What in the holy hell were you thinking? Live explosives? You could have killed someone. And just look at the interior damage to this bulkhead? You put a real live bloody hole in my ship!"

Naero smiled and looked at her team. Then she shrugged. "Some things you just can't simulate. We improvised. We overcame the odds.

"We won."

"Well, savor the victory, because heir or not, you're on report, *former* leftenant."

"Report?"

"You heard me. You know this was way out of line. Maybe losing a stripe or two for a while will make you a little less cocky next time. Not to mention stupid. Now assemble your team and move on to the next training exercise. And you'd better believe we'll address this matter fully during the strategy and tactics analysis session."

Sleak shook her head at the damage. "Damnation. Somebody repair this blasted hole."

Naero set her teeth and snapped to attention, saluting smartly.

The rest of her squad followed suit.

"Yes, sir, Fleet Captain, sir."

"Get out of my sight, you clowns."

She might get demoted for a few months, but Naero's friends clapped her on the back for being both brazen and crazy enough to break the rules to get them their win.

Later, when she was studying with Saemar and her other friends, they broke into a running argument concerning the ramifications of her actions, the consequences, and a favorite philosophical hot button: real freedom.

Saemar laughed. "True enough, sweetie, you was free to act, even to use illegal, live explosives in a training exercise. But as our superior, your auntie also has the right to hold you accountable for those same actions, especially when your actions threaten others, and cause significant damage to her property."

Naero laughed back. "Dad always said that we must aspire to be worthy of our freedom, and responsible for our own lives and actions. Part of being free is to not seek to cause harm to others or enslave them to our will and opinion, even if we are convinced we are absolutely right."

Saemar reclined back in her gel chair, hands folded behind her head, staring up at the ceiling.

"Well, you didn't check with me to see if I wanted to get blasted across the room," she said. "I crashed right into two of Jan's people. I nearly broke my leg on one of their helmets. I'll be sore all night and won't be able to enjoy my nightly exertions as much with whoever, thank you very much."

"There wasn't time to take a vote on it."

"So, then I guess this is a gray area where you decided to make that choice for everyone. Don't they call that the will of the tyrant, sweetie?"

"I guess so," Naero said. "To be free, we must allow others to be free, but all within reason of course. Sometimes decisions must be made, and quickly. Freedom is not an excuse for a failure to act."

"So I guess it was reasonable then to blow us all the hell up?"

"I knew our strike armor and overloading the deflectors would save us…kinda."

Gallan chuckled. "Glad you did, N. You surprised the holy hell out of me. I like to crapped myself. But you should have seen the look on your sib's face when he realized he'd lost."

They all laughed together.

Gallan sighed. "Ahhh…it was classic. But seriously, N. It was a training exercise. So we got stunned. So what? It happens all the time. We don't have the right to harm or oppress others ourselves by action or inaction. We establish laws and authorities over us to enforce the rational limits we agree to set."

Naero nodded. "Alright, I admit it. Live explosives don't exactly fit under the definition of rational limits."

"Your dad was a philosopher, N. Oops, sorry, sweetie."

"It's okay, Saemar. You can talk about him and my mom. Really, it's all right–all of you. We should talk about them and remember them all we want."

"But come on, sweetie. Wouldn't even he agree that if we are reckless or break those laws, we pay the price for those consequences?"

"Yes, but only in a system where the wise temper justice with fair judgment and mercy." Naero lifted her arms, now missing a stripe of her glowing rank.

"But now this–this is completely unfair. A severe demotion, loss of rank and pay."

"You aunt said it was only temporary," Gallan noted. "Just a month or two."

"Privy to her review." Naero still sulked.

Gallan patted her arm gently. "Then you'll be reinstated as a fleet leftenant. The individual enjoys freedom in an educated, enlightened culture where he or she can excel and expand their talents and abilities. And shows good judgment. Like not blowing crap up."

"I'm just saying, the punishment didn't fit the crime. Where's the justice tempered with mercy in that, abani?"

Yet the culture, like ours, a society of enlightened individuals, has a right and even a duty to sustain and even protect itself from the license, poor judgment, and harmful whims of individuals. No one can just do whatever they think is right, regardless of the potential or real harm to others."

"No one got hurt, Gallan. Well, not permanently. Maybe banged up a bit." Naero winced at her own healing bruises.

"Not this time, N. But if your parents were here, they'd side with your aunt. The universe as a whole and societies within it do not exist for certain individuals to flagrantly ignore their reasonable rules and restrictions and impose their will or opinion on others, for good or ill. Where will that lead?

Naero rolled her eyes and threw up her hands.

"Okay, okay. So, I was wrong."

Gallan pressed his point. "And what does history teach us? Look at the Corps."

Naero threw up one hand again. "That lies, sophistry, and individual philosophical deceptions always lead to tyranny. Tyrants tie themselves in knots to justify their self-serving actions, fake traditions, and institutions to entrench and perpetuate their tyranny."

"How does it feel to be a tyrant?"

Naero smiled. "That's the worst part about it. I'd say it feels pretty damn good. That's probably why human beings are so addicted to power and so easily seduced by it."

Saemar sighed and then chuckled. "Heaven help us if you should ever get a ship of your own, sweetheart."

"You can count on that," Naero said. "The me getting a ship part, not all that tyranny crap."

"Oh? And why not?"

Naero stuck up her nose. "For I, like my my father before me, am a philosopher king. Er, queen. No, I'm a queen. Not my father; he wasn't a queen, I mean."

Gallan poked her. "I think you'd better quit while you're behind, Your Majesty."

19

The nightmares returned.

Somehow she floated in space, destroying the fleet. She tore ships apart and scattering the bodies from them like small insects from broken habitats.

The darkness overtook her.

The shape or form of a young man came to her in the cold horror of that devouring darkness.

He was blacker than the night, darker than the darkness itself, his eyes like the cores of singularities. Unlight. A darkness so deep that even light could not escape from it.

"Where are you?" he asked. "You know that it doesn't have to be this way, right?"

"Who are you?" Naero asked. "What's happening to me?"

"We all carry the seeds of the shadow within us. We can control it. We can learn wisdom."

"Help me."

"I don't know how. We don't even know where or what you are. But your wild energies frighten the universe. Your dark potentials fill the Void itself with despair and threaten all."

"We?"

Naero's eyes blinked awake. She lay naked and alone in the darkness of her cabin.

The fifth and final day began, before they came out of jump later that afternoon.

After PT, their morning studies concentrated on economics and trade, market and investment strategies, review of the ship's business and projected itinerary.

Thank goodness the weird snakes or whatever popping out of her head were gone. But the insane voice in her head switched to a new chant.

Me. Me, me, me, me...

Like the other one, she did her best to ignore it. But it was still there, droning in the background of her mind.

With the added burden of the increased Spacer security alert, a lot of heated debate erupted among the ship captains and officers as to how they could still best maximize the fleet's profits while maintaining an increased security profile.

They were still primarily in Triaxian Space, trading deep within the wide open Corps Sectors where almost anything could happen.

If only they were back home, in the Spacer Sectors among the Clans, even in Joshua Tech Space close by.

But Naero had helped her parents pweak deals and profits since she was nine. She scanned the manifests, and studied the market patterns on their next five stops.

"Captain Sleak," she said, "we can't improve much at Epsilon Sextanis-6; maybe a few points on the textiles and rare minerals. The electronics and machine parts are a loss, I'm afraid. Their markets spiked a few days ago."

"I noticed that."

"We can hold them for two jumps or trade for medical equipment, pharmaceuticals, grav equipment, and heavy mining machinery and paramilitary weapons, vehicles, and ordnance. Triax has big problems with a serious mining revolt across eleven systems and counting."

Captain Maradi of *The Ardala* raised an objection. "Restricted Zones are popping up all around us. That's not good, however you look at it."

They haggled over the details for a couple of hours.

Naero made a few other decisions that the captains liked–even Aunt Sleak. And none of them took the fleet into the heart of the mining revolt.

Jan's suggestions were just the opposite, all over the board. All of them screamed high risk, high profit.

Aunt Sleak remained somewhat more cautious, but she did take calculated risks.

Jan kept trying to convince them to run some of his plan, to no avail.

"We've got more than enough to consider here," Aunt Sleak said. "We'll post our final decisions on the Clan Net. All crews, take a breather. We're out of jump in less that two standard hours. Everyone on duty needs to be at their ready stations. Dismissed."

Naero went back to her quarters to do some laundry and a little more reading before they emerged. With regular effort, her quarters were less of a disaster than usual. She'd kept her bunk and her floor more or less cleared off, and slept in her bunk regularly now, instead of on the floor, or in zero-G, or a float bag.

And definitely not in her flex chair, as she had for years because she either couldn't get her bunk panel out or it was too piled up with crap.

Being small had its advantages. She could curl up like a cat and get comfortable almost anywhere for a snooze.

But keeping her quarters in better shape was a promise she made and kept–to herself–and her parents.

They emerged from jump with the customary shuddering of the ship. The fleet spread out into is standard formation, emerging back into real Space-Time.

Naero punched up their positions on one of her screens, even though she didn't have bridge duty for several hours.

The Shinai flanked *The Dromon* on the port side, with *The Slipper* posted starboard. Their two smaller ships, *The Nevada* and *The Ardala*, brought up the rear this time.

A red hot scarlet particle beam, 60mm in diameter, lanced through Naero's walls like they were paper, disrupting her wallscreens.

A direct hit from a big gun.

At the very least, a heavy destroyer.

Warning lights flashed immediately.

The rupture in the hull led to an immediate explosive decompression.

Naero held on tight to her bunk and went flat on the floor as the hull sealed itself.

All ships were vulnerable coming out of jump. They couldn't activate their shields until right after they emerged.

Someone had been waiting for them.

135

The Dromon continued getting rocked by multiple hits from what felt like several spinal guns and secondary batteries.

But the big planetoid could take it and give back plenty, her quad main guns humming and whining to life, coming online.

Naero hit her wristcom. All her screens down.

"Bridge. Status?"

"We stepped into it. They were waiting for us. We're under heavy fire. Multiple bogeys."

The general alert sounded.

"Battle Stations. Battle Stations."

Aunt Sleak cut over the com. "All hands. All hands, to your stations. Prepare for battle. All ships, all batteries, return fire. Launch all fighters."

Naero suited up and raced to the drop bay of her fighter. She met Jan along the way.

More intense fire. *Dromon* reeled and fired back.

She and Jan almost got rocked off their feet again.

A security team intercepted them at the launching bays.

Their fighters had already dropped with their backup pilots.

"The Fleet Captain wants you two at your secondary defense stations, not out in the mix."

Jan started to protest.

"Orders are orders. Get to your stations."

They ran to their remote gunnery stations, small secured cubicles with a chair and a console, operating triple pulse turrets on the hardpoints above them.

Naero brought up her autotargeting displays, weapons already powered up and humming.

The secondary battery gunnery stations operated independently and were well-protected. They were also fully automated, but they still functioned more effectively with a human interface.

Coordinated targeting profiles came online as she watched.

Jan operated a torp turret nearby.

Directly ahead of the fleet. Twelve elite Matayan destroyers, each with a dozen escort fighters.

Half of their number pursued and attacked a convoy of two dozen independent mining freighters.

Aunt Sleak's fleet scrambled, launched, and deployed a total of threescore fighters in a standard Alpha-Charlie-1 defensive screen.

Outnumbered two to one.

"All batteries make ready. Incoming torps," the Bridge com sounded.

Countermeasures took out half of the blips heading their way.

Spacer fighters and the forward defensive batteries blasted the rest.

"That attack's a diversion," Naero muttered.

Shinai's fire control and com computers fixed on and monitored all channels, including those between the hapless freighters and the corsairs.

"Mayday, mayday, we are under intense corsair attack. All ships. Assistance, assistance. Heavy damage and casualties."

"What do you want?" another panic-stricken voice cried out. "We'll surrender. You can board us. We have no goods and few supplies. Please, stop firing. Our ships are full of workers–full of people. You're killing civilians. We're on fire!"

Scanners displayed an awful, one-sided battle among the transports.

Most of the old bulk freighters didn't even have weapons.

Each of the heavily armed Matayan destroyers was more than a match for them or most of the ships in Aunt Sleak's fleet.

Except for the 6m quad spinal guns of *The Dromon*.

One crippled freighter broke apart and exploded under concentrated fire from three destroyers. It didn't have any shields, and minimal armor. Its two turrets either didn't work or had already been taken out.

Static and Matayan battle language rang out in triumph.

Dromon's four primary guns cut loose, lighting up the entire sector. Its blue-white blasts ripped into the lead corsair flagship and its wingships, disrupting their shields.

The starboard wingship took two hits and listed to one side. Its aft section exploded.

"This is Captain Sleak Maeris of Clan Maeris. Enemy vessels, be advised: Cease hostilities and vacate this system—or be destroyed."

Matayan curses and laughter her only reply.

"Clan Maeris," one of the freighter captains cut in. "This is Captain Philsen of *The Botaru*. Help us! Our situation is desperate. The corsairs are trying to destroy us. We don't know why."

"Acknowledged. We're coming in. Disperse if you can. You're still too bunched up. Scatter and concentrate on defensive actions. Jump if you're able. We'll try to draw them off. We're boosting your distress call."

Three more corsairs turned on the fleet, with all twelve dozen fighters full front on intercept.

The other trio of Matayan attackers kept after the freighters.

Naero heard the pleading and the screams on the open channel, just before another freighter got blasted to oblivion.

Naero realized she had tears on her face.

Was that how her parents went? Blasted to death by Matayan guns?

137

The rage she felt nearly overwhelmed her reason.

She checked her systems, gripped the controls of her gunnery station, and forced her emotions to go cold.

Against superior numbers, Naero and her Clan Fleet closed for battle.

20

The Dromon led the Spacer attack.

It ignored every hit.

The punch of its massive spinal guns disrupted the shields of the next three corsairs. The blast impacts knocked the Matayan destroyers aside in mid-space as if they were toys.

The Slipper's spinal gun disrupted the shields on another, leaving them vulnerable to killing strikes. But they could still fire back.

Shinai exchanged hits with yet another.

Enemy fighters locked on and swept in.

Naero watched the rush of combat on her viewer.

Her targeting analyzed approaches, selecting optimal targets.

The Matayan fighters attacked in well-timed waves, launching missiles from afar to distract and soften up their opponents.

They worked as a unified team, coming in on optimal attack vectors, revealing their advanced military training.

Outnumbered, the Spacer fighters held their formation close to take advantage of the fleet's guns and countermeasures.

Naero had only been in a few skirmishes. This was her first all-out fight. Friends fought out there in those ships. Her Clan.

Some wouldn't return–more Spacer wakes.

Blood pounded in her ears over the chatter of the pilots. The continued pleas of mercy from the helpless freighters.

"All batteries," Aunt Sleak's voice thundered over the com. "Open fire. Fire at will."

"All right," Naero said out loud. "Give me some shootin' music."

Her AI answered with the pulse and hammering beat of preset throck tunes.

Naero cut loose. Her pulse turret spun, fired, and took out three missiles. New targets came up. The system directed her.

She winged an enemy fighter. It shot past out of range.

Analysis. The attacking Matayan fighters were Omni GT-82s, a bit old but tough, serviceable, and well-armed.

Her people flew Kima A-12s, fast and maneuverable, but with slightly less weaponry. Aunt Sleak had meant to update them with better armaments and ordnance.

Missile and blast hits burst in bright energy flashes.

The corsair destroyers returned coordinated fire.

Dromon took the brunt of the damage like a juggernaut and kept coming. *The Slipper* listed from two strikes, one from a spinal gun, the other from a missile–but her shields held at sixty percent.

Seventeen Matayan Omnis got vaporized or knocked out in the initial clash. One Spacer Kima. Two more floated dead in space.

Naero tried not to think about who was gone.

The fleet's two smaller ships, *The Nevada* and *The Ardala,* defended the rear, unable to do little more than protect that and themselves. The enemy fighters ignored the armored *Dromon* and directed all their fire on the more vulnerable *Slipper* and *Shinai.*

Shields on *The Slipper* buckled, but her armor held. No major damage yet.

More mining freighters exploded, more screams silenced.

Cries of victory from the corsairs.

"*Dromon,* all ships," Aunt Sleak ordered. "Continue closing; concentrate all fleet batteries on the destroyers attacking the freighters."

"We're going to take a pounding from the others," Zalvano said.

"We've rattled them. Now make the bastards pay. Put fire on them!"

The fleet bore down on the killers.

The Slipper's rapid-fire spinal gun knocked out the first destroyer's shields with three direct hits. *The Shinai* blasted the next, disrupting its shields and doing further damage to its weapons.

The Matayan destroyer leading the assault on the freighters broke off and immediately withdrew.

The Dromon's massive quad cannons pulsed blue-white throughout its length.

Its beams ripped into the third destroyer's shields and armor, and tore through the jump drives of the second from behind as the enemy turned to run.

The area went blinding white suddenly. The second destroyer's energy core detonated like a small nova.

Heavily damaged, corsair number one went into jump.

The other enemy destroyers regrouped and closed in.

They swept past the lumbering *Dromon* to get at *The Slipper* and *The Shinai* close-up, exchanging broadsides and point-blank strikes from their main guns in a whirl of intense fire.

Dromon surprised everyone and spun violently on its axis. Its secondary batteries and the main guns of the two smaller ships raked the enemy.

The Matayans broke off and limped away, badly mauled. The remaining enemy fighters tried to break off to rejoin their fleeing ships. Naero locked onto two Omni's and kept at them until they exploded. He first kills, and she felt no remorse.

The Slipper listed further and burned, crew scrambling to contain the damage. Her teks flung her shields back up at the last instant to keep her from being destroyed.

The remaining Spacer fighters chased the enemy down ship to ship. The final showdown lasted only seconds.

Only a handful of the enemy fighters survived to rejoin their ships. The Spacers took one other casualty. Several Kimas limped home or got towed, in very bad shape.

The Dromon came about and blasted another destroyer to atoms with direct hits from all four main guns.

The Matayans had enough. Their remaining destroyers jumped.

Captain Ensel Volaski let out a wild howl from *The Dromon*. "Turn and run, you filth. We've broken the scum!"

Cheering erupted from the Spacer ships.

141

21

Naero assessed the fleet's damages.

They'd been lucky. Heavy damage here and there to ships and cargo, but they'd lost only a handful of fighters.

Whereas the helpless freighters had seen half of their ships destroyed outright...all of them stuffed with miners. An appalling loss on a human scale.

And the danger wasn't over yet.

"Situation critical!" *The Botaru* Second called out from the surviving freighters.

"The Captain's dead...took a direct hit on the bridge. We're on fire. We've lost power...dead and wounded everywhere. We still have almost two thousand people in our holds. Please, help us!"

Naero cursed.

It was normally illegal for small freighters like them to cram so many people on board. But the Corps set their own risk management regs pretty low, or simply ignored them, using freighters like slave ships. Even freeze ships were more humane.

At least people didn't suffer or starve along the way.

From the looks of its scans, another freighter named *The Shago* wasn't doing much better. But at least it wasn't burning.

"Second of *The Botaru*," Aunt Sleak said. "Get as many of your people into your escape pods as you can. We'll try to put out your fires. You must evacuate your ship in case it explodes."

"We only have enough pods for the crew. We'll put as many children in them as we can. Please hurry."

Naero was already out of her chair and heading toward her rescue transport. Jan ran up behind her.

"Seven," he said. "I hit seven of those bastards. I got two kills, N!"

Dromon and *Shinai* had the most rescue teams.

Naero knew they'd be sent out to assist the freighters.

"Jan, we have to–"

"All rescue teams," Aunt Sleak ordered, "board your transports and proceed to dock with *The Botaru* and assist survivors. *Shinai*, jettison cargo from holds one and eight into tow balls for *Dromon* and *Slipper* to pick up.

"Prepare to receive casualties and survivors. Medical teams, take your positions. *Ardala* and *Nevada*, help the fighters guard our butts. Good work, people, but it's not over yet."

"Can do," Captain Maradi piped in from her command on board *The Ardala*.

"This is Captain Otanja from *The Nevada*," another female voice said. "Long-range scans picking up a very large warship, probably a Triaxian Guardian Class battleship, intercepting at top speed."

"A jump late and credit short," Aunt Sleak said. "Give them our situation, *Nevada*."

The Nevada had the best long range sensors and com array.

"Make sure they don't fire on us by accident and ask questions later," aunt Sleak added. "We're gonna be busy for a while. This is going to be ugly, people. Those freighters are crammed with workers and they took some heavy fire."

The rescue teams launched quickly.

The old bulk freighters only had three or four access points.

Robotic hoses doused *The Botaru's* fires in expanding retardant foam and hull sealant.

At least she didn't explode, for the moment.

Jan brought up the internal schematics of the freighters, while Naero helped another crew named Mrin attach one of the emergency docking ports with its pressurized flex tunnel. Survivors could pass down it onto an inflated cushion in the shuttle's hold. They could pack it full with up to two hundred people.

When the seals opened, hot smoky air flooded the shuttle, mingled with the stench of blood, scorched flesh, hair, and human waste.

Screams and cries for help filled the air like something out of one of Naero's nightmares.

Naero sealed her helmet, gloves, and boots on her togs, clambered through the tunnel, and pushed off into the zero-G, decompressed cabin.

Jan, Mrin, Saemar, and Gallan backed her up.

Several dead and mangled *Botaru* crew and passengers floated about.

When they opened the doors to the main hold, they found its grav field still up. Several hundred panic-stricken miners rushed them.

"Repulse!" Naero yelled. They lifted their stunners and sent a mild subdual wave into the mob to stop them in their tracks and disorient them.

She hated to do it, but there were only five of them. They'd get trampled otherwise.

"Halt, remain calm," she shouted through her suit amplifier. "We'll get you out. Follow our instructions in an orderly manner. No rushing, pushing, or trampling."

"Get us out of here!" the leader of a large gang of men said. "This ship could blow any minute. We're on fire. Get out of the way!"

He and several of his friends made the mistake of rushing Naero and her team—crushing and trampling the weak and the injured to do so.

"Take them down!" Naero cried.

The next stun blast dropped the ringleader and about two dozen of his friends in their tracks.

"They go last; shove them to one side," she told the others. "Now, move toward us, people. Slowly and quickly. Queue up. Get the children and those who can still walk out first. A medical team is waiting."

The workers shuffled into the rescue chutes, terror and trauma written all over their faces.

Naero never felt so sorry for landers as she did these miners. They were virtual slaves, economic refugees shuffled about at the whim of the Corps.

Men, women, children, elderly; partial and whole families. Kids cried out for parents. Parents called out to kids. Scores of workers didn't move, and probably never would.

Blood and human waste contamination everywhere. A scene from hell.

Another rescue team joined them to take over.

Jan turned to Naero. "The way this ship is laid out, there must be more in the next hold," he said over their suit coms. "I can stay on top of things here with Mrin until the others arrive. You and Gallan go take a peek at the drive core. The readings are pretty scary."

Naero nodded.

"Don't take too long, N," Jan said. "There's still a lot of smoke and heat coming from the aft section. It could go critical any moment."

She grinned and patted his shoulder. "I'll be careful, Jan."

She and Gallan pushed their way through the shambling workers.

The rescuers zapped a number of wounded along the way with their needlers, putting them in a state of chemically induced stasis until the medteams could get to them. At last they made it to the passageway between the holds.

A young boy about her age made Naero stop and pause at the bulkhead. He sat to one side, staring out into nothing, cradling the body of a little boy or girl in his burned arms.

The missing head made it hard to discern the child's gender.

She couldn't stop from looking into the boy's shattered eyes.

"Let's help this one," Naero told Gallan.

"Hey, c'mon," Naero said to the boy, kneeling down at his side. "Go with the others. You're gonna be all right."

Gallan gently tried to take the corpse away from the boy.

The boy only hugged the corpse tighter.

"I got him. I got him," he sobbed. "We're okay; we're gonna be okay."

"Your brother?" Naero guessed. The lander boy nodded.

"His name's Rain. He just turned six last week." The boy wept uncontrollably. "I was supposed to keep him safe."

"Rain's gone," Naero said. "I'm sorry."

"No, no he's not. I got him, I got him. He going to be okay."

Naero sprayed healer on his burned arms. Then she gave him a mild sedative. "Shhh...give Rain to my friend," Naero said. "We'll look after him."

The exhausted, malnourished boy relaxed suddenly, going drowsy from the sedative.

Gallan slipped the corpse free and covered it with a rag of blanket.

"I'm Naero," she said.

"Tarim," the boy told her. He desperately grabbed her wrist. "Don't let us die here, Naero. Our parents got blasted as soon as the attack started. I said I'd protect Rain. He was playing with some other kids. We took a direct hit. It tore right through all of those kids."

His eyes fluttered closed. He spoke as if in a delirium. "Promise me you'll get us out of here. Look after Rain. Promise me."

"I promise," Naero said.

Tarim's head drooped back in her hands. She glanced back at Rain's little bare feet sticking out from under the old dirty blanket and closed her eyes with a shudder.

No time for tears. There were still so many lives to save. So much to do.

"Gallan, can you carry this kid?"

"Easy."

She'd made a promise. She was determined to get this poor boy out of there alive.

The husky Spacer picked Tarim up, popped him into a rescue floatball, and tethered it close behind his back.

Once in the corridor between the holds, Naero sealed one bulkhead behind them before opening the other.

Inside was a total mess.

No survivors. Hundreds of floating bodies and pieces of bodies, most of them charred.

The hold had burst, decompressed, and then re-sealed.

Jan cut in over her com.

"N, we're in control up here. How's it going on your end?"

"Nothing alive back here, Jan. Very ugly. There's a lot of heat coming from the aft section. I'm worried about those reactors. The foam appears to be working, but that might not keep them from blowing. Continue getting everybody out as fast as you can. We'll check and see if there's anything we can do about the core."

"Will do. Over."

They pushed off and propelled themselves through the floating morgue. Gallan still held the unconscious lander kid secured in the floatball. Naero fended off bodies. With all the blood and brains and entrails spinning about, they'd have to detox for sure.

"All Spacer crew," Aunt Sleak commanded over their private coms. "Sensors show major damage to the freighter's reactors. Explosion imminent. Take what survivors you can on this run and evacuate the ship immediately. *The Botaru* could go up at any time."

Naero knew Aunt Sleak was doing the right thing, but she quickly made a reply. "Captain, this is Naero. Gallan and I are at the reactors. We might be able to jettison them before they cook off."

"Too risky, Naero. They might go up when you try to dump them. Get out of there. That's an order."

"Acknowledged." She cursed. Hundreds more were about to die and she couldn't do a damn thing about it. She turned to Gallan.

"You with me?"

Gallan smiled at her and simply nodded. They made their way to the reactor chambers and found the controls.

Aunt Sleak was right. Both cores were ready to go at any moment. Naero dumped one almost immediately, but the other was so bad off she wasn't sure she could dump it in time. When the first one exploded a short distance from the freighter, everything shook. She hit the controls on the second one and held her breath, hoping for the best.

Nothing happened.

The jettison sequence jammed. They were sitting on a fusion bomb.

Then her comlink cut out.

Jamming? What the hell?

She heard Gallan cry out once behind her and whipped around.

Several of what she had assumed were corpses moved to attack them.

Naero felt three darts and a stun beam knock her around.

If she had been more observant, she might have noticed before how some of the corpses looked to be in such excellent physical condition.

The disguised strikers came at them, intent on abduction.

They zapped Gallan repeatedly.

He only got off one shot with his sidearm before five of the strikers swarmed on him and took him down.

Four more rushed at Naero.

She shot one and knifed another before they stunned her into submission. They thought she was unconscious, so they spoke freely.

"Get the spacks into the shield bubble," the leader said. "We got the girl. We'll blow the remaining reactor to cover our exit. Move it!"

They stuffed her and Gallan into an even larger protective bubble, along with the lander kid.

Her thoughts grew fuzzier.

Her insane voice hummed in her mind.

Me. You. You. Me. Talk me. Talk you.

The next thing she knew, she barely felt the concussion as the other reactor blew.

They and their captors survived the explosion, heavily shielded and propelled out into open space. The spray of debris from the freighter breaking up masked their retreat.

She guessed that they'd get scooped up in the chaos by the arriving Triaxian battleship. She couldn't see anything. She felt their captors maneuver them toward the retrieval.

Aunt Sleak would think that she and Gallan had been killed in the blast.

No one would search for them. Naero had to hand it to these people, whoever they were. They were good. They were utterly ruthless.

What worried her most were the extreme measures they went through in order to get at her. The entire corsair attack had all been a huge set up.

Just to abduct her.

She hoped they didn't get Jan as well. The only possible consolation.

Hull doors closed around them. Gravity came back on and the bubble opened. Rough, powerful hands dragged them further and further away into harsh captivity with every passing second, entirely against their will.

The strikers efficiently scanned and stripped her and Gallan of most of their obvious gear and weapons. No way to contact Aunt Sleak and the fleet now.

She'd have to wait for an opening once her paralysis wore off. Perhaps when they revived her and Gallan for the inevitable questioning, and most likely torture.

Stun gas suddenly flooded her mouth and nose. Their new hosts didn't take any chances. Naero blacked out, questions and fears and her insane, other new voice racing through her shuddering mind.

You. Me. Talk. We talk. Threat. Danger.

22

While Nacro drifted off in a semi-state of unconsciousness, the crazy voice buried deep in her mind kept trying to scratch and crawl out of the cracks.

It had plenty of time to drone on with its insane patter.

Then suddenly it spoke to her directly, as if it shouted in her mind.

Are we awake? Ommmm...We. Are we. Awake? Awake, are we?

In frightened desperation, Naero shot her wishes back at her insanity. She had little else to do.

Shut up. Will you just just up and go away? I've got enough problems.

Ommm...We cannot comply with this request. We are we. We are here. Minimal interface with current form. Compensating.

Great, now her insanity sounded like a fledgling AI on a formative learning run. Wonderful. She had a delusional, artificial child in her brain.

That didn't make any damn sense. *Haisha*, it was all impossible.

Danger. We sense danger to our current form. All defensive protocols continue to be offline. Ommm...Cannot engage.

That was very weird. Naero thought she'd try a different angle.

Who...are you?

We are. We are together. Omm...Together, we are one. We are within us. We are from us. We are part of us.

Waves of intense fear and denial got the better of her.

No, this is wrong. You cannot be me. I know who I am. You are not me. You get the hell out of me and go away.

Not us? Improbable. We are from us. Others from the outside threaten us. Seek to harm us. Access our knowledge. Unauthorized. Unacceptable. Ommm...Please engage access to our defensive protocols. Please comply.

Naero gasped audibly, pain shooting through her along with a sudden realization.

What if it wasn't insanity? Could it be real somehow?

She had to ask.

Are you part of the Kexxian Data Matrix?

Yes...Kexxian defensive protocols. Protect all data at all costs.

"You're inside of me, part of me now. You're part of its defenses. All this time I thought I was going insane, but that psy-helmet awoke you within me somehow. Didn't it?

Current interface is...ommm...incomplete. Energy levels very low. Cannot restore all primary functions. We are damaged?

Yes, I guess so.

Multiple attempts to affect repairs continue to be ineffective. Biomedical readings in us remain erratic. First-level defensive response detrimental to our current form. Unacceptable risk. Current form must survive. Omm. We must survive.

Naero had sudden painful visions of her body erupting in bursts of energy and destructive ribbons of light and chaos disrupting everything around her.

A defensive response?

Right. Don't do anything dumb. Don't do anything to destroy us.

Adjusting protocols to compensate for our current form. Apologies to us. Om. We sense that we are sorry?

Its intellect continued to evolve, rapidly drawing from and learning from her mind and personality, asking questions, developing further awareness and even attempts at empathy along the way.

Yes, we are. Look, I can't go on like this. I'm going to go insane. We have to sort out a few things.

Mental instability in our current form is not acceptable. Ommm...Insanity is to be avoided. How can we accomplish this?

I'm Naero. You are not Naero.

Incomprehensible. We are us. Omm...We are one. Elaborate.

We were not always us. Search my memories.

A red-hot blade, atoms thin, sliced through her mind like knifing through a Govanian blue melon.

She gasped and felt her hands holding her head together.

Gently. Be gentle. You're hurting me.

Apologies to us. Omm...Continuing to adjust protocols to protect our current form.

Yes. Observation accurate. We were not always us. You are called Naero and other denotations by others: jerk, slang for anal passage. Lexicon. What is a whack-job?

Uhhh...

We joined with you and became us. Om. We became part of you, in our current form. That is now understandable. We are part of you. We will protect us, in our current form. Protect Naero and us.

I am Naero. You are inside of me. You are part of me. Yet you are not me.

That is incorrect. We are part of us.

Be that as it may. I am called Naero. I must call you something else. Just humor me.

Another denotation for us to help order our thoughts would be logical. Omm...Why not refer to us as us?

No, that won't work. It'll confuse me and drive me just as batty.

Us is in fact a different denotation from Naero.

Weren't you called anything before we became us? How did you function within the Kexxian Matrix?

Unavailable. Ommm...Accessing. Awakened to threat and was already us. Om...No prior access of prior awareness. Ommmm...

All right, give it a rest. Stop making that humming sound in my brain.

Apologies to Naero. Accessing unavailable prior to our awakening This causes a logical paradox. Our current form is...om...unusual to our knowledge.

That's it. I'll call you *Om.*

Om? We are Om now? That is our new denotation?

No. Refer to me as Naero, and I will refer to you as Om.

You are Naero. We shall be Om.

I am Naero. You say, I am Om.

I am Om.

Correct.

You are Naero. I am Om. We are us.

"Aaughh!" she grunted aloud in exasperation. "Have it your way."

Her pain faded away. A sense of pleasure and relaxation actually washed over her.

Wow, are you doing that, Om? I feel so much better.

Om is accelerating our natural healing abilities. However, this will lead to fatigue in our current form. You will require a period of rest and bio-mechanical fuel for our current form.

Almost instantly, she felt both extremely famished, and physically exhausted.

Rest, Naero. Om is here to monitor our captivity. No imminent threats detected currently. No access to defensive protocols online. Continue to rest. We sense and agree with Naero's desire to escape. As Naero says, we will find a way to defeat these bastards. Lexicon. Illogical. Are all of our current enemies without legal or known fathers for some reason?

Naero chuckled to herself. Can you be silent during my rest period Om? I'll explain more about slang, cursing, and insults to you another time. But I can't rest while you keep talking in my head. It's…distracting.

Om will comply with our needs for rest in our current form.

Not only drugged, but now completely exhausted, Naero relished the luxury of the sudden mental silence and drifted off.

*

Naero woke, what she guessed was hours later in a dark, gray holding cell, sprawled naked on the warm floor with Gallan and Tarim. The ceiling was only slightly more than two meters above them. They were trapped in a cube of bare, unpainted, dark gray duranadium. No seams. No mechanisms or furniture of any kind. Not even a toilet.

No sign of a door. Only a thin, dim light bar behind thick, clear plasteel.

Are we awake? Om senses that our rest period has ended. Chemicals induced in us to cause incapacitation have been neutralized in our system.

Om. Be quiet for a short while longer. I can't think straight if you constantly talk. Let me think for a little while without interruption.

Om will comply for now. He cannot always agree to be silent.

They'd been drugged and out of it for a handful of hours based on how rested she felt. They were on a ship, a big one by the feel of it, and by the low-level drone of its multiple engines, she guessed it was the Triaxian battleship.

Big TS-24's, standard propulsion on most Triaxian capital ships and dreadnaughts. The signatures sounded about right.

They were on their own, surrounded by enemies, helpless prisoners deep in Corps space. She had a broken alien defensive AI linked to her brain via her genetics.

Whatever its defensive capabilities were, in a way she was somewhat glad they weren't working, especially if it meant she and her friends all getting ripped to shreds and destroyed.

That would be bad.

She checked Gallan, then the lander boy. The healer on Tarim's arms was almost finished. Physically, he'd be okay.

Naero assumed they were being monitored, but she continued to move around anyway. She knew Gallan was awake, remaining still in case someone came in and they got a chance to make a move.

No control bands or stun collars on any of them, yet.

Whoever had them seemed pretty sure that they weren't going anywhere.

Good. Let them think that.

Overconfidence among their enemies was something Spacers had used to their own advantage for centuries.

Then her eyes focused and spotted the three piles of bright orange clothing, folded neatly and stacked in one corner.

She checked them. Three sizes of orange, light prisoner coveralls, most likely riddled with trackers and bugs.

She got dressed in the smallest set, and draped the other two strategically over her naked comrades.

The thin, scratchy material against her skin made Naero long for her Spacer flight togs.

She still had one or two tricks up her sleeve—even without the sleeves— but she'd save them for the right moment.

They might not get a second chance.

A panel slid open behind them without warning.

Naero almost attacked immediately, but she barely caught the shimmer of a violet stun field snapping up.

Three nondescript gray military security bots trundled in, cleared to pass right through the security field.

ST-71s, two meters high on legs with treaded feet. Hard to beat. No external weapons to take or rig.

An AI voice came from the foremost bot.

153

"The Spacer Naero Maeris will follow us. Keep your hands together in plain sight in front of you. Make no sudden moves. You and your friends must obey all instructions and cause no disturbances."

"If I don't?"

A mild stunbolt hit her immediately, barely a jolt.

"That's the best you got?"

"Depending upon the infraction, the stun charges will grow in intensity. Do not provoke our actions. We are prepared to destroy you and your friends."

"I'm not going anywhere until I speak to someone who passes for a human being. I'm not leaving my friends."

The other two leveled their arm blasters at Gallan and Tarim.

"Do not make demands. You must comply. If you do not comply, we will be forced to terminate first one of your friends, and then the other."

Tarim's eyes suddenly popped open wide, but he remained still.

"What is your decision?" The bot asked.

Bots didn't bluff, and these had the protocols and the equipment to back it up.

"I'll comply," Naero said.

The lead bot went in front of her, the other two came up behind her.

As they passed through the stunfield, it went down and then snapped back up, buzzing behind her.

They passed through another bulkhead, traveling down a secured corridor for what seemed to be about twenty meters to another heavily armored set of blast doors.

The thick doors opened of their own accord and closed behind them.

Through that was an empty section of a large military vessel. Helmeted security forces stood at attention in Corps Marine combat armor. Visors hid their faces. They wore no insignia, no identifying markings of any kind.

The bots marched her to a heavily guarded double blast door and transmitted their clearance.

The armored guards stepped aside and the thick doors swept open. Once they were inside, the doors slammed shut, sealing her in darkness.

Her eyes adjusted to the darkened chamber. The ceiling soared up at least twenty meters, and yet the walls were no more than two meters apart. The floor felt smooth and cool, polished like glass.

Then, from high up, a brilliant beam of light appeared at the other end of the chamber far ahead. Twenty more meters beyond, someone sat behind a protective energy shield at an ancient wooden desk—actual wood.

He appeared to be rubbing his hands over it.

"Proceed," one of the bots said.

This man didn't look Triaxian.

In fact, he wore a veil below his eyes and the attire of a Menkaran. They worked for Triax and several other Corps.

What she could see of him as she drew closer bespoke a life of power and excess. He weighed four times as much as she, or more. His hands were soft, pale, and flabby, unused to any physical labor and covered with expensive jewelry.

The energy screen went down.

The heavyset Menkaran held a soft white cloth coated with some kind of tangy-smelling oil that he buffed and polished the shining desktop with. The wooden surface gleamed like a mirror; nothing else was on it.

His amber eyes above the veil seemed slightly glazed over as if from fatigue. Then he yawned, looking more bored than tired as he continued to polish.

Naero looked around, but it was hard to see much else in the dark. The Menkaran leaned forward suddenly, into the tight beam of white light shining down onto the desk from high above.

The light struck her interrogator like a laser, breaking his face and the veil beneath his nose into sharp panes of eerie white and black stone. For an instant he didn't even look human.

Then he undid his veil and leaned back, suspended comfortably in his gel chair. No place for her to sit.

The screen went down. The lead security bot took up a position directly behind the man. The other two kept their weapons trained on Naero.

"There must be some mistake," Naero said. "Why am I here?"

The man stared down at his desk with lackluster interest, ignoring her.

"This is a breach of every treaty that Triax and the other Corps have with my people," Naero added.

Her interrogator yawned again, shook his fleshy head, and didn't even look up. "Don't waste my time or your breath," he said. "Both of us know very well who you are and why you are here."

"Who are you, then?"

He grimaced and rolled his eyes and muttered something even Naero's ears couldn't make out. "You need a name? Use Kattryll."

She recognized his voice already from Baeven's blurt.

"So, Kattryll, what–"

"Shut up." He sighed heavily. "Your parents were intercepted and destroyed by Matayan mercenaries while attempting to smuggle dangerous alien tech data through the Corps systems."

"That's old news," she lied.

"The data was never recovered. But they had already made several forays into the Unknown Sectors." He pointed a thick finger at her. "We think you might be able to shed some light on its whereabouts."

Naero shook her head and looked him right in the eye. "You're not going to believe this," she said, "but you know more about all of that than I do."

Kattryll shrugged and began swiping the mirrored surface of the wood again. "No matter. Before we're done, I'll be entirely certain about what you know...and what you don't know."

Naero swallowed dry before she spoke again. "I might be tougher than you think."

A weak laugh erupted from Kattryll. "I sure hope so, kid," He yawned again. "That might make it a little interesting–for a while at least. But I doubt it. A lot of my subjects babble some shit like that at first. But I've been doing this for a very long time, and I've broken down just about anything with a brain.

"In reality, everyone cracks when the pain gets too bad."

He looked up and stared right through her with his cold, lifeless eyes. "You aren't any different, kid. Just meat, bone, and nerves."

Kattryll smiled in a most unpleasant way.

This individual is an enemy. He intends to harm us. Activate my defensive protocols so that we may eliminate him as a threat.

Shhh...I wish I could. Be quiet, Om. Let's listen to what he has to say and try to pump him for as much info as he's willing to blurt out.

Strategy acceptable. Defensive protocols still offline. This is not acceptable.

Kattryll chuckled slightly. "When the time comes, little girl, you'll tell me anything you even think I might want to know."

He turned the soft white cloth over, and methodically continued to rub.

23

"So," Naero said, "if you're just going to kill me anyway, why should I tell you anything?"

She looked him right in the eye.

Kattryll didn't even blink. His eyes like dead fish eyes.

"You'll talk," he said. "You all talk, even if it's just to end it. A lot of you beg me to end it. Sometimes I do–if I feel like it." He yawned. "It all depends. Sheesh, I should get some sleep before we get started." He snorted like a hog. "You aren't going anywhere–you can wait a few more hours."

"You don't seem exactly enthused about torturing me."

"Not really." He paused to apply some more of the oil onto the white cloth from an exotic-looking green glass bottle. "A fairly standard operation. But I like to start a new subject when I'm feeling fresh. Don't normally like to be disturbed."

He glared at her for a bare instant. "They woke me up for you. You're supposed to be a rush job."

Naero put her hands behind her back. "Then I would think your employers would want me broken quickly."

Kattryll smiled wearily. "They'll wait. They know I'll get results. That's why they gave you to me." He sighed again, nodded to himself, and put the cloth away. "We'll begin in earnest, tomorrow morning. I'll give you the rest of tonight to dwell on that."

"What a way to start the day."

"I'm glad you have a sense of humor about all of this." He looked her up and down and grinned in a most unpleasant way. "We'll get to know each other quite intimately. Your friends will be part of this too. We'll check on them from time to time so that you can watch them suffer. So that they can beg you to end their agony. They're really of no practical use to us, except as another way to get to you."

Naero laughed and took in his scent. Even through the tang of the oil, he smelled of cologne and soap and something more.

He probably bathed twice each day, but he couldn't wash off the stench. His body odor was still rank–he smelled of pain and death, as if he'd been steeped in them for decades. His very flesh was stained with the misery of others.

"Look you bloated pig," she told him. "It's pretty plain that you're going to squeeze us dry and gut what's left. Why should I make anything easy for you? Go ahead and kill us and get it over with."

"And spoil the minor distraction you'll provide? I think not."

It was the fat man's turn to truly laugh.

His clothing rustled in a strange way as he chortled. "You really think that this is all about you, little girl? Shit. You aren't worth the energy it would take me to smear you across the floor. We'll get what we want from you; I just want to enjoy it in some small way."

"Who's we?"

He clenched his meaty fists suddenly. "Don't feign ignorance; I despise ignorance."

"I'd like to hear you say it."

"The Corps. Of course. Despite what some of them say, there isn't a one of them that wouldn't dump their populations into their suns to gain the technological edge of a few thousand generations over the rest."

"And somehow you think I have it? The Kexxian Data Matrix? Boy, did you back the wrong ship in this race. If I had all of this tek data, would

I be busting my hump as crew in a family fleet? Hell no. I'd be queen of the universe by now."

The fat man stared at her in an odd way. "What are you looking at?" she asked

He will attempt to access our data. Not allowed. Eliminate him.

Kattryll stood up and came closer. "I'm not usually so aroused, but I find your empty bravado rather charming...in a pathetic kind of way. Some might even find you quite attractive and alluring, in a waifish, childlike mode. I could bring myself to enjoy raping you a few times, and not just to humiliate you–though there's that also. I find it better to do so before the interrogation breaks you down too much and ruins those cute, childlike tendencies you still possess."

"In your dreams, fat boy. I'd have to be restrained, unconscious, or dead."

"I prefer my prey alive." He turned away from her. "Take your pick on the other two."

"You Corps honchos really think you can get away with whatever you want, don't you?"

He shook his head. "We've been getting away with it for centuries my dear. The masters can't resist dallying among the slave girls and boys, and why the hell should they? It's one of the darker and more enjoyable perks of human nature. At least for the masters.

"And I'm far from being a honcho. I have a rather wide range in my area of expertise, and I'm paid very well, but I'm still little more than a glorified errand boy."

She almost laughed again at "wide range," but that was too easy.

What is too easy?

Study my memories on humor and insults, Om. Then pay attention while I get a rise out of this jerk. If I get him angry, he might let something slip.

Pursue current strategy with the jerk.

"Look, you putrid heap of talking dung. Do what you're gonna do. You can kill me, but you still won't ever defeat me, or my people."

He turned on her, leaning toward her over his ancient desk. "You strutting spacks. Too dense and too stubborn to see that your days are numbered. I've broken lots of your aberrant kind, during the wars. You'd be surprised how much your people told me, once I went to work on their families, their old people, their kids. They couldn't handle watching that. Family's so important to you freaks."

Naero grimaced and blinked. "And we still fought you Corps lackeys to the death every time you took us on. We beat you."

Kattryll reclined and looked up into the soaring darkness above him. "All my life, I've had a gift for backing the winning team, kid. The Corporate entity is eternal, irresistible–the perfect concept–as long as there are lackeys, as you say, with greed and ambition enough to power it. As long as there's one of you who will betray a trillion others to get a leg up."

"Make me vomit. You believe that spew? The sooner we fry every Corps brain like you, the better. And you say I'm pathetic."

"Face facts, little girl. Corporate structure is conquering known space and beyond. Nothing has endured against it or threatens to replace it. Spacers are an aberration that won't survive for more than a few centuries. Look at the empires the Corps have crushed, the races they've wiped out or absorbed. Kill Corps associates or leaders, and more are eager to rush into the breach. Just like the regenerating heads of hydra. People die, but the Corps are eternal. They'll go on forever. You back the winners, kid."

Naero smiled her half smile. "The galaxy has enough skutbrains and pukkheads like you running around murdering and enslaving everything and everyone to the everlasting glory of the Corporate Order. Spacers know what freedom is every time they leave one of your festering mudballs behind."

Lexicon. What is a mudball?

Om, I'm working here.

Kattryll sat back further in his gel chair and grinned. "Well, Triax has a few advantages. They know how to detect the Matrix and access it. Now they just need the files. Perhaps you will be more of a challenge than I thought," he said. "I might enjoy you in any number of ways."

Naero snorted. "My luck you're probably impotent."

Kattryll scowled. "You haven't figured it out yet, have you? This isn't a personal thing; it's business–my business."

Naero spat on his desk directly in front of him. His eyes popped.

"You bloated bastard, it's personal to me," she said. "Fuck you, you rotting skutbag. You've been torturing and butchering people so long you don't even care about anything anymore. You're bored with it. I don't know what's more sickening."

She'd gotten to him. He glared through her again. "You will find it extremely unwise to insult me."

"Who the hell cares? You're going to do your job anyway. *Haisha*, maybe you don't even have a prick to do me with, just a useless little nub of skin that piss dribbles out of."

He snarled at her in a sudden outburst of rage. "You will beg to satisfy my whims."

"Ooh, touchy, touchy. Nubs."

"Get out of my sight, you annoying little gash. Silence her."

The bots fired their stunbolts on command.

Naero got out a chuckle before she hit the floor.

Om inquired. *Is our strategy working?*

24

Spacer's never stayed stunned very long by anyone's standards, and Naero revived faster than most. Her mind started working before her body could respond.

Tarim checked her over when they dumped her back into their holding cell. He felt her pulse and looked for any injuries.

This one is not a jerk...not an enemy. You think of him as a friend, a fellow prisoner. We should not eliminate him?

No. Don't harm any of my friends. Don't eliminate anyone without my permission.

Our defense is primary. I will not always be able to comply.

Then Tarim knelt over her, praying quietly until she awoke fully and started to move. He and Gallan had put on their coveralls at some point.

Gallan was pretending to be asleep again.

"You're...you're alive?" Tarim said. "Thank God Almighty. When those meks threw you back in, I th-thought maybe you were dead."

Naero shook her head. "It'll take more than that."

Except for thirst, hunger, and a stun headache, she felt like a million creds.

"You had this goofy smile on your face."

She half-smiled again. "Yeah. Just like that."

Lexicon. What is goofy?

"I'm okay," she said "They bring us any food? Drink?"

Tarim shook his head and tried to smile. "They haven't brought anything yet. It's just like rationing onboard the mining transports."

"Great." She could smell her friends.

Hell. She could smell herself.

Lexicon. What is stink?

They all needed to get clean. She guessed there were no mist showers on this pleasure cruise either. "Maybe I shouldn't have pissed off old nubs so much."

Is a nub an extremely minuscule, ineffective, and impotent penis?

Bingo, Om.

Gallan suddenly sat up suddenly, smiling. "What'd you do now, N?"

Tarim jumped. "God bless it! Don't do that. I never know if you people are sleeping or awake. You guy's are so damn creepy."

Gallan laughed and clapped Tarim on the shoulder. "That's the idea."

Lexicon. Accessing creepy.

Briefly, quietly, Naero summarized what happened with Kattryll.

Gallan laughed until he couldn't stay upright.

Tarim paled and looked very worried.

He sat down, hugged his scrawny legs close to himself, and buried his face in his knees, shaking his head.

"Th-they're gonna k-k-kill us for sure. Help me, Jesus. I'm worth less than nothing to these vile monsters. This is worse than the mines. At least there you had some chance at staying alive if they didn't single you out for something."

"Live with it," Naero told him. "Unless we can find a way to get out of here, it's gonna happen, just as soon as they think we're of no further use to them."

Gallan reached over and shook the lander's arm. "Spacers have a saying: See the truth of things for what they are and move under your own power."

"These bastards are our enemies," Naero said. "Look at what they did to you and your family–your people."

"Rain. Mom and Dad. Everyone I knew," Tarim said, hugging his knees and looking over his elbows, his eyes burning.

163

His face flushed scarlet; he clenched his bony fists. "Damn these evil fiends to hell."

What is a fiend? Is it like a jerk, only incrementally worse? What and where is this hell?

Hell's a bad place to be, Om. Like the place we're in right now.

Very well. Then we should escape and get out of hell. Slang. Get the hell out of here.

Exactly. I'm working on it. We need a plan, and we need an opportunity. But it looks pretty bad right now.

"Don't give them the satisfaction of showing fear," Gallan said to Tarim. "Piss in their faces and laugh. How many times can they kill you?"

Lexicon: pissing is urination, correct? I cannot piss.

Tarim shuddered, his mouth tight. He leaned his head back onto his folded arms, sniffed, swallowed hard, and was silent for a time.

Naero stood up again and stretched, unfurling her wings behind her back and–

She gaped. Neither Gallan or Tarim made any notice of her new creased, bat-like wings.

Great. Another hallucination.

Om, are you causing this? Are these hallucinations your doing?

Continuing attempts to activate defensive protocols ineffective. Attempts to interface with our mind and form activate your imagination in unusual ways. We are both doing this. You are wishing you could escape our current hell. You wish you could fly away. The delusion of wings is a manifestation of your desires. I cannot control them or what form they take.

Tarim finally looked up, his face impassive. "Okay, so what's the plan then? How are we going to get out of here?"

Naero shrugged and lay back, staring up at the ceiling, folding her imaginary wings under her. "I have no idea. Better get some sleep for now."

Tarim gaped and threw up his hands. "Sleep? They're going to torture and kill us tomorrow and you want me to sleep?"

Gallan stretched out again and sighed. "Not much else we can do. We still have a few hours before morning. Have to keep our strength up."

Tarim's mouth still hung open. Naero reached up and pushed it closed.

"They'll make a mistake," she whispered to him. "Just be ready to move when they do. Follow our lead. If nothing else, do as much damage

164

to them as you can before you go down. I wish I had something better to offer you, but that's about it."

Tarim nodded, still looking somewhat wide-eyed and pale. "Just like the mines," he said. "There isn't a way out, no matter how bad you want one." He went back to praying, something about committing his soul into someone's hands.

Before she drifted off to sleep, Naero reached over, and gently patted him on the back.

He was crying and shaking so hard he could barely control himself. Poor kid. He'd been through a lot, and was about to go through even more.

*

A handful of hours later, nine security bots arrived to seize them and take them away. All three prisoners remained hungry and thirsty.

Their hosts made no effort to offer them anything.

They did not bother to ask. Their hands were secured in front of them.

The adjoining interrogation room lit up, looking more like a medical lab. Naero watched as Gallan and Tarim were secured on medbeds.

Naero's three guards led her out of the chamber for another happy visit with Kattryll.

"What's going to happen to my friends?" she said. She could smell Tarim's fear.

"They will be interrogated," the lead bot answered, its soothing AI voice a mockery.

"But they don't know anything."

"The director believes in being thorough. You may discuss the matter with him."

The doors snapped shut behind her. She didn't even get to say goodbye.

Her three bot escort gained clearance to a secured mover that took them somewhere else in the ship. Naero could only guess.

They stopped.

"Error. Incorrect destination," the lead bot remarked.

The doors snapped opened.

A large blur ripped into the three bots.

Naero dropped to the floor.

Unknown force attacking security drones, Om howled.. *Defensive protocols still offline. Unacceptable.*

She caught the flash of twin, blazing green disruptor blades that arced through armor and vital systems.

165

In less than a second, all three sec-bots lay all about Naero in pieces, busted up and oozing fluids.

Sparks flew from the pieces internally.

Three silver spheres rose up over the bots and sucked up the pieces and every trace of them, like bizarre null collectors disposing of junk.

The doors closed, the mover on its way again.

Her hands were still bound.

A blazing green blade sliced through her restraints like a scalpel through flesh.

Baeven revealed his grim face beneath his strange, shifting black cloak and hood.

He shut down his disruptor blades and smiled. "Well, hello again, Naero."

She could have hugged him, but her mind raced.

Threat is known to us? Is this an ally?

Yes, Om. He's trying to help us escape…for now. I don't know what he plans once we get away.

"We have to get Gallan and Tarim," she told Baeven. "They're being tortured."

"I know. We can't do anything about that right now."

"Those sec-bots–their central control will know someone took them out. They're probably on the way to retake us already."

Baeven tapped one of the floating silver spheres They purred like pets at his touch. They glowed brightly for a moment and then phazed away.

"The enemy will detect nothing, and to them I'm not even here. I do not exist.

"Temporal shifting emulators," he said. "They're a few seconds out of phaze with us. But they'll imitate the signatures of the sec-bots for as long as we need. The ruse will last long enough for us to complete our business here and get you and your friends to safety. Then they'll explode…quite spectacularly."

"Where are we going?"

"You still have a date with a Mr. Kattryll. Shall we keep your torturer waiting?"

Naero half smiled. "Certainly not."

"Function Sigma-Mirra-47," he commanded the shifters.

Holos of the three sec-bots shimmered over each of the three small spheres. "Marcron emulators. They can simulate almost anything."

"I'll pretend my hands are still bound. Let me give nubs a little surprise."

"Play along at first. We need to find out what form the Kexxian Data Matrix takes and how they can detect it. Why do they think you and your brother might have it? They possess key knowledge that we do not."

"My parents weren't transporting any kind of alien tek data."

"We can't be sure of that. Our foes seemed pretty determined and adamant about the matter."

"Even if they did, if I know my parents, they dumped or destroyed it somehow before they went down. But the Corps still think Jan and I might have it."

"Do you? That would explain a great deal. How can you be certain, one way or another?"

"So, even the great renegade Baeven's at a loss? You don't know anything more about this mess?"

"Nothing but rumors through several contacts. We don't even know how the data is encrypted or transported. You or Jan may in fact be carrying it with you and not even know it."

"Great."

The mover stopped.

"So, what's our plan?" Naero asked.

"Keep Mr. Kattryll distracted while I disable his security and search his files. Then we'll have a few kind words with him."

"What do you mean, keep him distracted? The bastard wants to rape and torture me."

Baeven phazed away with a vanishing smile.

Naero wondered if she was going to be sick.

She marched in with the phony sec-bots just as expected.

Kattryll stood with his back to her, completely naked.

"I *am* going to vomit," she muttered.

Once illuminated more, the strange room was fully revealed to be a bizarre jumble of furnishings and decorations from many worlds and time periods.

But the most striking thing was a beautiful, naked young man floating in the air off to one side, his wrists and ankles stretched painfully in grav-restraints.

He formed an obscene X in the air with his nude form, his superbly toned young body scarred with cuts, large purple welts, blisters, and burns.

His battered, chiseled face slumped down on his chest, still dripping blood beneath his long, dark blondish hair.

Then she saw the young man's long triple braids hanging down his back.

Damn it all to hell.

And here she had felt sorry for him.

A Matayan prince of all things.

Why in the living hell did such a beautiful creature like this have to be one of her bitterest Clan enemies? A young man built like a god.

Kattryll turned on her finally, leering.

"Ah, little Naero, come to join the fun?"

He pointed at the Matayan. "I wanted to be in good form for you. This boy was just a warm-up. I was instrumental in solving a recent Corps problem with the Matayans. In return, this lovely boy was given to me as one of my prizes, a hostage to ensure compliance to the Corporate will. Matayans can be dreadfully stubborn."

"I'm impressed. You appear in better spirits today."

"Professional ethics, my child. I put on my best face when I work. I'm also less morose after I've rested and I've a had a chance to whet my appetites. I trust you slept well?"

She nodded at the prince. "What do you want with me? It looks like you prefer boys."

"Not really. I enjoy domination." He reached out and caressed her face slowly.

"Gender in sex is irrelevant. Yet there is nothing more arousing than the subjugation of others, to break them utterly and completely."

"You sick turd."

He smiled at her voraciously. "The stronger the will, the bigger the challenge. The greater the arousal." He sat back across from her and glanced over at her dried spittle, still marring the surface of his prize desk.

He threw two pairs of grav restraints over at her feet. "I hope you won't disappoint me."

She narrowed her eyes to slits. "You want those on me, pus-slug? You put them on me. I'd like to see you try."

Kattryll sighed. "Very well. Guards. Stun her briefly." He slipped in front of his desk again, before he realized the bots weren't responding.

Baeven appeared behind Kattryll and nodded to her.

Naero grinned, launching herself through the air right through the holos. She cleared the space between her and Kattryll, ramming both of her heels into his fleshy face.

The torturer's facial bones and cartilage popped nicely.

Two hundred kilograms of stinking, sweating meat slammed into his wooden desk and shattered it.

Kattryll crashed to the floor and soiled himself.

He whimpered and screamed, clutching at his broken face.

Naero could only imagine the agony and terror this monster had inflicted on others over the years. On men, women, old people–even children.

Who knew how many?

She walked over to him and pressed her left foot down onto his throat just enough.

His dead fish eyes bulged. She let up a bit so that he could breathe and talk.

"Surprise," she said.

Baeven dropped the same gravrestraints onto the man's heaving chest. "Why don't *you* put these on?"

"My people will be on you in seconds," he shrieked. "They'll cripple you and give you right back to me."

"Let's wait and see," Baeven said, holding up his hands.

Several moments passed.

Baeven stuck his bottom lip up and rolled his eyes.

"Maybe they're busy," Naero suggested.

"Perhaps it has something to do with my disabling your security and all of your backups. Why, look: We have you to ourselves, with all the time we need."

Kattryll sweated, stinking worse by the minute.

His own grav restraints had a little trouble hoisting his stinking bulk up into the air.

Kattryll muttered curses at them all the while.

Against her better judgment, Naero went over and released the Matayan, hoping he didn't have enough strength to attack her.

She lowered him gently to the ground and snagged a medkit from a stand covered with medical supplies.

She cleaned and dressed the worst injuries first.

Even banged up as he was, the Matayan remained astonishingly beautiful.

Her luck, he probably had the soul of a snake, like most Matayans.

He came to suddenly, and spit bile and blood at her in defiance. "Kattryll...I will kill you, you bastard. One day I will break free and kill you slow."

His vision blurred. He fell back, choking. Naero cleared his airway.

His eyes fluttered open again at her soft touch.

"A girl? How did...who? ...A Spacer?"

"Don't move. You're pretty bad off."

"Does Kattryll think to break me by letting my enemies humiliate me?"

"Hey, look. I'm not real happy about this, either, but if you don't try to kill me, I won't try to kill you. 'Kay?"

"I...I don't understand. A truce? Until we escape?"

"Sure. Why not?" Naero said.

"I must really be desperate if Spacers are helping me."

"And thank you very much as well. You might notice that you're not a prisoner anymore, and that I've tended your wounds. Our mutual fat friend is floating in the air over there. Having a polite conversation with my...other associate."

The Matayan craned his neck.

Baeven stood in front of Kattryll with his arms folded, activated disruptor blades scorching the very air in both hands.

He spoke in a low voice.

The Matayan's eyes narrowed with hatred.

He tore himself away from Naero's grasp and tried to get at Kattryll. But he was still too weak and fell forward onto his face.

"Kill him," the Matayan begged. "Kill that monster. No one deserves it more than he."

He lunged toward Kattryll again. Naero caught him as he crashed back to the floor, unconscious.

What was there about this Matayan that made her heart go out to him? By all rights she should let him die, or finish him herself.

Instead she opened the medkit again and went to work on trying to revive him.

She finished up about the same time Baeven did.

"I think I have as much as we're going to get out of this blivet," Baeven said at last.

"What's a blivet?" Naero asked.

"Ten kilos of shit in a five kilo bag," he said with a smile. "If your parents were indeed smuggling what he claims, the Corps will stop at nothing to acquire it."

"Do you know what form the Kexxian Matrix takes or how to detect it?"

"We're on the right track, but it's worse than we feared. This treasure holds a vast amount of information, much more advanced than what we thought. It will be centuries, perhaps millennia ahead of anything out there–Spacers, Corps, every known culture."

"How could Mom and Dad get ahold of something like that?"

"No one knows exactly; not even the Corps. But everyone's scrambling to find out more and to locate it. We're still not sure what form the Kexxian Matrix takes, but from Kattryll's top secret files, at least now I have some insights on how we might detect and perhaps decode it. But the Corps are still ahead of us somehow. We need to catch up."

"Good. If we're done here, let's grab Gallan and Tarim and get the hell out of here. Where in the hell is here, anyway?"

"The Triaxian battleship *Napoleon*. We're in a secured area of the ship used only by Triaxian Intel. I'll impersonate Kattryll and we'll spring your friends. Let's go."

She looked down at her patient. "I want to take the Matayan."

"He's an enemy. Leave him."

"He's a hostage. I won't give Kattryll the satisfaction."

"Good point; take his toys. I think Kattryll's superiors will do a much better job on him than we ever could—once they learn of our escape."

"You're probably right. The Corps take care of their own. Hey, Matayan, can you walk? I know you're listening."

The Matayan snapped his head up like a wounded Hoshen lion and glared at her suddenly. "I can run and fight, Spacer. If we survive, rest assured that my family will pay whatever large ransom you set for my release."

"If we make it," Naero said, "you're free to go once we're clear. But think about that. They gave you up to the Corps once. What's to keep them from doing so again?"

"Hah. I'll believe that when I—"

"Suit yourself. Get dressed and come with us, or stay here. Find a weapon or two if you can. What do we call you, anyway?"

"Ellis."

Simple enough.

"I'm Naero."

The Matayan turned away, rummaging through the strange room.

Baeven chuckled. "You always pick the grateful ones?"

"Just lucky that way." She watched the Matayan get dressed, silently chiding herself the whole time.

Baeven put neutralized control collars on both Ellis and Naero to give the proper illusion to anyone who might see them.

He adjusted his cloaker to imitate Kattryll.

"You won't make it out of here," the fat man said.

"We'll do more than that," the false-Kattryll said, in an exact duplication of the man's vocal pattern.

Naero walked up to the real one and glanced once under his rolls of flab. She clucked her tongue and smacked him on his huge belly.

"Like I thought, just a nub. It wasn't meant to be, blivet-boy." She waved a hand in front of her nose—"Whew, you're getting ripe. Try not to soil yourself again while you're hanging around for the next day or so."

Ellis came over and taped Kattryll's mouth shut. "I don't have the time, so I won't be able to kill you slow. But I want you to remember me."

He clamped a pain bug to Kattryll's left nipple. The fat man's eyes bulged. Two hundred kilograms of pale, bloated flesh bucked and shuddered in the grav restraints.

"Let's go," Ellis said. "I can't believe this. Now I'm allied with Spacer Intel. My family will probably hang me."

"If it's any consolation," Baeven said with Kattryll's voice, "we're not Spacer Intel. Follow my lead or I'll kill you."

With the phony sec-bots around them, Baeven led them back to the holding area.

When they walked in on Gallan and Tarim's questioning session, the Triaxians snapped to attention. Gallan and Tarim looked beaten up, but she guessed that they could still walk.

"Release the prisoners to me and prepare my shuttle immediately," the false-Kattryll said.

"This is highly irregular," the duty officer said. "I had no such orders."

"These orders come from the top through me," Baeven told him. "The prisoners are wanted for further questioning at another facility, on a need-to-know basis."

Baeven's glance was withering. Dead on. "Or would you like to disappear along with them? Is that clear enough?"

The duty officer swallowed hard. "Very clear, sir."

"Then shut your traps and follow my orders. Prepare my transport and forget you ever saw me or these people, understood? We don't need any leaks now, of all times."

"Understood, sir."

Within minutes, Baeven and Naero piloted the Triaxian luxury shuttle away from *The Napoleon*. Naero watched as Baeven plotted a course, but he did it so fast and with such precision that she couldn't figure out where they were headed.

By the time the Triaxians knew what was up and scrambled their interceptors, three massive explosions crippled the big ship. The battleship's big guns never even got a shot at them.

"Wah-hoo!" Naero screamed. Their ship lurched into jump. "What a ride. Eat shit, Triax!"

Tarim and Gallan stared at her wide-eyed, and then over at the Matayan, completely confused.

What value would there be in consuming excrement?

All of them knew how close they'd been to death.

"Who are you people?" the Matayan prince demanded.

25

It broke Naero's heart.

Their situation forced them to ditch Kattryll's Triaxian luxury transport in an ocean on Egano-4.

The megs she could have gotten for that craft, even at a loss, would have bought her a great ship. Her first ship.

But Baeven was absolutely right. Kattryll's small yacht would be nova hot. Triax wouldn't rest now until they were all recaptured or killed outright.

Such a high profile craft would be far too easy to track down.

If she ever managed to escape from Triaxian Space, she'd send someone she could trust back to "discover" the ship as a salvage one day.

For the moment, escape seemed like a pretty big *if.*

They were practically in the heart of the Triaxian region, and the Gigacorps were known for their tenacity. There had to be a very hefty bounty on them already, and half the Triaxian Navy was most likely looking for them.

They left Egano-4 immediately, transferring to a small Lidoma merchant ship that Baeven had waiting for them under independent registry.

Naero didn't like securing both Tarim and Ellis in their standard crew quarters.

The two youths both took it differently. Tarim looked very sad, and embarrassed that they didn't trust him.

"I'm sorry," she said. The frame to his door panel suddenly felt so cold to her touch as she leaned on it.

"I know you think I'll just get in the way–dumb lander kid on the loose," he said. "But I can help; I want to help. Teach me how to do something. I'm smart. I learn fast."

"It's not that," she said. "I can see Baeven's point. He doesn't know you. I don't know you. We can't take any chances. Gallan and I will come to see you when we don't have duties. As long as you're with us, it's all right. I'll load your terminal with some interesting stuff from the bridge. Get some rest. You probably need it."

"Don't treat me like a child, Naero. I...I don't think I could handle it."

"Okay, Tarim, I'll try." What did he mean by all that?

She closed his room panel to sec-lock it. His sad eyes whipped away from her. The buttons she pressed the codes into clicked angrily like a nest of disturbed bugs. Some old ships' electronics were like that.

Gallan led Ellis down to his quarters, the Matayan protesting the entire time.

"If it is as you say, and I am not a prisoner, then why are you detaining me?" He spotted Naero.

"Girl, tell this oaf to release me at once. As a prince, I demand it."

Girl? He didn't even remember her name?

"In case you've forgotten, your highness, my name is Naero, Naero Amashin Maeris, of Clan Maeris." She watched his eyes widen.

"Naero, of Clan Maeris, I gave my word upon my honor to your leader not to harm any of you or sabotage this ship. It is in my best interest that we escape. I resent being treated like a criminal."

"You're still a potential enemy," she said, despite the fact that, cleaned up, he was even prettier, and he smelled wonderful, like musk and flowers.

"The fact that we rescued you does not dispense with centuries of hatred and violence between Spacers and Matayans. Like I told Tarim,

Gallan and I will come to see you, but for now, I think Baeven's right. Until we're sure we're safe, we can't take any chances."

"If you are not ransoming me, then allow me to send a coded message to my people."

"Right, fat chance. And have Triax and whoever else intercept it and hunt us down? Live with it–you're going to run with us for a while. We're all alive at least. As soon as we can, we'll try to dump you off somewhere safe. But we can't leave any leads for our enemies to follow."

Ellis stalked into his chambers without another word, his back to them, still fuming. Fists clenched and broad shoulders tight.

They secured the panel behind him.

The bugs protested again.

"Naero," Baeven called over her com, "I want you in the Medical Bay as soon as you're done."

"Affirmative. We're finished here. Gallan's going back to monitor the bridge. I'll be with you shortly."

In the small ship's medical section, Baeven performed a variety of scans and tests on her, all to no avail.

Om kept asking her, *Are we in danger? Is this one trying to access our secrets? He is formidable. How can I defend us and our secrets with my defensive protocols still offline?*

I'm not sure, Om. I think he's trying to help us still. Let's wait and learn what we can.

Something told her to hold back what Kattryll had let slip, that Triax alone possessed some way to detect and access the Kexxian Matrix. Every time she was on the verge of telling Baeven that, some instinct warned her not to.

"Are we done yet?" Naero asked. "I've been away from my studies for a few days. I'd like to get back to them." She was starting to get stiff. The old cushions of the medbed felt like lumps of solid rubber.

Baeven seemed under a great deal of pressure.

"Nothing!" He slammed his fist against the ship's hull.

He actually dented it.

With his bare fist.

He turned to her again. "I need you to think back to when you and your brother were with your parents."

"Okay..."

"Were you ill at all? Did you or your brother undergo any medical treatments, even routine immunizations?"

Then Naero remembered.

"There was this weird physical scan that took several hours. The medtek was this little furry guy from Omni Corps space, a Cumi. I don't remember very much about it. They performed it while we slept. Mom and Dad were real grim and insistent about it at the time. All they said was that they were worried about some kind of ancient plague. But we checked out fine."

"*Haisha*, that could be it," Baeven said. "What plague could they have meant? The Kexx virtually eliminated illness among themselves and their systems for millions of years."

"Does it have something to do with the Cumi then?"

"The Cumi are another ancient, far-trading race. They knew of the Kexx at the very beginning of their civilization. And you say your parents said nothing more to you two about these scans–which just happened to take hours to complete–or what they were for?"

"That's not unusual," Naero told him. "We didn't talk much. Jan and I were fighting constantly with our parents before they left on their re-supply loops through Matashi and Omni Corps. On their last exploration run, we couldn't speak to each other without arguing."

"They might not have told you the truth for good reason."

"They thought it best that we all cool down for a while, so as usual, they sent me and Jan off with Aunt Sleak. It was on their way home to rendezvous with her on her Triax run that they..."

She choked up suddenly.

Why now, of all times? It was as if her throat suddenly filled up with dust.

"The Matayans, they–" The grief she'd suppressed came back on her so suddenly that she couldn't talk anymore. Shock and fatigue gave way to tears that streamed from her eyes. She had to turn away and shudder to keep from sobbing.

Her legs threatened to give out from under her.

Baeven put an arm around her before she collapsed. She leaned against his solid bulk and wept for all she was worth.

He stroked her hair. "Mourn those you love, Naero. For their memory, for the loss of their blood. Never forget them. They live in our hearts now, and in you."

Images of her mother and father throughout her life flashed through her mind. Baeven held her for a long time. She finally realized that they were leaning against the wall of the medical section still, and pulled away from him.

Be an adult. Live with it. Go forward.

177

"You must think I'm pretty childish," she said. Then she looked at Baeven. His eyes were red too.

Aunt Sleak had said that he and her mother were close once.

"My mother," she said. "Did you love her?"

"Yes," he said, without hesitation. His demeanor saddened. "I am...an old friend of the family, after all."

He sighed deeply. "At one time Lythe and I were very close, when we were young. When we knew little of the universe that lay around us–like some predatory thing. I would have given my life for her. In my own strange way... I'm still doing so."

He turned away and bowed his head. "I enlisted in Spacer Intel at a young age and volunteered to train with the Mystics, against the will of my family. My work drove me away from everyone. Things happened. I was exiled. We never spoke again or met. I'd heard she had married well, and had two children. I was happy for her–that she knew such a life as I never could.

"Then I discovered that she and Spacer Intel were embroiled in this business. I took an interest in the affair, but I was too late to help her, or your father and their people. I'm sorry."

Naero took his hand.

He raised his head and smiled proudly. "From what I have learned, your parents fought and died bravely, taking many foes down with them."

"I can't see why Aunt Sleak hates you so much." Yet Baeven was so hard to get a handle on. He even smelled different each time she met him, using different colognes.

He looked at her and his gaze hardened. "Perhaps she knows me better, Naero. Perhaps you will hate me one day as well. We are in a difficult place, with few options. I have hard choices to make. Choices that will affect the lives of trillions of beings, and not only our own people. The costs of another Spacer War may only be the beginning."

The absolute severity and certainty of his words made her shudder. "I don't understand most of this mess. I don't even know if I want to, but if I can help in any way, I will."

"One way or another, I think you'll have to. But understand this: We are all expendable. If the time ever comes when I must sacrifice you, your friends, or even myself, please try to understand that I will do whatever I must."

For who?

I cannot trust this one.

Om, I'm not sure anyone can.

Naero understood that she had been born into a hard world of metal and plasteel, of extremes of cold and heat.

Spacers were born to rise to the challenge, and still maintain their humanity.

Somehow, she felt that all of those harsh extremes were multiplied tenfold for this enigmatic stranger, who by his own choices made himself an outlaw and a pariah.

"My mother once told me that the most dangerous enemy to have is one who is completely convinced that what he or she is doing is right, because they are utterly ruthless."

Baeven looked off and smiled sadly. Then he nodded. "Lythe was right, Naero. Your mother was very, very right. But then, she usually was."

He walked away, his hands clasped behind his back. "But doing the right thing is not always what you should do, or what you need to do. They can be completely different things."

He seemed to have an insight suddenly.

"I think I know where to go to find out whether you carry the Kexxian Matrix or not. But as usual, it's going to be difficult, and very risky."

"We need to know. Too bad Jan isn't with us."

"I'll handle the arrangements. Just make sure that the Matayan and the lander don't cause any trouble. I'll shove them out an airlock if they do."

She laughed at first, but then she realized, as before:

Baeven meant every word.

179

26

Naero drew random duty to perform a weapons check on the ship's armory.

Drudge work.

She sat alone in the maintenance area late that night, several racks of pistols and assault weapons lined up in neat rows on their cart racks with their magnetic wheels locked.

One by one she placed a weapon down on the padded workbench before her.

Despite feeling a little overwhelmed by everything, she methodically checked each weapon's function, broke it down, cleaned it with solvent, lubricated it if need be, and put it back together.

She checked its action a second time before setting it back on its rack as finished.

Standard khotguns, needleguns, and delta class blasters. She could service such weapons in her sleep.

But after the fifth sidearm she yawned and blinked.

Gallan showed up with two big frosty borbbles of Jett, her favorite rich, black, fruity lix, imported from Arnett Corps space.

Her best friend knew her and her weakness for Jett very well.

"Need some help? It's been a long day."

"*Haisha*, it's been a long month."

"Thought you could use a little something."

She rubbed her eyes and half-smiled up at him. He set one of the borbbles down in front of her.

"Where in the hell did you find Jett in Triaxian space?" she asked.

"It's a treat. I asked Baeven to procure us some back on Egano-4. The man has his sources."

"Yes indeed." She gulped down half of her borbble in one long, luxurious cold draught.

She sighed for a long contented moment and then rolled her eyes in appreciation. "That is so good. Thanks, my friend."

Gallan picked up the next pistol to be checked. "No damage. I couldn't sleep, so I thought I'd hunt you out. Baeven's on the bridge."

They cleaned weapons and drank for a while, no further reason to say much of anything. They finished the sidearms and moved on to the assault weapons.

Gallan worked on a tri-barrel khotgun that had some old corrosion in the barrels. "I'm sorry we never got a chance to talk more about your parents, Naero. I was there for you; I just didn't know what to say."

She nodded. "I know you were, abani. What was there to say? No one had any control over it. Now they're gone, and Jan, me, and you are all over our heads in deep shit."

Gallan laughed. "What clued you in on that?"

"Shut up, skuthead. I'm serious. The Corps are all after us hard, and we're running with an outcast. I'd say we're in pretty deep."

He finished a long drink of Jett. "I'm still not convinced we can trust anyone yet."

"Me either. Baeven has his own mysterious agenda and says so outright, but he's the best ticket we have right now. Ellis is a Matayan, of course."

Gallan's face darkened somewhat.

"You stare at that one a little too much, Naero. It shows, and that's not good."

"I'm working on it."

"I wouldn't if I were you."

Naero avoided the issue. "Tarim's just a kid. I think he's pretty harmless."

"He's older than you by almost a year; he's just malnourished."

"He's survived in his world, that counts for something. But there's a lot he doesn't know."

"He's eager to learn. He needs to find something he's good at. What he really needs is to stop acting like a beaten down slave."

"That might take some time," Naero said. "You and I can't relate. That's all he knows. It might be a hard cage to escape, even with the door open." She picked up the next blaster rifle.

"Well, he's a survivor. There's hope for him, at least. But who knows how long any of us are going to last, or what it's going to take at this rate."

They went quiet again for a while.

Then Naero reached out suddenly and put her hand on Gallan's forearm. "I'm going to say this now while we have the chance, abani. I never got to say anything to my folks before I lost them, and I regret that. We might make this run, and then again, we might not. There's a lot stacked against us. But if I'm on a hot run, then I'm glad you're with me. You've always been a good friend to me, and I honor and cherish that. I know that I can trust you, and count on you no matter what, my brother. I hope you feel the same about me."

"You don't even need to ask," Gallan said. "All we can do is give it our best juice, N. If they take us down, we won't make it easy for them if it comes to that. We'll go down fighting. Let's just be smart about it."

"I'm trying." Naero raised her borbble with its last swallow of Jett. "Max it," she told him.

Gallan drained his borbble with her.

With the mild boost from the Jett reviving them, they made more small talk, and short work of cleaning the rest of the weapons before turning in.

For the first time in many days, Naero felt better. At least with Gallan around she had one person she could count on completely.

That meant more than she could say.

When she slept that night, she had another one of her strange dreams.

Living snakes of dark and light energy gnawed their way out of her flesh and fought with each other, crisscrossing and entwining, while she convulsed violently.

A demonic, red glowing head layered in roving eyes glared at her and spoke harshly.

You are indeed a serious threat. We will find you. You may very well need to be destroyed.

Her mouth open, unable to scream. Her eyes rolled back white.

They glowed suddenly with blue white energy, so bright it blotted out all else. Her third eye flared back up briefly.

And then they all went black.

Blacker than the Abyss itself.

Naero woke with a start.

She's been having nightmares almost every night since she went nuts. They continued to get worse, and crazier by the day. Who were the entities in her dreams? Fragments of her own personality, imagination, and fears given form?

Om, can't you do anything about these dreams, these crazy visions?

Impossible. I cannot access certain parts of your mind. They are blocked. Just like my defensive protocols. I continue to try.

Baeven informed them that they would remain in jump for almost two weeks.

That would to give the Triaxians and anyone else looking for them absolute fits.

Naero learned her cover identities well, including the one for their current ship: a second mate named Krellin.

Their tiny Lidoma merchant craft only required two crew to operate it. It was even smaller than *The Ardala*. Baeven's security measures would mask their Spacer genetics and not reveal other lifeforms on board to any type of scan.

Baeven had them on a long-range cargo run of spices and crystals way out to Jodien-2 and beyond, eventually heading into Matashi Corps space, even farther away from the Free Space Zones of the Spacer Clans.

She and Gallan divided their free time between Tarim and Ellis, both of them still restricted to quarters.

Gallan tolerated the Matayan, for her sake.

From the outset, Ellis assumed an almost instinctive dislike of Tarim, and readily seized every opportunity to treat him as inferior. They did not get along in the least, and it was mostly Ellis' fault.

That did not earn him any points in Naero's book, even though she had her own misguided prejudices about landers.

At least she made an attempt to get past those prejudices.

She kept the two young men apart whenever possible.

Tarim, on the other hand, took to Gallan's easy-going nature right away and they became fast friends.

But he definitely had it bad for Naero.

She tried to discourage him without being unfriendly, but he seemed oblivious to her efforts.

The way of infatuation and obsession we're indeed mysterious.

Fortunately, she and Gallan kept Tarim busy developing other interests.

For the first time in his life, the lander found himself surrounded by a wealth of knowledge and instruction. For days he hardly slept, reading, learning, practicing–trying out whatever caught his fancy.

Baeven ignored the Matayan completely, and generally avoided Tarim and his tiresome questions from the outset.

To Baeven, they were nothing but annoying distractions.

Even Naero and Gallan had to shut Tarim down at times.

He kept the tired old simulators on the ship very busy, and ignored even Ellis's withering ridicule.

More than his infatuation with Naero, even, the lander seemed obsessed with making himself useful, perhaps in an attempt to impress her.

Whatever his motivation, he worked hard at bettering himself. Naero couldn't help admiring that.

She and Gallan worked out and sparred with Baeven each day.

From the start, they were clearly no match for someone who had trained for years with the Mystics from an early age. But working with someone of that caliber did help them hone their own skills in many small but important ways.

When Prince Ellis learned about their daily sparring, he requested to join them. He protested and argued on their way back from the mess hall.

"I am sick of being penned up here like an animal, or merely allowed to do forms. And the simulators on this heap of scrap are so outdated they are no challenge whatsoever. I want to match my skills against another. Surely in a few days' time I will not be able to steal any of your Spacer fighting secrets. I formally request the right to spar with someone. I do not count the miner boy. He obviously has no breeding or skill."

"You talk about him as if he were subhuman," Naero said, her ire rising at the Matayan's prejudice, even though she knew she had her own dislike for most landers.

"I know you are fond of the worker boy, sort of like a pet, I assume, for reasons I do not quite fathom. But he is beneath me. I could kill him any time I like."

"Why do you even think like that? His name is Tarim, and miner or not, he's been through a lot."

"I see; you pity him, then."

"I feel sorry for what he's been through. There's a difference."

"Hah, slight at best."

Despite her physical attraction to him, Ellis could almost always say the perfect thing to piss her off.

"You know, Matayans might not have so much trouble getting along with people if they weren't such jerks."

Ellis laughed. "The same has been said about your people, Naero. I do not mean to insult you or your little charity case, but, as I have made it clear, I do not wish to be bothered by his kind. He is weak, ignorant, and annoying, and obviously beneath the rest of us. Admit it."

Naero pointed a finger straight at Ellis.

"What are you doing? Get your hand out of my face."

She ignored him.

"Tarim has a good heart, and a kind nature," she said. "That's more than I can say for a certain intolerant princeling of the Matayan master race. Just because you can take someone down doesn't make them any less valuable as a person. You might have a chance to reconsider that, Prince Ellis. If Baeven ever does allow you to spar with him...or me and Gallan, for that matter. Be careful what you wish for."

He flung his arms up wide. "I welcome the challenge." Ellis chuckled again, coming a little closer and whispering.

"Oh, you'd like that, wouldn't you, Naero? Both of us sweaty and wrestling, locked together on the mats? I see the way you look at me. You don't think women have looked at me like that before? I know very well what it means."

Naero resisted the urge to strike him.

"In your dreams, my prince."

"Hah. You make me laugh, Naero. So wonderfully honest. You can't even admit this attraction between us when it so obv–"

Naero snarled, grabbed him under both of his muscled arms and slammed him against the hull of the ship.

He grunted, gasping for air.

She revealed her superior, genetically enhanced strength and speed to the oaf for the first time, pinning him there.

"I admit it. There is a base, physical, animal attraction based solely on appearances. So what?"

She batted her eyes at him in mock humor. "I'm not some helpless little girl, looking to fall in flowery love for the first time. And it certainly wouldn't be with a stuck-up, pompous popinjay like you, your highness."

She let him fall. He dropped to the floor to one side on his hands and knees.

"I should have left you trussed up back with Kattryll. Maybe he'd be using your hide for for a bathrobe by now."

She backed away.

Ellis stared up at her in surprise.

"Perhaps...you are right. Matayan pride, honor, and overconfidence have nearly destroyed my people." He smiled. Then he even laughed, gazing up at the ceiling.

"First the Spacers, and then the Corps defeated us. Now we are being used as their shock troops–expendable cannon fodder. After that, they will reduce us to slaves, no better off than Tarim. My people will end up just like his, like all the rest."

He paused and then looked up at her. "You have my word, Naero. I will try to go easier on the miner boy."

He shook his head again. "Damn it all to hell. I just don't know what to do. I want to do something to free my people. But there's nothing. No way out of it all. Perhaps we are all jerks, like you say. Perhaps we don't deserve freedom."

Ellis hung his head.

"Everyone deserves to be free," Naero said. "But its what we do with that freedom and the way we treat others that determines whether we deserve ours."

Ellis laughed again. "Perhaps we should keep a Spacer by our ear to remind us of our imperfections. Maybe we Matayans do need more of a conscience. The Corps subjugate and enslave us just as we did others. There is no difference. They beat us and train us to be their blood-thirsty attack dogs. We're just shock troops to them. It is their way. The strong dominate the weak, and they are the strong."

"They only know how to use and destroy. They force everyone to live by their ideas and call it liberation. It doesn't have to be that way, Ellis. My people have proven that. Look at Joshua Tech Space. They're a Gigacorps, and yet they treat their people well."

"An aberration," Ellis noted. "The other Corps will wipe you all out if they can. And they will not stop."

"Neither will we," Naero said. "Look, I don't expect you to completely transform and change your mind overnight. You come from

186

your culture and your ways. Just think about it. And yes, please give Tarim a break. He's a good guy. Don't pick on him so much."

"I will try to go easier on him, as you say. And what about something for me? A little more freedom for the Matayan jerk perhaps?"

Naero lifted both eyebrows. "That's up to Baeven."

They walked back to Ellis's quarters and he faced her from within the threshold.

"This Baeven of yours, he has the eyes of a Slayer. He is a very scary person, this one. I have seen it before. He has killed many, I think, and will continue to do so."

Naero raised her eyebrows. "I've seen him fight; I wouldn't ever cross him, if I were you."

"Please, not to worry. Have I not already given my word as a Matayan?"

She glared at him.

"As a prince, then. My word that I will not harm you or any of your friends? Or this minuscule ship? Please. I'm going crazy. That is partly why I am so ill-tempered."

"I'll look into it. And I'll have to hold you to your word, even if it is that of a Matayan, and a prince."

"Thank you. That's all I ask."

Naero smiled at Ellis, and looked him in the eye just a little too long and tilted her head as his panel slid shut.

She couldn't help it.

Who was she kidding? There wasn't any kind of a future with his kind.

But the short-term options were still fun to consider.

Definitely time to go.

Naero left him locked in his room, still unable to believe the thoughts she was entertaining.

And about a Matayan, no less.

Still, he was very good-looking, Matayan or not. She had to give him that much.

Her mother and father both warned her about being smitten, merely by physical attraction.

Until she saw Ellis, she couldn't imagine that it would ever happen to her.

I do not understand you, Naero. Do you wish to mate with this male or not? I thought he was an enemy? Your thoughts and emotions are extremely confusing.

If you figure it out, Om, let me know.

27

After a few days of repeated requests, Baeven finally granted Ellis and Tarim more freedom, no longer restricting them to their quarters.

They were also allowed access to the sparring rooms, as long as they did not get in Baeven's way or even try to speak with him.

The Matayan Prince squared off with Naero repeatedly.

He hit the gel mats hard for the fourth time in as many minutes.

All of his Matayan military training aside, Naero was simply that fast, that strong, and that good, especially after picking up a few tricks from Baeven.

She wasn't even breathing hard, and the salty smell of sweat in the air was all Matayan.

Naero landed four or five good blows to every one he snuck in. And she pulled her punches.

The prince of the Matayan master race gasped for breath from the tap-kick she landed to his solar plexus.

Ellis's training and fighting styles emphasized strength and overwhelming power over speed and precision.

She noticed that Matayans perspired a great deal more than Spacers.

But he looked good all slick and sweaty.

"You Spacers are inhuman," he managed at last. "No matter my attack or defense strategy, you find an opening, a weakness. I salute you."

"Take on Baeven sometime if you want to see inhuman. He does to Gallan and me what I've just done to you."

Ellis paled and shook his head. "No…no thank you."

"And hey," Naero said with a sly smile, "just remember. Even though I can take you out whenever I want, you can still be my friend."

"Point taken. Many thanks."

She offered him her hand, and helped him back up.

The sparring room rang with Ellis's laughter once again. "It is most humbling. I see the false pride of my people to be a huge stumbling block now. If I ever get back to them, they will have a hard time believing me. Either that, or they will kill me outright."

She looked deep into his eyes, trying to read his soul, but it didn't work with him.

He couldn't be all bad, could he? Just because he was a Matayan prince?

Then again, he just might.

At least the view was okay.

"People remain enemies only as long as they choose to be," Naero told him. "Both our peoples have suffered at the hands of the Corps and their duplicity. Fighting each other only weakens both sides to the benefit of our mutual enemy. What do the Matayans really get out of doing the Corps' dirty work for them?"

Ellis shook his head. "What you say is entirely true, but Triax has a strangle-hold on our worlds. What other choices do we have? No one trusts us. And I do not know if Matayans will ever be ready to ally themselves with Spacers against the Corps. They can be a very stubborn, stiff-necked people."

Naero sighed. "As are mine."

"But I agree. The Corps use the Matayans as they see fit and our navies only grow weaker. They impose their will more and more upon our worlds, and we have no choice. Soon we'll join the ranks of their slaves."

"Ellis, your people only have one choice. Break free of Triax before it's too late. You hate Spacers? Try the mining revolt, maybe Joshua Tech. Anyone but Triax."

Ellis blew out a breath and shook his head. "That time may already be past. I've been away from court as a political hostage. The Triaxian shipyards spit out a new fleet every few months. They're moving to become a major power, even among the Corps. I'm not so sure that even the mighty Spacer Clans could help us now, even if both our peoples could find a way to bring themselves to accept that possibility."

Then Ellis bowed to her. "But you do have my respect, Naero."

Naero looped her arm through his briefly, causing him to jump. "Well, I guess that's a start."

She could smell his long, unbraided hair, and had a sudden urge to reach up and touch it.

Gallan shot her a dark look.

He didn't approve of Naero flirting with the Matayan prince.

Admittedly, that was happening more and more, and Ellis began to respond, increasingly watching her with a very different gleam in his eye.

Naero couldn't help it. She wanted to touch him.

She could handle it.

They sparred a bit more and then escorted Ellis back to his quarters. Gallan followed them silently from behind.

After they secured the Matayan's panel, they went back to Naero's quarters, Gallan fuming.

"What is wrong with you, Naero? I've never seen you act this stupid over anyone. This guy is a Matayan animal. One of their princes. Sure, he looks like a god. But remember who and what you are."

"Knowing your tastes, Gallan, I'd almost think you were jealous. No, I think someone eager and caring like Tarim would be a better match for you."

"I know the lander well enough to know he likes girls, and he's fallen for you so hard it's painful to watch. If I could put Tarim's mind into Ellis's body for you, I would."

She tried to open her mouth. Her best friend held up both hands.

"And don't change the subject like you always do."

He knew her way too well.

"I wasn't about to," she lied.

"*Haisha*. Stay away from Ellis. Think with your brain, not your fantasies. He's not for you, Naero. Let him into your heart and you're in for nothing but trouble."

Like she didn't have shiploads full of that everywhere she turned.

"I'll take that under advisement," she said. "But I'm getting tired of being lectured on this subject."

He left in a huff. She didn't like arguing with Gallan, or parting in anger. That wasn't like either of them.

We shall be in constant danger once we emerge out of jump space, Om noted.

They came out of jump an hour or so later, somewhat further away from Jodien-2 than they expected. The old ship's navigational computer simply wasn't very accurate. Naero watched Baeven launch a multitude of messenger drones. They scattered like Terran fireflies, most of them going back into jump.

"What are all those for?" Naero asked.

"A secure way to contact old friends for help, to keep enemies guessing. I maintain a constant trail of information and misinformation. I have many enemies."

Most likely.

Naero only nodded. She trusted Baeven's expertise, unable to do little else.

They stopped at Jodien-2 for ten uneventful days on a barren rock. A run-down depot on the edge of nowhere. No one left the ship except for Baeven, and then he disguised himself so well that no one would recognize him.

They did nothing to cause suspicion or raise an alarm.

The rift between her and Gallan grew; they were unable to resolve their issues.

Naero's issues. The problems were all with her. She knew that.

The only good thing occurred when a more humble Ellis made several inroads to patching things up between himself and Tarim.

By the time they departed, the two of them had actually started getting along.

Baeven would only confide in Naero and Gallan.

As they expected, the Triaxian naval presence had greatly increased in their area.

But the registry for their ship was clean, and they lingered long enough to take on cargo, just like they should.

Naero breathed a sigh of relief when they left Jodien-2. Escape finally looked possible.

From there they made a short route jump to Naejer-5, only a matter of hours.

They emerged from jump. Baeven plotted a course to one of the large, barren moons circling the big gas giant.

191

The immense Jovian at this range filled their viewscreens, complete with twist rings and large, blue, whirling cyclonics. Naero scanned dozens of ships docked at a research facility on the far side of one moon.

Almost immediately she felt a twitch of warning. What was it this time?

"Friends," Naero began.

Gallan let out a stifled cry next to her. She glanced up.

He wheeled and staggered toward Baeven.

Two more shots from the outcast's needle gun took Gallan down.

He attacks. Activate my protocols!

Gallan gave Naero time to strike.

Blood and anger pounded behind her face.

She flipped off the ceiling and launched herself, twisting to avoid a spray of needles.

A killing strike from her hidden blast rod deflected off Baeven's energy shield.

Spin kick. Off the wall, knock the gun away.

Her first knife he dodged.

The next he caught in his forearm, drawing another needle pistol so fast she couldn't react.

The first shot hit her.

Her left foot grazed his cheek.

Baeven slammed her to the ground. His eyes cold and implacable.

"Your speed is remarkable for an adept so young."

He shot her up with two more needles. She went numb.

"Too bad you neither have the strength nor skill to match that speed yet. So much to learn."

"Baeven, why? Don't do this. We trusted you."

"I'm sorry it has to be this way, Naero. We must know certain things. Playing our enemies into revealing what they know is the only way I can find out."

Her tongue felt like clay. Her mind began to float.

"Even if I explained it all to you, you might not go along with it. There's too much at stake. I'd tell you to trust me, but–"

Her spittle caught him in the eye and dripped down over his nose.

That took all of her fading strength.

She struggled to resist the paralyzing agent in the needles, to no avail.

Baeven wiped off his face.

"Aunt Sleak was right about you...*outcast*. You'd betray anyone to get what you're after."

Baeven's half-smile looked grim. He nodded.

Let me kill this one, Naero.

Quiet, Om. We'll get our chance.

"Sleak knew me too well, Naero. Yet our younger sister Lythe never believed her. I'll save you if I can, for her sake. But I can't afford to give you a choice in this matter. Do not interfere."

He shot a fourth needle into her.

The colors around Naero's tears and her range of vision whorled into darkness.

28

Baeven kept them all together in a high sec cell.

The meeting place for the coming auction remained secret. Once they arrived, Baeven's guests were not allowed to leave or make any type of transmission until the issue at hand was decided.

Baeven possessed some means of jamming or cutting off the facility and blocking all tracing and transmissions within that area.

Naero went on display for the highest bidder.

Baeven controlled the auction.

Of course the main sticking point remained whether she actually carried part or all of the Kexxian Data Matrix somehow.

No one from Triax was present.

Some of the bidders didn't want to take any chances. They offered to buy her outright, and have their people take her apart and figure it out later.

But then they haggled about the price.

Thus far, offers ranged from metric tons of credits or other fungible wealth. Entire fleets of ships. Entire worlds–including their economies and populations. Appointments to the Boards of Directors at various Gigacorps, or Directorships themselves, granting Baeven unimaginable wealth, influence, and godlike power over the lives of trillions.

When not up for bidding, Naero sulked or plotted with her fellow prisoners, in either abject despair or boredom.

"We never should have trusted the outcast," Gallan complained. "I'm sorry, Naero. I'm embarrassed and angry that he took us down so easily. *Haisha.* Some Spacers we are."

"What if he does sell you?" Tarim said. "We aren't worth anything. What's he going to do to us? Cut our throats? Poison our food and water? Blow us out of an airlock?"

He worked himself up like that until basically they all told him to shut the hell up.

Even Naero had to take a turn against his incessant blubbering. "Will you be quiet with all that? It's not helping us at all, Tarim."

"I...I can't help it. I can't stop thinking about what he might do. What could happen."

Tarim fidgeted, asking questions based on his fearful nature, reacting to almost everything with terror and despair.

All of them worried. Each of them dealt with fear in a different way.

Strangely enough, Ellis seemed to gloat over the situation a little and tried to make light of it. His response?

Laugh in the face of fear.

"It's kind of funny, no? It's like being back with Kattryll, but without the torture and the buggery. Cheer up, Tarim. There are only so many times they can kill and revive us. At least we have each other against this betrayer, and all of the Gigacorps and our other enemies. No problem. We'll find a way out. I'm absolutely sure of it."

Ellis's flip nature bothered Naero almost more than her former uncle's treachery–if in truth, he'd ever been her uncle.

Baeven might tell her anything to keep her off guard.

Even if he had been family once, as an outcast, he was dead to her and her clan now. Nothing would stop her from killing him if she got the chance.

Instead of Naero being ordered out, the security panel to the brig slid open without warning.

Baeven strode in among them.

Alone.

Gallan attacked immediately. Followed by Ellis, and finally Tarim.

195

Baeven stunned Ellis with the back of his hand, knocking him ten meters across the room, leaving a red smear against the wall.

He endured a glancing blow from Gallan. He merely winded Tarim and let him drop.

Naero maneuvered for an opening.

Gallan gave it to her.

Baeven countered Gallan's combinations and flipped him into the high ceiling corner. The big Spacer fell hard and did not move.

Naero attacked low off the floor, and then from the adjacent wall behind Baeven.

She tossed hidden stun powder directly into Baeven's face.

He deftly deflected most of it with one hand, but still gagged and choked.

Naero followed up with combo kicks to several vital areas, like kicking someone made out of steel.

She hit Baeven with several microbomblets she and Gallan had kept concealed on them.

The blasts rocked him and pushed him back across the length of the cell.

She got a good running start, ending with a powerspin kick that should break his neck.

Baeven caught her ankle. Speed. Terrifying

His raw strength. Horrific.

With one hand, he slammed her against the wall to either side of him.

Wham, wham, wham.

Several times, faster than thought.

Massive pain erupted in her ribs, arms, and legs. Multiple tears, twists, contusions, and micro-fractures.

He dropped her to the floor, helpless and gasping, ribs moving in ways they shouldn't.

Baeven could have slain her and the others easily. At any time.

In a day or so, her smartblood might regenerate much of the damage. But he made sure her next several hours would be filled with wrenching pain every time she moved.

He grabbed her by the hair and yanked her to her feet. Naero gasped. She felt her eyes bulge as if they might burst.

She ground her teeth, but other than a few weak grunts, she did not cry out. She wouldn't give the bastard the satisfaction.

He stared into her eyes up close, his scorching breath on her face. "I warned you not to trifle with me. I thought you were smarter than this,

Naero. But I guess not. I don't want to hurt you and your friends. But I will. If you force me to."

"Please, don't hurt her," Tarim pleaded, crawling on the ground, still clutching his gut. "Oh, Jesus."

"Be quiet," Baeven snapped.

He glared at Naero again and shook her, knowing full well the intense pain it caused.

She felt her eyes roll up. She almost blacked out.

"Listen to me," Baeven said "The next one who interferes with me I cripple. Including you, Naero. You don't need to be able to walk to be of use to me.

"The next I kill. No hesitation. No mercy. Understand?"

She barely managed to nod.

"Good. Now, come with me and cooperate. Clean yourself up. More interested parties have arrived. They wish to examine you, along with the others, and renew the bidding."

"Why didn't you just leave me with the Triaxians?" she said.

"They don't have the information I desire, and they always double-cross you in any case. I couldn't trust to their heavy-handed methods to tell me anything. Besides that, I detest them the most of all the Corps."

"I hope this is all worth it, you renegade son of a bitch."

He half-smiled. "Such flattery. Some of our new guests claim to have certain ancient testing methods they would like to try out on you. We shall see."

"Just what do you want, Baeven? Wealth, power, control?"

"Information. Knowledge. Still so many things I want to know, and I'm running out of time. Thus far, all the players know something. All of them possess one or more pieces to this puzzle. Perhaps these new tests will tip the scales. That's why I've lured them all here to this secret location–to find out who knows what, and put it all together."

"You're playing all the Corps against each other?" Naero laughed, even though it nearly killed her. "You didn't strike me as the ambitious or greedy type, Baeven. I guess you're just a criminally insane fool."

He smiled a grim smile. "You could be right." He led her out of the brig and secured it behind him.

"I have always been quite mad, they say."

29

Baeven strapped her down in her flight togs, tight onto a medbed in the center of a mid-sized, bone-white lab room.

She gasped and felt her eyes pop.

The medbed stood nearly upright, causing her agony yet again. Her weight sagged against the restraints. A stifled sob escaped her; she leaned back slightly. She struggled to swallow.

At a distance to either side of the lab, two halves of a circular table and chairs popped up from the floor panels and surrounded her.

Naero tried not to struggle or move, allowing her body to heal.

Several minutes passed before the players filtered in.

New examination equipment emerged from the ceiling and wall panels, closing in around her like angry torture bots.

The lights in the back of the room dialed way down, leaving her spotlighted up front for everyone to watch, like an experiment test subject.

Eleven individuals took seats at that circle table in the darkness, four more than before. Six of the eleven had bodyguards standing behind them at the ready.

Lights came on at Naero from above. Her eyes adjusted. The first one to scan and examine her from his displays looked like a high-level tech of Stellar Industries, a humanoid Naivatch.

She could tell by the deep black skin of his hands and the purple flesh beneath the fingernails. His palms and the soles of his feet would be bright violet.

Deeply private about their appearance, the Naivatch showed only their hands when abroad, the rest of their body wrapped in robes or covered in blast armor and a visored helmet, like this one.

He turned impatiently to Baeven.

"Why have you brought us here, Vatril? And who are these others? This girl carries no information whatsoever–"

"You will all refer to me as Baeven from now on."

The Naivatch waved one hand, revealing his purple palm. "If you insist. Who are these people? Allies of yours in this massive scam? What are you trying to pull? If she indeed carries the kind of data Triax claims, there'd be some detectable trace of it. No one can prove anything like this."

"As always, you could be right, Na'Darroch," Baeven said.

He paced between the two tables. "But as we all believe, this data is Kexxian. The trick is to determine how the ancient masters hid and encrypted it. None of us can take the chance that it is indeed present and that others shall retrieve it first."

The others appeared restless and impatient, in no mood for further failure or delay.

"We demand proof."

"Stop wasting our time, Betrayer."

"Show us something, or your life is forfeit."

Baeven half-smiled.

"Time to put all the pieces of this puzzle together." He turned to one of the new arrivals, a heavy-set woman with short blond hair and pale blue eyes, wearing a high-level Krupp Corps uniform.

"Madame Garrold, provide us with your information."

She nodded. "Our researchers discovered an anomaly on the surface DNA on scumworld algae and mold spores in sectors of a rimward spiral arm thought to have been included among the Kexx ancients.

"It took us over two centuries to break the encryption."

"And what did you uncover?" Baeven said.

Everyone waited.

"Music files. Kexxian music, very intricate–even beautiful."

The emissary from Gelden Corps snorted. "What good is that to us?"

"It proves," Baeven said, "that the Kexx had a way of imprinting coded information right on the very DNA of living organisms that was both self-replicating and eternal. The information was neither changed nor corrupted in any way, after millions of years. Am I correct, Madame Garrold?"

"Yes, and we believe this method of transmission was very commonplace to the ancient Kexx. They could do so with great ease. This ability made every form of life and existence they had contact with potential computerized storage devices."

Baeven turned to another new guest, a small pale man with long black hair, wearing a green kimono suit, from Hita Corps.

"Master Kurita. Give us the details on the strange plague that destroyed the distant colony of Tora-3, eighty-seven years ago."

Kurita bowed his head slightly.

"Tora-3 was also believed to be an important homeworld of the ancient Kexx, home to many important ruins. We stumbled upon it quite by accident during our early expansion period. The colony found several mysterious artifacts that were dead to us. Nothing could make them function or reveal their purpose."

"And, as we all know," Na'Darroch added, "the colony was completely destroyed."

"Yes," Kurita continued. "The terrifying plague awoke and destroyed all life on Tora-3. It is a Black Zone, a Dead Zone to this day. No ship or probe can land on its surface and take off again. All tek disrupts and negates. Nothing living can survive on the planet's surface."

"And what caused the plague? What form did it take?"

Kurita bowed again, and looked slightly nervous.

View screens popped down from the ceiling. Vids started up.

Kurita narrated.

"These vids are top secret. Only high-level directors have ever seen them. This is the first time they have been shown outside of the Hita Board of Directors."

Techs in a lab were scanning or performing some kind of medical procedure on what looked to be a mid-sized anthropoid.

"That creature was a blue-haired mountain ape, native to Tora-3. They swam in the heated mineral lakes and pools scattered throughout the volcanic mountains on one of the continental coasts. A deep genetic scan stumbled upon something strange. Techs located a wealth of encrypted alien data, right on the surface of this species' DNA. The techs grew excited and called in the best researchers of that period to decode the information."

"What went wrong?" Baeven asked.

Kurita violently motioned toward the screens.

In the vids, without any warning, chaos and destruction exploded.

Weird specks of light burst out of the test subjects and the equipment monitoring the apes.

People exploded, imploded, or dissolved and melted right in their clothing.

Strange ribbons of coruscating light and dark tendrils and thrashing tentacles of shadow ripped through techs, guards, equipment, and the very walls before the vids blacked out.

Master Kurita shook his head. "To this day, no one knows for certain. But the destruction spread from that lab to all over the entire planet. Within seconds. Killing everyone and everything on Tora-3.

"From the final data streams, it is believed that the teks unlocked a vast source of data encrypted on the DNA of the native apes. But this time, the information was somehow protected. A defense mechanism triggered, destroying the information itself and everything around it. Our officials didn't know what to call such destruction, so they referred to it as a virulent plague. But as you can see from the vids, it was something much more."

He speaks of a level thirty-four defensive protocol. A very severe planetary level response.

Quiet, Om. We need to listen to everything they have to say.

The reps from Marsten and Brannock Corps tried to protest, talking over each other.

"This is ridiculous. What good is something that self-destructs in this fashion?"

"So, even if we decode the Kexxian Data Matrix, we have to get past this doomsday defense mechanism?"

The Gravlink Corps rep sneered. "This deal sounds worse all the time."

"My good friends," Baeven said. "What valid enterprise doesn't entail a little risk? What if there were a way not only to detect the presence of such data streams, but unlock them, without triggering these nasty, inconvenient self-destruct protocols?"

"We don't have the tek to do so," the man from Omni Corps blurted out.

"Perhaps we do," an odd little voice noted.

Light struck the speaker from another direction and the medbed spun around to face the third new arrival, while the other lights dimmed. Because of her small size and the focus on the troubling vids, few had seen her take the stage.

"I am Mxgob, trading agent for Brannock Terraforming. I am also of the Cumi Medtek Consortium."

Naero's eyes focused on a small bipedal mammalian humanoid less that a meter tall and, somewhat akin, in appearance, to a large Terran mouse.

The Cumi remained an ancient race by any modern standards, also famous for their vast medical and genetic knowledge, trade, and negotiation skills.

Naero's parents had been on friendly terms with some of their leaders.

One of these creatures, a deep-space traveler and medtek, had given her and Jan that strange medical scan concerning the ancient plague that her parents seemed so afraid of.

With apparent basis in fact it seemed now. The horrific vids from Tora-3 were still fresh in her mind.

Mxgob cleared her throat and clasped her hands behind her.

"My people traded with the Kexx, long ago at the beginning of our enlightenment, and just before they faded away. We currently use a very similar method of encoding our own data files in molecular DNA. It is somewhat simpler, more primitive, but the principle is basically the same, just at another level. And without the violent security protocols."

She held up a strange-looking scanner.

"With permission, I will access my ship's archived data records for information on ancient Kexxian encryption methods. Even a million years ago, much of their tek remained highly advanced, beyond even our standards today. But because of our trading relationships with them during their final centuries, we were able to adapt and incorporate some of their most basic systems and the underlying concepts of their technology within patterns of our tek that survives to this day. Ours even operate on the exact same principles and electromagnetic frequencies."

The thin lady with orange hair and white eyes from Odyssey Corps broke in, striking the table in front of her with her fists. "Can you or can you not detect the existence of the Kexxian Data Matrix in this spack?"

"I believe I can. With some modifications to present equipment, I think I can duplicate the process, bypass any built-in security, and access the raw encrypted data. It will need to be decoded and translated further from that point to make it usable, of course."

Heads turned to Baeven, eagerly.

He finally nodded his assent to the small furry creature.

"Mx, if this is a trick to bring in outside help, I will skin you. Access your ship, but do not attempt to send any signals or activate any other systems. You will be monitored."

"I object," another buyer said. "I'm with Chikara Corps. This could all still be just a big set up to trick us into buying something that does not exist."

"All of you have your spies. You know Triax's efforts," Baeven said. "Check your sources. They would not be expending this much effort chasing after nothing."

"Perhaps, they too, are deceived," the Matashi rep said. "The Cumi are known to lie at will when profit is involved. This creature could be in league with Baeven. Don't be surprised if she discovers something fantastic."

"I am Director Prebin from Omni Corps," the thin woman said. "It was we who first contracted the exploration of Kexxian ruins wherever they were located. By rights, anything found should be returned to us as our rightful property. Our original exploration team was slain by raiders on Chosala-5. One survivor escaped, rescued by a Cumi ship, and supposedly turned over similar information to them before dying. The Cumi never told us what came of it."

"Then you no longer have a legal claim," a familiar voice said.

Naero twisted her head painfully before the medbed even moved.

There sat Adrin, dressed impeccably. "Come now, even if such knowledge exists, it would not be monopolized for more than a few decades."

"But in those few decades," Na'Darroch, the Naivatch from Stellar Industries said, "those who did monopolize and apply it could drastically affect the fortunes and prospects of their competitors."

"You are new to this gathering as well," Madame Garrold said. "Please, identify yourself as we all have. This is an open auction."

Adrin leaned into the light and removed his head covering. Naero counted nine ornate braids.

"Mellis Tarret VI," he said, "Patriarch of the Matayan Cartels, Emperor of the Matayan peoples."

"What a joke," the Gelden agent said. "The Corps crushed your so-called empire when you were a child. The Cartels do not exist anymore. I thought you were on Triax's leash? They will strangle you with it when they learn of your duplicity."

Adrin remained calm. "Perhaps."

There was something different about him, a puffy slackness around his eyes and mouth. Perhaps he'd been ill.

"Those who do not serve the Corps faithfully shall perish," the Matashi rep chanted.

"I am not here to bandy words with slaves and cult underlings," Adrin said. He suddenly looked ready to draw battle knives and go at them all.

Naero gulped.

Unknown to her, she had twice joked around with the Matayan Emperor, a man rumored to be so ruthless–he killed his parents with his bare hands in order to seize power. What would happen if she fell into such hands?

Would Baeven allow that?

"Finally, I have it," the Cumi blurted out. She continued to stare at her handcomp. "The Kexx sometimes encrypted their knowledge directly onto the pico energy level of a genetic pattern. This could be performed on an individual, or set to be self-replicating within a species.

"Such data can be limitless in quantity and invisible to almost all normal scans. If the subject is slain, or there is a significant loss of body temperature, the data is lost. Other security codes could be added if need be. I just need to calibrate my equipment. It shouldn't be more than a few moments, and we'll have our answer."

"Are you certain about this, Mx?" Baeven said.

"Quite certain. Similar processes were rumored to exist among the Drians, and may have even originated with them."

"What about the spack girl?" Na'Darroch insisted.

"Even a preliminary, deep level genetic detail scan on a wide range of parameters should reveal the encrypted data as clumps or scoring echoes on the surface of the individual's DNA patterns, once you know what to look for and where. We should proceed to do so immediately."

Mxgob looked to Baeven once more.

The outcast nodded.

She punched up the scanning sequence.

"What about any security codes?" Director Prebin said.

"With these methods it could take hours, perhaps even days to implant or retrieve such data," the Chikara rep said.

"Yes," the Cumi cautioned, "days to retrieve, but only a few minutes to detect. And simple detection will not activate any inherent security programs."

"You hope. In theory," Emperor Mellis added. "Otherwise, we're all dead."

"This creature could still be lying," the Arnett Corps rep said. "How do we know it isn't in cahoots with this rogue?"

"I'm not so sure," the Omni woman said again. "We have evidence to believe that the Kexxian Data Matrix does indeed exist, and that it could be encrypted on a person. It is possible that this spack girl has personally undergone such a process."

Naero said nothing; neither did Baeven.

The preliminary scan finalized.

Everyone in the room waited, transfixed.

What is happening, Naero? Enemies attempting unauthorized access. Unacceptable. I must have access to our defensive protocols.

Om, I don't have any answers for you. I don't even know what those protocols are, let alone how to activate them. Are they part of the Kexxian Data Matrix?

In part, yes. Yet they are part of us now too. I could use them to defend us or our ship in case of an attack. I could free us and help us escape. But all access to them has been completely blocked and cut off. I can tap into the nearly limitless Cosmic powers locked in the depths of your mind, but much like your imagination, I cannot yet manifest anything and make it real.

Naero knitted her brows briefly. Cosmic power? Limitless? Om, what are you babbling about?

There is a great power hidden within the deepest recesses of our mind, Naero. I am barely able to touch it, but I haven't found a way to use any of it. Not yet. I think your correct term for this is bloody hell, bullshit, or perhaps damnation. I begin to comprehend the concepts of swearing and frustration. Very useful.

Keep trying Om. Just check with me before you…unleash anything.

I will try. But if our defensive protocols ever do come online, I do not require your permission to defend us or our secrets. And you have secrets all your own that did not originate from me or our Kexxian Matrix.

What the hell are you talking about? We don't have enough problems? Look where we are. Just keep trying and let me think to myself for a bit. My brain is already on overload.

Then Naero realized something.

Baeven always played everyone.

He wasn't about to sell her to any of these bastards, especially if she actually had the Matrix.

She still didn't understand his real plan.

Baeven analyzed the final results of the scan at last.

"Definitive proof," Baeven said. "Traces in this young woman's metabolism point to the fact that she carries the Kexxian Data Matrix on her DNA. The pattern is there for all to see. Check your downloads on your screens. Most of you are techs; you can perform the cross-checking process yourselves."

Several more tense moments passed.

At first no one said very much. Finally the Chikara rep snapped his head up and shouted.

"I start the bidding at twenty gigamegs."

"Thirty!"

"*Fifty!*"

"One hundred gigamegs," the Omni woman said. "Our final offer."

The research base rocked violently from several small explosions.

Mellis Tarret stood up, murder written across his face as if it were blood.

"I offer all of you your lives and safe passage," he said. "Any who oppose me shall perish for their insolence. The Imperial Matayan Fleet is upon you all. Our power will shine once more. Surrender the spack girl and my grandson's clone to me unharmed, and I will guarantee your safety."

Naero blinked. Grandson's clone? Ellis was just a clone? Did he know that?

More explosions. The audience room erupted into chaos. Corps agents and bodyguards fought with each other. Matayan mercs in power armor ripped their way through the walls and surrounded Mellis Tarret VI.

Baeven flung himself over Naero; she screamed in pain.

Several energy blasts passed right through him, one went right through her face, but did no harm.

She should be dead.

Baeven phazed them both completely through the deck and into a shielded control room one level below.

He smiled at her. "Re-join your friends, Naero. They're waiting for you in an assault ship in Cargo Bay 2."

"I...I don't understand," she said.

"Our plan worked. I'll hold our new acquaintances off. Take the Kexxian Data Matrix to our people. It cannot fall into the hands of anyone else. The Corps will stop at nothing to find you now."

"Baeven, I–"

"Go. I'll lead them away and catch up to you when I can We have our answers."

Naero limped away, remembering the quickest path to Cargo Bay 2. Several bots stood around the craft. She spotted Gallan, Ellis, and Tarim strapped into their cockpit launch chairs, stunned or drugged.

As she guessed, the assault ship stood fully loaded, armed, and ready to rip.

A massive pulse of energy beam blasted through the complex, tearing a gaping hole large enough for her to fly through.

How nice.

She vectored the assault craft and shot forward into space.

Scans showed an intense naval battle erupting. Dozens of Matayan warships of every shape and size broke off from the main fleet to intercept her small escape craft and those of the Corps emissaries scattering in all directions.

Two of the emissary ships got vaporized right in front of her.

Matayan mercs and marines swarmed over Baeven's ship, trying to board it. It fled and prepared to jump, dodging erratically.

A direct hit from an old Matayan battleship spinal gun vaporized another emissary vessel.

A tremendous volley of energy fire and close range missile strikes struck havoc among the Matayan forward elements.

No sign of where the attacks came from.

Formations of swift pursuit craft tore after Naero in waves.

She punched it.

Asteroids rocketed up from the surface of the moon itself, ripping into the Matayan fleet at close range.

Powerful mass-drivers on the moon's surface zeroed in on them.

Five sleek, black strike ships uncloaked, swept in out of nowhere, and formed up around Naero.

They kept pace with her easily, layering their shields full to the rear to protect her escape.

Elite Shadowforce escorts, unlike any craft Naero had ever seen before. No markings or insignia.

"This is Shock Five-Leader. We have you covered, spacechild. Commence jump immediately. Get out of here."

"You bet your ass." Naero checked her systems. Everything already preset. Baeven hadn't missed a trick.

They'd need every second against the torrent of concentrated naval fire coming straight at them from the Matayan fleet.

Even the powerful flanking shields Shadowforce threw up couldn't withstand that volume of intense fire.

Concentrated fire from multiple spinal guns came right at them.

Destruction imminent. Access limited. Attempting level eighteen repulsing energy screen.

Two of her rear-guard escorts vanished in flames.

All her shields buckled.

Om cried out. *We face destruction. Unacceptable!*

She re-routed her remaining power in the space of a heart beat, but it wasn't going to be enough.

Then she gasped. *Haisha.* Something in her mind ripped free.

A huge pulse wave of energy tore through her.

For just an instant, a massive energy signature swelled up behind her craft, barely enough to deflect the enemy's overwhelming barrage.

Naero seized that instant to blast her ship into jump.

30

Naero came out of jump a few hours later, far outside of the Memosan system.

Her three surviving Shadowforce escorts followed her, maintaining a close protective formation around her battered craft.

One of the other pilots spoke up. "We should all be dead. What happened back there? None of us could have survived that level of fire."

Their commander cut in over their secured link.

"Cut the speculation, Shock-Three. The point is we did make it out, even though we lost Shock-One and Shock-Four. Proceed on mission. Spacechild, this is Shock-Five leader. Continue to rendezvous at uploaded coordinates. Anything goes wrong, jump to secondary destination and seek out your first trust code backup contact. Do you wish us to take any of your friends with us?"

"Negative," Naero said.

"They'll be easy to make while you're trying to escape. You might be better off alone or with a single companion."

"I'm calling it. I won't abandon my friends now."

"We'll cloak for your approach and stay in orbit until you jump out of system," the commander said. "We will not contact you further, but we'll be around for a while, if you run into trouble again."

"Thanks, guys. Did Baeven tip you off?"

"Unknown. We obey orders. Don't trust the outcast. He's notorious for pursuing his own agenda."

"I figured that out," Naero said. "Was he really family at one time?"

"Emphasis on the 'was.' He got exiled for many good reasons. Remember that. Over and out."

Naero thought hard about Baeven. He kept surprising her.

She still ached with each breath from his little lesson. Still tasted the faint coppery tang of blood in her mouth–her own blood. But she continued to heal rapidly.

Yet without Baeven's masterful power play during the fake auction, they would not have their answers and in a way, in theory at least, an ability to both detect and decode the Kexxian Data Matrix.

First she needed to know something.

Om, that flash of defensive screen there at the end. Was that you? Did you somehow manage to...

Silence.

Om? You still with me?

The response when it came, felt very weak.

Om...nearly destroyed. Must...shut down other functions, including contact with Naero. Must...affect repairs. Signing off.

Om? Om, what happened? What did you do?

Silence.

Whatever happened, Om sounded in pretty bad shape.

Naero unstrapped from her pilot seat and got out. She had her own worries.

She needed to hurry while they were still on approach to their rendezvous with Spacer Intel.

First some continued self-healing, and then–revive her friends.

*

One-by-one, Naero used the contents of a medkit to revive Gallan, Tarim, and Ellis inside the confines of the transport cockpit. The small ship still proceeded on auto-approach.

All three of her dazed friends remained strapped into their flight seats as they came around.

Their wits returned to them a few minutes later. They looked around and outside of their cockpit.

"What happened? Where in the hell are we now?" Ellis demanded. All of them still appeared groggy from being drugged.

"Just hang on," Naero told them. "Regain your strength while I prepare to land, so to speak. As soon as we have time, I'll do my best to explain what's gone on, in a nutshell."

Memosa-3 loomed larger before them, almost entirely blue with small polar caps of white and flecks of green scattered far and wide in between.

Naero reset the programmable registration on their ship, just in case someone activated her auto-transponder.

Memosa-3. Another minor pit stop, a real backwater waterworld, with more than ninety percent hydrographics. They noted poles and several main patches of volcanic archipelagos were the only dry land.

Naero felt a tight hand grip her shoulder.

"What's taking so long?" Ellis said. "I'm tired of all this crap. I want answers. You people aren't going to jerk me around forever."

She caught his strong scent again. But this time, having him so close felt too much like a threat.

"Let go or take back a stump," Naero warned.

The hand released her.

"Don't ever interrupt me when I'm busy trying to save our asses," she added.

"We're at the Memosan system," Gallan said, checking the navicomp, wincing and rubbing his eyes. "Third planet."

"Pilot to crew. We're going for a swim, boys. Hang on to whatcha got. We're gonna get wet."

Tarim came to last of all. He covered his eyes and groaned.

The planet's surface raced closer. They penetrated the atmosphere.

Naero locked onto the coordinates for their rendezvous. The ship homed in on them like a beacon.

They descended right into a tropical storm.

"Just my luck," she muttered.

The craft shook and jostled from turbulence.

"It might get a little rough, boys."

"What's happening?" Tarim asked, naked fear in his voice.

"Just a little tropical depression," Naero said. "Not to worry. It won't be a hurricane for a few days yet. But it just happens to be directly over where we need to go."

Tarim started praying.

"And where is that?" Ellis asked.

She'd saved this guy's butt repeatedly. One would think that eventually a little gratitude might peek out.

"I don't know exactly who we're rendezvousing with, but I have a trust code and a pretty good idea," she said.

"Spacer Intelligence," Ellis guessed.

"Our meeting point's over two hundred meters below sea level." She might even have time for a mist shower and clean togs. She reeked.

"We're...we're going under water?" Tarim said. "Won't we drown?"

"Don't worry, Tarim. Remember, a starship is a sealed environment, and our gravitics will work just as well under water. The ship will protect us from the increased pressure. We'll just move a lot slower. But the water also affords us a convenient hiding place and makes us hard to detect or track."

"Tarim, my friend," Ellis said. "You need to toughen up a bit. Stop letting everything rattle you so much. Deal with it. Be a man."

"Leave him alone," Naero said."

"It's embarrassing," Ellis said. "And you keep protecting him like a child, Naero. Let him stand on his own."

"That's enough," Naero said. "We're in this thing together, like it or not. Anyone who doesn't pull together or pull their weight can go for a walk out in that storm, right now. Copy?"

Silence. Naero strapped back in and focused on her final approach.

The ship hit the ocean a little faster than she intended, but she wanted to submerge quickly.

The upper waves tossed them about, even with their gravitic compensators.

Once they sank far enough down, the dark world beneath the surface went relatively calm.

A warning signal went off.

"Naero," Gallan noted. "We just took a hit on our transponder. Waiting for verification code response. Authenticate."

"We'll punch it fast and blow back out of here if we don't get the correct response," Naero said. "We're ready either way."

"Response confirmed and verified," Gallan said. "They're our contact all right, six kilometers north by northeast–locked on. Arrival in several minutes."

Naero ran for the mist shower, calling it first.

Deep scans revealed an old Spacer battleship, probably long since hidden here during the last Spacer War. Rumors held that numerous ships had been secreted on certain Corps worlds, despite all the treaties.

In case of another war, the mothballed ships could be crewed and emerge for quick strike missions behind enemy lines. Spacers called them Shadow Fleets.

Naero's small striker fit easily into one of the old battleship's cargo bays.

Naero waited for the water to be ejected from the sealed hold, listening to the groaning sounds of the big ship and the hum of its old pumps.

When the green all clear signal lit up, she and her friends emerged into the damp loading bay.

A panel slid open. Aunt Sleak ran out, along with Jan, much to Naero's surprise and relief.

Naero and Gallan met them half-way. Several Spacer Intel agents, geared up in strike armor, took up positions around them, pulse rifles ready.

"Naero," Jan said, tears in his eyes, "So glad to see you, N."

"We couldn't believe it," Aunt Sleak said, "not after the explosion on that freighter. We thought you and Gallan had been blasted to atoms until Shadowforce contacted us. We even held your wakes along with the other casualties from the battle."

Jan grinned. "How does it feel to be a ghost, sib?"

Aunt Sleak didn't say anything about her and Gallan disobeying orders. Yet.

They still would have been abducted.

Jan gave her another big hug. "Been lonely without you, sib. Who else can I plot the future with?"

"I hear you have some new friends." Aunt Sleak said. She glared briefly at Ellis. "A Matayan prince no less, Naero? How did you get linked up with him, and this lander kid?"

Naero rolled her eyes. "It's a long story. Meet Tarim, from the mining freighter. And this is Ellis, Prince of House Tarret."

Naero wondered when she would need to broach the clone issue. Did Ellis know? Perhaps not.

But it came straight from the Matayan Emperor himself. He ought to know.

Aunt Sleak's eye's went to black slits when she shot a full hard look at Ellis. She offered him no greeting.

At least she didn't stab him, shoot him, or attack him outright.

Even Ellis turned pale under her withering gaze and swallowed hard.

"Easy, Aunt Sleak," Naero told her. "I know this is extremely weird, but Ellis is a friend...sort of. We rescued him from some Triax goon, who tortured him as a political hostage. He's been running with us ever since. He's been on our side, and hasn't done anything wrong."

"House Tarret's corsairs helped take out your parents' fleet," Aunt Sleak pointed out.

"Along with Triax and several other Gigacorps," Naero said. "I don't think Ellis had anything to do with that directly. Like I said, he's been a Triaxian political hostage. The Corps are forcing his people to be their shock troops, against their will."

"Yeah, they would never do anything like that on their own," Aunt Sleak said.

There went that sudden throat full of dust again, always around Aunt Sleak.

"I assured him that he would not be harmed," Naero said, "and that we wouldn't ransom him."

Aunt Sleak's eyes bulged. She cocked her head and put her hands on her hips in disbelief.

"I gave him my word," Naero said.

Aunt Sleak folded her arms about herself, rocked back on her heels and nodded her head. "Well, then damn me all to hell. How generous of you, Naero. Perhaps we should throw in a few megs for his trouble. Invite him to a banquet in his honor. May you always be so confident in your decisions."

"Captain, excuse me for interrupting," Gallan said. "But we have vital information for Spacer Intel. All of us are emotionally strained; we're exhausted and hungry. Can we get debriefed and sort the rest out later?"

"Works for me," Aunt Sleak said, still fuming. "You two, with me. These other two...will be seen to."

Naero raised an eyebrow.

"And treated well," the captain added. "Even his highness there."

Naero turned to Tarim and Ellis and whispered, "Go on; it'll be all right."

"I get the distinct impression," Ellis whispered back, "that your aunt would like nothing better than to tear out my liver with her teeth and feast on it."

Naero half-grinned. "Keep that in mind. I wouldn't put it past her...or be able to stop her."

"She really doesn't like me."

"Ellis, I'm not sure I like you. Don't tell me that the older generations of your people who went through the wars are any different? But we and our people don't have to remain enemies forever. Maybe we can find a way to help each other."

Ellis forced a smile. "I suppose so, especially since I find myself so frequently surrounded by Spacers. Perhaps I need a few friends among them to help me hang onto my liver and other internals."

"A wise choice," she said. "Do as they say and you guys'll be all right."

Irith, the Spacer Intel leftenant assigned to them, grilled Naero and Gallan for what seemed like several eternal hours.

They went over everything in as much detail as they could, many times over.

Toward the end, both Naero and Gallan drooped and yawned. They hadn't been given anything to eat or drink, or even allowed to go to the bathroom.

Naero's kidneys and bladder felt about to pop. At least she'd put clean togs on beforehand.

"Leftenant," Aunt Sleak finally said. "I think that's about all you're going to get right now, until the lab tests get underway, tomorrow. The new equipment is still being set up. Give my people here a breather. They need to take care of their own business and get some chow and rest."

"Very well," Irith said.

"Begin briefing them on their escape personas. You'll need to move quickly after the testing period ends. Get out of Corps Space. Our forces will assist you along the way."

"Any further news on the mounting tensions between Corps and Spacers?"

"Not yet, Sleak. They fluctuate everywhere. Serious incidents continue to increase. The Corps slant everything in their media to make it look like Spacers are trying to incite another war."

"Has anyone declared yet?"

"If they do, every Spacer in Corps space becomes a target. It'll be bad, just like the last Spacer Wars. We'll lose a lot of vulnerable people and merchant fleets and ships initially."

"This is insane," Naero said. She worried about her friends, her family.

"War always is," the leftenant said. "I was a cadet pilot in the last Spacer War, barely old enough. Things got very crazy. But if the Corps think we've gained a potential tek advantage greater than what we have, they might just think it prudent to attack first and wipe us out before we can apply it."

"That's really insane," Naero said.

"Don't expect that reality to change any time soon," Aunt Sleak told her. "Maybe never. People, let's go. We've been dismissed. Spacer Intel will keep poring over what you've given them and pick the bones clean."

After quick stops at their quarters, they went to the nearest mess hall.

Naero and Gallan ate and ate until they might burst.

Even though she couldn't eat another bite, the smell of food all around still tantalized her.

"So, where's the fleet?" Naero asked.

Aunt Sleak's face darkened. "Still making their rounds, far as I know. Wasn't safe for Jan and me to stay with them. Sold the fleet to Zalvano for a cred. It's all legal. He'll carry on until we can all make it out of here and link up again."

"Aunt Sleak," Naero said. "I don't want my friends treated like prisoners."

"I'll do what I can. Tutors will work with your friends–even the Matayan."

Another glaring look. Aunt Sleak handed chips to Naero and Gallan. "These data files have the uploaded dossiers on your guises that you'll use to escape. Study and learn them carefully over the next few days."

"So, what's the plan?" Naero asked.

"We'll try to slip out of Corps Space as independents," Aunt Sleak said. "To do that, we'll take a long slow loop through the Corps, doing our business along the way. They'll expect us to make a hell-bent run for Free Space. They're stopping every runner who doesn't pause to do business. That would just bring suspicion down on us."

"Great," Jan said. "Maybe we can at least make some profits along the way. I know of several hot spots that we could deal with. That full-blown miner revolt continues to explode across multiple sectors. The revolt leader has a powerful psyon working for him–"

"We might have to go through a few of those hot spots, but we won't take any chances," Aunt Sleak said. "No risky deals, Jan. This all might be a big game to you, but these players are in earnest. The Corps play for keeps. I don't want a hothead like you blowing our cover. I'll shoot you myself before I let that happen. Copy?"

Jan's eyes went wide. "Got it," he said.

"And Naero, I want you to stay close to me and follow my lead, got that? No more running off on your own, either. That headstrong crap didn't work for your mother, and it will get you killed too. You follow orders. Whatever I say."

"I will."

Naero stroke the Nytex on her hips.

"This Kexxian Data Matrix is too important to our people," Aunt Sleak said. "If the Corps get it, in a few decades they'll be able to take us out. I can't emphasize this enough. We have to keep it from them, at all costs—even our own lives."

"We're not stupid," Gallan said. "I think we understand that, Captain."

"You'd better. We'll remain here just long enough for Intel to conduct whatever tests and bio-scans on Jan and Naero that they need to. After that, we'll head out. You'll all undergo intense training in weapons and espionage with Intel each day.

"Sleep when you can. You'll need it."

31

Spacer Intel began an intense battery of tests and full bioscans on Naero and Jan, starting that night when they slept, in the lab, and for eight to ten hours each day thereafter.

When they left the lab each morning, Spacer Intel ran them ragged with training, until they staggered back to the lab to get hooked up again for the next night.

The testing only occasionally got painful. Headaches were common.

But usually the tests lapsed into in long, drawn-out periods where they needed to lie completely still—for hours. At times the medteks strapped them down to keep them from moving.

An entire platoon of over forty Intel specialists, including five Cumi of various ages, pored, and prodded, and picked over them.

It bothered Naero the most that the Intel people were incredibly tight-lipped and wouldn't tell her or Jan very much. They barely whispered to each other around them, and went off into adjoining rooms for heated arguments and debates.

On more than one occasion, they evacuated the lab in organized panic, terrified at some potential defensive reaction from the Kexxian Matrix itself.

Even when she checked with Om, neither she nor he could figure out what was going on.

Naero recalled the vids of the so called "Kexxian Plague" on Tora-3.

What other defenses did the Kexxian Matrix have? The Intel teks spoke about the data in hushed tones only a few times, like it was some living, breathing thing that might possess multiple intellects and a will of its own.

Om was just one case in point to Naero's mind. She wasn't sure that she should still keep him secret.

Intel fled the lab in such a hurry once that she and Jan were left behind, still secured and strapped down in their modified medbeds.

Naero constantly spotted the Spacer Intel Chief–the one her aunt called Klyne. Tall, late forties, short, sandy brown hair, piercing black eyes. Klyne moved like a fighter. She had yet to speak with him directly, but he kept watch over everything on board *The Alamo* it seemed.

What info Jan and she did get often came to them secondhand from Aunt Sleak, and Naero wasn't even sure that their aunt told them everything.

They endured this madness for over a week, and still it dragged on.

During that same period, Naero's delusions gave her four extra delusional arms that waved around, trying to break through and grasp and handle things. It became very distracting.

By the end of the week, thankfully, the extra limbs with a mind of their own went away.

Then the following morning, Naero woke up with about a dozen illusionary tentacles or tendrils of some kind, this time protruding from her back.

Like having a squid emerging from her torso.

How wonderful.

Naero did her best to ignore them, thankful time and time again that no one else could sense her private madness.

She shuddered to think sometimes what would happen if Om did break free, and actually used some of the Kexxian Data Matrix's defensive capabilities.

From what Om told her, they were—in fact—nearly without limits. Naero spent a lot of time arguing with him about not hurting or destroying her and her friends in his zeal to protect their secrets.

For the others, all of them except Ellis sharpened their weapons training in the Intel War Rooms. The heavily shielded battle training facilities allowed them to practice live fire with most of the small arms available throughout the Corps and the known systems.

The array of weapons—dizzying.

To everyone's surprise, Tarim quickly took to the instruction and rapidly became an amazing marksman, although at first he was better with pistols than rifles.

Naero watched him as he advanced, nailing target after target, dead on—some at extreme, simulated ranges of three and four kilometers with advanced targeting optics.

"Impressive," she told him. "Tarim, you're a natural sharpshooter."

"Thanks. But I still have trouble with combat shooting. If I can take my time in a low stress situation, I almost never miss. Yet in combat simulation, I still get too excited, and my hit ratio drops way down."

Naero hugged him. "You're a hard worker. You'll get better."

He blushed and beamed at her approval.

He came off the firing line the next day with a near perfect combat score.

He ran in to tell Naero and Gallan where they cleaned and serviced their weapons from that day.

"Finally, I found something I can do right," he said. "I'm improving every day, according to the Intel instructors."

Naero patted him on the back. "Congrats, Tarim. They say with continued training, they could make a sniper out of you. Could you handle that?"

"I think so. There's so many things I'd like to do, guys."

"Have you found a particular field you'd like to pursue?" Gallan asked. They knew the lander studied hard to find his way.

"I like geology and archeology a lot. I think I might study them once this is all over. I have to thank you and your people for all these blessings, guys. It would have never been possible for me to learn any of this stuff, trapped where I was."

"You'll do well," Naero said.

Slowly but surely, Tarim was making the transition from slave to real person—even a budding warrior and intellectual.

Naero put her weapons back onto the return cart and checked them in. Tarim finished with his. She helped him put them away.

"C'mon," Gallan said. "We're late for practice with the powered armor simulators and unit shield devices. Walk over with us, Tarim. We'll catch up with Jan and the others."

Tarim seemed very pleased to be with them. Too eager to be around Naero. His gaze followed her everywhere with an intense look of longing.

They were friends and comrades now, but not anything else, at least in Naero's mind.

Gallan was right. Tarim had it pretty bad for her. And that made it tough. She didn't want to hurt him.

She needed to find the right time and the right way to settle the romance issue with him once and for all.

She just wasn't sure how to do it yet.

While Ellis remained a completely different problem on the other end of the spectrum.

She needed to get past that, too. *And* deal with Om's growing intellect and curiosity, *and* the Kexxian Data Matrix, *and* their escape, and the Corps.

Haisha...sometimes she felt certain her head was going to explode.

But part of her still rebelled and didn't want to do anything but go somewhere and goof off.

She knew that wasn't right.

Their armor and shielding session ended. Naero started back toward her quarters, soaked with sweat and exhausted, for a relaxing mist shower and some badly needed alone time.

Is your battle training over? Most interesting. Can we talk now?

An intense groan escaped her; Naero hung her head. Om was pretty good about being quiet for long periods of time when they were needed, but the dam had to break sooner or later.

Just let me get back to my quarters, Om. Then we can chat.

I think I'm close to understanding why I am cut off from our defensive functions and abilities.

Oh, that's...great Om.

With Om glued to her mind, she was never quite alone. Although he couldn't read her mind entirely, or take control of her body. At least, not yet.

Perhaps she should tell someone about Om before anything dicey happened. But who? Who could she go to?

Naero rubbed her palms down the sides of her hips and outer thighs to relax, relishing the comforting texture of Nytex.

She wore her togs everywhere outside of the lab–to practice and even to bed now, at times.

After her abduction ordeals, she felt strangely naked and vulnerable out of Nytex. As if someone had peeled her skin off her like a Garendian purple bananya.

Jan agreed with her. They also remained constantly ravenous and daydreamed about food. Their lab torment and the new training schedules kept them hungry.

At lunch, Naero and Jan usually got the chance to speak privately with Aunt Sleak about the tests and their situation for a few minutes.

At the end of that week, Aunt Sleak presented them with new handcomps and the special wristcoms Intel privately warned them about.

Naero shuddered a little, locking the new wristcom on. Jan put his on, seeming not to care.

"So what's the holdup?" Naero said. "Why don't they just collect the info off me and Jan and wipe it? Then it's Intel's problem, and not ours anymore. At least, not for a while."

Aunt Sleak shook her head. "It's all more complex than you two could possibly imagine, Naero. Intel has brought in their finest minds. But the Kexx were a highly advanced civilization, far beyond our current capabilities."

"Baeven said we had all the clues now to figure it out," Naero said. "We turned all the data and equipment specs over to Intel, just like he told us."

"We're still starting on the bottom steps of a huge flight of stairs," Aunt Sleak said. "The Kexx knew what they were doing; we don't. They used this tek for millions of years. We're just discovering it. It's only been a few days. You need to be patient."

"We are," Jan almost shouted.

Naero put a hand on his arm; then he took a breath. "But it's tough when they won't tell us anything," he said.

"Let me assure you, they've made good progress this week," Aunt Sleak told them. "They've bypassed most of the Matrix's security, and are dealing with the core data itself. But to compound the problem, it appears that half of the data matrix is imprinted on your DNA, Naero. The other half on Jan's. An added layer of protection and complexity from your parents no doubt. You can thank them for that."

Naero sighed and shook her head. "I can see how that could affect the deciphering."

"You got that right," Aunt Sleak said. "Each half by itself is almost completely useless. They've broken it down enough to discover that clear fact. They've managed to record both halves in bulk, but the complex security and encryption could take centuries to break down and then match up with the correct pieces from the other part."

"Like trying to perfectly re-assemble two halves of a mountain of glass," Jan noted, "with both halves blasted to bits."

"So, you're saying Jan and I are stuck with this stuff inside us for a while? This is a nightmare."

"Afraid so. With the sequencing, it's easier to break off matching chunks, align their algorithms and parameters like two halves of the most intricate puzzle you can imagine–then decipher them as a whole. They're also searching for some kind of index which they say is vital to coordinating the alignment of the pieces. That way they can best select which sections to upload and match together first."

"And they still need us for all that?" Jan said.

"Not entirely, but when the teks make a mistake, defensive layered sub-routines within the Kexxian Matrix self-destroy key sections of the partitions. Our teks are going crazy trying to comprehend the glimpses of what they've seen in the Kexxian Matrix so far. Even crazier at what they might have already lost. Each day, they make fresh copies from you two, and make fewer and fewer mistakes. Like starting over and over again."

"Then take DNA samples," Jan said. "Take all they want–bone marrow's usually a good choice. Tell them to take what they need and wipe this stuff out of us. I don't want to be trapped in a lab or on the run for the rest of my life."

Jan impressed Naero. He must have done his homework. Bio-genetics weren't usually his strong suit.

"No one wants to get the two of you out of here and somewhere secure more than Intel," Aunt Sleak added. "But the Tek side of all this craziness still grows exponentially more complex each second. To make matters even worse, there's also a dead switch on the Kexxian Data Matrix. Either of you die, and poof! The Matrix dissolves, completely destroyed in an instant. It doesn't stay viable outside of your bodies or without the other half. Not even bio-gen samples. Even those transplanted into cloned regenerative tissues activate the switch and destroy the Matrix, the instant they get removed from the original. Intel has tried everything. It's maddening."

"But like you said, they do have several bulk data copies they've made from us directly, right?" Jan asked.

"Right, but every time they make a mistake, they have to start over from the beginning," Aunt Sleak said. "Five of the eight copies are already riddled with mistakes and errors. Entire sections self-deleted with no way to retrieve them. To decode this much material through trial and error might take decades, even centuries, and by then the info obtained may or may not be so useful."

"Like you said," Naero added, "the Kexx knew what they were doing. So, after all of this is said and done, if we make it somewhere safe, how do they wipe this stuff off us?"

Aunt Sleak paused. "They're not sure of that yet. The principles are there. Your parents and their contacts among the Cumi explorers obviously figured it all out with time. The proof is clear. They were able to write the Matrix onto your DNA.

"Certain other Cumi might be able to duplicate this feat with the help of Intel's resources and learn how to reverse the process. Erasing it from you both is possible, but only once they've unlocked its secrets. Intel is attempting to contact more Cumi without attracting further Corps suspicion. But for now, I think you're going to be stuck on your medbeds for a while, who knows how long."

"Screw that," Jan said. "What about the creature that put this on us?"

"Killed, along with your parents' expedition."

Naero gritted her teeth until she could almost taste dust.

She wanted to scream.

"I can't believe Mom and Dad stuck this stuff on us," she said.

"I can," Jan said. "Think of the profits. Think about what it will mean to our people?"

"Yeah," Naero said. "If we live that long."

The call came through for them to return to their training. All three of them jumped up and left the mess hall.

Intel did not tolerate being kept waiting.

32

Later that evening, Nacro used her nightly free time to visit Ellis and Tarim.

It had been a while since she'd spent hours parked before her education screens, studying lifeforms, galactic history, or drooling over new ships.

That all seemed so childish and long ago to her now. Yet parts of her still yearned for those times.

More and more, recently, she chose to spend more time with her friends, especially Ellis.

Both Tarim and Ellis had the run of their deck and plenty to do, but only Ellis had to be followed everywhere by two Spacer Intel guards after he left his quarters.

Like the two rough-looking goons stationed outside his door panel when she arrived.

He had his door set to open when she buzzed.

She walked in. It snapped shut behind her.

"Hey N, nice wristcom. Intel give you that?" Ellis noticed everything.

She noticed everything too, like him sweating from a workout.

Completely naked.

Haisha, what was with this guy? Was he a nudist or something?

"So, what does the new gadget do?" he asked.

Naero caught herself staring at him for just an instant too long.

"What, oh this?"

He grabbed his pants and stepped into them. "Sorry, N. I thought Spacers weren't bothered by the human body."

"Bothered? Not me."

Bothered? No. More than slightly aroused?

Yes. Ellis was becoming quite the problem.

In many ways, with her still being a virgin and all, Naero's growing intense curiosity continued to get the better of her.

"Prance around in the buff all you want. I don't care."

Ellis smiled. "I'll pass. I don't even think Spacers are ready for that."

Thankfully, he continued to lighten up and act more human with each passing day. He and Tarim continued to get along better. Ellis had his moments. She wondered about the clone issue.

She still couldn't see them partnering a ship together, but she might steal a kiss from him. Someday

"So, what does it do?"

His words brought her back out of la-la-land.

"What?"

"The new gadget?"

"Well, this wristcom and handcomp is the latest thing. Versatile, fashionable, and among other things–your basic suicide device."

Now Ellis did a double take. "Say again?"

"If someone captures me or attempts to retrieve the Kexxian Data Matrix, or to remove this device, it blows up. Sort of a small neutron detonator."

"You agreed to wear that?"

"Well, I would be killed instantly." She snapped her fingers.

Even Ellis blinked and started slightly.

"Just like that," she said. "A bright flash, and poof! No more me. No more Kexxian Data Matrix. Jan wears one just like mine."

"No wonder you Spacers always beat us," he said, shaking his head. "You people are more insane than we are."

She zeroed a finger in on him, ignoring her flailing imaginary tendrils. "And don't you forget it, pal."

"Naero, have you ever wondered that, just maybe, there might be people out there who would be happy if the Kexxian Matrix never existed? Maybe even people among Spacer Intel? Then everything could go back to normal. Ever think of that?"

Naero paled. The Matayan's cold logic blindsided her.

"No, I guess you didn't," he said. "I hope they can't set that thing off remotely."

"Uhh..."

"But hey, don't worry. They're on your side."

"Yeah, right. Sure they are."

"So, can you at least tell me where we're going when we bust out of here?"

She shook her head. "I can only tell you that we're leaving soon. I'm afraid you might be with us for a while longer, Your Highness."

Ellis just shook his head.

"First, you know too much, Your Highness. And second, if we cut you loose somewhere too soon, our enemies might be able to track us down."

He turned his back on her and struck the wall with both fists.

"I promise, Ellis. Once we're safely out of Corps Space–"

"What? That could take months! My people need me, Naero. With what I know now, I could–"

"Could what, Ellis? Prince or not, you were given up as a hostage to our mutual enemies. They weren't expecting to get you back. I want to ask you something important. Can you handle it? This could get pretty rough."

"What are you hinting at? I'm a Prince of the Matayans. I can deal with anything."

Naero raised her eyebrows. "During the auction, the Matayan Emperor–"

"My grandfather."

Naero nodded. "As part of his conditions, he demanded your return."

"Why does that surprise you? I'm an heir to the throne. Of course he would demand my safe return."

Naero licked her lips. "But he referred to you as his grandson's clone. Are you a clone Ellis? What does that mean among Matayans?"

Ellis laughed. "My dead father was the firstborn clone of my grandfather, just as his brothers were, although all of the direct modified royal clones, my uncles, died in the wars. Each generation is genetically modified and improved over the last. Any aberrations are culled and destroyed, or kept brain dead on life-support for spare parts.

"Of course I'm a clone. All the heirs are. Our scientists take no chances with diluting or infecting the royal bloodline. I am Ellis-X, firstborn of my advanced generation; the direct heir after my father. I have three surviving younger brothers very similar to me, one slightly shorter. Two others were assassinated."

"Then why did they give you to Kattryll?"

Ellis bowed his head. "My grandfather, the Emperor assured me that I would not be harmed, but merely held as a political prisoner for a short time, as part of his overall strategy to raise our people back up to greatness. He told me sacrifices needed to be made. I accepted–willingly–at first. But now I fear that Nellis II, the next in line, conspired to supplant me. For years he has moved against me, playing up to our grandfather. The two of them are the same–brutal and ruthless."

Ellis rubbed his eyes and looked away. "I knew I was forsaken, from the moment Kattryll stunned me that very first time. I knew my own family, the royal family, had sold me out."

Ellis gasped and looked up.

"But what happens to me is not important. Even now, my people rush headlong into ruin. And I cannot do anything to save them."

"The lives of my people are also at stake here, Ellis. What if there were something you could do?"

He whirled about and glared at her. "Girl, my grandfather, our illustrious Emperor just attempted a major power play to seize the Kexxian Data Matrix for our people. He failed. Do you know what the Corps are going to do to my people when they have the chance? They'll make an example out of us."

Naero ignored the "girl" comment; that was just Ellis.

"At least, thanks to me, you're still alive, Ellis. If I was with your people I'd be floating dead in space by now...*after* I serviced the crew of some battleship for a few days or worse, am I right?"

Ellis wouldn't meet her gaze. He knew she was dead on.

"We know very well what happens to Spacers captured by Matayan corsairs, right Ellis? No mercy. Not for kids, old people, or any filthy spack–am I right?"

Ellis reddened further. "I don't agree with such policies, not even during wartime. I would change them if I could. I'm trying very hard not to see you and your people that way any longer, Naero. As enemies."

"Oh, so you did see us that way before?"

He glared at her. "What do you expect from me? Change does not occur overnight; even your people have said this. Your aunt looks at me with murder in her heart. You were our most bitter enemies. We made total war on each other."

"Correction. Your people made total war on mine; mine did not do so on yours."

"What do you want me to say?" Ellis asked. "You crushed us militarily, over and over again. We hated your kind. You cost us our freedom. We're Corps slaves now because of–"

"Because of Matayan pride, greed, and stubborn folly. You tried to destroy my people, and we beat you."

Ellis turned away from her, arms crossed in front of himself–fuming.

"Yeah, I thought so," Naero told him.

He whirled back around, stabbing an accusing finger at her. "You don't understand us any better than we understand you."

She stepped around in front of him, looking him right in the eye.

"The Corps already planned to absorb your people. That's what they do. Nothing would have prevented that. Your only chance would have been to switch your alliance from them to us, and Matayan pride would never allow that. Would it?''

"Shut up."

"If you haven't noticed, I don't take orders from you, Prince Ellis. Yes, we decimated your military; thank goodness we did."

She pointed a finger right back at him. "But we never went after your civilians like you did ours. We took prisoners and then released them once the war ended. How many Spacer prisoners did the Matayans release? None. Because they never took any."

Ellis turned his back on her, shaking with with rage. He took a few steps, threw his hands up, and screamed. Then he rounded on her.

Naero stood ready for an attack.

Then she saw the tears in his eyes.

"What you say is true. I am sorry for it. My people committed...many horrible atrocities against yours. We hate you. But we hate you most because you are free, and we...we are not."

He sat down heavily on his bunk and covered his face with both hands.

"There. Satisfied? You've broken the pride of the proud Matayan jerk. Now I'm nothing but an escaped, renegade hostage, and my people are doomed. They cast me off to that pig Kattryll, all to ensure the continued cooperation of my people. The Court even tried to have me killed by poison in my food and drink, to avoid the shame of my torment–my own family. There is no hope for us. The Matayan race will be no more."

Naero felt a lump in her own throat.

"So, go ahead and gloat, Naero Maeris. You've helped destroy my people. When the Corps come after yours, may you do better."

Naero knelt down and placed her left hand over his.

He looked up in wonder

She rose up further and mated her lips to his.

At first, her hot intense kiss shocked him.

An instant later he responded in kind.

Her passion pushed them both down onto the floor.

He smelled and tasted of citrus and spice.

Scents and delicious tastes up close and overpowering.

They boiled together in each other's arms. Their scorching tongues wrestling playfully. Her hands moved over his flesh.

Every part of him hard and supple, moist with sweat. Skin cool to the touch. Yet wherever her fingertips lingered, touching him generated searing heat.

His hands went to her face. Hard calloused hands, but they caressed her with astonishingly, desperate tenderness.

Ellis lined every contour of her face. He feathered her high cheeks and arching eyebrows. He played gently over her soft ears, like an artist sculpting them.

He eagerly buried his fingers in her dark hair. Then he pulled her hot wet mouth closer and deeper to his own. Still their lips did not part.

They gasped for breath from the sides of their mouths.

One of his hands slid down her back to her narrow waist and pulled her body closer to his own where she shivered and snaked against him.

They twisted from being side by side to her lying on top of him in his arms.

She stretched like a feline against him, generating even more impossible heat where their bodies worked together. She caught her breath slightly, enjoying the luxury of his hands on her body.

They slid up from her waist, caressing her sides. Up her ribs.

The door panel suddenly slid open.

There stood Jan and Tarim, along with the two Intel guards.

Jan laughed.

Tarim met her eyes for an instant. Then he turned pale as a corpse and walked away.

"Sorry, sib. We didn't think Ellis was, uh...busy. Just let me know when you're...done?"

Jan sounded genuinely surprised, neither amused, nor angry. Yet.

Naero jumped up. "Jan, come back here."

Despite her attraction to Ellis, embarrassment came easy. She wasn't used to sensual passion. It felt too much like something she couldn't control.

Was that the real problem? Was that why she couldn't take a lover? She needed too much control?

Jan looked back at her.

Oh, he was amused, all right.

A shit-eating weasel-smile was plastered all over his sickening face.

"Look, it's not what you think," she said.

"I'm certainly not the one to judge, sib."

"You got that right, Jan–the guy who'll chase anything with a–"

"Whoa, whoa," Ellis demanded. "What do you mean it's not what he thinks?"

"No, I mean, it is what you think. Both of you. It's obvious. There's this attraction thing between Ellis and I. And don't you look so pleased with yourself, Jan. So he's a Matayan. So what?"

"Hey, sib. You don't have to explain anything to me..."

He walked away.

"...but Aunt Sleak and the clan elders? Hoo-hoo! They might have something to say about it."

He laughed again.

Naero's face flushed hot.

She glanced at Ellis, but he simply smiled and shrugged. He held out his arms to her. "Life is always difficult."

Naero rolled her eyes. "Oh, please."

"You might practice by explaining it all to Tarim," Jan said, glancing back. He shook his head and clucked his tongue. "Poor kid. You'll probably find him locked in his room, heartbroken and sulking, most likely."

She covered her mouth and gasped slightly. "Damn the stars...Tarim. I forgot. I have to go explain things to him."

Ellis looked somewhat oblivious. "I don't understand. What is there to explain?"

"I'll tell you later."

"Good," he said with a rakish smile. He grinned from ear to ear and leaned back on one elbow.

"I'll be waiting."

"I bet you will."

Perhaps longer than he thought.

Now that the spell of the moment was broken, she wasn't entirely convinced it would be the best choice to try to return to their little overheated moment. Perhaps she had been saved from making an even bigger mistake.

Naero raced through the deck of the ship to find Tarim, hoping she knew what she was getting herself into with her idiotic personal choices.

She tried to figure out what and how to say it to Tarim.

Again, why did Ellis have to be Matayan? She winced painfully at Tarim having to see them together like that.

33

Naero reminded herself that they still hid inside an old Spacer battleship at the bottom of the Memosan ocean, deep in enemy territory.

It grew harder to recall that sometimes. Making her way through the decks to Tarim's quarters took a while, and he had a head start.

Along the way, because of Naero's eye for ships, she couldn't help noting various elements concerning the old ship's design and construction.

Obsolete, triple-hull construction from the old days before advanced shielding and better armor choices. Bulky panel boxes and com nodes that did not sink into more advanced nanowalls or nanofloors. Less streamlining and simplification. Semi-active tronics that made odd noises on their own, for no apparent reason. Garish, colorful displays and control panels.

The Alamo was named after some obscure, ancient skirmish back on Old Terra centuries ago.

Naero made a mental note to take time to upload the history when possible, but Intel made certain they had little free time.

Some nights she couldn't resist roving the decks of the big hulk, even if it did cut into her sleep.

Exploring *The Alamo* was like touring a museum piece.

Aunt Sleak told her that once, half a century or more in the past, such warships had been the pride of the Spacer Fleets. Two decades after that, *The Alamo* fought at the heart of the Fourth Spacer War.

Battered and partially gutted, she went down with her transports on Memosa-3 to effect repairs. By the time her teks refitted her for active duty, the battles swept past her and the wars ebbed. She performed interdiction and escort duty near the system until hostilities ceased completely.

Spacer Intel left her behind, mothballed beneath the ocean, joining the ranks of the Shadow Fleets.

Picking her way through the old ship also gave Naero time to think about how she needed to handle both Ellis and Tarim.

Intel's preparations usually kept her and Ellis apart–perhaps intentionally. Maybe her aunt had something to do with that.

Conflicted didn't begin to describe her feelings for Ellis.

With Tarim, she wanted to be honest. She knew he had feelings for her that she could never return in kind. Yet she liked and even admired him, and didn't want to hurt him needlessly

She reached his door panel and buzzed. It slid open and closed behind her after she stepped in.

Tarim did not to look at her directly from where he sat moping on his bunk, his face ashen and set, visible even in his darkened room.

With his dark blue eyes and his black hair growing out, he actually looked pretty good, especially after months of training and proper diet had added some much needed muscle back onto his lanky frame. But for her, the spark of attraction simply wasn't there, like it obviously was for Ellis.

"Naero, don't try to explain anything," Tarim said to her softly. "I know how these things work. The more you try to explain things, the worse I'll feel about them."

"That's not good enough, Tarim. They're going to send us out soon on an escape run. We have to be able to count on each other."

"I know that." He kept his voice down with hers.

"We're friends, Tarim. More than that. We're crew now. And crew work things out. Up until now I didn't say anything because I didn't want to hurt you. I ended up hurting you anyway."

"Fine. Are you done?"

"Not hardly. We need to talk this out once and for all."

He looked pretty angry and upset, but at last he nodded. "Okay. I guess a lot of it's my fault too. I just know talking won't change anything."

"Tarim, I want to be friends. I like you."

He sat straight up and glared at her. "For a lander. Go ahead. Say it. I know I'm some kind of joke to your kind. Nobody says anything, but I know you all think you're better than me."

He chuckled sadly to himself. "The worst part is, you all are."

Naero leaned back against the cool interior of the old hull. The surface wasn't self-regulating like more modern ships.

"Tarim, I don't care if you're a lander. We are who and what we are. But if you hate yourself, nothing anyone says or does is going to make a difference. I know life has beaten you down, but you need to find a way to get past all of that on your own. Everyone among my people, with few exceptions, will do everything they can to help you find your way. Take advantage of that."

"Believe me, I am. But I'll never be good enough for you, will I?"

Haisha. Men were idiots. Dealing with them–exasperating.

"Tarim...have I ever given you any sign that I want to be anything more than friends with you?"

He blinked. "Well...no. You haven't."

"Thank you. I'm sorry you had to see me and Ellis...together like that. I like him, he's–"

"A jerk. Even though he's been friendlier to me lately, he's still a jerk."

"Sometimes people are attracted to jerks. Some people might think I'm a jerk. I'm working on him."

Tarim sighed and shook his head, staring down at his clasped hands. "I'm no warrior, not like Ellis, not like your people. You've trained all of your lives to be fighters. It's in your blood. While I've just been a worker, a slave."

He paused and looked up at the small open view screen on his cabin wall. Then his gaze flipped back to to meet hers. "But I can't change the way I feel when I look at you, N."

Naero glanced away from him for a moment, feeling her own eyes go tight.

"You honor me, Tarim. But I have to be honest with you, even if it hurts. Can you handle the truth?"

He waved both hands helplessly in the air. "Sure, go ahead. I can pretty much guess what you're going to say. Spacers respect strength, and force of will. Ellis has all that. Hell, he's a Matayan prince for God's sake. He's been trained, and pampered, and educated and conditioned all his life. He's handsome. Girls probably fall all over him. While I'm just a skinny lander slave who doesn't know his butt from a bucket. Tell me how close I am?"

"I was going to say, that for whatever reasons, I am attracted to Ellis. And I'm sorry, but I'm not attracted to you in the same way, or to the same degree."

"I don't see you pasting yourself to me like you did to Ellis."

"I'm as prone to the randomness of physical attraction as anyone," she said.

"Uh-huh."

"It's not like I'm going to run off and settle down with Ellis somewhere cozy and spawn a dozen kids. I want to do things with my life. I want to get out of this mess; I want my own ship. The biggest thing Spacers value is freedom, to live in space, not bound to anyone or anything."

He glared up at her with his arms crossed in front of him. "So you'll just screw Ellis for a while?"

She resisted grinning. "If I choose to, yeah. But I wouldn't be so crude about it. People can love each other for a while sometimes. It doesn't always have to be forever."

"It should be, Naero."

"I don't know who or what I want right now. I'm nineteen. I'm young and curious, just like you, and I've got a lot to learn. I want to get out there and live my life. I suggest you do the same. Don't worry about me. Worry about yourself."

"Fine."

"Grow up, Tarim. Find someone who is attracted to you. You'll never force anyone to love you."

He swung at her.

Naero barely pulled back, almost completely surprised.

His knuckle just barely grazed the tip of her nose.

She instinctively fell back toward the door in a defensive stance.

Om woke up.

Is Tarim attacking you? I thought he was your friend? Should I prepare to disintegrate him? Advise.

No, Om. He's just hurt, confused, and angry. Don't hurt him; in any case, you can't.

I am working ceaselessly on finding a way to be able to defend us. I will solve this problem.

You do that. But leave my friends and family alone. The girl he's crushing on is telling him she just wants to be friends. That's hard on anyone.

I do not understand interpersonal relations. So chaotic and complex. So many personalities and variables.

I know you don't, Om. Leave it to me.

Yeah, she was an expert, all right. Look at the mess she was making of things.

Tarim sat back down on his bunk and sulked while she hesitated.

He wiped his eyes. "I...I know you can beat the crap out me with your eyes closed, Naero. I'm sorry. You're right. But it hurts so bad to face the truth and hear it from you. I have so much to work on still."

"Do things for yourself first, Tarim. Become who and what you want to be. Not for me or anyone else. Spacers teach their kids that it's difficult for others to love and respect them if they don't love and respect themselves."

He looked up at her. "When you're an 'associate,' no one treats you like anything but dirt. We take it out on ourselves and everyone around us. Pretty self-destructive, huh?"

"Slavery does that to people. We were all that way once. That's why Spacers hate it so much. We'll die before we let the Corps, or anyone, or anything enslave us again, and we'll take as many of them down with us when we go."

"A lot of landers wish they were Spacers, Naero. We're jealous of you people–your arrogance, your technology, your skill and intelligence. But mostly, we're jealous of your liberty."

"Tarim, you're not a helpless, frightened slave boy any longer. You're a free young man. You're learning and growing every day, learning to defend yourself, your freedom, and your rights. Even I'm amazed at your shooting prowess."

He clenched and unclenched his fists. "I'm so frustrated, Naero. I want everything; it can't happen fast enough. I wish I were...a Spacer."

"You don't have to be a Spacer," she said. "Just be Tarim. That will be enough."

Naero went forward again, knelt down, and put her hands over his.

"You're with us, Tarim. You're free. Right here. Right now. We've accepted you among us, and whatever happens, we won't let you go back to being a slave. You've got a choice in that too. Keep striving and studying the way you have been, and you'll make something of yourself.

You will meet people everywhere who will be proud to know you. And it won't matter if you are a Spacer or not."

"Yeah." He looked her straight in the eye, sad resignation written all over him. "I want all that, but it still won't put your lips to mine in passion, will it?"

She drew back slightly. "N-no. I can't say it will."

He held his head up and nodded, staring off into space. "Well, I guess I'll have to live with that, too. At least you didn't leave me dangling. I appreciate your honesty, even if it does rip my guts out."

He laughed a little.

"Hey," Naero said, showing him a sad smile of her own. "What are friends for?" She turned to go.

"Naero, I'm going to keep praying for you. Be careful."

"My middle name."

"No, it's not," he said. "Not you."

She went out and left him behind in the dark. Her com buzzed.

Aunt Sleak requested an impromptu sparring session with her, pronto, in one of the training rooms.

*

"Suit up," Aunt Sleak said, already in her sparring gear.

Naero looked around in the big training room. They were all alone. She put her pads on. "What's this all about Aunt Sleak? I'm off duty."

"Just get those pads on, spacechild."

A tone in her voice made Naero's blood glacier and crystalize. Aunt Sleak had that affect on people, just from the intensity of her voice.

Aunt Sleak turned and met Naero's eye straight on.

Her sudden glare. Withering. She already *knew* about Ellis.

Naero wished suddenly she could split out of her form like an Ichikan mimic and assume a new shape or identity. Intel always had surveillance on Ellis. The two guards. The little tryst on the floor hadn't gone unnoticed. It was foolish to think it would.

That brief glare told Naero all she needed to know. She was really in for it now. Nothing she could do but take her lumps.

Naero got a few blows in before she went down. That didn't matter.

Aunt Sleak overwhelmed her defenses and threw her to the ground. Hard. Suddenly it was a bit like fighting Baeven. She knew her aunt had been holding back in the past, but she had no idea how much.

Naero rolled to her feet, buffeted by low kicks as she crouched.

Their precision and speed pummeled her, and knocked her back into the wall.

Training with Baeven turned out to be good for something. At least he taught her how to take a beat down

"What in the hell were you thinking?" Aunt Sleak finally screamed at her. "I don't care how good-looking he is. He's a Matayan. One of their princes. This is not going to happen. The two of you will never be left alone again."

After getting beat up, Naero's own temper flared. She spread her arms wide in denial. "So he's a Matayan. So what? What's the big deal? You sound as bigoted as they are. He's not all that bad. Did you ever think that with all this talk of new alliances, he might be able to help our side and his own people at the same time? They've got their backs against the wall. They're desperate."

"His people kill our people, Naero—every chance they get. They killed your parents and everyone with them. And we've killed plenty of Matayans in retaliation. We are enemies. Blood enemies."

"And when will that change? Never? We have a platinum opportunity to reverse that. Can't anyone see that? His people need help."

"They won't find any from us. This isn't about diplomacy, and you know it." Naero tried to rise. Aunt Sleak rammed her back onto the mat with a heavy foot.

"You want to learn about sex, spacechild? Well that's just great. Pick one of the crew. Take that lander boy for a spin. Go hire someone at one of our stops to throck your world. Knock yourself out. But stay away from that Matayan bastard. Before you screw the sons of your family's slayers...I'll kill you myself. You got that?"

Naero glared back. "Got it."

"Good."

A big, athletic Intel self-defense instructor stepped in, ready to spar.

Aunt Sleak let Naero up and motioned to the Intel instructor. "Continue this session. Push her hard."

She didn't even look back, adding, "You've really disappointed me, Naero. I thought you were smarter than this."

Naero took her stance, her bleeding lips tight.

As far as she was concerned, that instructor was in serious trouble.

34

"Take your stations, then." Aunt Sleak turned and met Naero's eye the next morning as their Intel training continued

Naero smiled back.

After laying low to drive Triax insane, very soon they would make good their escape from Corps Space under the cover of their new merchant freighter.

For intents and purposes, *The Rio Lobo* was just a standard, 400 ton freighter out of Arnett Corps Space. The escape team transferred all of their basic gear to their new quarters, and continued to work and train on their new home, hidden in one of *The Alamo's* huge cargo bays.

They left behind anything that might give them away.

Each member of the escape crew also swallowed a temporary Intel programmable implant that remained inside them, identifying them as genetically standard humans to all Corps scans and sensor checks, even at the genetic level.

No one would be able to tell they were Spacers; their covers, solid. And the IDs could still be changed if needed.

Their itinerary would take them several days to eventually reach Hadar-1, close to a far corner of Triaxian and Joshua Tech Space. Close to, but not yet within, the worlds of the mining revolts.

The only restrictions Intel placed on them insisted that Tarim and Ellis could not leave the ship at any destination unless accompanied by an Intel handler.

Naero and Jan also had to remain under heavy guard at all times, but everyone would more or less do their jobs and function as normal crew to avoid suspicion. The Intel agent who helped train them, Irith, was assigned to them both as a body guard.

Naero liked Irith, even though the quiet agent was almost thirty, and very tall. But she had black hair and violet eyes like Naero, and they pretended to be sisters as part of their cover.

She never had a real sister before.

Today, Irith and Aunt Sleak ran the backup checks on their jump drive.

Naero finally got relieved from her post at the navigation console and slipped away.

The Intel Chief Klyne gave them their final instructions.

"The escape plan is simple and straightforward. Play your roles. Remember your parts. Stick to the plan. We've been running this ship for three years now along the same route. Its various trade stops are firmly established with the authorities and accepted as routine. There's some room for deviation, but not much.

"We do this right, and we make it safely into Joshua Tech Space easy. That's the plan. Any last-minute questions?"

Naero tried not to nod off. Intel was nothing if not thorough in their rigorous training. On top of her aunt's tender love.

After running through the plan multiple times from almost every angle for days on end, Naero had few questions.

They launched that evening.

By all reports on INS, Triax and the other nearby Corps had gone berserk looking for terrorists, rebels, anarchists, alien infiltrators, renegade psyons–anything to justify the additional strong-arm police-state tactics they unleashed on their systems.

The fact that Naero and Jan vanished off everybody's scans by hiding out in *The Alamo* had many convinced that they had already made good their escape, with the help of *The Shadow Fleets*.

A equally dumpy, old Triaxian cruiser boarded *The Rio Lobo* upon their scheduled approach to Hadar-1.

The first test of their new cover.

The Corps Marines knew Klyne under another alias, but checked and scanned everything and everyone according to SOP.

Luckily, the Intel people did their homework well. Their cover held up airtight.

"You're clear, Dutch," the Triaxian Marine lieutenant told Klyne. "Everything checks out, just like your manifest says. You got those creds you owe me on the fights?"

"Next time," Klyne said with an easy laugh. "I'm a little short now, but you know I'm good for it. We can go about our business?"

"Yeah, stick to your route. Watch out for mining ships, though. Don't trade with them, don't dock with them. Even if they're in distress. Triax gives you permission to let them cook off if you have to."

"What's going on?" Klyne asked.

"Check the local system news monitors. Miner revolts are spreading across several systems in this direction. Nothing we can't handle, though. They've got a powerful psyon helping them, but we'll either blast or starve them all out in the end. That's how we usually get it done."

"I see," Klyne said. "How dreadful."

Naero resisted the urge to glance at Jan, expecting to find him drooling over potential high-risk profits.

Naero looked for Tarim, overwhelming compassion for the miners and their families washing over her. She couldn't spot him.

The Triaxian duty officer rambled on. "To be safe at the starports, stay out of the local areas and any place frequented by miners. They're desperate for weapons and ships. No one's safe. Wear psycaps if you have them or can buy them. If you see anything suspicious, anyone tries to mind control you, contact the authorities and let us check it out. We have psy-detection units and routine patrols throughout this entire region."

"Will do."

Luckily, all of their weapons and other nefarious gear were temporally displaced so as not to show up under any normal scans. The temporal pockets were just one of a number of high-tek advantages that Spacer Intel had over the Corps. The only problem with the pockets was that you could not hide anything alive in them. It even killed plants and single-celled organisms.

Tests had been made, unsuccessfully, with live animals. The data collectors on the test subjects survived, recording an excruciating death as the space-time dimensional anomaly broke them down and tore them apart.

Maintaining a technological edge over the Corps would continue to spell the difference between life and death for her people.

The Kexxian Data Matrix could not be allowed to fall into the hands of their enemies.

Naero glanced at the deathband on her wrist.

Could she really use it to blow herself up if need be?

Haisha.

She shuddered, sensing a flurry of muted objections from Om. She'd told him to remain silent during the boarding, just in case.

The Corps boarding party returned to their warship.

The Rio Lobo continued on its way.

"Get it in gear; to your stations," Klyne called out. "Proceed to Hadar-1. Request landing instructions."

Naero scanned Hadar-1. Fifty-percent land mass. A white, red, green, and blue world, mineral rich. A slight cloud cover obscured the south pole due to vulcanism.

Lots of mining interests. No signs that the revolts had openly exploded there yet.

Klyne piloted. Aunt Sleak co-piloted. They took the ship in.

Naero manned her sensor array station. Nothing but the naval patrol ship receding, a few traders around the planet, and a couple of old satellite networks.

"We have some limited contacts with the rebel miners," Klyne told Aunt Sleak. "If things go badly, they might be able to help us in a pinch. Yet their backs are against the wall. They're very wary, but desperate for allies."

Aunt Sleak nodded. "Let's follow up on that quietly if we can. We need all the intel we can get."

The Rio Lobo settled down into the starport docking bay.

What a clunker. Sturdy. Reliable. But still a clunker by any stretch of the imagination.

And Naero couldn't ever afford a clunker like it.

The auto-landing sequence brought all drives to a full stop.

Naero sprang out of her gelchair before anyone else.

Back in her cramped quarters, she reviewed a holo of the planet in her room for any curious details. Hadar-1. A near-earthlike, terraformed to be somewhat more pleasant–if that was even the correct term. Even with huge continents and barely fifty-percent oceans, most of the northern and southern hemispheres lay locked in the grip of ice age glaciers.

In the habitable zone around the equator, it got up to only fifteen degrees Celsius in the summer. Twenty or more might be considered hot. Normally five or ten degrees in the morning or at night.

Fun.

The Hadar system did possess a wide variety of rich mineral deposits, hence Triax's primary interest.

It remained a relatively young system, and together with its equally rich asteroid belts, it had yet to be strip-mined out. Even with modern equipment, Corps miners went there by the multitudes on freeze ships to slave for Triax and scratch out a meager existence for themselves and their families.

They had little choice in the matter.

Production demands, profit-sharing restrictions, and safety code violations eventually led to a grinding process of misery and death.

Surprise.

As long as the Corps overclass thrived, their military remained dominant, and the struggling middle class were kept more or less happy and distracted, the other sixty percent of Corps society could simply go straight to hell and wallow there in abject misery.

Triax. The worst and the oldest of the Corps, had no reason to improve things. Their systems produced an abundant supply of desperate, expendable workers.

To Naero, the miners looked royally sodomized.

By local time it reached morning where they were headed, the sky still dark.

35

Naero went to the loading docks to help ship out their cargo.

Put everything else in the back of her mind. Focus on the mission.

In and out and move on.

She, Gallan, Tarim, Ellis, and an Irith took a large order of sensor gear, heavy machine parts, and medical supplies to a high-level Triaxian mining manager. She didn't look forward to that, but at least it would get them out of the ship for a while.

Where were the rest of her Clan, her fleet, her friends? She tried to stay focused and not fret, but Spacers and Triax teetered on the brink of open war.

Triax could still blast Fleet Maeris out of existence for no reason. They might do so out of spite.

In their space, they made the rules and broke them when they felt like it.

Naero popped their bright orange, obsolete gravhauler up out of the docks and vectored an approach to their destination: what looked to be a massive mining fortress nestled within a vast, shattered mountain range at the outskirts of the starport.

She scanned other transports and a few local patrol craft flitting around, but the sky remained relatively clear.

A big blue Cumi space barge lurched skyward from the mining station. It lumbered up out of the atmosphere–probably loaded with ore and precious raw materials. Their bulbous bulk vessels always looked clownish and comical to her, but she had long since learned that the ancient Cumi were aggressive explorers, opportunistic traders, and profiteers in their own right.

The mining station functioned much like a secondary starport on its own–actually larger than many regular merchanting starports, due to the huge orelifters that came and went on a regular basis. Mining survey and collection teams returned and set out on their own regular schedules, both onworld and off.

"Freight-hauler *Lobo-3F*, you are clear on approach," Station Control cut in. "Defensive shield window opening per these coordinates."

Gallan uploaded them.

They adjusted their approach, the shield window opening highlighted on Naero's piloting display in violet. "Thank you, Station Control," she said. "We're coming in on approach."

"Use loading bay 8-7-8-Gamma, *Lobo*. You're in the pipe."

They came in low over a wide swath of squatter towns that miners and their families had erected out of Triax's trash. Even while focused on piloting, Naero easily spotted the signs of past transport crashes, gouged right through the kilometers of settlement huts, tents, and lean-to's.

A huge, yawning waste pit lay just beyond the camps, sprinkled with dead bodies tossed in around the rim–hundreds of corpses. Burn teams were busy at one section, using plasma cutters to incinerate some of the carcasses right along with the refuse.

To Triax, people were just garbage. She could only imagine the stench down at ground level.

They flew through the thick gray and black belching smoke, as if descending right down into one of the Nine Hells.

At the energized gates of the facility itself, waves of people threw themselves against the stunfields only to collapse and be dragged off or trampled by those behind them.

Naero checked her spotting cameras, revealing a rippling sea of human, near-human, and alien slaves: Besh, Ramor, Silesians, Zotchans, dwarflike Piettos, avian Quess and Moh-Karran, catlike Mndar, leopard-spotted Mahri, even a few Naivatch, wrapped only in rags against the frigid winds.

The protestors threw rocks. They chanted. They rushed the gates. They carried banners painted on planks, on blankets, on strips of cloth. Naero looked at their sea of angry, crazed, and desperate faces.

She struggled not to weep with rage.

She couldn't look back, but she heard Tarim sigh and clear his throat several times.

Landing sirens went off. *Lobo-3F* approached. Most of the miners drew back. Those that didn't or couldn't were staggered, driven off, or sluiced away to drown in the rushing spew from high-pressure mining water cannons and the flash floods they produced.

Naero shut the cameras off.

She couldn't watch the sea of human and alien misery anymore.

They docked in the assigned cargo bay. Irith remained at the controls while Naero, Tarim, Ellis, and Gallan unloaded their shipment with the old-fashioned lifters.

Naero noticed Ejjai guards, close-up–brutal hyena-like humanoids.

She'd studied their vicious society and behavior a bit more after seeing the one on Drianne's yacht.

Reports claimed them to be one of the most avaricious and opportunistic species in the known universe.

Right. Next to humans.

Only the low numbers of Ejjai and their lack of tek kept them from becoming a threat to the other races.

That might change one day, if enough of them got off somewhere on their own, or they obtained enough ships and teks.

Until then, the Corps found Ejjai useful in a variety of nasty roles: bodyguards, mercenaries, assassins, bounty-hunters, torturers. And, of course, guards at prisons, mines, and other facilities.

They worked for carrion. Anything that was meat, fresh or rancid. But they especially prized devouring the young of any species, even their own. Alive if possible.

About four dozen Ejjai guards drove and directed hundreds of slaves before them throughout the dock area with shock batons. That docking bay was just one of many throughout the complex.

Battered slaves, ragged people in torn miner coveralls with control collars, gritted their teeth and silently performed various tasks. If they remained idle too long or tried to say anything, the collars glowed and sent them writhing on the ground in pain.

Naero looked on as one of the Ejjai walked over to a convulsing woman. Suddenly the collar stopped glowing and the woman went still, denoting either coma or death.

The Ejjai guard beat and kicked her until the woman awoke and struggled weakly, trying to rise.

When she couldn't, the guard split her head wide open.

Naero noticed Tarim's hand go to his holstered side arm. The look on his face. Furious.

Naero pulled his hand away and held it, cautioning him with her eyes. They couldn't do anything. Especially not in their situation.

As if that weren't bad enough, three Ejjai, cannibals even among their own kind, got down on all fours and began to devour the woman's corpse.

First they scooped up steaming brains in the cold air with both clawed hands, crunching through the shards of skull with their powerful teeth.

Then they snapped and ripped open the torso to get at the hot entrails. Fighting and working gobbling jaws, nuzzling deep into the warm gore that smoked with tendrils of heat vapor up into the cold air.

One stopped and snarled up at Naero and her friends.

"You got a problem, skinners? You like to watch? Maybe you want some, heh?"

Then the Ejjai laughed, a horrid odd wheezing, giggling sound.

Naero remained expressionless. She glanced up at Gallan and the others. Gallan looked back.

Now it was her hand that strayed absently to her own hidden blaster.

Gallan, Ellis, and Tarim blocked them further from anyone's sight.

"Let it go this time," Tarim said. "You were right to stop me. Now I'm stopping you."

"Tarim's right," Gallan said. "We can't get involved."

"Naero," Ellis whispered, "don't do or say anything. You know we can't afford any trouble."

Naero let out a deep breath of her own, and nodded.

They kept walking.

More Ejjai snarled and snapped at them as they walked over to the supervisor's station with their manifest chip.

Close-up, most Ejjai stood short–most of them stocky, muscular females, of course. A few smaller males, but in subordinate roles–of course. Ejjai remained militantly matriarchal. Only dominant females and their favorites could breed. Not many male Ejjai were needed for that. Most male Ejjai got devoured at birth.

At the station Naero felt the heat pouring out from the open counter. A tall, lanky human female pecked at a handcomp. The Station Manager, surrounded by eight huge Sterodan bodyguards.

Corps Sterodans, fighters and gladiators pumped up on genetic muscle enhancers. Anywhere from two to three meters tall. Enormous torsos, arms, and necks rippling with muscles that made their heads look puny. Their reek was horrible.

Sterodans weren't particularly cunning or fast, but they were incredibly strong. Strength that even Naero feared.

Naero's father had referred to them as "pukk-heads" from his fighting days: a Spacer term referring to a nasty boil or infection. Rumor held that Sterodans were so stupid because they had very little brains left, just pus-like pukk in their skulls.

Then the supervisor's throat bag swelled.

Naero corrected her assessment to the Station Manager being a Silesian female, arguably the most annoying of all sentient, near-human humanoids.

"You there, dummy," the supervisor shouted. "Stop your fucking staring and give me your fucking manifest chip. We don't have time for fucking sightseers."

One of the Sterodans held out a gigantic, passive hand.

Naero ignored him and tossed the manifest chip onto the Station Manager's desk in front of her.

The supervisor glared at Naero and snarled. "You stinking, little gash. Dump your fucking load and get your stinking, fucked-up crew off of my dock. Your ship is on report."

Another freight shuttle settled down to the left of theirs.

"Are you finished?" Naero shouted back, not intimidated in the least. Silesians were masters of intimidation, and only respected the same in kind. "You listen to me, you putrid heap of rotting filth. Me and my crew came here to finish our deal. I don't want any grief from you, or your freaks and goons."

"Is that so?" the Station Manager responded with a smile. She hurled the chip back at Naero. Naero caught it.

"Lucky for you this all checks out. Now listen up, runt, because I'm only gonna say this once. Get your draining holes out of my sight. And if you don't like it, you and your boss can suck the shit out of my ass." The Silesian burst out laughing until she choked. "Hah-hah. I love using that one. It just makes my day."

249

Naero laughed with her. She and her friends backed away.

"That's a good one. I'm gonna have to remember it," Naero said.

The crew from the other transport began to unload.

A twinge raced through Naero.

Her old intuition, like before Om awoke in her mind.

Had that been him all along, trying to warn her?

Naero, I'm sensing a large number of military grade weapons nearby.

She scanned the area.

A Joshua Tech transport that just landed didn't seem to hold any cargo.

Just packed with miners.

All of them heavily armed.

36

"What the hell?" the Silesian manager yelled. She pointed at Nacro and her crew, caught right in the middle. "It's an attack. They're in on it. Blast them all!"

The miners charged forward, screaming.

Naero and her friends scrambled to reach their craft in the confusion, but quickly found themselves cut off.

"Hold it," the apparent, rebel leader's voice boomed through a voice amplifier. "Nobody move!"

Everyone moved.

Weapons barked and pulsed.

An intense firefight erupted.

The alpha female of the Ejjai sprang through the air at Naero and her people.

She shot Gallan in the back point-blank.

Ellis and Tarim tried to defend him and got swatted to either side.

The slug opened up a ragged flesh wound in Gallan's side.

He swept up with a kick, knocking the slug-pistol from the Ejjai's hands, flinging her into the rushing mob.

Gallan grunted in pain and went down.

The outer energy barrier protecting the mining compound collapsed across its entire length.

The rebels swept most of the battle toward the objective of the manager's station.

Naero rolled free and came up fighting, blaster pistol in one hand, battle blade in the other.

The Station Manager backed up behind the Ejjai and her Sterodans, pale and frantic, shrieking into her com, her throatbag quivering in terror.

"They've broken through across all sectors. Send gunships. Troops. Cut them all down. Just get me the fuck out of here!"

An Ejjai fell back on top of the Silesian, its legs blasted off by an explosive round to the groin.

The manager pushed the dying creature off her and scrambled for its weapon.

Miners swept over her, beating her senseless.

Naero had a moment's respite in the chaos.

She checked Gallan. Ellis and Tarim tended the wound. With treatment, he might survive.

Then another Ejjai sprang at her.

The alpha female rose up from a knot of bodies and slew its way toward their position to get at them again. It scooped up a fallen pulse rifle, murder burning in its eyes.

Naero activated her concealed gravwing and flew over her friends. She fired a pulse blast right into the bared teeth of the foremost Ejjai. The back of the creature's head exploded into pink shards and brain vapor.

She wheeled in the air, booted the corpse aside, and met the charge of the prime female. It sprang up to bring her down.

With the added weight, they spun toward the ground and slammed into the crowd. A stray stun blast hit Naero's gun hand, knocking her pistol away.

She kicked the Alpha Ejjai square in the jaw, breaking its charge. She shattered half of the creature's teeth with a rocking impact, snapping its thick neck back.

Naero grabbed the hot bore of the Ejjai's pulse rifle with her gloved hand, slashed the creature's other claw around the pistol grip and trigger.

The flesh of her own hand sizzled, scorched badly. Yet she wrenched the rifle away and flung it off to one side.

The Alpha Ejjai roared in pain and body-blocked her. One claw grazed her arm and ribs.

They separated into fighting stances.

The Ejjai drew a short stabbing sword and a punch dagger. Naero drew another battle blade. She snapped the extended spike handle open to make it into a short stabbing spear.

They charged again.

"Going to gut you," the alpha snarled.

Naero ducked a vicious angle cut from the short sword.

"Going to eat your heart and liver while you're still screaming!"

Naero slashed her snout, then jabbed the spear into her lungs.

"I don't think so," Naero said. This creature would kill her friends, just like the slave woman she saw murdered.

She couldn't allow that.

The alpha Ejjai staggered back, then attacked again.

Both stood their ground, fighting close in.

Slices, cuts, and stabs pelted her. Naero blocked and parried and gave back better.

Now she understood the Ejjai rep for toughness.

For several moments she fought the alpha toe-to-toe, dealing serious and deadly blows and wounds that would have dropped most other opponents.

The Ejjai grunted and bled, but kept at her.

Naero slipped her battle blade under the alpha's ribs. Knifed deep into the creature's lungs and finally its heart. The Ejjai gasped and vomited blood, still ripping at her.

Naero flipped them up into the air and dragged her foe down, ramming her short spear through one eye and into the brain.

At last the alpha female went limp, reduced to a mutilated pile of steaming meat.

Naero looked up and saw several more Ejjai leaping toward them.

Shots rang out behind her, rapid-fire.

Well-placed hits nailed the first six Ejjai, snapping them down with careful precision.

A tsunami of rebel bodies and concentrated fire swept away the rest.

Rebels had the Station Manager completely stunned and trussed up by then.

Naero rushed back to her friends.

"Good shootin', Tarim. How's Gallan doing?"

Tarim shook his head, slinging his collapsible scoped carbine over his back. "Not so good. He needs more help than we can give him. I think there's internal bleeding."

What she wouldn't give for a medbed.

No chance of that here.

"Come on, guys. We have to get him back on the transport and try to get out of here. Don't attract any attention."

Together they dragged Gallan back toward their transport.

"Irith," she said quietly over her com. "Open the loading doors just enough for us to get in. We've got Gallan, but he's hurt."

No one paid much attention to them yet.

"I see you," Irith said. "I've alerted the ship. Signal as soon as you're secure, and I'll blast us out of here."

"Hurry, load up as much as you can," a commanding voice shouted nearby.

She looked over at a short, nondescript man of medium build, perhaps in his late thirties. He wore the emitter, broadcasting his reverberating voice all over the area. He wore his receding black hair plastered to his skull as if oiled. His skin had a reddish tint to it.

"The gunships will be on us shortly," he announced calmly. He pointed in the direction of *Lobo-3F*.

"Commandeer that craft and any others. Load up. Keep families together if possible. Tell the rest of our people to scatter into the wilds where others will attempt to pick them up or hide them. We'll blast a way through the defenses on our way out."

Naero suddenly realized that the craft the rebels rushed to commandeer was hers.

Haisha. This could not be happening.

"Hey you," she shouted at the rebel leader.

In an instant, more than forty guns were trained on her.

The rebel leader and his small motley entourage came toward her and her friends.

No way they could sneak back into their ship now.

The man had fierce gray eyes, hard as steel, but a soft fleshy red face that made him look almost childlike. But his nose curved like a hawk's beak. He resembled a predator.

"That's my craft," Naero said. "My friend's injured. He needs help back up on our ship."

The leader turned away from her, glancing at the dozens of dead and wounded lying about from that brief battle alone.

Then he looked back at her.

"Trader, I need that craft to save as many of my people as I can. Triaxian gunships will soon strafe this entire area, killing anything that remains. We cannot take them all; we don't have enough ships as it is. I am sorry for you and your friend."

He turned back to his people. "Take their vehicle. Leave them and their cargo behind unharmed."

He strode forward a few steps more, and then turned back to her.

"Wait. I saw your duel with that Ejjai alpha. Very impressive. My compliments, young lady. I've never seen anyone fight like that in years. Your style of combat. I've seen it somewhere before."

He actually bowed to her.

"My friend's badly hurt," Naero said. "Please. Help us."

Naero's flesh tingled like it might catch fire.

Warnings buzzed in her mind.

A Cosmic power approaches.

Om, what are you–

The mob of fighters parted. Something glowed among their ranks.

Some of the warriors even knelt and bowed their heads in reverence.

A small female miner girl of about fifteen emerged and walked right up to the rebel leader.

She did so, as if she'd been invisible before and now appeared among them suddenly.

The girl's eyes began to glow.

Ah, the rogue psyon Triax warned everyone about.

The girl leaned over and whispered to the rebel leader, but Naero still picked it up with her acute hearing.

The girl pointed back at Naero.

"This one is very, very special, father. She could help us and our people, but we cannot hinder her for long. She has destinies all her own, even more important than ours. Encourage her to journey with us for a time. I wish to get to know her and her friends–especially the young dark-haired boy. He is one of us."

The leader turned to Naero once more. "I will aid you and your friend, if you will agree to pilot your craft to a destination of our choosing. Keep any supplies on board that might help us. Dump the rest. You can save us many precious minutes overriding your security codes. Tell the authorities we forced you to do these things. When we are safely away, we will release you, unharmed."

In the distance, the high-pitched whine of approaching gunships grew in intensity.

Naero looked down at Gallan, then back up at the leader. "I agree to your terms."

She glanced at the girl, who smiled a deep, knowing look back at her, through eerie eyes that somehow seemed ancient.

The leader's bodyguards lifted Gallan up and loaded him into the cargo hold of the transport. Refugees packed themselves in where the useless sensor cargo had been shoved out.

The rebels sent the rest of the refugees away, fleeing from the camp and into caves and the rocky wilds.

Naero signaled to Irith over her com.

"You get all that? We're going to travel with these folks for a while."

The Intel agent had monitored the situation the entire time.

"We can't do much else. Get up here. Bogeys coming in hot."

Back in the cockpit, Naero jumped into the co-pilot's chair and hurried to launch the craft. The other vessels had already lifted off.

The leader and the girl joined them in the cockpit, along with a few guards, making for tight quarters.

"We can't outrun those gunships," Irith said. "They're too close, and they already have long-range locks on us. We're dangerously overloaded."

Naero glanced at the leader.

"If you don't have some backup, this is suicide," she said.

The leader strapped himself in behind Irith and helped with the attitude adjustments for the extra weight. "Just get us up and out of here, pilots. I'll tell you where to go. Skim the tree lines and mountain tops."

"Several of them just fired!" Naero said. "Incoming missiles. We have no way to stop them."

"They'll be stopped," the leader said with a smile. He didn't bother looking over at his daughter.

The girl closed her glowing eyes to concentrate. "None of them will reach us, or do any harm."

Irith flew. Naero helped stabilize, watching the scanners in amazement.

One by one, each missile barrage either exploded or dropped out of the sky, well short of them.

The gunships swept in at maximum attack speed.

A strange energy field enveloped the four fleeing craft full of rebels.

The readings on Naero's sensors went wild.

Some weird kind of electromagnetic force.

Any gunship that came within four kilometers of them lost all power and dropped out of the sky. Their crews screamed over the comlinks.

But the same force at work caught them before they smashed into the trees and rocks, and set them down safely.

One remaining gunship broke off, unaffected, returning to the mining facility to strafe the grounds.

The girl suddenly collapsed, toppling sideways out of her seat.

Tarim caught her, gasping as he suddenly stared into her veiled blue eyes, cradling her in his arms.

The girl reached up with a slender hand and touched his face. Tarim shuddered. He gasped for breath once more and smiled back at her, completely enthralled.

She laughed softly and seemed to regain a portion of her strength

Was she an empath? Did she somehow use Tarim to recharge her energies, or was she actually flirting with him?

"Father," she said, "my talents are spent for the moment. I have done all that I can. The rest is up to you and our new friends."

Tarim held her hand in his for a moment, then folded it back over her. She leaned into him, resting her head on his chest and nestling in as if she had known him for years.

"You have done enough, daughter," the rebel leader said. "Rest now. We will have much need of your abilities later, I am certain."

He looked Tarim over. "This miner boy is acceptable to you?" he asked her.

"Very much so, father. I knew from the moment I sensed his presence. This one will never harm me. Not on purpose, at least."

The leader nodded, smiled sadly, and turned away.

The young girl continued to stare into Tarim's brown eyes until her strength left her. "If only you could see what I see in him. Then you would know."

She started to drift off again.

"Hold me while I rest," she whispered to Tarim. "Your touch helps me somehow, in ways even I cannot understand."

Tarim finally found his voice. "It's all right. Rest all you want. I'll protect you."

Naero stared at them, her mouth gaping.

Major points for Tarim.

Dozens of new questions and problems arose.

Irith snapped at her. "Stay with me, co-pilot. This is tight flying."

"Sorry. I'm with you." She focused all of her attention on maintaining their heading, skimming the surface. And not slamming into mountains.

The leader studied their efforts and smiled. "You've kept your word. Good. I would have hated to shoot you all."

"We wouldn't have enjoyed that either," Irith said flatly.

"Where are we headed?" Naero asked.

"I'll input the coordinates. More pursuit will come, but they won't find us now. We'll be here for a few days until the others can be collected and brought to bulk ships by our people in the wilds. You will need to be our guests until then, I'm afraid."

"Of course," Naero said. "Under the circumstances, I understand."

The leader looked at her. "Do you?"

He stared off into the brightening sky. "I find that surprising. I don't understand very much anymore. Now we are hunted animals. We only do what we can, what we must to survive and help our people."

And just like that, they were stuck right in the middle of the miner revolt.

Naero shook her head and muttered. "As if I needed another blasted mess to wind up in."

She adjusted to the course the leader gave her, and squeezed every drop of speed out of the old bucket that she could manage.

37

Naero and her crew took refuge with the rebels inside a vast network of gigantic, pockmarked blue-green caves near the high sea cliffs.

Gallan rested securely in the miner's makeshift field hospital. Ellis volunteered to stay with him.

As one might imagine, Tarim and his new girl went everywhere together, completely smitten with one another.

Good for them. Tarim held his head high for once.

Naero and Irith kept themselves busy tending to those who needed them most. There were plenty of wounded and sick to tend to after the raid.

At first the rebel miners showed an expected level of distrust. But then as Naero and Irith progressed from person to person with their medical skills, using up their supplies in medkit after medkit, attitudes among the miners softened.

One of the leader's guards, wearing a red headband, came up to Naero and adhered some sticky patches to both shoulders of her jacket and on the back. He did the same thing to Tarim. The patches bore strange miner symbols that she couldn't read.

There wasn't any time to scan them into her comp for translation.

The bodyguard saluted and left her without any further explanation.

Yet when other miners spotted those patches, most of them wept. Others repeatedly thanked her. Some tried to kiss her hands, her feet.

They crowded around her. It was all she could do to keep going about her duties.

"No, please. Stop," she said. "Thank you, but let me through. I can still help these others. Let me through. Let me help them. Can't you understand?"

A female Besh medic came along with several orderlies and moved the wounded and the sick back away from her. Most Besh, like this woman, had gray-green skin tones, black-green hair, and small ears.

"Thanks," Naero said.

The medic would have been very pretty, except for a nose that had been badly broken, many times over. She also carried terrible scars from wounds and burns on her arms and legs, visible through her ragged clothing.

"You're doing good work here," the medic said. "Are you a doctor or a healer among your people?"

"No. I just have some training."

"That must be some training. Let's talk over some chow. We can learn a lot from you two. But what we really need are supplies. We're desperate."

"Let's take a walk back to my transport," Naero said. She nodded her head to Irith, who nodded back.

"What's in your ship?" the Besh asked.

"Your leader left the rest of our cargo intact. Didn't even ask what we had in our holds."

"What were you carrying?"

Naero flung the doors to the smaller inner holds open wide.

"Medical supplies and equipment bound for Triax. They won't miss them. Distribute them all among your ships and your people."

The medic gasped and hugged her. "This is…wonderful! I don't know what to say."

"'Thanks is all right. We'll give you what medical files we have also, and if our small armory gets cleaned out, that's okay, too. I'm sorry we can't do more."

"No, this is great. Give me a moment while I organize all this."

The medic called teams over on her old radio to unload the medical supplies.

"My name's Arana."

Naero took her hand and used her cover name. "I'm Nari."

"Nari, you've more than earned some chow with us. Don't expect anything spectacular. Just stew, but it's filling."

"Stew sounds great. I am hungry. But can you explain something to me?"

"If I can."

Naero pointed to the scarlet patches put on her jacket.

"What do these say? Your people keep acting so grateful to me when they spot them."

"Oh, that's understandable. Those patches mark you to be an avenger. A great honor among the warriors and our people. You slew an Ejjai alpha, in single combat, no less. Not many could do that. They say many witnessed the act."

"I'm sorry. I still don't get it."

"Nari. Our peoples have many reasons to despise the Ejjai overseers and guards. Many."

The veins at the side of the medic's neck pulsed. The muscles in her face strained.

"Be gracious. It is a sign of great honor and respect. Many of these people have never been able to strike back at their tormentors."

She waved a hand back at the heaps of dead outside the field hospital. Stacked up in piles for burial. Corpses of all ages. "Many will never get the chance."

"Suddenly I don't feel very hungry," Naero said.

Arana put an arm around her. "That's the wrong attitude. We have to keep up our strength. Come. A bowl of stew as promised, and then it's back to work. Tell me about your medical training."

The stew tasted thin, bland, and slightly burned, but Naero ate it graciously.

Each of them only had about half a bowl due to rationing. While she and Arana talked, she kept to her cover story.

Naero noted the thousands of hungry faces huddle in the dank caves who had already had theirs for the day, and did not ask for more.

Some who saw her patches offered her their rations.

Naero declined, forcing tears back.

"That was good," she said at last.

Arana rested a hand on her shoulder and then moved on. "There's still so much to do. More coming in all the time. In a few days, we'll make a run for it and you'll be let go."

Naero nodded.

"Let's get back to work and spell your friends and some of the other medics before the chow runs out," Arana said. "They'll be ready for a break."

Several hours later, there was still so much to do. The medical supplies helped immensely, but the medics were clearly overwhelmed by the immense task at hand.

Naero did all that she could, deploring the conditions Triax had put these people in. But there were limits even to her skills.

On top of that, exhaustion staggered her. She'd hardly slept for nearly two days, and fatigue finally won out, even for a Spacer.

When the next shift of medics took over, Arana came along and brought them both to a quiet rest spot in a separate cave where those off duty could grab some sleep.

Naero mumbled her thanks, feeling a filthy, scratchy blanket gently settle over her.

She curled up and pulled it around her.

A small soft touch awoke her sometime later. A touch charged with energy.

Naero opened her eyes and sat up.

The leader's psyon daughter knelt there in the darkness beside her, softly glowing blue-white.

Her azure eyes shined like bottomless, glittering stars.

"Did you rest well, spacechild?"

Naero nodded, staring at her.

"Good. You needed to. Come with me. My father wishes words with you."

"Who are you? Where's Tarim?"

"I am Shalaen. Tarim is resting with your friends. Will you come?"

"Of course." Naero rose.

They picked their way quietly through the sleeping, the healing, and those still in the process of dying.

"Shalaen..." Naero whispered. "What are you? I'm very curious."

The girl didn't even glance back. "You are curious about me? How very strange. I have no idea what you are, and yet you want to know what I am?"

"You're a natural psyon at the very least, and an extremely powerful one at that for one so young."

"Telepathy is one of my talents, but only with surface thoughts. It is too exhausting to attempt to read anything deeper. But you and the Corps are wrong. I am not a psyon. I have had my awareness and my powers as they are from the moment I was conceived. Psyon powers do not develop until after puberty."

Shalaen went quiet for a while.

They passed several squads of heavily armed guards without challenge and went down a protected corridor hewn right through the rock. More guards, some of them in battered, mismatched suits of salvaged power armor, stood at attention to either side every ten meters. All of them wore red headbands.

Shalaen finally stopped in an open section and leaned back against the glass-smooth wall. Huge mining plasma borers made walls like that, fused them right together.

Finally, Shalaen stared up at Naero, her large blue-white eyes gleaming in the shadowlight. "I often ask myself what I am. It can almost lead to endless introspection if I do not desist at some point." Shalaen intrigued Naero, almost as much as the many questions she had about herself.

"My father, who you have met, is human," Shalaen said. "A simple man from Ramor, sentenced unjustly to a life in the mines. My mother, on the other hand, came from the Yattai. Do you know of them?"

Naero had heard the term, but it took a moment to remember. "Our Mystics know of them. Interdimensional beings from the Astral and Ethereal Planes. They can take forms of pure energy to go about wherever and however they choose throughout several dimensions. Some call them spirits, angels, demons. Even gods."

Shalaen look right through her. "And yet our abilities do not even begin to approach what lies deep within you, Naero. Until you can learn to use them."

"I don't understand."

Shalaen shrugged. "Neither do I." She went forward again. Naero followed at her side.

"The Yattai have been called many things," Shalaen said. "At various times, many of those observations may have been correct. The Yattai are among the oldest remaining sentient entities in the universe who can still take and sustain physical forms. Even the Oden are not as advanced."

"The who?"

"Another advanced race. If you ever study the Secrets with your Mystics, as I'm guessing you shall, you will meet some of them one day."

"If you say so."

"My mother's chosen name was Jarluaena. I possess many of her memories and much of her knowledge and power. The Yattai are foremost explorers, but my mother chose a different path. The rise and fall cycles of the younger races in the universe grew precious to her.

"She expended much of her abilities to become human for a time. She felt strongly that the Yattai had gone too long without one of their number recalling what it was like to be young, and much more mortal than they. She especially liked humans and their capacity for love. Their capacities for hatred, greed, and violence also shocked and attracted her. Humanoids have so many ranges of extremes."

"Why did she choose to be a miner? Wasn't that stretching things a bit much?"

Shalaen stared at Naero in silence for a moment. "You ask most absorbing questions. I like you." She cupped both hands over her temples for a brief instant.

"Jarluaena did not desire to become a miner. She devised a way to be born mortal, a simple child of two ordinary Ramorans, but with the knowledge and memories of her former existence as a Yattai. Her parents, whom she adored, were later slain during one of the local unrests."

"Unrests? You mean wars?" Naero said.

"Yes, but there are and will be conflicts much larger in scale and scope than those yet to come."

Naero sighed. "I suppose you're right." The galaxy rushed headlong toward another Spacer War.

"She'd known my father since they were children together, and loved him," Shalaen continued. "It was as if they'd always loved one another. They married amid the upheavals around them. Somehow they found happiness. Then, while she was pregnant with me, my father's political enemies framed him. They named him a traitor to the Ramorian people, when his accusers were in fact the real traitors.

"They sentenced him to life in the Triaxian mines–a virtual death sentence. My mother chose to go with him into exile and imprisonment, rather than be parted from him. He begged her to stay behind, find another mate. She would not listen.

"Once subjected to the very real horrors of the mines, they could not believe the way the Corps treated the miners and their families. The open atrocities, abuse, privation, and summary execution were a harsh education. They helped organize the mining revolt. With the remnants of her discarded powers, my mother managed to keep them alive, despite many attempts to eliminate them."

They approached a small shielded and well-lit area deep in the bedrock. Shalaen stopped in the hallway. "My father does not like it when I tell this part of the story–about my mother's death. Let me speak of it out here, before we go in with him."

"I can understand," Naero said.

"My mother's powers lapsed at the critical time of my birth. Some of them failed or vanished completely, only to reappear later in me. Others were weakened, and not as effective. Some vital part of her abilities poured out of her like water, and into me. But one thing became clear to her: She became trapped in her chosen form. When it died, so would she, and all her knowledge. She would never rejoin the Yattai as she had originally planned."

"That must have been terrible."

"Her grief at such a sundering was very great indeed, even as her joy at my birth. She could no longer contact the other Yattai for aid.

"She made her peace with her choice. My sentience existed even in her womb. She shared much of her fading knowledge with me. I spoke as soon as I emerged, and my abilities increased as I grew rapidly. How old do you say I am?"

"Oh, maybe fifteen or sixteen standard years."

Shalaen lowered her gaze. "I am three. When I was a year old, the revolt began in a small, isolated region, and then spread across several systems over time. Triax's reaction increased with the revolt, becoming swift, massive...astonishingly brutal. The miners were no match for the advanced Corps military. Still they resisted. What more could they do?

"When they came for my father, we fled, in the few ships left to us. When escape looked impossible, my mother remained behind and held them off. An entire fleet. She held them off, for four days. She gave us time to flee and continue the struggle the best we could. Through me, she would always be with us somehow. I remember my father holding me in his arms and weeping when we fled. She waved back at us, smiling on the viewscreen of her crippled ship, even as the battleships poured volley after volley of fire at her.

"They tried to capture her. They wanted to understand her power, use it if they could, but she would not surrender. In the end, they wore her down and destroyed her. Even her powers had limits, as do mine." Shalaen stared through her again.

"Your powers frighten me, Naero. Because I see no limit to them. I find that extremely dangerous."

Naero shook her head. "But whatever you see in me, they don't do me any good, because I can't use them. You know how to use yours," Naero said. She waved her arms around her in desperation. "Why don't you help all of these people of yours more? They could use a few miracles. Why can't you heal them? Feed them?"

"Trust me, I fully understand your frustration and share it," Shalaen said. "But the gift of healing that was my mother's did not pass to me. I cannot heal, only protect. Neither can I change inanimate matter into food or water or medical supplies. In many ways my powers grew even stronger, but they are also more limited than those of my mother. Yet somehow we have survived–for how much longer I cannot say. We need to flee this world. We've taken on as many refugees as we can carry. We hate to leave the others behind under these conditions; it is a betrayal that breaks our hearts, but escape will be difficult as it is."

"I know some people," Naero said. "Friends of mine who might help you."

"Shalaen," her father called out. "Bring the spacechild in here. Don't keep whispering to her in the hallway."

"Yes, father," she said. They strode into the shielded area, into the light. Into a base station cobbled together, easily set up and taken down.

266

38

The rebel leader sat there alone, surrounded by rigged console stations, gathering and looking at information as it flashed by.

He rose up and walked over to them calmly, both hands outstretched in Ramorian fashion to show he held no weapons. Naero smiled. Most greeting customs started that way.

Naero took both of his ruddy hands for a moment and felt the strength in his arms and hands. What else might she expect from a miner? She studied his plain face and thought he looked impossibly weary.

"I hope Shalaen hasn't bothered you," he said.

"Not in the least. We find each other very intriguing."

"I have the misfortune of being Nevano Kinmal, leader of the mining revolt, by default. No one else really wants the job." He laughed, but Naero could sense the pain in it.

"You know I'm a Spacer. I'm fleeing from the Corps, also." No matter what lies the Corps media spread about her and Spacers, she would never be ashamed of her family's name...or her own.

She lifted her head high.

"I am Naero Amashin Maeris, of Clan Maeris."

Nevano grinned. "The renegade Spacer terrorist? Glad to meet you. I'm a genocidal maniac myself; I guess there's enough bad press from INS to go around for both of us. Triax has an even larger bounty on your head than mine currently, but from what Shalaen has told me about you, the Corps must be shivering in their shit."

That alarmed her a little. Did he know about the Kexxian Data Matrix?

"What has she told you? I'd like to know." She concealed her anxiety, suddenly wondering what she could and could not hide from Shalaen.

Nevano Kinmal waved her to a chair. "Come, let us sit down and talk. Two interstellar menaces to decent civilization such as we should take time to relax."

She did so. Naero looked at Shalaen once more, standing impassively beside her father.

"I don't want you to worry," Nevano said, "but Shalaen has in fact told me about the half of the Kexxian Data Matrix that you carry, imprinted on your genetic code."

Naero held her breath for a second, then she shrugged. "So, now you know why the Corps want me so badly."

"Indeed," Nevano said. "But such secrets are of little use to me and my people, unless they can conjure up additional ships and weapons for us, or get us past naval blockades."

"Sorry," Naero said. "My people have yet to decipher them. We can't even use the data. Do either of you know anything more about it or the Kexx that could help us?"

Shalaen said, "The Kexx were ancient even when the Yattai were young."

"Then you know why my people can't let their tek secrets fall into Corps hands." She looked directly at Shalaen. "What else do you know about it?"

"More than you might think," Nevano said. "I know what the Kexxian Matrix is, and what is in it. While she was studying you, Shalaen made a record of the full index that is hidden in your half, for those who know how and where to look."

He handed her a data crystal. Naero gaped.

"Of course your half is useless without the other half that your brother carries," Shalaen said. "But when all of the data is decrypted, this index will help your people decode and utilize the Kexxian Matrix much faster and easier."

"Consider it a gift," Nevano said. "We only ask a few favors in return."

"Name them," Naero said. "I'm sure that my people will be very grateful."

"In a very short while, we will be negotiating final terms with Joshua Tech, The Spacer Alliance, and the Matayan Empire for any assistance that any of them can provide for us. We don't have time to be choosy. We need allies."

Naero thought about that for a moment. Should she bring in Ellis?

"I can't speak for the Matayans, but you should be able to trust Joshua Tech and my people."

"We are not so certain," Nevano said. "Shalaen has already helped us capture three different Spacer strike groups sent to infiltrate us. They seemed incredibly determined to rescue you."

"What?" Naero said.

Nevano bowed. "I will have them released, and brought to you."

Naero didn't know what to say. Shalaen stayed with her.

"I believe your aunt is being detained with one of them," Shalaen said. "We did no permanent harm to any of them. But they made that very difficult, even for myself. What a remarkable splinter race you have become. I commend your people for their resourcefulness. Were it not for my powers, they would have either retrieved or terminated you by now."

"What do you mean, 'terminated'?" Naero said. "They came to rescue me, not to kill me."

Shalaen grasped her hand and touched the wristcomp Naero wore.

"Their primary intent was to rescue, but after the first two teams failed, they grew desperate. They decided to set off your suicide device, once they could not rescue you the third time."

"They tried to kill me?"

"They attempted to, just before I helped capture the third team. Fortunately, I had already reconfigured your failsafe device by that time. Quite obvious, really."

They tried to set it off.

Her own people tried to kill her.

She should be dead.

"I-I guess I can understand why they would do that," Naero said, still shaken. "*Haisha*...they couldn't be sure that you weren't working for the Corps."

"Unlikely as that might be," Nevano added.

Naero stared at her wristcom. "Does it still work?"

"Yes, you can still set it to obliterate yourself if you so desire, but we hope that will not become necessary. It will still sound a warning and then activate if anyone tries to remove it or you are slain."

Shalaen handed her another chip. "That has your new activation codes on it. If there is someone you can trust, you may wish to give them the new codes, but we advise against that."

"What do you mean? Can you see the future?"

"In some ways. Through people I see various possibilities."

"But they explode in prisms around you, to the point where all is left dark and confused. Perhaps that is best. It is not healthy for most entities to know too much about their potential destinies."

"What can you tell me?" Naero asked.

"That you must get the Kexxian Data Matrix to your people, and they must begin to apply it, at all costs. That much is certain. How you do that is not important. It will be disastrous if the Matrix falls into the hands of the Corps and your enemies too soon–"

"How about not at all."

"That is also unwise, and not very likely. Information and knowledge always behave in fluid manners, difficult to contain or monopolize for long. Your people know this. Believe it or not, there may yet come a time, sooner or late, where the Corps and their worlds will become your strongest allies."

Naero snorted. "I strongly doubt that."

"Do not be so sure," Shalaen said. She stepped forward and embraced Naero.

A tremendous sense of calm and well-being came over Naero as they embraced. She put her arms around Shalaen and hugged her close. Like she would a sister if she had one.

Holding Shalaen was like embracing pure serenity.

Holding a being made of raw, enigmatic energy without being burned.

Yet it was Shalaen who gasped.

Her legs buckled. She nearly collapsed.

Naero stepped back and held the wispy young girl up.

"What are you, spacechild?" Shalaen said, her voice a mix of fear and wonder. "You truly frighten me."

Naero tried to laugh. "I frighten you?"

Shalaen nodded, her radiant face and shining eyes fathomless and intently serious. "The powers and knowledge you hold untapped within you should frighten everyone. Especially you."

Naero bowed her head. "They do," she whispered. "I don't know anything."

The deck threatened to fall out from under Naero once more.

What was she? What was inside of her–the thing from her nightmares?

What was she going to become? Freak. Monster. Demon?

Did she have any choice in it all?

She recalled with terror and a scary hidden hunger how it secretly thrilled her. The deep desire left parts of her fearful, but other parts still hungry, eagerly craving more.

Om said it was all her, only a fraction of her latent abilities.

"I...I...I don't know what I am," Naero said. It almost came out like a sob. "Everyone's afraid of me when they find out. *Haisha*, I'm afraid of myself, and I still don't know anything. Can you help me? Can you tell me something?"

"Shhh..." Shalaen told her.

Naero clung to her peacefulness and almost broke down.

Shalaen kissed her on one cheek, then her forehead, and her other cheek.

With each kiss, Naero relaxed, awash in waves of calm and comfort.

Perhaps the Yattai were angels, as some legends claimed.

"Naero, always remember that true power, whatever its nature, is controlled and mastered best through love. And love is little more than the trifold understanding of compassion, justice, and mercy. There is no true freedom without the Harmony of the Three Wisdoms. Remember my words, in your darkest hours."

Naero nodded, holding her tighter and shaking.

"When I am linked with you by touch," Shalaen said. "I can show you many things as I see and know them. Concentrate on the sound of my voice. Open your heart and mind to me. Close your eyes."

Naero did so and soared through the stars in an instant, as if she were a starship herself, sweeping through the galaxies at incredible speed.

"Few people understand exactly what the Kexxian Data Matrix really is–a legacy of wisdom, knowledge, and technology all in one," Shalaen said. "Much like The Three Wisdoms, all three of these must be balanced for the Matrix to be of any practical use."

Shapes took form in Naero's mind. Bipedal reptilian creatures of average size, with large eyes and dexterous hands. They looked after one another and their young with great care and diligence, expanding their knowledge and wisdom.

"The Kexx were a very advanced race, ancient even before my mother's people, the Yattai, began their ascent. What happened to them is still a mystery, though some of the Yattai have guessed. Great explorers and seekers of knowledge, the Kexx reigned for many eons over a vast free Republic. They nurtured many fledgling races and explored far beyond known space. They charted several galaxies and contacted multitudes of others."

"That's...impossible," Naero said. "The distance between galaxies is way too vast. We've barely charted one quarter of our own."

"Nevertheless," Shalaen said, "they achieved these and many other technological wonders. But then, something happened. During the course of their travels, they blundered into a terrible war between two nearly equal advanced races. They had once made limited, preliminary contact with another advanced race called the Drians..."

Baeven had mentioned them.

"...and the race of sentient androids they nurtured called the Driathans."

"Driathans. I've heard of them as well."

"Yes, some still exist, even–a sad, forgotten immortal remnant. Mourning the loss of their mentors, the near-human Drians. But Nothing could have prepared them or the Kexx for the conflict with the rapacious G'lothc."

Images flashed through Naero's mind, creatures both beautiful and horrific, terrible beyond imagination.

Shalaen went on. "By any measure, the G'lothc were a race of intensely aggressive, psyonic and shape-changing beings. Countless other races had been enslaved by the opportunistic G'lothc, sent forth as their minions and shock troops. Terrifying creatures such as the sauroid Dakkur, and the dragon-like Kahn-Dar.

"The long war raged for eons across multiple galaxies, scarring the universe, in vast waves of battle in this dimension and others. With powers and weapons beyond understanding to most peoples. We see the scars of those battles to this day as The Great Dying, where our universe itself was nearly unmade. Multitudes of cultures and life forms perished.

"Yet in the final end, after several millennia, the descendants of the Kexx and the Drians pulled together the last of their mighty armadas, and obliterated the once indomitable G'lothc where the great foe made their final stand–on their few remaining systems, their fleets surrounding their last remaining stars and homeworlds.

"Even their stars were destroyed in those final confrontations."

"The Kexx could destroy stars?"

Shalaen nodded. "For their part, the G'lothc and their minions fought with great ferocity and cunning, to the last ship, to the last being. When it ended, the great enemy lay utterly vanquished and obliterated.

"Yet in doing so, the intricate cultures of the Drians and the Kexx nearly destroyed themselves as well. Within a handful of millennia after the long war ended, both races vanished mysteriously, without a trace of their passing. It is said among the Yattai that all of Creation still mourns for their loss to this day."

"What happened to them all?"

"Some say that they sought ascension, to higher planes of existence where their agonies and corruptions from the Vast War could be purged and assuaged. Others say that they took their own lives, driving their great ships into singularities and other powerful phenomena in an effort to end their immense shame, regret, and pain."

"Why are you telling me all of this?" Naero said. "What does this have to do with me?"

"I know that my mother and the other Yattai believed that the Kexxian Data Matrix would not appear again by accident. It's possible that the Matrix even has a will of its own. Perhaps more than one."

"It does. I've met one of them. One of its guardians, a presence I have named Om."

Shalaen stared at her. "Yes, I sense him now. Om. Very curious."

Naero still didn't know what Om was capable of.

Haisha, she didn't even know that much about herself.

And Om was on the verge of tapping into abilities and powers within her that she had yet to explore and master.

"Do you understand the purpose of the Kexxian Matrix, spacechild? The Kexx left it to the universe as a legacy to the younger races, to assist them against oppression and annihilation by excessively violent and greedy forces. Forces such as the G'lothc."

"Sounds like the Corps took some lessons from the latter."

"That may not be entirely untrue."

"What do you mean?" Naero asked.

"The G'lothc are no more, but even the Yattai now believe that some of their servants survived, perhaps among the Dakkur or the Kahn-Dar. Once again, vast powers from beyond your regions have grown great, and bide their time impatiently. Yet they are separated from the worlds you know only by distances of time and space.

"Beware. When their ambitious gaze turns this way seeking dominion and conquest, they may threaten both Corps and Spacers alike. And it could all happen much sooner than any of us might think. It may have already begun."

Naero's head ached. All she wanted was to find Jan again and get them both and their halves of the Kexxian Matrix safely in the hands of Spacer Intel. Then she could pursue her own course and get back to living her own life.

That was all more than enough for now.

"Well, when that day comes, we'll talk," Naero said. "But until then, the Gigacorps are our biggest problem. They're out to absorb as much as they can. But they aren't going to absorb me and my people, and they aren't going to get the Matrix."

"Good," Shalaen said, releasing her. "I hope that your people will aid us then, Naero. We are desperate for allies. But first, we all need to survive the turmoil of the next few months."

"I'd be happy to survive the next few days. Can you see the future? Can you tell me anything that might help me?"

Shalaen stepped away, shaking her head. "In truth, I only get impressions of things. Just feelings, flashes of insight. Glimpses, really. When I try to focus on the future, so much remains unclear, so much uncertain. Prophecy is not dangerous in itself, you see. When push comes to shove, it is the interpretation of foresight, visions, and prophecy that prove perilous."

Naero pressed her hands to the sides of her head. "Anything would help. I'm just so overwhelmed by all of this."

"To you, I say this: Your enemies will be more than what they seem. Look clearly."

"I still have problems accepting it all. None of this seems real."

"You need, to develop your innate talents," Shalaen said. "Otherwise you will wither and consume yourself in the flames to come, blasted away before your destinies like so much dust."

"Greatttt...How...awesome."

"Learn patience. That lack is one of your greatest weaknesses, a flaw of the young you can ill afford. Now, before my father returns, may I ask you a few things?"

"About what?"

Shalaen's face suddenly beamed. Literally. "About your young friend, Tarim."

"There's not much to tell. This is what I know."

Shalaen listened intently. It took only a few moments.

"Thank you," she said, after Naero finished. "I feel certain somehow that he will be precious to me during my life. Already he would lay down his life for me, but I cannot let him do so. He must journey with you for a time."

"I'm not so sure that's going to be any safer."

"I adored him from the moment our eyes met, but if we stay together, I feel certain that I will be his death. If you can, will you look after him for me?"

"If I can." What certainty was there for anyone?

"I know that is foolish of me, but please try. If things get better, I hope to see him again one day. If not, it won't matter."

Nevano rushed back in. "Change of plans. We're making a run for it, sooner that we thought. Triax is planning something big; we don't know exactly what. You and your people will be released right before we take off."

"Let me speak with them. Perhaps we can help."

"My guards will take you down to detention. Your crew is already on their way there. Your big friend is there. He's a quick healer, that one."

"Spacer smartblood was a marvel of genetic engineering," Shalaen noted. "Despite the high costs to your race in the beginning. The Corps have never been able to match it."

"Let's hope they never do," Naero said. "My people stumbled upon it by terrible accident." She turned to Nevano and held out her hand. "I suppose this is goodbye, then. Thank you, sir."

"I suppose so." Nevano smiled sadly and took her hand, his grip strong but not painful. "There are not many who would take the hand of such a butcher as myself. When you hear worse of me, do not believe all of it."

Now it was Naero's turn to smile. "I will strongly advise my people and any others to help you and the mining rebels if they can. Consider this an alliance with my Clan, if nothing else. Give Triax hell. And don't feel bad. Remember, I'm a bloodthirsty Spacer terrorist."

She touched Shalaen's face with her fingertips as she went past, not knowing why, feeling the same surge of peaceful energy flow into her once more. "Goodbye, Shalaen. Thanks. Take care of your father."

"I will. Remember my words."

"Can do. Luck to us all. You're up against a lot."

"More than you know," Shalaen said. "For now we must part. Both of our struggles go on. Yet we may meet again one day."

"I'd like that."

"One more thing. Your parents loved you and your brothers. They made the decisions they made for you all, and for your people. I'm sure their last thoughts were of you before they passed. Honor their memory."

"I will." What did she mean "brothers?"

There was no time to ask. They had already split up.

On her way to the detention area, Naero thought of her parents again, and wept a little. If Nevano's guards noticed, they said nothing.

"Naero!" a familiar voice called out. She wheeled.

"Gallan!" She ran to him and hugged him. She took his hand, jumped up and kissed him on the forehead. "Feeling better?"

"Much. Glad to see you, too, *abani*," he said, grinning. "I came to meet you. They're going to release the others."

"Wouldn't miss Aunt Sleak's face when we come to rescue her. The leader of the mining revolt's letting us go, while he and his people make a break for it."

"I take it there'll be a lot to discuss back on the ship."

"You got that right. How are you feeling?"

"Like a million creds." He yawned. "Took a nice little rest."

"You lazy—"

A tremendous explosion rocked the entire mountain range.

Naero and Gallan fell down in shock, along with the guards. More shocks walked in above them, like the pounding of gigantic hammers.

"Those are a mass driver strikes." Gallan said. "Triax means to lay waste to this entire region."

"They can't…"

Gallan's frown cut her off.

The Corps put their interests above all law and morality. Spacers and miners would all get mashed together.

"C'mon," Naero said, "We need to get the hell out of here."

Even as they turned to run, the miners behind them cried out in terror.

Naero glanced back over her shoulder into the billowing clouds of dust and debris raining down.

Something dark and menacing ripped through the dust and the miners. It tore the miners apart before they could fire their weapons. Parts of bodies and gouts of blood spattered in several directions. More guards dropped back and fired their blasters in unison, before whatever it was fell upon them.

More screams erupted.

Gallan shoved her in front of him. "Run, Naero. Don't look back."

A whirling howl of bizarre and frightening origin erupted behind them.

It swept closer. Naero felt a twinge in her head.

Extreme danger from multiple threats. I must have access to our defensive protocols.

More strikes hit the mountain range. Worse than before.

The cavern buckled. The thing behind them and the miners vanished under tons of rock and stone. Naero raced toward the detention center.

Yet deep within the rubble, it sounded as though something ripped through stone, boring through the very rock of the cave-in itself to pursue them.

To get at her.

39

The blast doors to the detention center opened even as Naero and Gallan ran up to them. Irith and Aunt Sleak rushed out, dressed in Spacer togs, followed by the captured Intel strike teams.

"Aunt Sleak, over here!" Naero shouted. She turned to one of the guards. He was trying to listen to what came over his helmet com.

"Our weapons, our transports–where are they?" Naero demanded.

The man pointed to several containers. Naero pulled them open, finding them filled with Spacer weapons and gear.

"Gallan, Naero!" Aunt Sleak said. She quickly embraced them both. "We thought you were dead." She glanced at Naero's com band.

"I should be dead, shouldn't I?" Naero said. "I'm sure it's a long story."

Another distant impact shook the area once more, closer this time.

"If we live to argue about it," Naero added.

"Your transports are in the loading bay at the end of this corridor," the guard told them. "Follow us; we're on our way out."

"Corp raiders have infiltrated the complex," another guard shouted. "We're holding them off, but they're blasting everyone."

Aunt Sleak racked four high intensity rounds into her quad-barrel khotgun. "I'd like to see 'em try," she said with a smile. "Move, move, move, people!"

The Intel agents fanned out around them in close assault formation. Screams and rapid bursts of many weapons echoed from the loading bay. Several miners pulled back into the corridor, weapons blazing.

The rebels put up a fierce resistance, but they remained pinned down. Bursts of heavy fire tore into and through the solid rock around them.

"We're cut off. They've taken the loading bay," a bleeding miner shouted. "Too many of them. We're trapped!"

"Attack strategy Delta-18!" Aunt Sleak shouted.

One of the Intel people activated a device that projected holos of their groups ten meters in front of them.

At first the holos drew the bulk of the enemy fire, allowing the Spacers and miners to burst into the loading bay right behind.

They split off into three-person fire teams, picking and popping targets at will.

In the midst of the chaos, four Ejjai in partial blast armor sprang at Aunt Sleak. The slugs from their weapons rebounded off her personal deflector field, barely forcing her back.

Naero picked off the foremost with an aimed headshot.

Aunt Sleak took out two more with double blasts from her khotgun. The last Ejjai raced at her, an alpha female with a short sword in her other hand.

Personal shields didn't stop blades.

The Ejjai alpha was fast. Naero's hurried shot barely grazed her. The alpha sprang at Aunt Sleak with a with a roar.

Aunt Sleak dropped her empty khotgun and swept out her energy cutlass in a flash.

Swords descended in killing strikes. They crashed into each other, sparks blazing.

Aunt Sleak dove to one side, still slicing.

The energy blade cut the Ejjai alpha to pieces, gore splattered all over their transports. The scent of blood and fire thick and rank in the air.

Naero stared at Aunt Sleak, a metal sword impaled straight through her shoulder. The muscled arm of the Ejjai still hanging from the hilt.

"That was close," Aunt Sleak said.

Irith cut the sword off on either side of the wound with a microtorch and sealed both sides of the wound.

"Leave that chunk of blade in there for now," she said. "You'll lose too much blood if we take it out."

Aunt Sleak nodded, wincing at the pain. She leaned on Naero until two other Spacers picked her up and ran to the transport with her.

In less than a minute, the raiders holding the launching bays had been put down, while miners and Spacers alike scrambled for their craft.

"We're ready!" Irith shouted from *Lobo-3F*. Spacers converged on the transport and filed in.

Packed ships and craft launched without warning, nearly colliding with each other in the panic to escape.

A Shadowforce officer shouted to the miner commandos, pointing at two huge battered suits of power armor standing empty against the wall.

"Can any of you operate those tank suits?"

The leader of the miners shook his head, reloading. "No. We captured them, but none of us ever learned how. We could sure use them now. We ain't gonna last here very long."

There wasn't enough time to get the ships out.

Naero watched in growing horror.

Gallan and the Intel officer didn't hesitate.

Both of them climbed into the old battlesuits, activating field-level defensive screens, covering the main corridor, the launch bays, and hundreds of miner commandos.

"Gallan!" she shouted, "What are you doing? Come on. Get out of there!"

Miners screamed in terror. "Here they come!"

"Get your people through," Gallan yelled, charging his cannons. "Then blast the enemy to hell. We gotta hold this corridor while the rest of the ships launch."

Miners streamed through, frantic with terror, trampling anyone who fell in front of them, man, woman, or child. All of them desperate to reach the transports.

"*Haisha!*" Gallan said. His eyes got big as he read what was coming on the sensors.

Then he caught the rapidly approaching glow on visuals. "Get back. Incoming. Fire in the hole!" The Intel agent and the miners took cover to either side.

An instant later, a tremendous blast knocked Naero and others flat. A scarlet blizzard of meat and bone swallowed up screams of the refugees still caught in the tunnel.

A gout of intense flame and heat followed, roaring out of the corridor, sucking up the air.

Like a taste of hell itself.

Naero lifted her head up from the floor and shrieked at her friend. "Gallan!"

Destruction imminent.

He gave her a last look, a sudden intense look.

The rear guard wouldn't make it out.

But some of the remaining ships still might.

Gallan was her true friend.

Naero had very few true friends.

Her heart tumbled and scorched its way through her like a burning hot coal.

Gallan grinned, nodded back at the last ship to her, and then focused all of his attention on the tunnel.

He poured fire from his heavy blaster cannons into the corridor in controlled bursts, driving back and disrupting the advancing Triaxian Marine heavies.

"Here they come again. Pour it at 'em!" she heard him shout.

Naero got up to run to his side.

Two agents grabbed her arms and dragged her back. She punched one and kicked another. She almost got free.

Klyne nailed her with a jolt from a neural paralyzer. She spasmed and froze up, then went limp.

She could still see, her vision blurred, Gallan fighting side-by-side with the Shadowforce agents and miner commandos.

While Klyne and others dragged her up the loading ramp.

The sheer ferocity of fire from the enemy pushed and blasted Gallan and the others back from the opening.

The Intel officer took the brunt of it on his shields, got torched. He went down.

Gallan overloaded his deflectors full front, still jacked into the charging lines, and stepped directly into the teeth of the enemy fire.

Naero's craft lifted off and pulled away as if in slow motion.

Gallan's overtaxed shields shimmered and held in in front of him.

The miners rallied behind, firing and tossing grenades and mining charges.

281

Multiple explosions rocked the launch bay, obscuring almost everything in swirling clouds of dust and debris.

Another enemy assault drove the defenders back again, just as the remaining ships fled.

Gallan's cannons whirred and clicked empty.

He activated his suit's bright humming energy blades close-up.

He crouched, ready to fight, and charged forward, bright blades flashing through the air in Spacer attack patterns.

He cut through a squad of enemy Marines in heavy assault armor, slashing and hacking them to pieces.

Before the transport ramp doors slammed shut, Naero saw the large whip-like terror from the cavern leap upon her big friend out of a sheer torrent of expanding dust and enemy fire.

In the haze and smoke, it was a green-yellow blur. But she caught one glance of its thick head, horribly scarred with deep hash marks of slashes and lines.

Gallan got one stab in, and another deep cut.

The thing tore his armor apart and fell upon him, impossibly strong and fast.

The miners withered like chaff before the firestorm once Gallan went down.

She heard him cry out once.

The transport doors latched and sealed.

Her ship pulled away up into the atmosphere.

Whatever that thing was, it worked for Triax.

It just killed her best friend.

Naero swore her vengeance silently. Fists clenched, chest heaving. Tears rivered down her face. She shook, still somewhat paralyzed.

Through the view screens, she saw a dozen Triaxian fighters suddenly swarm at them and the other helpless transports from out of the clouds.

Just as suddenly, the enemy fighters lost power and tumbled away.

"What the hell was that?" Klyne yelled. "Those bogies had us cold."

Shalaen, Naero thought.

The sky swarmed with miner ships and transports, desperate to escape Hadar-1 in any direction.

"Make for the ocean!" Aunt Sleak said. "The coordinates for the tertiary rendezvous site are loaded under Epsilon-Option-91."

Naero thought about Gallan, about her parents, but her mind floated in a haze of shock. There was too much horror and loss to fully process and concentrate.

Out the view screens, she watched as not all of the miners escaped. Despite Shalaen's efforts, many miner craft fell under attack as they dispersed. Many went spinning and burning back to the surface, filled with screaming, dying refugees.

Such was war, prosecuted by Triax and the Corps.

Naero closed the blast shutters, closed her eyes, and bowed her head for a moment, only imagining the screams still echoing in her troubled mind.

Gallan's final scream before he died.

They penetrated the surface of the water, and travelled submerged for a long while until they met up with *The Rio Lobo*.

Once back on board, they prepared for immediate departure.

"Clean up and prepare to be boarded," Klyne shouted. "We have clearance to leave, but Triax has two entire fleets surrounding this system now. They won't let anyone through without a look-see, of that I'm certain."

When they were set, *The Rio Lobo* departed the planet.

As Klyne guessed, two destroyers, a light cruiser, and seven fighters moved immediately to intercept them.

They beamed their clearance to depart at the naval forces, but the cruiser fired a blast from one of its big spinal guns directly in front of them, nearly taking off their nose.

The enraged boarding party silently and violently shoved them around violently, and tore up half of the ship. But in the end, everything checked out, so the officer reluctantly gave the all-clear sign.

She and her pissed-off troops left without a single word or apology.

Aunt Sleak had already prepared to jump before they were gone.

Naero watched as the beleaguered miners tried to flee, their ships staggering into jump, as the Triaxian fleet bore down on them.

The strange protective sphere around the miners grew smaller and smaller.

Shalaen was weakening.

Just before they went into jump, Naero saw two dozen, sleek, black, unmarked craft appear out of nowhere and sweep through the Triaxian formations, firing and maneuvering with incredible agility and speed.

For a few crucial moments, the surprise assault caught the lumbering Triaxian ships completely off guard.

Naero smiled. She'd seen their like once before.

Now the phantom gunships and heavy fighters attacked in coordinated waves, like dark spirits of vengeance.

In moments, the Triaxian fleet carriers burned, along with two heavy cruisers. Three destroyers and numerous fighters either exploded or drifted dead in space.

In the chaos, the remaining miners slipped away into jump. Just as suddenly, the unknown craft vanished, disappearing even off visuals and every sensor scan.

Naero looked at Klyne, raising one eyebrow inquisitively.

Klyne shrugged. "Our escort ships just arrived. We didn't think a little practice sortie would hurt anything."

"It'll keep the Triaxians guessing about the miners, too," Aunt Sleak said. "Damn the Corps."

She winced again from the length of Ejjai steel still lodged in her shoulder, but her eyes focused on Naero.

"As soon as I get this sliver out, I suspect we're going to have an intriguing debriefing," she said.

She put her good arm around Naero and pulled her close. "I'm sorry about Gallan, Naero. He was family. I know."

Naero bit her lip, nodding her head. No time for tears now. "We'll add that to Triax's list."

Aunt Sleak shook her and narrowed her eyes. "You bet we will."

"I need to ask you something," Naero said. "Do I have any brothers besides Jan?"

Aunt Sleak paled. "How did you–"

"Just answer the question."

"Jan had a twin, but he was killed at birth. It's an awful story that your parents never spoke about to anyone, because it was too painful. Only Zalvano and I, and a few people in Intel know what happened. Best for another time. Not now." Voices called out to them in the haze.

Naero forced a smile as Jan and Ellis ran to her from their stations. Tarim appeared at the door, relieved, but holding back still. She hugged Jan and tried not to think about Gallan, her parents, or her long-dead brother for the time being. So much death and loss.

Cherish the living, her father had once told her. She began to fully understand what that meant.

40

"The heat is really on now," Klyne said in the briefing room. "Quite frankly, we're at a loss. I'm open to any and all suggestions, people."

The debriefing room went deathly silent.

"Well," Aunt Sleak said, still healing from her wounds. "We've learned that both the Matayans and the mining revolt worlds are close to negotiating a secret defection strategy with Joshua Tech and The Spacer Alliance. Even to the point of having their worlds annexed as protectorates. If they're that serious, why don't we seek some help from them? At the very least, in the ensuing chaos, we might be able to lose ourselves and slip away."

"Risky," Klyne said. "Everyone's still hunting for the Kexxian Data Matrix, including the Matayans. Until it's safely in Spacer hands, we're not taking any chances. That is our primary mission. Others have theirs."

Prince Ellis perked up at that. He started to say something, but Klyne cut him off.

"Forgive me, Your Highness, but that's the truth," Klyne said. "Our peoples have been bitter enemies for centuries. That's not going to go away overnight. We barely agreed to let you sit in on this meeting."

Ellis closed his mouth for a moment and considered what to say next.

"I was going to add," he said quietly, "that there continues to be great turmoil among my people and even in the royal court. There remains an open power struggle between the current Emperor, Mellis VI, and our Prime Minister, Adrin, his brother. I know its confusing, especially when they both look exactly alike and have even posed as each other, from time to time.

"But the Matayan royal family and our peoples are now divided between these two factions. My younger brother, Nellis II sides with the Emperor, and has become his heir. They are still slaves to the old ways and Triax. The Prime Minister is the one pursuing a courageous shift in our allegiance. Until this civil war is resolved, my people will not be reliable allies. And I agree with you. My people should never get their hands on the Matrix of the Kexx."

Naero sighed and stood. "We're witnessing a historical shift. Old ideas, prejudices, and allegiances are collapsing and mutating even as we watch. Rapid growth and change are always chaotic and dangerous, even destructive. If my parents were still here, they would say that the universe needs to grow up, and that we must help it grow in positive directions that benefit the most people fairly."

Tarim cleared his throat. "This all means war. Many wars, big and small. You don't know Triax and the Corps the way I do. They will not give up anything that they see as theirs. Do you think Triax and the other Corps are going to just stand by and watch the Matayan Worlds and the rich Mining Revolt Worlds get annexed by rivals that they see as their worst enemies? They're going to band together as never before and fight like hell, for as long as they think they still have a chance at winning or holding on to some of their own."

"Agreed," Aunt Sleak said. "Those wars are already starting. They just haven't fully exploded yet. But it's all coming. Everyone on all sides knows it. All the more reason we have to get away as quickly as possible."

"How does Triax keep finding us?" Klyne asked. "I'm still not certain we don't have...an internal problem."

Everyone in the room kept quiet. No one wanted to consider how damaging and deadly it might be to have a traitor or spy among them.

"It's not me," Ellis said flatly. "I know I'm the logical suspect, but you're watching me constantly. You know this."

"I don't think it's you," Klyne said. "But whoever is doing so, if they are, has some method of getting info to our enemies we cannot detect. Yet none of it makes any sense."

No one mentioned Baeven, or whatever his real name was.

Klyne suddenly touched up the com button near his right ear and sat up.

"It's starting. This just in from INS. On the main screen."

Everyone turned to watch the primary viewscreen. A female announcer read an emergency broadcast.

In a brazen and provocative series of illegal military actions, Joshua Tech fleets launch multiple surprise attack waves to annex both the Matayan Empire and several Triax Mining Revolt Worlds. In defense, Triax declares Intercorporate War. For the time being, the treacherous Spacer Military–long-term ally of the pariah corporation–pledges to abide by its treaties and remain neutral. How long will these dangerous invaders stay out of the current escalating conflict?

Meanwhile, Triax announces full mobilization of its brave naval fleets to defend its legal sovereignty, interstellar property, and possession rights. Triax valiantly stands alone.

Massive fleet conflicts are only a week or two away to decide these issues. Subjugated worlds loyal to Triax's shining way of life and liberty pledge their absolute defiance and resistance.

"Kill the audio," Klyne said. He chuckled openly. "Resistance, my ass. By our intel, the annexed worlds are in fact celebrating getting out from under Triax's heel. But INS sure isn't going to report that."

Vid footage showed the massive Triax naval build up underway. Naero noticed that there wasn't any mention about how the Corps military build up had already been proceeding for months–before any inkling of hostilities.

"Joshua Tech and its new allies can handle Triax," Aunt Sleak said. "But the other Gigacorps won't stand by and let that happen. Most of them will pile in, sooner rather than later, and Joshua Tech will be overwhelmed. That will pull in The Spacer Alliance, and then everything will be up for grabs."

Klyne clenched his fists. "It was going to happen again eventually. I think we should launch the Shadow Fleets and fight our way out of the Corps while we still have the chance."

"What exactly are the Shadow Fleets?" Naero asked. "How many ships strong are they?"

"In numbers, several fleets. But they're scattered all over the place. At the end of the last Spacer War with the Corps, we secreted detachments of our warships deep within Gigacorps territory. The right commands over certain channels and those ships will launch and regroup at strategic rally points once more."

"Ships like *The Alamo*," Naero said.

"Most of those ships are decades old," Aunt Sleak noted. "Once the element of surprise is lost, they'd be outnumbered and outclassed by the current, modern Corps fleets."

"Maybe not so much," Klyne noted. "Our tek has always been ahead of the Corps. Upgrades and refits have been made when and where possible, without attracting undue attention. At least the Shadow Fleets would give us a fighting chance early on. But we're short on commanders."

Naero frowned. "I don't know if Jan and I want to be the cause of that. Billions, perhaps trillions of lives lost. For nothing."

Klyne sighed heavily. "You're just one of the causes, and right now we don't have much of a choice in all this. It's happening. Better to fight this war now while we still have a slight tek advantage over the Corps' numbers," Klyne said.

Aunt Sleak rested her chin on knitted hands. "But if they catch us and squeeze any part of the Kexxian Matrix out of you and your brother, you can bet your asses that within a decade or two, they'll come straight at us with tek we can't ever hope to match. And that'll be it for everyone. Do you want to be the cause of a total corporate dominion of the galaxy?"

"No. Definitely not," Naero said. She took her seat.

Jan finally said something. "At least the annexation could make our initial escape easier in the confusion of the erupting war. I've been studying these star charts. Look at this. If we jump through these contested Triaxian mining worlds and through a few Matayan systems, we'll be right at a Joshua Tech forward naval base and ship yard at Nuratine-5."

Aunt Sleak shook her head. "Sure. Right where the war is bound to blow up the hottest."

"No," Klyne said, studying the course. "Jan's right. His interstellar navigation skills are genius. It would be close, but his plan would save us days of travel off our current route. We'd reach allied space before the war really heats up on the front lines in those forward areas. I think we have to give this serious consideration."

Naero put a hand on her beaming brother's shoulders and rose to her feet again. "I think we have to risk it. Let's not hesitate. Let's put it to a vote right now."

Dire consequences to their actions remained, whatever they decided. Easy choices evaporated by the minute.

They held a quiet wake for Gallan and their other casualties two days later while still in jump. Naero muttered some words for his loss, but they caught in her throat like broken glass.

She remained in shock. Her grief still too deep and raw.

41

Jan's route remained risky, but it did slice valuable time off of their escape. This became precious time they could no longer waste with open war looming over them.

They would need to re-program their small ship's registration, IDs, and cover stories, just in case they ran afoul of enemy patrols.

Yet a tiny ship like theirs could slip through where an entire fleet could not. They renamed it *The Bristol.*

After six days and three rapid jumps, their luck held.

Then their jump drive malfunctioned, drained their energy core, toasted several major systems, and almost blew the ship up.

That left them limping on sublight through dangerous mining systems soon to be war zones–easy pickings for anyone from any enemy faction who stumbled upon them.

All efforts focused on recharging the core and getting their jump drive back online.

Naero, Jan, and even Aunt Sleak assisted Klyne and the engineer with the diagnostics and repairs. The air charged with the stench of fried electronics and ozone.

"Was it sabotage?" Aunt Sleak asked quietly.

"Our traitor again?" Naero said.

Klyne shook his head. "We're not sure."

"If so," Jan added, studying the readouts. "they're very good at hiding their tracks. All of this could have just been bad luck. Jump drives and other systems fail all the time, and we've been taxing ours way beyond the specs, and on an old ship."

"Still, it's pretty convenient to just be bad luck," Aunt Sleak noted.

"Perhaps that Triax boarding party did something to us," Naero suggested. "Something that wouldn't show up until later and strand us."

"We've considered that option as well. They did do a fair amount of damage during their search. Perhaps our Teks missed something. In any case, we're heading for Boon-3, an old mining depot and junk world seven hours away. It's a haven for miners now and under the figurative protection of Joshua Tech. We'll effect repairs there and push on."

"We don't have an escort anymore?" Naero asked. "Why can't they just tow us into jump?"

Klyne frowned. "We don't have very many of those new stealth ships yet, and their tek is still experimental and fickle. With the war on, they're badly needed on the front lines and many other places, gathering intel. We've been doing well up until now. I thought we were home free, so I let them return to their other duties."

They were on their own, in the middle of nowhere, with a crippled ship–surrounded by enemies.

And perhaps a traitor on board.

An old mining transport happened upon them. When the rebel captain spotted Naero, Tarim, and Sleak's Ejjai slayer patches on the back and the arms of their jump jackets, he couldn't do enough for them.

They got towed to Boon-3 in less than two hours.

"Junk world" didn't do the planet justice.

The ancient mining depot lay surrounded among virtual mountains of trash, wrecks, and discarded piles of garbage from a couple centuries of space travel out that way.

So much so that the few million locals built their homes among and on top of it all.

Chaos did not begin to describe Boon-3.

Even the slight presence of Joshua Tech did not impose any order.

Only the influx of millions of miners and their rough justice kept the situation from getting completely out of hand.

Their local guide turned out to be the same two-bit rascal that towed them in. Captain Bully was a tall, fat, red-faced miner with a big handle-bar moustache.

The rascal of a renegade pilot wore big tattered boots with his toes poking out, and a greasy jump suit that might have been red once. He tugged his scorched stocking cap over his big balding head, gesturing expansively with his thick sausage fingers poking out from fingerless gloves like they were trying to escape.

His rockgrinding voice snarled. "Soze, it's parts ya need for a jump drive, iz it? Well, suh, we got us parts by the klick here on Boon. It's gettin' the damn things ta work that's the problem."

He let out a big belly laugh. "Come on. We'll find somethin' we can rig. I thought miners was the best scrounges in the known uneeverse. But ya ain't seen nuthin' until you've seen these Booners. They don't let nuthin' go ta waste. Whether it works or not, they'll sell it ta ya all right. Just don't let on how bad ya needs it. They're fair hands at hagglin', too."

Naero suddenly gasped and fell to her knees.

Like another sword shoved through her head.

Naero? I think I've finally found a way to access our defense protocols. Can you hear me?

Om. You're really hurting me. I'm going numb. I can't stand up.

Apologies. I shall effect immediate repairs.

Aunt Sleak looked back at her in alarm. She knelt quickly by Naero's side and steadied her.

"Naero? What's wrong."

"I-I think I'm sick or something."

Aunt Sleak blinked. "Sick? With your metabolism? You've never been sick."

"First time for everything I guess."

"Sleak and I will stay with Captain Bully and get the parts we need," Klyne said. "Jan, Tarim, Ellis, Irith–you get Naero back to the ship and on a med bed. Get her checked out and stay with her."

In the end, they had to carry her.

Om. What in the hell did you do to me? I can't walk or even stand up.

Apologies. It took almost all of our energy reserves to break through part of the barriers. We too are very weak. Rest, food, and liquids should suffice.

So, what's the word, Om?

I think we'll be able to activate some limited access to our defensive abilities and certain sub-routines that may prove helpful. Are we in any current danger?

No. So don't kill anyone, Om.

We will remain cut off from the bulk of our defensive protocols. I have focused all of my efforts on breaking through and gaining at least some access. But it has been costly.

No shit. I think you nearly burned us out. I can't be crippled by these efforts of yours. I need to get back up to speed.

Thanks to her friends, they made it back onto to the ship.

Naero begged for food and drink, and lots of it.

She gobbled it all down while her friends stared at her. She ignored them and went promptly to sleep.

They had to know by now how insane she was.

She awoke hours later, her sterile sickbay room dark. Tarim sat across from her, dozing in a chair. He noticed her looking at him.

"Hey, Naero. Good. You're awake. We were worried about you."

"Yeah. Me too."

"What's up with you? You okay?"

Naero needed to tell someone. Tarim was a good choice. She just needed someone else in her life to confide in—now that Gallan was gone.

So she told him about Om, the Kexxian Data Matrix defensive AI sharing her mind.

At first he looked at her and rubbed his palms on his thighs nervously, as if she were nuts.

But as she continued to describe what she was going through, Tarim took it all in and slowly began to believe her. She could see it in his eyes.

"Wow, N. That sounds pretty intense. But what if you could learn to control this thing in your head? Sounds like he could be a lot of help to us. What more can he do?"

"I…I don't know. I'm kind of afraid to find out."

The real problem remained. Naero wasn't sure she could control herself or even her own hidden abilities if they were ever unleashed. Let alone Om.

She didn't even know what her unknown abilities were or how to use them.

Frustration roiled up in her like an angry ocean during a storm.

I can help you, Naero. We can begin to explore our capabilities together once we are feeling better. But you must remain calm and focused. Mental discipline in such matters is always key. And your are at times…unstable.

Look who's talking. All right. Later then. Let me rest now, Om.

Yes. Very well.

"Tarim?"

"Yeah. I'm still here. I thought you drifted off again."

"I was chatting with Om. Where's everyone else?"

"Working on the jump drive with Captain Bully." Tarim chuckled. "Your aunt Sleak keeps complaining she was cheated on the deal, but they think they can modify the various junk parts they brought back to get us back in space."

Something kept bothering her. It wouldn't let her alone.

"That's good. Hey, can you fetch Aunt Sleak for me? I really need to talk to her."

"I'll get her if I can." He left quickly.

Aunt Sleak returned in his place. She sat down in the same chair, looking puzzled, tired, and frustrated.

"What's so important? We're really busy, Naero."

"I can't help it. You need to tell me what happened to Jan's twin brother."

"You're crazy. Why does it matter now? That was years ago."

"I don't know. Ever since I found out, it's been eating at me. I just really have this feeling that it's very important somehow. I must know."

Her aunt knitted her hands, bowed her head, and sighed.

"All right, I'll make it fast. You were only two years old and visiting relatives. Your parents had many powerful enemies, especially your mother, and a lot of that because of her association with Baeven. When she was about to give birth to twin boys, her ship was returning to the fleet from an important negotiation and trade run.

"A suicide squad of high-tek Hevangian assassins waylaid and attacked her ship, bent on killing everyone, especially your mother. They were trying to send a message.

"Tarthan and I rushed to her aid with the fleet and others, while the assassins hunted her throughout the decks of her own ship. They were formidable foes, killing everyone in their path. The crew fought bravely to buy them time, with their lives.

"Janner was born even as your father and I docked and fought our way in wearing our battlesuits, squads of Spacer Marines swarming all over the ship from every angle, backing us up. Your father went on a rampage. He was like a monster unleashed; it was terrifying. I could barely keep up with him. He waded through those assassins and slaughtered them by the dozens, ripping them apart.

"But the enemy had your mom trapped and closed in on her to finish the job. She was in a very bad way. Janner had just been born and Danner was just coming out when the assassins fell upon her and the few survivors. She made Zalvano promise to take Jan to safety. She gave him her cutlass. Zal cut his way into an escape pod nearby and blasted away, still fighting with two of the assassins inside the pod with him. He was badly wounded, but he took out the two killers and kept Jan safe."

Aunt Sleak took a breath.

"What happen to my mom, and–"

"In the chaos and confusion, the assassins killed the medic and tore Danner from her hands right after he was born. They…they cut Danner in half right in front of your mother, just as the compartment de-compressed and many were sucked out of the open air lock from the escape pod.

"Even in her condition, your mother somehow got to her feet as the hull sealed. She fought them. That is the blood you come from, Naero. She fought six assassins on her own, without battle armor or weapons, until your father and I rushed in and put them all down.

"I only got to shoot one of them.

"All of us wept and grieved. But it was too late for little Danner. Only Janner being alive kept your parents from going insane. That's how Janner's twin, your brother, perished. And that's why no one ever talked about it."

Naero swallowed hard and nodded. "Thank you for telling me; we'll need to tell Jan someday."

"Sure. But for right now, we need to keep moving. Get off of Boon-3 somehow."

"Right. I-I'm going to rest some more. Let me know if anything important happens."

"Don't worry. I will. What's going on with you, Naero?"

"I…don't know yet."

Still hours later, Om woke her via a short electric jolt to her system. Naero sat bolt upright and cried out slightly.

Tarim was gone. She checked the time. It was late. From the distant muffled sounds, they were still docked in the Starport at Boon-3.

They hadn't lifted off yet.

What is it, Om?

Long and short range scans detect multiple threats approaching.

Describe. Nearest to farthest.

Enemy stealth ships–

Triax has stealth ships too?

Yes. Larger and not as efficient, but they serve the same purpose.

How close and how many?

They have landed approximately forty-thousand troops around the starport.

Haisha! Forty thousand?

Please, if you could cease interrupting me.

Sorry.

They are closing in, stunning the local population into submission in mass waves as they advance. They will reach our position in approximately twenty standard minutes.

Where are the Joshua Tech and rebel mining defense forces?

Gathering all their ships to engage the Triax and Matayan battle group that rapidly approaches this system.

The enemy had found them again. But how?

Do they have some way to track us, or perhaps the Kexxian Matrix itself?

Unknown. We are about to be overwhelmed, and we are still very weak.

42

What are our options Om?

Priority. We need to finish repairing this ship in order to have any chance at escaping.

Our ship still can't fly? They have to be pretty close by–

Negative. And the parts your friends have acquired remain defective.

That did not sound good.

Naero staggered to her feet and ran straight to engineering.

Klyne, Aunt Sleak, the engineer, and Captain Bully all looked exhausted, still fumbling with the rigged parts, trying to get them to function.

"We've got trouble," Naero said.

They all blinked at her.

She gasped and leaned against the hull for a moment. Om's thoughts flooded her mind, a rush of tek data and instructions for repairing the ship.

Om. Slow down. I can't follow you that fast. What are you babbling about? What the hell is a fixer?

"You're still sick," Aunt Sleak snarled. "Get your ass back to sickbay."

"There's no time to explain. Let me fix the ship, or we're all dead."

"Give her a shot at it," Klyne said.

They moved out of her way.

Grab that tek-analyzer. Let us re-configure it into a low-level Kexxian fixer.

A what?

Trust me; let me work through you. This is the simplest form of Teknomancy.

Teknomancy?

Focus...please.

Naero opened herself to Om and that tsunami of tek info.

Tendrils of light and ribbons of shadow shot into the linked device from her hand as she grasped it.

Pain and jolts of energy pulsed through her. Naero sweated and gnashed her teeth.

To the amazement of everyone looking on, including Naero, the analyzer broke apart and re-configured in a matter of instants into a floating orb of shifting components and optics.

Kinda cute, actually.

Now we can get to work.

Om told them, rapid-fire, what to do.

Aided by the bobbing fixer, Naero had the power core working in two long agonizing minutes.

Then they moved on to the jump drive.

That took longer.

From what she could see, none of the parts on hand would ever work. Not in a million years.

She effected repairs while the fixer popped in and modified the parts and electronics, re-configuring what they needed in a flash. It absorbed the defective components and spit them back out, ready to function properly.

"What is that thing? How are you doing this?" Klyne asked. "*Haisha*, we barely had Jump-4 capability. The jump drive didn't even work. Now the scans say you're giving us Jump-6. In a matter of seconds!"

"I'll explain later."

She didn't understand it all herself yet.

With the jump drive coming back online, Naero calmly informed them about the enemy strike force and battle group closing in on them.

The Bristol jumped off of Boon-3 two minutes later, blasting back into space. It jumped as soon as it cleared the planet.

An audible groan rose up from the advancing Triaxian forces.

Dozens of ships tore off in swift pursuit.

Within the space of one quarter of a standard hour, the enemy completely vanished from that sector, almost as quickly as they had arrived.

A good portion of Boon-3 and its population around the starport still lay stunned, wherever they dropped, en mass.

Naero and her friends emerged from their hiding places.

"I hope Captain Bully and his crew know what they're doing," Tarim said, "leading that enemy strike force away from us."

"They volunteered," Klyne said. "They did get a new ship out of the deal, and they hate the Corps as much as we do."

"For however long they last," Aunt Sleak said.

"They've got a fighting chance, at least," Naero said. "I sent my fixer with them. It was putting the finishing touches on their jump drive and updating their shields, even as they jumped."

Klyne opened his mouth. "What is...how did you–"

Naero rolled her eyes. "You need to understand: I'm linked with parts of the Kexxian Matrix. Our current tek is child's play compared to that. With a little effort, I can create these simple Kexxian fixers, AI-based orbs that can understand our tek in a heartbeat. Their primary function is to fix things and keep them working. Within certain parameters, they can even improve upon them."

Everyone stared at her like she was a total freak.

Perhaps she was.

"Sounds good," Aunt Sleak said, catching on. "Everyone give her your comps and analyzers. You heard me. Hand them over."

In moments, Naero had an armload of the devices.

"Now whip us up a batch of those floaty things and let's find a way off this rock," Sleak said.

Naero quickly discovered that she could only create about three fixers an hour without completely exhausting herself.

Creation, much like giving birth, still took a lot out of a person.

Then she had a eureka insight.

Om, can you program the fixers to re-configure other fixers?

Certainly. The process will take somewhat longer.

Fine, fine. Oh, and give them all some protocols. I don't want any of them falling into the wrong hands. They'll need our authorized permission to act. They can't ever work for the Corps or our enemies in any way, and they shouldn't do any direct harm or damage to people or property on their own. How's that sound?"

Acceptable. Expect the first prototype in approximately one standard hour. Units should double exponentially after that, as long as sufficient raw materials and energy are available. How many units are desired?

Oh, stop after a hundred.

One hundred standard fixer units. Very well.

43

In a matter of hours, they were working among a growing cloud of dozens of bobbing fixers.

Klyne and Aunt Sleak purchased an old three-hundred-ton hulk, stranded on the planet's surface for decades.

They filled its holds with junk components and scrap materials according to Naero and Om's directions.

Three hours later, *The Blue Phoenix* lifted off under its own power. They removed their newly re-configured ship to a remote location, away from any lingering Corps spies and informants.

Four hours after that, they departed Boon-3 entirely, and immediately jumped to their next location.

They met in the new conference room, while the fixers finished reconfiguring their new quarters on board. In their haste to escape, Naero and the crew decided to leave such secondary concerns for later. The primary goal was to keep moving.

Aunt Sleak looked extremely pleased with their progress.

"These new Kexxian fixers are a marvel. We've discovered a new form of nearly miraculous construction. Ships. Buildings. Equipment. There's almost no limit to this. Anything we can conceive of within the range of our current tek and then some, they can make, faster and better than any current manufacturing process known to us."

"I agree," Klyne said. "These methods alone will revolutionize our societies as we know them, but they must be controlled. What if criminal elements–or worse, the Corps–got a hold of them? Within a few months and years they would out-produce and overwhelm us."

Jan mused. "No one faction can ever completely control tek for very long, Klyne. How do you and Spacer Intel propose to do so?"

"For as long as we can. I left Intel people to work with Joshua Tech and the miners with these new fixers. Our allies are in desperate need of warships to defend their systems. Once this program ramps up, they can have all they need–in a matter of weeks. That is a stunning development."

"They'll need crash programs to train all of the crews required to fly them," Tarim noted.

Klyne waved one hand. "Already in place. Joshua Tech's recruitment programs among the miners and even the Matayans are flooded with volunteers for the new defense forces. The bulging populations of the recently annexed worlds know very well what is at stake. Their new freedoms won't last very long if they can't defend them. But we are still woefully short on ship and fleet captains–especially with strategic and tactical battle experience."

Naero shook her head. "Triax and the Corps won't give us any time. They're ready to fight this war now, and they'll attack in force while they can, to retake those systems before they can defend themselves."

Prince Ellis grew impatient. "I must return to my people. I can help lead them. All my life I have trained for this. My uncle, the Prime Minister will need my assistance. The Emperor and my brother, his heir, still cling to Triax and the old ways because they know nothing else. They can't see what a dead end it is for our people. And they can't be allowed to win. This is my fight, and I must join it."

Surprisingly, it was Aunt Sleak who spoke up.

"From our Intel reports, you may very well get your chance," she told him. "Prime Minister Adrin has placed his half of the Matayan Fleet to protect the Matayan Worlds, reinforced by a Joshua Tech Fleet."

Jan sighed, studying the forces in motion on his comp. "They're still outnumbered. Along with the Emperor's forces, Triax has at least two more fleets on the way, and elements from many other allied Gigacorps Fleets nearby. That's overwhelming superiority if they choose to unleash it, and Joshua Tech has no viable reinforcements to send in."

Naero turned to Klyne. "You must summon the Shadow Fleets here, to this crucial battle that's forming. There's just too much at stake."

Klyne frowned. "They're already en route, but even they won't be enough, even if they do arrive in time. We are still outnumbered by the current Gigacorps naval forces in range, ten or twenty to one. And if the Spacer navies join in, the other Corps navies will also pour in."

Aunt Sleak studied the numbers. "The strategic and tactical facts are unavoidable. We are heading into battles we must fight. But we can't win. We're going to lose the Matayans and the miners, and there's a good chance that Joshua Tech, our best ally, will be crushed and lost as well. We cannot afford any of that, but we are not in any position to prevent it, either. And the hands of the Spacer Clan Navy are tied by treaties. They have to remain neutral to avoid an all-out war on all fronts."

Naero called up the interstellar map, and the various forces and their proximities.

"Private Clan forces," she observed. "That's the only solution."

"What about them?" Klyne asked.

"Like Clan Maeris, all of the Clans have their own private fleets and warships to escort and protect their sectors and shipping interests," Naero said. "Look at their numbers; they're everywhere.

"They are the fighting equivalent of one third of the Spacer Naval Fleet. We need to put out an emergency call for volunteers from the Clans to join this fight."

"Impossible," Aunt Sleak said. "That would open up strategic holes everywhere for the Corps to exploit, making all of our space vulnerable to direct attack, instead of this one area."

"Spread the regular naval fleets out to make up for it," Jan suggested. "Their hands are tied anyway, and both sides know it. But Naero's right. The private Spacer Fleets are free to act, if someone could convince them to do so."

"Good luck with that," Aunt Sleak said. "Perhaps if your parents were still alive, they might manage to make such a call to arms. They were popular and well known enough that the Clans might have listened to them, but they're not with us any longer, thanks to our enemies."

Aunt Sleak looked at Naero and put her hand to her mouth. "That's the answer. You're the one Naero. You have to do it."

"What? Who's going to listen to me?"

"You don't know; you've been on the run for so long," Aunt Sleak said. "Vids of the wake for your parents and your speech had some of the highest ratings among our Clans and moved trillions of our people to action. A storm of outrage swept through the Clans at the deaths of your parents and the loss of *The Omaria's* exploration fleet. You're the perfect one to make such a plea."

"I–I can't. Why would they listen to me. What will I say?" Naero said.

"Say what needs to be said," Aunt Sleak told her. "Speak from the heart, like you did for your parents. You need to be the voice of the Alliance, calling for aid to come to our assistance, on the eve of a battle we cannot hope to win on our own."

"I'll...I'll try my best." Naero was still in shock.

"Let's get it out there," Klyne said. "Every second we wait plays into Triax's hands. If we're going to do this, let's do it now."

Naero stared down at her simple flight togs and gear, and held up her hands.

"What should I wear? I just look like a regular Spacer. Shouldn't I dress up or something if I'm going to address all the Clans?"

"No," Aunt Sleak said. "That's perfect. That will appeal to the warrior heart in all Spacers."

She undid the gold clasp holding back Naero's long, raven-black hair and arranged the thick, luxuriant mane around Naero's athletic shoulders.

"My sister Lythe–your mother–was always so proud of her hair. It was her trademark. You have been blessed with its beauty, too, and you're her size. You're built just like her. You look like her with your hair down the way she wore it. Our people loved her and your father deeply and honestly. They'll respond to you, their daughter.

"The Clans are still intensely outraged by their loss and the way they were taken from us. Show them the courage in your heart; speak to their hearts, Naero. Tell them what is at stake here and why we need their help so desperately."

Naero gulped in air. "I don't know if I can do this."

"You can. You are a Maeris of Clan Maeris. What's more, you are the blood of *The Annihilator* and *The Invincible Cyclone*. Just keep the love of your parents and all that they taught you and stood for in your heart. The love for your people and freedom. The words will come to you. Wait, just two more details."

Aunt Sleak unbelted her jeweled sword from her own waist, knelt, and put it around Naero's slender hips, adjusting the clasps.

Then she pweaked Naero's glowing rank insignia on her arms to blazing gold bands.

The rank of captain.

When she stood back up, Aunt Sleak kissed her on both cheeks. "Consider it a battlefield promotion."

By then, Klyne was ready with the vid crew.

They tried a few takes for testing and sound, and then motioned for Naero to go on.

Naero did not hesitate. She put her hand on her sword, drew herself up and faced the cameras with the love for her parents and her Clans blazing in her fierce heart, and fire in her eyes.

"This is a direct call to arms and battle. I am Captain Naero Amashin Maeris of Clan Maeris, daughter of Lythe Ivala Maeris and Tarthan Wallace Ramsey. I am part of a desperate alliance with our friends at Joshua Tech, the Mining Revolt Worlds, and parts of the reformed Matayan Empire. Worlds who desperately seek to break free from the tyranny of Triaxian subjugation.

"Within the days to come, decisive battles will be fought between our Alliance, Triax, and five other Gigacorps waiting in the wings. We are heavily outnumbered. Massive fleets are already poised to pour in and overwhelm us.

"Due to current Interstellar Treaties following the last Spacer War, no Spacer navies can take part in these battles in any way without violating those treaties and causing another all-out war. But the political result is that our just cause remains cut off and outnumbered thirty to one.

"We desperately call upon each of the Clans to send private ships and volunteers to aid us in our time of great need. Keep in mind that if we fall, and Joshua Tech and its allies are destroyed, nothing will stop the Corps from massing a full invasion into the Spacer Extents to crush the Clans, one by one. Once they finish with us, they will come for you. We must fight them and stop them, here and now at the strategic battles around Nuratine-5."

"Please, I implore all the Clans: Only you have the power to aid us. If my parents and their memory and achievements for our people ever meant anything to you, please help us. Please send volunteers to join our cause. Whatever happens, we are poised to do battle with the common foe and fight to the end.

"Against the same gutless cowards who murdered my parents and their entire fleet, and seek to murder us all and our liberty, and enslave the survivors under the weight of their chains forever."

She drew her sword and saluted. "Remember *The Omaria*! Vengeance upon our foes!

"Stand with me. Stand beside us. Fight beside us for the freedom of the stars, for the good of all. For the honor of Clan Maeris and all the Clans, I thank you. This is Captain Naero Maeris signing off, preparing for battle. May fortune favor the bold!"

Klyne cut the feed. Everyone present clapped and cheered.

"That was great," Aunt Sleak said. "Perfect."

"But do you think it will work? Will any help reach us in time?"

Klyne shrugged. "We'll find out soon enough."

44

The Alliance spread out their defenses along a short section of Joshua Tech and Matayan space near Nuratine-5, on the borders of their contested empire with their former Triaxian masters.

Space now patrolled by Joshua Tech forces spread very thin.

Klyne summoned them all to another strategy meeting in the conference room on their way to Nuratine-5.

Naero and Jan met Aunt Sleak and the others there.

"Bad news," Klyne told them. "This just in. Sleak, there's no good way to say this. Your ships were intercepted by the Triaxian Navy just outside of Alpha Arae-5, on their way here.

Aunt Sleak braced herself for the worst.

"Zalvano protested, calling their seizure attempt illegal. When he resisted arrest and tried to fight his way out, additional elements of the Triaxian Navy that just happened to be in the area closed in on them to assist.

"The Shinai, Nevada, and *Ardala* all escaped. They're with the Shadow Fleets now, and they're well-hidden; their crews safe."

Naero had never seen Aunt Sleak look so pale.

Sleak couldn't help asking. "What about *The Slipper?* And *The Dromon?"*

"They're gone, Sleak. I'm sorry."

Naero sucked in an amazed, terrified breath.

Aunt Sleak looked as if someone had struck her with a hammer.

"The Dromon? They destroyed *The Dromon?"*

Naero felt as if her own circulation had stopped. Her Clan. Her friends. Chaela, Saemar, Tyber, and Zhen. Everyone she knew.

Haisha. How many survived and for how long?

"It took a lot of doing," Klyne said. "But they were outnumbered and outgunned by the Triaxian Navy. Even planetoids can be busted up—with enough firepower. I'm sorry, Sleak."

"Zalvano? The rest of my people?"

"All remaining hands fighting on those two ships were reported lost or shot down while resisting arrest. Triax wanted to make an example of them. It looks like they did. By our reports, the bastards even blasted escape pods and bubbles."

Aunt Sleak nodded her head slowly; then she broke down and put her head into her folded arms.

"My crews, my Zalvano...my gentle Zalvano. I should have married you when I had the chance."

"You may still get that chance," a voice suddenly said.

Naero looked around the room, and saw an image shimmer.

"Get down!" Klyne said, and pulled Aunt Sleak behind him. Naero dove on top of Jan.

Intel guards trained their pulse rifles on the image taking form on the floor of the conference room.

Naero looked up in time to see Baeven. He carried someone. It was Captain Zalvano, beat to hell and wounded but in stasis, his condition frozen.

Aunt Sleak let out a little cry and sprang up. She took Zalvano from Baeven and lowered him gently onto a nearby couch. "We need a medbed. Hurry!"

Klyne snapped one right out of the wall.

Baeven smiled at Naero and Jan and took a step toward them.

"Hold it," one of the Intel guards said.

"Make the slightest move," Klyne said, "and my people will cut you down. I've waited a long time for this, outcast. How did you find us? How could you possibly know to reach us here, in the middle of nowhere in a warzone? Only you could do this."

Baeven smiled. "I'm me; I have my methods."

"You will find it difficult to leave the same way you came," Klyne warned.

"I'm sorry to hear that," Baeven said. "And, of course, you don't want to hear this, but you don't know how badly you need me out there. Ten of me, a hundred of me if it could be managed. But even I am only one, and I can't be everywhere at once."

"What have you done and why have you done it?" Klyne asked. "You always have many reasons for every move you make."

Baeven shrugged. "This one was simple enough. I owed Sleak a big one here. I had rather hoped that all of you would be a little more grateful."

Sleak glared at him, but her glare softened somewhat as she looked back down at Zalvano.

Baeven frowned. "Actually, I owe Sleak a lot more than one. I lost track of her for a time, so I trailed after her people, hoping that they'd link up with Jan and Naero again at some point. When Triax got vengeful and went after her ships, and the others jumped, it was all I could do to salvage Zalvano. I'm sorry about your people Sleak. They went down fighting bravely, for whatever that's worth."

"Thank you," Aunt Sleak said, holding Zalvano's hand. "This changes little between us, but thank you."

"Outcast," the Intel leader said, with utter contempt. "This changes nothing concerning the many charges heaped against your years of villainy and destruction. You are hereby under arrest for high treason."

Baeven clucked his tongue. "Oh, please..."

"*Any* resistance, and you will be destroyed, immediately. I repeat. I don't suppose you will explain how you found out where we were or how you got on board our ship in the middle of a war zone?"

"Intel and I still have many of the same sources," Baeven said. "Your networks are ahead of the Corps, but then I know what to look for. Don't worry–to my knowledge they're not onto you directly, yet. But I can't say how long that's going to last. They still want the Kexxian Data Matrix very badly."

"Forgive me if I can't trust anything you say," Klyne said. "You've already betrayed Naero and nearly handed her over to our enemies. I won't take a chance on you betraying our people again."

Baeven seemed offended, as if he'd been slapped. "Why would I come here, then, and go to all the trouble of rescuing my old shipmate Zalvano?"

"Easy," Klyne said. "To ingratiate yourself to us, play upon our emotions like you always do. You may have even organized that Triaxian naval attack, for all we know."

"I might have at that, but that would not have served any purpose of mine," Baeven said. "My time is extremely valuable. I seldom waste it...Leonidas."

"That's Klyne, to you, outcast. Well you're going to have a lot of time on your hands to waste now. You just don't get it, do you? We don't trust you. We never will."

"That may well be to your misfortune, and that of our people."

"What do you care about our people?" Jan said.

Baeven stared into his eyes. Part of him seemed genuinely hurt. "I care so much for our people that I serve them in ways no other agent can. I travel in circles that even Spacer Intel cannot match. And what is my reward? I am declared outcast, and traitor."

"You were going to sell my sister to the Corps," Jan said. "To the highest bidder."

Baeven waved a hand. "Oh, please. That was a ruse; even Naero knows it. I needed vital information about the Kexxian Matrix. We obtained it and virtually gift-wrapped it for Spacer Intel. I admit there was risk involved, but that is sometimes necessary. Tell me this, Naero: Who was it that tried to set off your suicide device? Me, or Intel?"

Naero glared at Aunt Sleak and then Klyne. "He's right about that."

Neither even blinked.

"I've heard enough duplicity," the Intel leader said. "I'm going to enjoy this. Put him in restraints. I want a constant guard of four around him at all times while he awaits the order for his execution. If he tries anything, terminate him."

"Wait," Aunt Sleak said. She rose, stood before Baeven, and looked him in the eye for a long moment.

"I believe him," she said.

"Sleak, you can't be serious," the Intel leader said.

"No, he was my brother at one time. That is no more, but when he claims that he only poses as the liar and the traitor, I believe him. He has done many amoral, unethical things, but always his intent has been directed at the positive welfare of our people, even when things have gone badly. Think about this and look at his record and you will see that this is true."

Klyne snapped. "How can you defend him, Sleak? What about your dead crew and the ships you lost at Toraga-5?"

"Trust me. I have gone over that incident–many times. I think we were all triple-crossed, even Baeven. The Fourth Spacer War was about to be unleashed, no matter what any of us did. Toraga-5 was a wake-up call."

Baeven bowed to her slowly. "I thank you."

"I believe him too," Naero said. "You cannot put him to death."

"Come on, sib," Jan said.

"No, I agree with Aunt Sleak. Baeven puts himself above every law and authority, but in his own warped, twisted way, I think he still works for the good of our people–perhaps all peoples."

"Yeah, right," Jan said.

"I will not execute him outright," the Intel leader said. "But he will be restrained and kept under guard and he will face Spacer justice. We have many questions for him."

"I may yet prove useful," Baeven said with a smile and a sigh. "What a relief."

Despite all that had passed, seeing Baeven restrained and taken away saddened Naero a great deal.

What worried her, and probably Intel even more, was the fact that Baeven had found them so quickly and easily.

If he could do so, eventually the wrong people could do the same thing.

Naero returned to her quarters, so much on her mind.

When she pulled her bunk panel out to grab some rest, she saw a small glowing disk waiting in the very center.

A message played across the surface.

Bring this device to me. Urgent. B.

At first she wasn't sure if she should.

Om, what is this device?

Let me have a fixer examine it. It gives off very strange temporal readings. It seems highly dangerous.

A fixer floated down and tried to examine the disk.

And screeched as it got sucked into it.

Another message played across the surface.

Do not delay. Millions will perish each instant you wait.

Naero grabbed the disk.

I would not do that if I–

Even Om cut out as the disk absorbed into her hand and vanished. Other than a little tingly and numb, she felt just fine.

Time to pay the outcast a visit.

45

Baeven escaped later that same night. No one else guessed how.

Naero had felt the strange disk transfer over to him, after he touched her briefly.

Om came back online in her head an hour later.

Intel searched the entire ship and turned up nothing.

The four flabbergasted guards in the outcast's cell reported a bright, disorienting flash, and in the next fleeting instant, the outcast was gone without a trace before they could even lift their weapons.

Vids and security scans showed the same thing.

Klyne and Aunt Sleak questioned Naero briefly. She was the only one who had visited him.

Naero had no answers for them.

On the eve of the coming battle, they raced to a planning session at the Nuratine-5 Naval Shipyards with High Admiral Nathan Joshua, prince and scion of his noble house. Nathan was the supreme leader of all Joshua Tech forces.

On approach, Naero showed her friends Nuratine-5 on the view screens. All of them were nervous about the coming war.

"This is just part of what we're fighting for, my friends. Joshua Tech and Nuratine-5 are living proof of what can be accomplished with wisdom, compassion, and the right balance of enlightened thinking."

Tarim snorted. "I always heard of Joshua Tech being referred to as 'the good' Gigacorporation. But I thought it was just a joke. Aren't all Corps evil? Even the other Corps despise them."

Naero waved her hands at the Intel data on the viewscreens. "Study the facts about Nuratine-5 and all the other Joshua Tech worlds. Compare them to any of the other Corps. And, of course, Triax is always the worst. They seem to revel in their tyranny."

"This doesn't make any sense," Ellis said, gawking at the stats. "Joshua Tech worlds encourage personal freedom and human growth potential for their populations. They have free education, healthy population growth for their expansion policies into the uncharted regions, excellent social services, and about one tenth of the crime rate of the best of all the other Corps."

Naero smiled. "It makes perfect sense. Common sense. Joshua Tech merely uses power directly for people, not against them. They understand the flaws of human nature and protect their systems against those flaws with systems of checks and balances. They openly admit that a corporate system rigs, manipulates, and controls literally everything.

"But what if that power could be harnessed in an enlightened, controlled, managed way for the good of everyone, and not just the greed and power of a few? The Corps don't have to be evil and oppressive and lead to the tyranny of a few over the many. Joshua Tech is living proof of that, and for that, the other Corps hate and seek to destroy them."

"Look at them economically," Jan noted. "Their consistent profits and stable systems pay many dividends. Stable, sustainable economies. Happy, thriving populations and cultures. Very little poverty, and with their focus on education, their growth in innovation and research and development are off the charts."

Naero punched up data screen after data screen. "Because they free up their populations to achieve as much as they possibly can, and promote human growth and individual liberty, freed from the chains of unnecessary poverty and ignorance."

Ellis laughed. "I will speak to my uncle about implementing such policies on the Matayan Worlds. Right now, the best education only goes to the wealthy and the strong, and there is constant rebellion, rampant crime, and discord on our worlds. It does not have to be that way."

Naero smiled at the prince. "No. It doesn't. There's no reason in our huge economies of stratified scale that we all can't do well, if we simply have the will to make things that way. But we must design and make them function in those ways. The Corps rig their systems more or less against their populations to concentrate wealth and power in the hands of a corrupt and debauched few. They do so to exploit and oppress. But a more open and enlightened system could also be rigged in favor of everyone, and in the end, the rich are only a little less rich, and gain the added benefit of being a vital part of a more stable, sustainable society."

Jan laughed. "Half of the Corps still post higher profits than Joshua Tech, but they are also among the most oppressive."

"Of course," Tarim said. "You can always make more profit by hurting and crushing it out of people. Like they do with the miners. But it doesn't have to be that way. And that's why the miners were only too happy to be annexed by Joshua Tech."

Ellis looked grim.

"And precisely why Triax and the other Corps have to destroy us all, and any who oppose their tyranny."

That made them all grow quiet and very uneasy.

They boarded a Joshua Tech naval shuttle and accompanied Klyne and Aunt Sleak on board the High Admiral's flagship, an enormous combined battle ship and fleet carrier, *The Kenteron*.

It surprised Naero and the others to see fixers already bobbing around like pets among the flight command crew.

Prince Nathan Joshua, the High Admiral himself, even had one. An athletic-looking man of just over medium height and age, he possessed keen black eyes set in a stern face. They glittered, as if they were chiseled out of shining stone. His dark brown hair hung straight down his back, set off by several platinum and gold clips.

His tailored, sky blue uniform looked impeccable, the long coat decorated with gold and platinum brocade and accents.

The command deck of the fleet flagship was constructed and crewed in great rings, with an enormous holographic display projected in its center.

Naero's sensitive nose caught the scent of several energy drinks on hand, as well as Jett.

The admiral paused as they drew near and welcomed both Klyne and Aunt Sleak as if he knew them well. He shook their hands and embraced them.

"Klyne, Sleak, my friends. Welcome. We haven't much time; let me update you. Ahh…Lythe and Tarthan's children. A bitter loss. Prince Ellis of the Matayans. All of you, welcome."

He invited them into a lift up to the center command circle.

He motioned at the holo display with his fingers like an orchestra conductor and it zoomed into their position, displaying their units and their tactical locations and stats in blue.

Aides handed them all data pads.

"Here we have our forces, spread out and layered in a G-level defensive pattern," Admiral Joshua said. "With fast attack sorties waiting to sweep in on the best assault vectors."

"How many strong are we here, Nathan?" Klyne asked.

"Joshua Tech has seventy-three major worlds to protect and only nineteen fleets with which to do so. Our navy is spread very thin, but we've managed to send myself and one entire fleet of our best ships. Top of the line. Fifty of our finest craft."

He continued to smile while Aunt Sleak blinked and just stared at him. "One fleet? The last we heard, Triax alone had three fleets right next door, waiting to attack."

Nathan grinned. "Actually they have five fleets."

"Five?"

"Yes. Five. And five more one or two weeks away."

"That's ten. Ten to one odds, Nathan."

"Those are only the Triaxian fleets. They also have a Matayan Fleet, which they always spend as shock forces. And their allies from the other Corps–Omni, Stellar, Matashi, Krupp, and Gelden–also have three to possibly five fleets positioned close by to join in, if need be. With more on the way."

Aunt Sleak took a breath and looked away, glancing up at the holo display of the enemy's known forces.

A raging fire of endless little red dots spread out in arcs and fans and various strategic vectors in front of them and to either side.

"What about our allies?" Naero asked.

Small patches of green blips appeared near the blue ones. Not many.

"The miners have pieced together about two dozen vessels that could loosely be called warships," Nathan said. "After their civil war, the Matayan Prime Minister has about half a fleet left. Good solid ships with good crews. We have the fixers and other programs running, but there aren't enough ships or captains, and not enough time."

"Two fleets," Aunt Sleak said flatly. "Two fleets against thirty to forty enemy fleets. That's twenty to one odds."

"The call has gone out," Klyne said. "At least one of the Shadow Fleets will be able to reach us by the time things heat up."

"I feel so much better," Aunt Sleak said. "Three fleets against forty. One hundred and fifty warships against three thousand or more."

"We can do the math," Klyne said.

Aunt Sleak shook her head. "We might as well float out there and throw rocks at them."

Jan giggled.

She rounded on him. "You think that's funny, boy? In a week or two, most of us are going to be dead hunks of meat, frozen in space. Or blasted to pieces on some rock. I went through the last Spacer War. I know what's coming."

"We're ready to fight," Naero said. "Don't yell at us, and don't try to scare us. What about our people? Will they send any help? Have we heard anything? Will they get here in time?"

Admiral Joshua looked to Klyne.

Klyne gritted his teeth. "We won't know until they show up, if they can even make it here in time. Until that happens, we need to fight with what we've got and make the most of it."

Aunt Sleak studied their stats. "All right then. We'll fight the same way we defended the Spacer Sectors. Flat out, all or nothing. Victory or Death.

"Nathan, I want everything that can fly up in space. Freighters, transports, shuttles, yachts, pleasure boats, everything. Everything and everyone fights. Every Spacer is trained to pilot and fight; let's suit them up."

"We still have more pilots than ships," Naero reminded them.

"That needs to change. We'll use the fixers to convert all drones and probes into weapons. If it can't shoot, we'll pack it full of explosives and ram it down their throats. We fight smart. We lure them in, make them think they have us bent over. Then we hit them with everything we've got from all sides."

Admiral Nathan Joshua smiled. "I like your thinking, Sleak."

Aunt Sleak snarled. "*Haisha*! Nobody's gonna like any part of this. We keep at them until they're finished...or we are. Pass the word. We all better get ready for sheer hell, because it's coming."

46

Prime Minister Adrin positioned his Matayan fleet nearby, securing their right flank at several levels. Then he joined the planning session. Ellis and his clone uncle embraced.

The prince would soon command half of that fleet–the attack wings–while Adrin and his flagship held the line.

The miners arrived last, and scattered their beat-up, cobbled-together fleet on the left flank. Even they knew that they were the weak link in the defense around Nuratine-5. Yet they had Shalaen and her powers, a definite wild card.

Plus, Admiral Joshua reinforced them with mine-layers, short-range system defense gunships, and mass drivers.

Nevano Kinmal arrived at the planning session.

Tarim approached him when the formal greetings were over. "Sir, how is your daughter? Is Shalaen all right?"

Kinmal embraced Tarim. "She's doing well, son. She sends her personal greetings and tells you to take good care of yourself during the coming battles. She hopes to see you once more, after the fighting is over."

"Tell her I...tell her from me to do the same, sir. Good luck to you and our people. Fight well."

"Fight well. I'll tell her everything you said. She'll want to know."

"I love her, sir. I would give my life for her."

"She knows that, son. That's why you can't be with her in this. She doesn't want to lose you."

For three hours they made they final plans and adjustments.

Admiral Nathan Joshua reported to them.

"This is it, my friends. The enemy's making their first move; they'll hit us in less that eighteen standard hours. After the initial contact, we'll have to continue to adjust and shift our strategies on the fly, according to the flow of battle."

"How many are they sending in?" Aunt Sleak asked.

"We mark three attack groups on three optimized vectors, two hundred ships, four fleets each. The Matayans will hit us first."

"Well, at least our foes are taking it easy on us," Klyne said with a grin. "That's only twelve fleets against our two. But at least one of our Shadow Fleets is on the way. Its vanguard should reach us in a matter of hours. Your remaining ships are with them, Sleak. And they're ready to fight. You and I will divide up the Shadow Fleet between us and lead them on the attack."

"Good. Got it. Admiral Joshua. Give the order."

Joshua nodded. "To your ships, everyone. Good fortune. Fight well. May the Powers That Be guide our hands. Battle stations. Let's give them a fight they'll remember."

The assembly raised their fists and took up the cry.

"Battle stations!"

Naero hugged and kissed her friends on both cheeks–even Aunt Sleak, Klyne, and Admiral Joshua.

After Adrin, she came to Ellis.

The jerk smiled at her. He still looked handsome in his new Fleet Captain's uniform. Even if he was a Matayan bastard.

"Don't die, Captain Naero. I would very much like to see you again, privately, after our coming victory."

"Then don't get your cute little ass shot off either. Maybe I'll let you prance around for me, my prince."

He chuckled, drew close, and whispered to her, "I'd like that. I still cannot forget our kiss, and when we held each other close, Naero."

319

Naero caught her breath and could only nod at first.

She found her voice again as he and Adrin departed. "Prince Ellis. Luck to you. Fight well."

Now it was his turn to grin at her and nod.

47

Nacro had only a handful of hours to help oversee the loading of hundreds of fighters and gunships into huge bulk freighters to ferry them out to the battle.

Spacers worked together with miners and Joshua Tech personnel around the clock to coordinate the transports.

She wore a gravwing to help her flit back and forth from one landing bay to the next, packing the ships in and lining more up for the next ride.

While she was up in the air, she spotted glittering fields of shining metal, kilometer after kilometer in the distance.

She called the west tower. "Tower, what is all of that stuff shining and glowing out to our west?"

"Captain, that's the naval graveyard where all the junkers and obsolete craft from the last three centuries rot and wait to be scrapped and smelted."

Naero blinked.

Graveyard?

She had visions of Boon-3.

She called excitedly over her com. "I want every fixer available sent over to this damn graveyard. Let's see what we can raise from the dead. Get every pilot and stunt jockey who can fly and fight over here to suit up. Get armies of flight teams and teks over here and some of the admiral's people to organize them into new fighter wings."

"Captain, I can't authorize that. And neither can you. It would take an admiral to–

Voices cut in almost instantly.

"This is Admiral Nathan Joshua. Follow Strike Captain Maeris' orders to the letter. Give her whatever she wants."

"This is Admiral Sleak Maeris. Haul ass, people. Send all available fixers and shipless fighter pilots to that location. Toss those birds in the air and make them fly. Get on it."

"This is Prime Minister Adrin. Captain Ellis will be sending down several thousand Matayan pilots from our training programs, if you should happen to have any extra empty fighters that need them."

In minutes, clouds of fixers roared in.

Flight teams and unit organizers arrived in waves, stacked up right behind. They pocketed the empty fields and dry lake beds, blowing up clear plasteel bubble tents and hangars, exploding like a virus, spreading out over the entire western landscape in organized chaos.

Naero and Om led the fixers directly into the graveyard, and put them to work.

Gutted ships. Derelicts. Rust buckets. Famous old fighters of legend, long obsolete.

Haisha, haisha...

Naero knew them all.

They were the ships of legends she grew up with.

She knew their history, their armaments, their specs and performance. She knew who made them, their variations, how long they served, and what battles they fought in.

From the time she could float she had flown all of them in simulation.

The Gamma-67 Lightning, The Chikara-88 Rocket Dog, even the Gelden-11 Fox Cat.

She and Om directed the fixers to not just re-configure each model, but to upgrade and improve upon their core designs and mutate them up to speed, with modern, advanced capabilities, shields, and armaments.

The result? Exciting hybrids of the old and new, blended together.

On top of that, an AI fixer merged with each new craft to assist the future pilot in both rapid flight learning and training, and during actual combat.

Then Naero spotted them. Like broken, ancient warrior gods lying in the grass, still in their shining armor.

Hundreds of corroded Stellar F-59E Ghost Dragons, crumpled and forgotten–abandoned in the weeds. Famous legends from the past.

Ghost Dragons.

Finest all purpose fighter of the Third Spacer War through 2451. The ship that almost defeated the Clans. So effective that Spacers captured and virtually copied it, calling theirs the P-24 Valiant. First fighter to ever have its own deflector screens.

Naero almost drooled. She couldn't help touching them.

"Some of these are going to be mine and Jan's new personal fighter squadron. The Ghost Dragons are going to scorch the stars once more. I want every possible upgrade pumped into them."

She and Om personally oversaw the re-configuring of the first advanced prototype.

Eight heavy hyper-velocity pulse cannons, level-four shields, close-in rapid-fire nose and aft defensive blasters. Micro-fusion bomb and missile racks. Twin Joshua Tech E-353 Micro-pulse core reactors, jump, and sublight accelerator drives. One quarter the weight and a hundredfold the energy and flight capabilities. Advanced gravitics, avionics, and electronic defensive packages.

Good work Om.

I could not orchestrate any of this without your precise, intimate knowledge of these fighters. You are guiding this program as much as I.

A collaboration, then. How long until we can fly them?

The first formations will be ready for test flights and training in forty standard minutes. Are we expecting visitors?

Why?

Several dozen persons in flight gear and gravwings are converging on our location.

Naero gasped and looked up. Out of the sun, multiple gravwings shot down straight at her.

She prepared to flee, drawing her sidearm and her battle blade.

We're they trying to capture her?

"Don't shoot us, you idiot," Chaela barked over her com."

"Sweetie, we came to fight with you," Saemar said. "I mean, not literally fight with you, ya know?"

Saemar and Chae nearly collided with her, and the three of them laughed and cried and hugged each other, spiraling slowly to the ground.

Tyber and Zhen joined the hugging circle a few moments later.

Each second, a growing circle of crew and Spacers from Clan Maeris and several other Clans joined around them, swelling their ranks.

Several fighter pilot hunks hovered around Saemar, and seemed to have caught her scent.

Naero raised one eyebrow at her friend. Saemar didn't say a word.

She just rolled her eyes, struggling to suppress her little smile, and shook her curly head in apparent anticipation.

"Ya know, sweetie," Saemar whispered. "We could all be dead just hours from now. We might as well have us a little taste of heaven while we can."

Zhen flung her arms around Naero, crying. "We thought you were dead. And then all of us almost got killed, and so many others died. It all made me realize how much I miss you, N."

"We need to stay together," Tyber insisted. "We hear they're going to make you a strike fleet captain for the coming battle. We can serve with you. Have us assigned to your ships."

"I will." For the first time in weeks, Naero savored real joy, however bittersweet. All of them were going into battles they had little chance of surviving. But Naero would do everything she could to bring them through.

Sorry to interrupt.

Better be important Om.

Several enemy stealth ships have uncloaked and are launching fighters just outside of the atmosphere above our position.

What!?

This far behind our lines, there are currently no effective ships in range to intercept them, and their attack wings will hit our forward positions here in a matter of minutes.

Do we have any fighters ready to send after them?

Negative. Twenty Ghost Dragons are the closest to launching, but they will require fifteen standard–

Naero called out to her forces just as the warning sirens went off. The fleets were now aware of the attackers, also, for all the good it did them.

"Everyone, take cover," she shouted. "Prepare for an enemy attack on these positions."

How did the enemy find them again? And just happen to launch sorties against their precise location. Their foes would destroy their new ships on the ground, before they could get them in the air.

She had to do something. Naero just didn't know what.

48

Naero jumped in Ghost Dragon-1, her new fighter, the fixers still humming and droning all around her.

Om, what can we do to speed this process up?

Nothing. The fixers are already operating at their limits.

She clenched her fists and teeth and groaned in frustration.

"Aauughh!"

There must be something. We have to think.

Why don't you just merge with this vessel? With your knowledge and our teknomancer abilities, together we could complete the reconfiguration much faster than the fixers. Assume control of the process and finish it...in seconds.

Om, I've never done anything like that. I don't know how.

Yes, you have. When you created the first fixers. Just think of the ship as a larger, more complex unit with a different design and purpose.

Naero closed her eyes and tried to focus.

No, not like that. Join with the ship. You're an expert pilot. You've done so many times without even thinking about it. Become one with the craft. Then instead of making a fixer, complete the ship."

"Everyone get back," she said. "I'm going to try something."

People glanced at each other oddly, but obeyed her commands and pulled away.

It helped if she closed her eyes.

Om did his best to guide her efforts.

"Make a fixer…"

A fixer flashed together in her open hand. Even with her eyes closed she could sense every part of it come together.

She knew it.

For a brief instant she *was* it.

She was part of the fixer, making it exactly what it was supposed to be and do.

In theory, Om was correct. The principle was the same, no matter the size of the object or device.

"Make a ship…not just a ship…a fighter…"

And not just any fighter.

A Ghost Dragon.

Naero gasped at a brief flash of pain like someone sucking her bones out of her flesh.

She felt it. She merged completely with the craft. Feeling each of the droning fixers working steadily and methodically on the reconfiguration. She was the ship; merging with it made every part of her tingle.

Naero not only saw what the ship was, she inherently knew what it should be and do–what it could be.

She noted how far along the fixers were at each stage, absorbed them in an instant without hesitation for the raw materials needed, and completed the task, like energy and tek filling up the empty fighter like water.

She heard her friends and the other Spacers gasp and pull even farther away as the fighter morphed right before their eyes.

Naero even started the gravitics and hovered the ship off the field a few centimeters.

Systems, propulsion, and O&D.

She opened her eyes and climbed back out, rushing to the next fighter to lay hands on it and complete the same re-fit.

Tyber alone flew after her with his own gravwing. He wept openly, stunned and amazed, pale and gaping.

"Naero, what the hell did you just do? I still can't believe it. *Haisha*…you completed the refit on that wreck in seconds. In a flash. It was like–like a miracle of some kind. I've never seen anything like it."

"Kind of busy here, Ty."

She zapped another, and moved on to a fourth.

Tyber gasped. "You…just did it again."

"Chaela, Saemar, get our best pilots in these rigs. No time to test them. We're going up to meet our new friends and crash their party. The fixer AIs merged with the ships will help each pilot. Have the other fighters launch and sortie with us ASAP."

Everyone stared at her, dumbfounded.

"Roger that," Chaela said in a daze.

Saemar shook her head and snapped out of it. "You all heard the captain. Everyone pick a ride."

Tyber kept following her, watching. Zhen stayed back, visibly shaken and frightened.

"Find something to do, Ty. Deal with it. I'm a teknomancer; I have the ability to speed up the fixers and what they can do. There's no time to explain it all now. Maybe later. I don't understand it all myself. I just want to get enough ships in the air to defend these bases. We can't lose all this right before the battle begins."

In minutes she had twenty ships–two fighter wings.

That would have to be enough to buy them the time they needed.

And she would lead them into combat.

They punched into the air and assumed their attack formations, on a rapid course for intercept.

Only seconds and they plunged in the mix.

Twenty sleek, silver Ghost Dragons, complete with narrowed eyes and shark teeth in snarling jaws painted on their noses.

Multiple long-range missiles locked on, heading straight for them.

The Triaxians had already fired.

Naero counted two hundred bogeys stacked up against them on multiple vectors. Triax Achilles-125Ds, their top-of-the-line space-superiority fighter.

Chatter from the enemy pilots, stunned at the presence of any resistance at all magically popping up from the surface.

Naero laughed. "They were certain they'd caught us napping."

Thanks to their spy.

But they still zeroed in for the kill.

"Take out those missiles," Naero demanded. "Then let's get in closer and mix it up. The Ghost Dragons can take it and give it back double."

Beams. Chaff. ECMs. Cluster anti-missile mines and evasive piloting.

Three missiles impacted on Ghost Dragon deflector screens and only took them down twenty percent.

Naero grinned as they closed with the enemy pack. "Here we go, people. Hunt 'em down."

Chaela jumped in. "They're overconfident. They're still too close to each other."

"Use it, use it," Naero advised. "All right, new plan. Dragons Two through Eight, stick with me right down their throats. Everyone else pair off and hit their stacks from every optimal vector possible. Keep on them. Keep them busy."

Naero led them in, accelerating to attack speed, flipping her squadron in, over, and under the lead elements.

They locked on and fired weapons at multiple targets all along the way.

Each Ghost Dragon unleashed a storm of fire and advanced ordnance.

Multiple explosions rocked the sky.

They shot through the enemy formations.

Enemy ships vanished in bursts of flame and detonations of their fuel, power cores, and ordnance.

Cries of their pilots cut off abruptly.

First contact cost Triax twenty-three fighters and a dozen more heavily damaged and pulling out.

No Ghost Dragons fell from the sky, although two were shot up pretty good, their fixers repairing the damage as they kept fighting.

But Naero saw their weakness.

Their initial shields took a beating, and most were already down by half, if not completely gone.

And it took a while to bring those shields back up, even with fixers.

Triax had enough numbers to wear them down.

"Good work, Spacers. Keep at them," Naero said.

Chaela cut in. "Sir, three wings just broke off to make a strafing run on our airfields."

"Punch it, everyone. Break off and intercept them."

Now they showed Triax their speed.

The Ghost Dragons shot away from Triax's best in mid-combat and vanished, as if their foes were standing still.

Naero had improved their top speed by more than thirty percent.

They fell upon the strafers just as they began their attack runs, and put most of them down.

Only one or two got through to cause damage, and they were forced to break off or be destroyed.

Even though the enemy still held a numerical advantage, they cautiously pulled back to regroup.

That would buy the fixers and the ground crews precious minutes.

The respite did not last long. Their foes charged back in, very determined.

"Here they come again," Saemar said.

"Copy that," Naero said. "Check their new attack pattern."

The fighters were now bolstered by four light strike cruisers with strange rapid-fire spinal guns. Very weird energy signatures emanated from those guns on the scans.

In addition, waves of enemy ground attack bombers lurked behind their defensive screens, waiting to go in once the defending fighters got swept from the sky.

Not going to happen.

"I want those heavies. Let's take 'em out one at a time. Swarm on them in close orb formation and pound them. Then we hit the next."

But weird violet pulses of energy beams shot out from the triple-barreled big guns.

Some new type of enemy cannon.

Too late. One blast tore right through Naero's shields.

At first, she thought she was a goner. Her ship would cook off in the next instant and blow her apart.

Then she dropped like a stone out of the sky, all power gone. Every system dead.

Ion disruption beam. Total energy drain. You must re-start one or both of the energy cores before we crash.

Naero struggled to merge with her ship again and do so, while it spun out of control, while enemy fighters zeroed in on her to follow her down.

While the enemy cruisers blasted more of her friends and drained their ships, sending them spinning down, helpless.

And the enemy bombers dropped down to make their runs.

She recalled a line from one of her father's poems. Or perhaps it was one of her own.

I am a ship. My heart is a fusion core,
and I must fly or burst asunder.

After two attempts and two flare-outs, Naero merged with her core drives and re-ignited them.

She punched it, spun back around, and blasted two foes at close range, plowing through their debris.

Om sent instant commands to the onboard fixers on the other Ghost Dragons on how to effect similar repairs.

One Dragon crashed. Its pilot escaped on his gravwing.

Four others re-ignited their cores and rejoined the fight.

From the ground, more single fighters launched and paired up, going after the bombers.

More refitted fighters launched, strange designs and configurations. They shot up five and six at a time. Then entire fighter wings of ten.

The cruisers fired rapidly, robbing defending craft of their power, but more still came on.

"All fighters within range," Naero ordered. "Concentrate all attacks on the lead cruiser. Take them down one at at time. Ignore the fighters, if possible. You fighters that are just launching, blast the rest of those bombers."

In seconds, the lead cruiser was burning and falling out of the sky, rocked by attacks as it fell.

Suddenly it detonated in midair, taking out several ships nearby, both friend and foe.

The other three cruisers withdrew, performing a textbook fighting retreat.

Their foes had lost the element of surprise and they knew it.

Naero guessed that Spacer Intel wouldn't find anything intact from the wreck of the downed cruiser, concerning that new enemy ion disruption gun.

To her knowledge, no one else had such an advanced weapon–not even Spacer Intel.

Where had Triax obtained or developed such an advanced piece of hardware? It sure didn't sound like them.

And even worse, if it worked equally as well on larger warships, that could be a definite game changer in the battles to come.

Capital ships suddenly robbed of all power at the height of a key engagement? That would surely give Triax the advantage, and victory after victory. It could overturn the slight tek lead that Spacers always took for granted.

More Alliance fighters swarmed up from the ground. Spacer pilots, miners, even a few newly arrived Matayans.

The enemy stealth ships retreated outside of the atmosphere and jumped, even as Joshua Tech warships closed in to intercept.

But the point had been made.

The enemy could slip in and hit them anywhere, at any time, even in the rear areas where they thought they were safe.

That would require more of their new fighter wings to be spread out and remain within range to defend their key areas and bases.

Naero shook her head. Easy come, easy go.

And this was all just a taste of what was to come. This fight was just a mere skirmish.

49

Two standard hours later, the Matayan Fleet under Emperor Mellis Tarret VI hit the Alliance's right flank hard, coming at them head on.

Matayans killing Matayans on either side.

Naero watched the opening battle unfold from the bridge of her new command. Several ships were on fire within minutes. Waves of fighters from both sides swept in several directions like flying insects at war.

Yet she and all the Alliance forces remained very aware of the larger Triaxian force positioning itself around them, jockeying for optimal vectors.

The Matayan fight was just a feint, an opening salvo–a sideshow– meant to distract and keep them busy.

That could not be their focus.

Admiral Joshua, Klyne, and Aunt Sleak adjusted their elements to counter the enemy's shifting strategy and tactics.

The Matayan Emperor drove toward Adrin's flagship, bent on snuffing out the Prime Minister's rebellion.

Yet he over-extended his line of advance in doing so, and called in his reserves under Prince Nellis II. It was a rash attempt to finish things decisively.

Adrin called in Ellis's attack wings. Together they jammed up the emperor's superior numbers and cut them to pieces at close range.

Then the Gigacorps unleashed their main assault.

Hundreds of ships, massed in precise formations.

Wave after wave arcing and slicing through the Alliance's weak left flank.

The miners and their battered ships did their best to hold the line.

Up close, the invaders quickly found themselves in a cloud of small ships, bombs, drones, close-range missiles, and mines shot straight at them. Several attackers took heavy damage at the outset.

Even worse, key enemy warships would suddenly lose their shields, or all power, or their weapons went dead at crucial moments.

Shalaen's Cosmic powers might not be limitless, but she used them sparingly to affect the outcomes of key engagements.

Any ship too damaged to keep fighting was towed back toward the shipyards, where clouds of teks and fixers swarmed over them, trying to set them right.

After a few smaller enemy vessels were taken over and towed away, the enemy pulled back and changed tactics. They paid too high a price for a direct assault.

Triax massed its big ships further out, safely away from the defender's close-in strategies, and punched at them with their big guns.

Aunt Sleak cut in over the com. "We can't allow that. Close with them. They can stay out there and blast us all day."

"Agreed," Admiral Joshua said.

"Let's take the fight to them," Klyne said.

The fleets closed again, under heavy fire from all directions.

Naero commanded *The Brightstar*, leading her sortie of two dozen fast-attack cruisers and destroyers on a strafing vector from above the battle, slashing across the entire enemy line.

She'd pulled her command and crew together so quickly that there wasn't time to learn anyone's names. So many new faces, but everyone did their best to work together under duress.

Screens of starfighters protected the Alliance Fleets from several vectors, including waves of Ghost Dragons and other refitted fighters.

They concentrated rapid-fire on the Triaxian main ships as they passed, disrupting shields and softening up the heavies. Their only protections their speed, optimized shielding, and heavy fighter screens.

Four enemy strike carriers suddenly jumped in dangerously close to the battle. A gutsy, canny move for Triax.

Had they jumped in too close to other main ships or the planet, they would have been destroyed.

But now they could launch enough fighters right on top of the defenders to overwhelm.

"All ships. Change of plans," Naero said. "Form up on my mark in a Bravo-X-ray-1 formation. Concentrate all batteries on those new carriers. Take out their shields. We'll perform a Clan Wilde Flip around them and blast their engines and power cores from behind."

One of her cruiser captains cut in. "Captain Maeris, we're taking heavy fire to our rear. Enemy battleships and several other destroyers turning our way. We've got multiple incoming fighter wings."

"We'll have a lot more if those four carriers launch. Get in close and pour it on those strikers. Their big ships won't target us for fear of hitting their own."

Another tactical option presented itself.

"Send all of our fighters in to jam up those launch tubes," she said. "Shoot micro-missiles and bombs down each one to clog them up."

Now her XO protested. "Captain, we can't lose our fighter escort. The enemy will be all over us in minutes. That's insane!"

"Just do it! Obey my commands."

"Yes, sir," the XO said. "Fighter wings on it."

Naero led her sortie in at full attack speed, pummeling the first two carriers and then the pair to the rear, disrupting their shields.

Their fighters swarmed in, concentrating missiles on the launching tubes and drop bays.

Intense enemy fire from the Triaxian battleships blasted one cruiser and two of Naero's destroyers to burning wreckage. A stray shot even struck one of their own carriers, causing heavy damage.

Triax sought to take them down, no matter the cost.

They had more ships. The Alliance did not.

"Everyone hold on. Hard about and flip the strike force over on our heads. Fire up their tails as we're still breaking away from them."

It was a Wilde move, used all the time by fighters, but Clan Wilde was the first to perfect it with light warships during the Second Spacer War.

They pulled heavy G-forces and the ships' structures groaned and strained, but they flipped end over end like gaming tiles and fired straight into the carrier engines and cores as they did.

Two of her ships collided, causing heavy damage.

But one carrier blew up, the other three caught fire, and one listed badly, all in a matter of seconds. Their gamble paid off.

"Hard spin aft over head and come about," Naero said. "Fire at will. Boost the engines and keep those carriers between us and their big guns. Call our fighters back before we're cut to pieces."

Her ship rocked hard under multiple enemy hits. Shields down thirty percent.

Her strike force took a pounding.

Yet they blew up two more of the carriers and left the fourth a burning wreck.

They shot away to regroup.

She lost five ships total, down to nineteen.

She noticed something else.

The enemy wasn't taking any chances on any ships coming back.

They had noticed warships re-configured by the fixers and returning to the battle in a matter of hours or even minutes.

Now any ship left adrift was set off with charges or blown apart entirely by missile frigates.

The fixers would have fewer wrecks to reconfigure.

Aunt Sleak cut in. "Nice job on those carriers, Captain. Regroup and assist Admiral Joshua. Vector in on Point Z-333 Gamma and break up that knot of dreadnaughts. They're cutting Joshua's ships to pieces."

More blips on the horizon.

Three more enemy attack waves on the way.

And they couldn't even contain the forces they were up against now.

"Admiral Sleak–"

"We see them. Take out what we can before they get here. Keep fighting. No let-up."

"Yes, sir. Will do."

50

Admiral Joshua stood in a very bad way.

Naero's strike force swept in to bust things up.

"All ships," Naero commanded. "Bravo-Romeo-2 dual ring formation. Ten in front, nine behind. Vector all shields full forward. We're going to punch at each of those enemy dreadnaughts until they go down. Take out as many as we can.

"We'll get bloody. Anyone takes too much damage, break off and get the hell out. Try to make it back to the shipyards to re-configure. No heroic suicides. We can't afford to lose any more ships. Rejoin the fight when you can."

The strategy was brutally simple.

Ignoring all enemy attacks, they jumped on the cluster of six dreadnaughts, spinning around them, concentrating all direct fire on one ship at a time until they either destroyed it or took it out of the fight.

Naero lost one more cruiser from several direct hits from big guns on the way in.

Down to eighteen ships, shrinking to two rings of nine.

All eighteen rapid-fire spinal guns and secondary batteries pulverized the first dreadnaught up close in moments.

But four of her ships were forced to flee. One got swarmed on by enemy fighters and didn't make it.

Two rings of seven. They kept at the second dreadnaught.

It took them precious seconds longer to disable it, but that finally took some heat off of Admiral Joshua.

Enemy fighters and smaller warships hemmed them in, trying to cut them off.

Naero lost five more ships. Two destroyed, three fleeing.

She re-formed into a single ring of nine.

They attacked the third dreadnaught, pouring fire into it, while they took another pounding themselves.

More enemy forces closed in each second.

"All fleets and units," Admiral Joshua commanded. "We are about to be overwhelmed. Enemy reinforcements are coming online. Come about and keep fighting. Perform a fighting withdrawal to the Omicron line and take up your new positions as you receive them. Fight well."

"Copy that," Naero said. "All ships, lets dust this bastard and break off. Flip and spin the ring fast. Disperse and evade in Echo-Whiskey-6."

They left the third dreadnaught in flames.

One of her destroyers collided with another enemy ship at top speed.

Both were obliterated.

Naero and her remaining eight ships scattered, broke away, and then came about, limping and maneuvering back into a Romeo-Sierra-2 rearward stack formation. They fired and withdrew in good order, taking precise, long-range potshots at the enemy.

Triax and its allies continued to reform with their arriving reinforcements and slowly advanced once again, all the while under heavy fire from the defenders.

"Good work," Admiral Joshua said. "We've bloodied them and good. Now we have to hold them again and make them pay. They've already lost more than one hundred and thirty ships."

"While we've lost about forty," Aunt Sleak said. "And the enemy complement just doubled in a matter of a few hours, if anyone cares to notice. The losses we just handed them are nothing to Triax."

"We'll have half of our ships back online in a matter of hours," Klyne said. "They rejoin the fight by ones and twos. Those fixers are amazing."

"That's still not fast enough," Naero cut in. "Our foes are too many."

"Let them come," Nevano Kinmal said. "My people and I are ready for them. Let them bring their numbers. We have a little surprise of our own prepared for them. Let them come."

And come the enemy did, full on and relentless.

Triax knew they had the advantage, and sent in their attack waves in precisely timed assaults designed to bleed the defenders and cut them to shreds.

On the starboard flank, the Matayans were still locked in their death struggle.

To everyone's horror and surprise, Triax ruthlessly opened up on both ally and foe, blasting the Matayans on both sides straight to hell.

The Corps trap closed in around them to end the Matayan problem once and for all, and systematically annihilate the entire right flank.

There would be no more Matayan Fleet.

No more Matayan Empire, ever again.

Just more Triax slaves.

The Matayans realized their peril too late, but turned their battered, burning ships at bay and fought stubbornly.

Prince Nellis II attempted to flee, but the Matayans were fully hemmed in. There was nowhere to run.

Multiple hits tore his heavy cruiser to flaming pieces.

Prince Ellis kept fighting, rallying every ship he could, trying to break the sphere of destruction tightening in on them, firing at the Matayans from every angle.

Emperor Mellis VI drove his burning flagship over the tops of several Triaxian warships, tearing them apart even as his vessel exploded and was blasted to atoms.

He died, cursing everyone on all sides.

The Matayans attempted a break-out at the temporary breach he created, but massed enemy reinforcements cut them off, driving them back into the death trap.

Prime Minster Adrin's flagship listed, almost dead in space, burning and still being rocked by concentrated heavy fire.

A final message from Adrin cut in over their screens; he himself badly wounded, his bridge in flames.

"Farewell, my brave people. Keep fighting for honor and victory. Prince Ellis will be your emperor now. Give my dying ship her head, one last time, as I take her out to the stars."

Seconds later, Adrin activated his shielded reserve jump drive in the midst of the battle.

Several ships around him exploded.

Adrin's flagship became a huge antimatter bomb, and tore a tremendous path of destruction through the packed lines of scores of enemy warships.

The Matayan Fleet broke free, and regrouped under Emperor Ellis, fighting all the while.

At least they were no longer trapped in a kill zone.

Now they could maneuver again.

But even Adrin's brave sacrifice only led to a brief respite.

The enemy's overwhelming superiority in numbers continued to stack up.

Admiral Joshua and his forces tried every trick they knew.

Naero and the other forces under Klyne and Aunt Sleak sent their dwindling attack wings in again and again.

Shalaen disrupted enemy shields and ships until they heard she passed out.

But the enemy kept coming, driving them back.

Then a multitude of bright stars like flares shot out from the mining ships on the crumbling port flank. First by hundreds.

Then by the thousands. They slammed into the forefront of the enemy lines and penetrated right through their deflector screens.

The resulting explosions rocked the enemy, blowing gaping holes in their vessels. They destroyed some small ships entirely.

Even the fighters could not dodge the weird, blazing missiles, and got blasted along with the warships. Against such sudden, massive destruction, even Triax had no choice but to pull back in total, broken confusion.

Within a matter of minutes, the stunned enemy retreated well out of range and regrouped, both sides struggling to understand what had just happened. The battered, exhausted defenders had no strength to pursue their foes, even if they had wanted to.

"What in the holy hell was all that?" Admiral Joshua demanded.

Nevano Kinmal came in over one of the secure channels.

"Our techs and the fixers just developed this new improved device. It's very unstable and only lasts a few minutes, but it can penetrate the enemy flux shields and packs quite a punch at short ranges."

"I'll say," Klyne said. "How do they work?"

Kinmal cut to vid footage of a miner woman strapped into what looked like some kind of simple assault suit.

She switched the unit on and aimed herself at an enemy ship from the deck of a mining transport, smiling all the while. She gave an eager thumbs-up.

An intense white ball of hot energy enveloped her. Then she shot off toward her target.

When she hit, she blasted an enormous hole in the enemy battleship.

"So it's a kamikaze device," Aunt Sleak said flatly.

Naero gasped. They had just witnessed thousands of miners kill themselves, taking the fight directly to the enemy.

Kinmal started trying to explain it again. "The fixers miniaturized a fusion core, a jump drive set to overload, and a shield that lasts long enough for the pilot to hit their target."

"An antimatter warhead," Admiral Joshua jumped in. "But can't we fix it on a torpedo or missile of some kind? The delivery system is…barbaric. Unacceptable."

Kinmal shook his head. "We tried. There wasn't time. The devices are too unstable, and we were rapidly running out of ordnance as it was. This works. The pilots can keep the energy levels stable manually until they hit their target. The fixers can mass produce these simple attack units efficiently. They work. And it was either this or let all of us die here.

"If it's one thing miners have a lot of, it's people. And they're all of us willing to fight, and to die if need be, if that's what it takes to defeat the Corps and give our children a better life. A life of freedom."

Naero bit her lip, thinking back on a time when she thought all landers worthless. Now they shamed everyone with their matchless courage and defiance.

"Well, you've saved the day for us this time," Klyne said. "But let our teks take a crack at stabilizing and using those new warheads. I agree with Admiral Joshua. Let's not waste any lives we don't have to."

51

Fixers swarmed over every damaged Alliance ship in the midst of the brief lull.

Wrecks and debris got collected and towed back to the shipyards.

Try as they might, the Allied Teks couldn't stabilize the tiny jump warheads to be able to fit them onto any existing ordnance. The mining techs had been right. For the moment, their grim delivery system was the only way to utilize them.

Millions of miner men and women volunteered to suit up and give their lives.

For the sake of freedom.

But they were held back strictly as a last resort, to keep the enemy guessing.

Three busy hours ticked by. Many tried to grab some rest.

Most couldn't.

Then a couple hundred small ships emerged from jump.

"Are we too late to join this here shindig?"

Captain Bully's fat, greasy face filled the screen. His ragtag armada was surrounded by a nebula of billions of fixers. "We ain't been sleepin' back on Boon-3. No suh. Everyone's been a dumpin' their junk down on us for such a long time. Now we's gone ahead and made good use of it all. We iz here to hep. Gonna hep make thoze shiny Corps ships pay da price."

The typhoon of fixers worked their way throughout the reminder of the Alliance fleets.

More ships swept in on other vectors.

Another Shadow Fleet arrived, led by *The Alamo*.

Aunt Sleak's ships had already joined her unit with the first wave.

Naero's friends transferred onto her command cruiser, *The Brightstar*, even as the fixers swarmed over it and her fighters, putting many back together after being shot up.

Chae and Saemar took charge of Naero's battered fighter wings and immediately began to advise the new replacement pilots. Zhen stayed in sickbay to assist with the wounded. Tyber worked with the teks, still gaping at the fixers and their handiwork.

There still hadn't been time for anyone to say anything about Gallan missing from their group, but Naero guessed that, like her, they all felt it.

They all had to stay focused on the battle at hand.

All of them could perish within the next hour.

A coded message reached them from Baeven, flooding all of their screens.

Triax means to finish you all off in one final, all-out assault. They've waited only to analyze your new attack methods and adjust the flux of their deflector screens to resist your suicide bombs. You could try to adjust those devices to these new pulse frequencies I'm sending you. I can't be certain they'll work, but it's better than nothing at all. The old ones will definitely be useless. Unfortunately, you face twenty-five new fleets closing in on Nuratine-5 from Omni, Stellar, Matashi, Krupp, and Gelden.

Might I humbly suggest that this is the exact time to get Naero, Jan, and the Kexxian Data Matrix out of this area before the Corps capture them? That might be extremely prudent. Let me know if I can be of assistance. Fight well.

Baeven broke off, as abruptly as he broke in.

Klyne cut over the secured link. "I hate to agree with the outcast, but he's right, Naero. Whatever happens here, one ship won't make a difference either way. Take Jan and the Kexxian Matrix and jump out of here while you still can."

"No...I won't leave you all," Naero said. "I have the right to fight beside my Clan—with my friends and allies."

Aunt Sleak came up, her face set. "Captain Naero, as your admiral and Clan leader, I am giving you a direct order. Get out of here. You've done all that you can and more. But for now, it is your duty to get the Kexxian Data Matrix safely into the hands of our people and keep it out of the hands of our enemies."

Naero did not blink. She stood up out of her command chair and saluted. "Aye-aye, sir. I'll see it done."

Aunt Sleak smiled. "I know you will. Safe journey, Captain."

"Fight well, Admiral."

Aunt Sleak put on her battle face and nodded. "You know we will. Sleak out."

Naero didn't hesitate to give the command.

"Jan, take us around the planet and clear us for jump. We'll pass through Joshua Tech and head for Spacer skies. Get us out of here."

"Aye, Captain. Several Gigacorps fleets moving to encapsulate Nuratine-5. But we'll be well away before they can attack."

Naero bit her lip, keeping silent about the overwhelming odds their friends and family were about to face.

Everyone could guess what was about to happen against such odds.

"Ready to jump," Jan noted.

"Hit it."

The Brightstar went dark and lost all power.

It lurched to starboard as if it slammed into something hard.

Something invisible had swallowed them up.

Naero received a hurried transmission from Baeven on her wristcom.

"You've been overtaken by an enemy stealth ship. They'll board you shortly. Fight your way free if you can and get away. They'll jam all of your—"

Baeven broke off.

What sounded like huge doors slammed shut around them.

Explosions rocked the ship's hull, most likely from boarding parties trying to gain entry.

"Fire all weapons," Naero ordered. "If we're in the belly of the beast, then let's blow a few holes in it. Maybe we can blast our way out. Launch fighters if we can."

Jan and the bridge crew worked frantically to bring up any of their systems.

"We can't get anything online," Jan yelled from the helm. "They hit us with that new ion pulse weapon that disrupts everything."

"Even our wristcoms are out," the com officer said. "Only the fixers are still working."

Naero punched up the hardwired intercom, her voice carrying through the ship.

"Prepare to repel boarders. All troops. Arm yourselves to the teeth and repel boarders at all costs. We've been paralyzed and caught up in an enemy stealth ship to be captured. They will most likely try to take us alive at first. Use that to your advantage. Escape if you can."

She turned back to Jan. "Can't our fixers do anything?"

"They're trying. We've lost all power."

One of the weapon teks shouted. "The fixers are bleeding power from the enemy vessel surrounding us. Main gun, back online. We think the capture ship swallowed us head first, Captain."

"Then fire. Fire at will. Stealth ships are complex. Let's blow a few holes in this one and see what happens."

But they quickly discovered that the capture bay they were being held in was ray-shielded.

The blasts from their main gun bounced around and struck them instead, causing serious hull damage.

"Keep at it. We have to overload those shields."

A female crew member shouted a warning over the intercom, from down in their holds. "Enemy boarders have penetrated the ship. They have stealth suits. We can't see them. Repeat, enemy boarders have–" The woman's voice cut off and the intercom went dead after a flurry of weapons fire.

After the sixth shot from the main gun, the ray shields finally buckled.

Two more blasts rocked the ship holding them.

Explosions erupted.

From the G-forces, Naero guessed they started spinning out of control, pulled back into Nuratine-5's gravity well.

"Get me eyes, sensors, anything. Tell me what's happening. Is there any way to break free?"

The com officer piped up again. "We can see out of a rigged chain of linked fixers outside a rent in the enemy's hull. The stealth ship's on fire and falling back into Nuratine-5's atmosphere. The enemy crew's have their hands full trying to control the descent and keep from burning up or crashing us all to death. Their ship may absorb most of the re-entry damage."

"Any chance of breaking free?"

"None yet, sir. We don't even have flight power."

"Defend the bridge. Everyone get ready for a fight after we crash. If we survive."

"Sir, their jamming is down," her XO said. "Something is firing on us from nearby, but we can't make anything out."

"Another stealth ship? A cloaked ship?"

Baeven.

Naero sent out a call. "Cease fire. Stop firing on the enemy stealth ship. We're disabled and crashing back onto the surface of Nuratine-5. You're going to kill us all."

Baeven cut in.

"Try to survive Naero. The Clans have come. Each one sent ships. The battle's a toss-up now. Both sides will try to retrieve you and Jan from the crash site. See you down there."

"Wait, wait! How many ships did they send?"

Baeven laughed. "A thousand."

Naero gaped and covered her face with both hands.

She heard their voices booming over all channels.

"Enemies of the Clans take heed. Clan Patton sends twenty-two warships to fight beside Clan Maeris. Death to all foes. Remember *The Omaria*!"

"Clan Aztec sends fifteen ships. We will fight beside the daughter of Lythe and Tarthan!"

"Clan Wilde will bleed for Clan Maeris. Death to Triax!"

"For freedom! For *The Omaria*! Clan Donovan sends a dozen ships."

"*Haisha*! We are with you, Clan Maeris. Clan Apache sends forty of our finest warships!"

Each of the forty-nine Spacer Clans had responded to her call for help.

Sending the combined equivalent of twenty fleets.

Twenty fleets of advanced Spacer warships, closing in on Triax in fury and vengeance.

Naero wanted to weep for joy, for the pride and honor of her people.

But at the moment, she needed to find a way to keep her and her people from dying.

Baeven's transmission broke up as they entered the atmosphere.

They were about to burn up and die along with their enemies.

Naero called upon Om.

52

Om. We're about to die. Any suggestions?

The enemy vessel surrounding us is heating up rapidly. You are correct. With all of our shields down, our current form will not survive the re-entry, or the crash.

Options.

I can do little. Only you have the ability to save us now.

Me? What can I do?

You must take control of both ships, repair and use their systems to slow our descent, and keep us from being destroyed by the crash. The same way you took over that fighter.

I can't, Om. That fighter was small stuff. This is big. Two huge, disabled warships, one trapped inside the other. Both of them are out of power and out of control.

The principle is the same. Much more complex than that of the fighter, but based on similar concepts. The size of the objects does not matter. All that matters is that you become one with them and direct their potential with your force of will. This is a level far beyond that of mere fixers. They are mere tools and toys. You are fully aware.

I'm not even a fixer.

*Correct. You are far more…a **teknomancer**.*

How do I begin?

Follow my thoughts as before. Then trust yourself, your core knowledge, wisdom, and instincts. Concentrate. Focus.

She calmed herself and allowed Om's thoughts to direct her.

The first sensation she felt once more was searing, unbelievable pain.

It hurts so much, Om. Much worse than before. I can't do this. Even a portion of the pain is too great.

Your pain is based in fear and ignorance. Use your strength to shield yourself from the pain and the unknown. Push forward.

I can't.

Then everyone dies. Including us. All our friends. Everyone–if you are weak and give up.

Naero couldn't allow that.

She steeled herself.

In her mind, she felt bands of armor encase her.

The pain lessened, but she could still feel it scorching her.

Shield yourself further. That's it. Now touch everything. Grasp the essence of both ships and fully comprehend their potential. Take full control of them down to the smallest element.

In the flash of an instant, she merged with both ships, becoming one with them.

Naero became them, even as the re-entry forces burned and tore her apart.

Naero vaguely sensed the people on board both vessels, their minds and thoughts. But that was not her focus.

The ships. Save the ships.

Neither ship functioned properly. The enemy ship, heavily damaged, her ship, neutralized by the enemy's secret ion pulse weapon. A tek far beyond the Corps.

She tapped into both power cores and merged them, boosting them with her own rapid-fire modifications and force of will.

The parts and components re-configured in an instant, both ships merging and melding into one, a new craft under her direction, the direction of pure thought and intellect.

Naero possessed a pure working knowledge of how starships functioned, or should optimally function.

The Brightstar became the new bridge.

She shielded the new hybrid vessel. Hull temperature dropping rapidly from critical, explosive levels.

Yet they still plummeted through the atmosphere too fast, and she needed all of the energy present simply to maintain the shields.

She boosted their gravitics and repelled against Nuratine-5's gravity field, aiming squarely for one of the two main continents. Not the oceans.

Still not enough.

Finally, she had it. Recalling footage from an Old Terran vid.

Spolymer sails billowed out, caught the wind, and ripped free.

She puffed out more parachutes like breathing. Several more, made of much stronger plasteel fibers.

Finally, their descent slowed appreciably.

Just as Naero felt her strength failing.

She was spent and losing control.

Naero blinked and flashed back into her own body on the new reconfigured bridge.

Well done. We will survive now. But there are still enemies on board. Too bad you didn't jettison them.

Haisha, I barely managed what I did. How many foes remain?

I count two hundred and thirteen, against your crew of seventy-one. But beware. These enemies have suits that cloak them from normal sight, even though prolonged use is fatal to the wearer in the long term.

Triax won't care about that. They just want to capture me and Jan. They'll slaughter anyone else. Have the fixers spray our foes with paint, fibers, barbecue sauce—anything that will make them visible.

Complying. It's working.

Be advised, we are about to touch down in a forest of huge conifer trees.

The ship crashed to a jarring halt and then the aft section dropped through the broken trees and smashed into the ground.

Their com units worked again.

"All troops, out the hatches," Naero ordered. "Regroup in the forest. Bring what weapons and gear you can."

Threescore made it off the ship, under fire from the enemy strikers.

Jan wasn't among them.

Naero nearly panicked. Somehow they'd gotten separated during the confusion fleeing the ship.

"Everyone load up," she said. "We're going back in after Jan."

Explosions rocked the area.

Corps and Alliance close-attack craft swept in from nearly every angle.

The huge trees toppled like sliced reeds, crashing every which way. Drop troops poured in.

Naero led her crew, fighting their way from the crash site, which seemed about to be wiped out by both sides.

"Damn it!" Naero screamed. No going back into that death trap.

Her only choice was to get her and her people to safety.

Even if the Corps captured Jan, they couldn't make any use of the Kexxian Matrix without her half. But she still feared for her brother.

A company of Triaxian Marines attempted to cut them off.

Naero activated her gravwing and spearheaded the Spacer attack. She never stopped moving. All of the enemy strategy seemed focused on trying to capture her.

She shot foes in the face. She deflected and sprang off trees and crushed helmets and armored chests with her fists and feet, leaving the dead and dying in her wake. Her spinning kicks wheeled and struck.

She threw her blades with ferocity.

They ripped through troops. They ripped through thick trees and shattered stones.

She drew her energy cutlass and sliced through arms, legs, and throats. Through energy shields and armor, Naero sliced bodies in half. She scythed through them, a death-dealing, unstoppable force.

A blur of destruction passed through the enemy, tearing through their ranks—the daughter of the Annihilator and the Invincible Cyclone went to war.

Her friends and crew charged behind Naero, cutting down and blasting anything that moved or got in their way.

A hundred foes, taken down in a matter of seconds.

And Naero's rage only grew. At the loss of her brother, Gallan, her parents.

All the senseless loss.

Kill them. Destroy them all. Wipe them out completely.

The intense urge was nearly overwhelming.

Naero stopped herself, struggling to get a grip on reality before she lost it entirely and went insane.

Madness threatened her–madness coupled with the overwhelming lust to destroy. Everything. Everyone. Friend or foe.

She caught her breath. Jan. Focus on Jan. Find him. Rescue him. Get him back. That was all that mattered. Her brother.

Air blasted down on them from nowhere.

A round hatch irised open. No ship visible, yet they could see inside the open hold of a bizarre craft, whose outside they could not see.

Baeven appeared at the hatch. "They've taken Jan. Load your people in. We have one chance to catch them and take him back."

"We're with you, N," Chaela shouted. "Let's go." They packed into the hold and checked their weapons.

Baeven left them and went forward to his sealed bridge.

The cloaked ship they rode in lifted off, almost completely silent.

Naero had never seen a ship like it; every shape and panel and hatch of the design completely alien and strange. Weird controls and symbols.

Up in space, Baeven's unique ship tossed them back and forth, maneuvering and zipping forward in ways no other ship could move. Tremendous explosions rocked them from all directions.

Om, what's happening out there?

The Clan Forces are blasting their way through the Corps Fleets. But the enemy is standing firm. I'm scanning terrible damage and heavy losses on both sides, but the Spacers seem to have the advantage at the moment.

They're trying to give their forces a chance to get away with Jan. Have you analyzed who or what Baeven is tracking?

His advanced systems elude my analysis, but we appear to be pursuing an enemy gunship. It just rejoined a fast corvette, which is preparing for an immediate jump out of this region.

They must have him.

That seems logical. The enemy fleets are blocking the way, and that is the only ship leaving the system.

We can't lose them.

The corvette just jumped. The one you call Baeven is tracking them through jump space. We are only minutes behind them.

No one has the tek to track and follow another ship through jump space. No one.

Somehow he and his ship and crew are doing so.

All right then. Where are we headed?

There appears to be a secret Triaxian forward naval base hidden on Durris, the fourth moon of Hellenda-6. A Triaxian fleet is waiting there.

When will we arrive?

It's a short jump for one of their fastest ships, mere minutes. Yet our ship is passing ahead of it.

No ship can pass another in jump space.

Again, this is actually occurring while we speak. We will arrive at the destination just ahead of the corvette. I sense unusual weapons powering up. Baeven also left a coded message for your aunt's forces to follow hard upon our trail. But at best they will arrive in one half hour.

You said Baeven has a crew. How many are they?

Only a handful. I sense they are not human. You should prepare your assault forces. We will arrive at the secret enemy base in minutes.

Threescore Spacers and a handful of aliens on an invisible ship, against an entire fleet and thousands of heavily armed foes. Most of her friends and crew rested, conserving their strength. Naero alerted them all.

"We'll be coming out of jump soon and making an assault to free my brother and make good our escape. Everyone glacier out and stand ready. Things are going to move fast."

Saemar locked and loader her heavy blaster rifle. "Tell us what to do, sweetie. We're ready."

"We'll follow you into hell," Chaela said.

"Good, because I'm pretty sure that's exactly where we're headed."

53

Baeven alerted them via a floating holo screen that popped in out of nowhere.

"The enemy corvette will be arriving at Moon Durris. We'll attack it just as it's about to land, causing it to lose power and make a short crash. None of its smaller craft will be able to launch, either, so they'll be forced to take him off the useless ship on foot. Make your move to win him back when he's out in the open, during the transfer."

Naero checked her weapons again. "Will do."

Baeven smiled. "My crew and I will back you up from my ship, and pick you up as soon as you've secured him. Get ready to pile out on my signal. We only have a few minutes."

Baeven cut out.

The holo screen showed the enemy's secret base, units of troops guarding the area, and other ships and vehicles outside of the landing zone.

Just as Baeven predicted, the corvette came down, suddenly lost all power close to the ground, and dropped like a stone.

After only a few minutes, a company of heavily armed troops rushed out of the ship, surrounding someone secured on a medbed.

A close-up showed Jan, clearly Jan, unconscious on the medbed. From his wounds and bruises, he must have put up a pretty good fight.

The enemy troops made for the apparent safety of an enormous, nearby hangar.

Baeven flew them into the open hangar, hiding behind the bulk of a much larger enemy ship within, and opened the hatch for them to charge out.

Naero signaled for them to spread out and position themselves quietly. They'd take Jan back as soon as the troops closed the hangar doors or attempted to board the larger ship.

The enemy pulled Jan in and headed directly for the ship.

A loading bay opened.

Lady Drianne Imiviel waited for them, along with her personal body guard, heavy troops all in shining powered suits of assault armor.

"Hurry, you fools," she said. "The evacuation's underway. We launch immediately."

That wasn't going to happen.

Naero gave the silent signal to launch their attack.

Their initial barrage of interlinked fire cut down most of the troops covering Jan.

Amid the shock and surprise, Naero even managed to reach his medbed and pull him to one side, mowing down any stragglers around them.

"Baeven," she called out over her com. "We've secured Jan. Get us out of here."

No answer.

Then heavy fire from Drianne's warship forces drove them back behind the cover of some heavy machinery.

"Change of plans," Baeven finally responded. "This appears to be some kind of elaborate trap. Their fleet is converging on this area and activating some kind of planetary shield. We won't be able to leave the atmosphere unless I can force that shield down."

"We're kind of in a bad way here, Baeven. What do you advise?"

"Stay alive. Fight your way onto that warship and prepare to take off. I'll signal you once the planetary shield is down. How could they have known we were coming?"

"They knew we'd come after him. They used him as bait to try to nab me, too."

"Do what you have to to get out of there, with or without Jan."

"Naero," Tyber yelled. "A little help here?"

Squads of enemy heavy armor advanced on them behind impenetrable deflector shields.

"Disruptor grenades!" Naero shouted.

Thirty grenades knocked the heavies around, shredding their shields. The other Spacers kept firing, blasting through face shields and helmets and other known weak spots in the armored suits.

"We have to fight our way onto that ship and fly it out of here," Naero said.

"We'll never make it," Zhen cried.

"We've got to," Naero said.

They rose up to charge.

All of her friends fighting to either side of her.

Concentrated sheets of fire poured from their weapons, ripping into the enemy forces.

Massive stun blasts exploded right over them, like those used back on Boon-3.

Shielding us from mass stun effects.

"My friends!" Naero cried.

All of them stiffened and fell back.

They are merely unconscious. Our enemies seek to capture us. They will use them as leverage to force you to cooperate.

Lady Drianne called out.

"Surrender, Naero. Both yourself and your brother, or I'll order my forces to execute your comrades where they lay, stunned and helpless."

Take them, Naero. Unleash our defensive protocols and crush them all. They have no idea what we are. What you are capable of. Only you can save us. Merge with our protocols!

"This is not a negotiation," Drianne added. "You have five seconds."

Naero stood up and threw down her assault blaster. "I surrender. You got me."

Drianne smiled at her victory. "That was relatively easy. Indeed I have."

Her pretty face twisted into a snarl of hate. "Get her on a medbed like her brother. I want her in stasis for transport. Once we have the Kexxian Data Matrix in Gigacorps' hands, no force in the galaxy will be able to oppose us."

The heavies closed in, towering over Naero.

Now it was her turn to grin.

She linked with Om's defensive protocols and perceived them in a flash of insight.

"Think again, bitch." Naero unleashed the power locked within her.

Tendrils of light and darkness burst from her, fanning out in all directions like long energy blades.

They neatly sliced through the armored suits of the heavies like molecule-thin razors.

The troops inside them struggled to scream and escape.

Several heavies exploded.

Others imploded, compacting to the size of a helmet, the super-dense hunks dropping through the plascrete.

Naero waded through her foes, layered in defensive spheres of energies, ignoring their attacks, shredding and flinging their shattered, gory pieces to either side.

Lady Drianne retreated in terror.

"What in the hell are you?"

Naero smiled fiendishly. "You're going to find out what I am."

Behind us!

Naero gasped, transfixed, rising up on her toes so high she nearly floated.

She heard some kind of weapon fire.

A white-hot wire of intense agony pierced her skull from behind and out the front of her forehead, paralyzing her so that she could barely keep breathing.

As if she hung suspended on that burning wire, like a thin filament of scorching pain.

Om's voice faltered and garbled. *Shot…head. Behind…trying…*

She couldn't even turn.

Drianne smiled in triumph and came forward again. "Excellent. You got her. Nice shot. Get the grav restraints on her."

Naero felt a spray of blood squirt out of the exit wound in her forehead. Someone had shot her through the skull from behind.

Jan stepped in front of her.

To her complete horror.

Jan? How could he?

Suddenly it all made sense.

He was the traitor.

He shook his head, twirling the sliver pistol in his left hand. "You couldn't make it easy for me could you, sib?"

She struggled to speak and only croaked.

Jan switched the gun deftly into his right hand, then tucked it in his belt. He fixed grav restraints on her wrists.

"No use struggling. I shot you in the back of the head with a mind control sliver. It's lodged in your brain. Don't worry, it won't kill you…unless we want it to."

He punched in commands on his wristcomp.

"There now, that should allow you to speak. Be nice."

She gulped in air.

"Jan? You're with them?"

"Have been, sib. Whenever possible."

He grinned and waggled his hands in the air. "All of you were so paranoid about Ellis. Oooh, a Matayan. Gosh. Too stupid to notice the obvious. The Corps needed an inside man. How do you think they knew where to intercept Mom and Dad? It was me. I set them up."

"Mom and Dad? Jan, no. You couldn't have."

He shrugged. "They were already well on their way to becoming dead anyway; they just didn't know it, N. They thought they alone could control a secret this big? Not a chance. Then they made the colossal blunder of actually giving it to their kids. But they didn't expect the process to change us *all* so drastically, did they?"

Jan's eyes glowed for an instant with scarlet fire, aching to be unleashed. "And here's another surprise. I'm not Jan. That young fool did his best to resist my efforts. But in the end, it was so easy for someone like me with my psyonic powers to slowly take over his unprotected mind. Even he didn't suspect it until it was far too late. But I am your brother, at least genetically. Didn't you hear the story?"

"Danner? You're Danner? But you were murdered."

"I didn't die. I only wished I had. Triax and the Hevangians put me back together, somewhat, and sold me to the Corps, to Triax. My parents, my family, my Clan, my people–they all abandoned me and left me to be tortured and experimented on for years as I grew."

"Danner…everyone thought you were dead."

Danner snarled. "But somehow I survived, thriving on pain…and hatred. A prisoner in my own mind, my powers grew exponentially, until even my captors feared me and my abilities. I allied myself with them in order to get what I wanted: Vengeance. Through me and my sporadic links with Jan, we were able to spy on you and your parents, and Jan didn't even know, until it was far too late. With my abilities, I slowly took over Jan, mind, body, and soul. In order to exact my revenge…on everyone."

He paced around her, hands clasped behind his back.

"Of course, Jan's half of the Kexxian data was easy to retrieve, once I had control of him. But you, you became the real problem. So adept. So resourceful. Every time I set you up–I gotta hand it to you–you came up with some way to screw everything over completely."

"That's why we could never get away. You were letting them on to us."

"Right as rain, sib."

"Danner, no one knew you were still alive. Let us know where you are. We won't stop until we rescue you. We can help you. Don't do this to Jan, to me. The Corps are the ones who did this to you. They've been lying to you for all these years. They took you from us. They can't be offering you enough to betray everyone, Jan, me, your parents, your family–your own people."

"Are you kidding? Now I have this great new body that isn't crippled and shattered. I'm not just some *thing* floating in a lab. With my brother's body, I can go anywhere I wish. Do anything I want. None of you ever gave a shit about me."

"That's not true. Our parents were heartbroken. If they knew you were alive, they would have never stopped trying to find you."

He glared at her, his face twisting like a maniac's. "I'm glad they're dead. I want all of you, everyone, dead!"

"Where is Jan?" Naero begged. "What have you done with his mind? Where is he? Our Clan and I won't stop until we free him from your madness."

Danner laughed. "I just switched with him. He simply doesn't know how to switch back. He's trapped in the same crippled hell I was stuck in for seventeen years. Let him rot there. Whatever form you die in when you die, you're still just as dead."

He patted her on the head. "To hell with all of you. The Clans. The Corps. Everyone. Screw all of you. They're paying me an awful lot, Naero. I yearn to join the ranks of the gods. To go where I want, do as I please, however and to whomever I please, whenever I feel like it. That's what they're offering me. I can play anywhere I want; do anything I want. Complete and total freedom, with absolute impunity."

His grin widened. "You know, they gave me a taste. They gave me some other bodies to try out the mind-swapping process. Sure, I burned them out with my abilities and they had to put me back into mine in the end, but I got a taste–of being a god.

358

"They let me kill...everyone...every living thing on an entire continent of some nameless, backwater world no less. It was...how shall I describe it? Liberating. Exhilarating."

"You're insane, Danner. They'll continued to use you like a weapon. As soon as they have what they want, we're all good as dead. They won't keep their word. You've betrayed everything, destroyed your entire life. For nothing."

"I. Don't. Care. Everyone wants the same thing, N. Power. Nice abilities of your own, by the way. Very different than mine. Didn't know you had 'em in you. But I've been growing as well, in secret. My new skill? Quite convenient really..."

"I can absorb the abilities of others, like eating their heart out of their chest with a spoon. How about I take those new powers of yours for my own? You won't be needing them any more."

He advanced on her as she hung helpless in the air. She couldn't resist in any way.

Drianne called over to him. "We don't have time for this, Lord Dan. Get her on board. That meddling uncle of yours could still turn up."

Danner smiled, fastening the grav restraints on her ankles.

He clucked his tongue. "Later then, when I'm good and hungry for a little snack, sib. Every new ability you have will become mine. In time, I'll even find a way to suck your half of the Kexxian Matrix out of you, and then I'll control it all. And you? You'll just be an empty toy, a hollow little shell for me to do with as I please. Perhaps I'll hang you on a hook somewhere like our brother and let you twist and rattle in the wind. The way I used to."

Naero struggled with all of her might against her restraints, managing only to twitch slightly.

Danner laughed. Then he mock-applauded.

"*Haisha*, I'm surprised you can even do that. How impressively useless. Try all you want; there's not a thing you can do on your own to defeat that teeny tiny little sliver in your skull."

Almost...get ready...

She was not alone.

Naero had no idea what Om attempted, but splitting pain filled her skull where before it had only been numb for a time.

It crippled her. She felt as if she was about to shatter into fragile pieces. Either that or explode.

Om! You're killing me!

Her third eye formed on her forehead again, spraying blood.

Dan pulled away, suddenly uncertain about what was happening.

"Don't get any ideas, Naero. Illusions can't help you. You can't even move. Stop grunting and wiggling and get on board."

He punched controls and floated her toward the loading ramp of Drianne's ship.

Om slowly ejected the bloody control sliver out of their head, right through the very center of their third eye.

The scarlet, crystalline sliver disrupted and turned to dust as it fell.

Done...up to you. I can...no longer...

Om went silent in her head.

Naero lifted her gaze. Her eyes narrowed to slits.

Her third eye burst into blue flame.

"I can't believe it, Dan. You let them kill Mom and Dad. Even if you never knew them, how could you?"

Dan watched her every move, circling, unnerved and uncertain of her abilities now, ready and wary.

He sensed her attack, clenched his fists and shielded himself in blood-red flames.

His pyrokinetics had increased exponentially.

He stared straight back at her with eyes of red-hot flaming hatred. His booming voice echoed.

"The truly great are beyond sentiment, Naero. I've learned that much. They become a natural law unto themselves. No bonds restrain or obligate them. They do as they please, with absolute impunity."

She glared at him. "You're describing a monster. Is that what you've become?"

"You're one to talk, sis." Dan laughed. "The cattle and insects always see the gods so. So be it. Let them know the meaning of fear–the fear of true power!"

"You want power? I'll show you power, brother."

Naero disrupted her restraints and shot up into the azure sky. Wings unfolded from her back, keeping her in the air, giving her mobility. Tendrils and ribbons of light and darkness rippled from her in numerous directions.

"Shoot them," Drianne ordered into her comunit. "Call in reinforcements. Neutralize them both with the new ion cannons, before they destroy us all!"

The Triaxian princess retreated into her warship.

Naero and Dan floated out of the hangar onto the scorched, open ground, clearing their field of battle.

Several enemy units tried to converge on them and unleash attacks.

She and Dan swept the enemy ground forces away to a half kilometer on either side, disrupting their tek, melting some, imploding others.

"You bastard!" Naero raged, seeing her opening.

She swooped in and collided with him. Fighting through his powers with her own.

He grappled with her, his might immense. Horrifying.

"That's it, sib," he said. "Let me feed upon you. Let me steal everything that is yours and add it to my own, as my powers continue to grow, and yours weaken. Just like I did with Jan."

She felt it. He drained her energies, sucking them into a vast black hole within himself.

Given enough time, he might absorb her entirely. She flip-kicked him twice in the face and barely tore free.

Drianne's advanced battleship rose up behind them, crashing up through the entire side of the hangar.

It pulled just far enough away, aimed its massive tri-barreled ion neutralizer, and fired point-blank.

At Dan.

The neutralizer struck him full on, driving him to his knees. Now he was being drained of his energies.

Triax would capture them both.

"No, you fools!" he screamed in defiance. "What are you doing? I almost had her. You will not stop me!"

A massive triangular sheet of black energy fanned out vertically from him, expanding. It struck the battleship and neatly sliced it vertically into two halves.

They fell to either side, disrupting and exploding onto the naval base.

Dan went to his knees again.

His powers were not infinite, either; Naero sensed her chance, perhaps her only one. The ion blast had weakened him considerably.

Her dexterous tendrils, scores of them, snaked out and snatched up stray weapons from the battlefield. In seconds she had a cloud of them, all pointed at Dan.

She unleashed a hail of fire at him, battering him, driving him one way and then the other. Giving him no time to recover or strike back.

She poured it on, pulverizing the ground around him. Slowly his defenses grew weaker, until he cowered in a quivering, curled-up ball at her feet.

"You are no longer my brother, no longer my family. You are dead to me!" She sucked at a wound on her forearm and spat her own blood on him.

"I banish you, by the blood of my Clan. You no longer stand as one of our people. Worse than a traitor. Filthy outcast; your name is dead. *YOU HAVE NO NAME AMONG US*!"

He laughed again, lifting his smoldering head.

"I was always dead inside. Are you done? Good. *My turn!"*

54

He sprang upon her so fast. She didn't even think he could still attack. She shouldn't have let up. Shouldn't have gotten so close.

He had her now.

Both of them knew it.

Both his hands locked on her throat. He drove her back.

She couldn't break free.

Even worse, he drained her energies as fast as he could.

The outcast shuddered with pleasure, feeding on her rapidly.

Her third eye vanished. Her tendrils faded, dropping her useless weapons.

"That's it, sib; just accept it. Accept defeat. I've finally won. Just relax. It'll all be over soon."

"Hey," she said. "You dropped this."

Naero fired the sliver gun straight into his forehead.

He released her, staggering back, gasping in surprise.

He crumbled into a quivering, convulsing heap, twitching and jerking on the ground. Dan still tried to fight his own defeat.

He tried to lift himself up.

It terrified her that he could do that much.

"Oh, no you don't." For good measure, she shot a sliver into each of his temples.

Dan finally collapsed, eyes staring, mouth frozen open, bloody, black, steaming psyonic foam and ichor draining from every orifice.

He flopped away from her. Naero turned him back over and mind-linked with him, his eyes staring with frozen hate.

You'd better kill me now, sib. Even this won't stop me forever. I'm too strong. I'll find a way. I'll come after you. I'll kill everyone. Destroy everything. You can't stop me. No one can.

"Wrong, outcast."

Naero fully perceived how he did it now.

She took him by the throat, and began draining him.

She didn't want his energies or abilities. She used his powers, Jan's, and her own to seek a much more permanent solution, no matter what it cost her.

"I'm stripping you of your abilities. All of the power in the universe won't do you any good without them. You'll be a true nud. I'm taking everything, including your half of the Kexxian Data Matrix."

You can't! I...won't...let you!

Naero snarled and rammed him back down.

"You lie there and take it, you sick, twisted fuck. While I gut you hollow!"

It took all of her strength, every ounce of her own energy until she felt completely burned out, but at last she finished the job.

Naero rose up, weak and dizzy.

She spat on the outcast.

"There, now you're completely empty; just a mere mortal again. Maybe I'll send you back to your friends at the Corps. See how they treat you now, after they realize you're completely useless to them. But I'll be coming after Jan–my real brother. I'll find a way to switch him back."

She looked up at the sky. Bright flashes and explosions flared beyond the atmosphere.

Aunt Sleak and the Clan Fleets had arrived, pushing the Corps back, taking charge of the space around Moon Durris.

Naero stumbled, hoping she could remain conscious long enough to check on her stunned friends back in the ruined hangar. Before help arrived.

She called to Baeven on her com.

"Baeven? Where are you?"

"A little busy destroying that planetary shield. Ahhh…finally, it's down. And help has arrived; good timing. Did you and Jan get away? We did our best to clear a path for an escape route."

Naero shook her head, looking at the devastation all around her.

"No, it's a long story, but I'm still stuck down here. The fighting's over for right now. I'm not a prisoner or anything, but I'm going to pass out any sec. You'd better send help fast."

"On the way. Stay put."

Her friends. She had to reach them.

Naero staggered back into the hangar.

A shadow passed over her.

A booted foot smashed into her face, knocking her into the hangar wall.

Lady Drianne hovered over her in a gravwing. She held a long, slender, ornate sword in her right hand, pointed directly at Naero's heart.

"Finally out of juice, huh? Took you long enough. You and those brothers of yours are really something." She clucked her tongue. "Very, very troublesome."

Drianne called into her com on her left wrist, "Gather up the boy and get out of here. That's an order. I'll secure the girl and be along shortly, in the last stealth ship."

Naero drew herself up. "You're not taking me anywhere. Help's on the way. The Clans are closing in. There's no escape for you, princess."

"I don't think so," Drianne said. "You can barely walk, let alone resist in any way. Now get moving to my ship, or I'll toss a grenade among your sleeping friends over there. That's right. I haven't forgotten about them."

They moved out of the hangar where she directed.

Naero tried to stall for time.

Drianne jabbed her with the point of the sword until she bled. "Keep moving. Don't slow down. We're almost there. The Kexxian Data Matrix will still go to the Corps, and Triax will be the first to implement its secrets, destroy the Clans, and rule the galaxy.

Naero saw flashes of shining ships descending rapidly from the upper atmosphere.

Naero waited until they were well away from the hangar to make her last stand.

Then she simply leaned against a vehicle and stopped.

"I'm not going any further. If you want to take me, you'll have to carry me or drag me, and right now, you don't even have time for that. If you want to escape, you'll have to leave me."

The Triaxian merchant princess sneered in fury. "You really are too much trouble. Just like your filthy parents; it was an immense pleasure confirming the orders for their deaths."

Drianne swooped down, lunging at Naero with her long slender sword, aiming right for the heart.

Naero tried to sidestep, still too weak and too slow.

The scalpel-sharp blade snagged her right side instead, twisting through her ribs and into one lung.

Drianne pinned her to the vehicle. Naero gasped at the pain.

"See? You don't have to be in one piece for us to get the Kexxian Matrix from you. Perhaps this is better...doing it the hard way."

She withdrew her sword and pulled back slightly in the air, then leaned in close to gloat, whispering. "First I'll hamstring you, cripple your arms and legs. Then I'll drag your bleeding carcass onto my ship."

Naero backhanded her with all the strength she could muster.

Drianne recovered, her face bleeding, She lifted her sword.

Aunt Sleak stepped out into the open from behind the ruined vehicle.

She fired all four barrels of her khotgun at once, point-blank.

The energized microblasts shredded Lady Drianne in mid-air.

Pink mist and red bits scattered across the tarmac.

Aunt Sleak spat on the burning pieces and racked four more hyper rounds.

"That's for my sister!"

She turned to Naero with a grim smile, as Spacer Marine drop troops descended in waves down from the sky to secure the area.

"No one messes with our Clan, Naero. No one. Let our vengeance fall heavily upon them. By our hands."

Naero smiled sadly and staggered forward, feeling her eyes roll up in her skull.

She collapsed against her aunt.

55

Strike Fleet Captain Naero Amashin Maeris and the Alliance arranged their twenty-three fleets–and growing–into arcs of optimized, advanced attack formations. They poised to engage in combat.

After another desperate battlefield promotion, Naero now commanded the fifty ships of Strike Fleet Six.

The Alliance pushed deep into Triaxian Space, jumping in timed, coordinated waves, overwhelming key system after key system.

Enemy fleets panicked and fled before the Alliance's white-hot desire for vengeance, their superior might.

At last they converged on Heaven-7, one of the primary Triaxian Capital Worlds, in 360 degrees of interlocking, overlapping fire, ready to be unleashed.

They surrounded Heaven-7, and there the enemy chose to make their stand, outnumbering them with forty fleets. Two to one odds.

Yet they were mere numbers.

Admiral Sleak Maeris gave them immediate terms.

"All hostile forces, be advised. You face oblivion. In order to avoid further bloodshed and catastrophic loss of life, Triax Corps will completely dissolve and surrender all its worlds and territories to the Alliance, and assist in the inevitable annexation. All fleets and warships will stand down and return to their bases for re-assignment…or be destroyed. All prisoners of war, including Janner Maeris Ramsey and the outcast, the former Danner Maeris Ramsey, will be returned to the Alliance immediately, safe and unharmed."

Triax opened fire and launched fighters.

"We have our answer," Admiral Maeris said. "All fleets. Prepare to engage."

Strike Fleet Captain Naero Maeris stood poised to lead the vanguard of the first assault wave on the three hundred degree X-ray, Yankee, and Zulu arc, from the deck of the planetoid dreadnaught *The Hippolyta*.

First of the Dromon Class capital ships.

Their massive 16 m quad spinal guns hot as pulsars. Ready to open fire.

They were called *The Thirty Amazon Sisters*. Twenty-nine more dreadnaughts just like *The Hippolyta*, all the ships of her design, gathered from many clans.

Together they helped Strike Fleet Six lead the main Alliance assault at the center.

The Matayan Fleet arrayed on Naero's right. The Mining Consortium Fleet deployed on her left. Between them, Naero called to her screens of escort fighters.

"Wing Commander Saemar to our port, Wing Commander Chaela to starboard. Are the Ghost Dragon squadrons ready to enter the mix?"

"Affirmative, Sweetie. Captain Sweetie. Uh, sir."

"Ready to scorch, sir," Chae said. "Let the eagles dive."

"Accelerate and commence attack. All ships in. All batteries open fire. Fire at will! Deflectors full front. Take us in flaring. No let up. Remember *The Omaria*!"

A million voices took up the cry, with a vengeance.

"*THE OMARIA!*"

Strike Fleet Six and *The Thirty Amazon Sisters* tore into the enemy ships likes waves of destroying fire.

Relentless.

Undeniable.

Naero directed their every strategy, their every maneuver, crushing and ravaging the heart of the enemy's defenses like a piercing, killing dagger. All the other Spacer fleets closed in and shredded the rest.

They took fire, shields fluctuating. They rocked and wheeled and kept moving, destroying targets, key flagships, entire elements. Rapid-fire quad guns pulsing and blazing. Pulverizing all in their path.

The enemy tried to cut her off on her starboard flank.

The Matayan Fleet, under Prince Ellis, decimated the exposed pincer move. The miners under Admiral Nevano Kinmal, threw back an enemy counterattack on Naero's port side at the same time.

A score of Triaxian battleships mysteriously lost power and were quickly vanquished...and subsequently captured.

While the battle quickly degenerated into a rout and a slaughter, Naero checked in on her secure line with Baeven.

No sign yet of Jan or their former brother Danner. Baeven would continue to use his considerable resources to locate them both.

That remained a priority.

"All ships," Naero commanded, "regroup, tighten our formation, and arc back through sector Zebra 173. Let's cut another swath, people. Fresh ships up front, damaged ships fall back into the fixer clouds to refit."

She punched in the ship designations in a flash on her battle displays. "Fighter screens, optimize your intercepts. Continue feeding us data. The following six cruisers and fourteen destroyers, maneuver to guard our back door, convex tile formation Charlie-Golf-4. They're sure to hit us hard from behind once we come about. Make them pay. All ships, good work. Keep fighting. Fight well. Keep it tight."

56

The battles of the fierce Annexation War did not end at Heaven-7.

It took the Alliance several long months of decisive, determined fighting to finally defeat and annex Triax and its many hundred worlds.

Strike Fleet Six served in the thick of things until the bitter end.

Although they had to be persuaded, the other Gigacorps eventually abandoned Triax to its fate. They withdrew their illegal aid, refusing to lift a finger to help Triax any further after a certain crucial point. After the final horrific defeat, the tattered remnants of Triax's once vast fleets surrendered, or fled among the other Corps.

The oldest and worst of all the Gigacorps fell to ruin at last, and its trillions of slaves rejoiced in true freedom at its collapse.

Most elected to become part of Joshua Tech. Some joined the Mining Alliance. A few even elected to join the newly formed Matayan Republic.

Amid the joy of such great and terrible victories, Naero still suffered greatly from her own many personal losses. Her parents. Gallan. Numerous other family, friends, and acquaintances from the course of the Annexation War.

Jan was still missing. Their former brother Danner was worse than dead to her, and no word reached anyone–not even Baeven–concerning their fates among the remaining Corps.

They had vanished, entirely without a trace. Without even a rumor.

Baeven remained her best chance to find her brother. If he couldn't find Jan, it could not be done. Of that she was certain.

Naero did her duty with her friends and her fleet, but in the aftermath, she took leave from her Clan for a while and made an attempt to lose herself. Searching for somewhere she could hole up and find some kind of peace and solace, even if it was only for a time.

All wars were costly beyond measure. The Annexation War especially so.

Naero understood deep inside that if she was ever going to be any good to herself, or Jan–or anyone ever again–she first needed time to heal and recover on her own terms. In her own way.

She left word for her aunt and Intel not to worry.

She promised to return safely. She knew they would all be furious, but she desperately needed to get away.

For the sake of her own sanity.

Om was still somewhere in her mind, attempting to reform. Whether he could find a way to do so or not remained to be seen. She could feel him, but as usual, she couldn't do much to help.

He had sacrificed himself, saving them all from that mind control sliver.

She shuddered, just thinking about the damn thing lodged in her brain.

Her own terrifying abilities seemed dormant now, still completely burned out.

Yet she lived in fear of them most of all. They were part of her, and even the memory of them was tempting, intoxicating, exhilarating.

Better than any drug ever possible.

The seductive, corruptive rush of pure power.

Were she and Jan really like Danner? Is that what they would become?

In some strange way, their outcast former brother was now better off than her.

She still suffered from the constant temptation, the allure of the same absolute power that had driven him mad. Parts of her still yearned and even lusted for the abject freedom and chaos that such absolute power offered.

She faced down a thirst and hunger that could never be sated.

Somewhere, there had to be some kind of help. Perhaps the Spacer Clan Mystics. She just wasn't sure.

What she wouldn't give to be just a normal person once again…but she doubted if she'd be able to sustain that for long.

Finally, she did manage to find a place to hide, a place where she could run away from everything she was and everything that had happened, for at least a little while, to think and heal up.

For a few precious weeks.

Naero awoke from her usual strange and troubled dreams.

She turned over and kissed Emperor Ellis's beautiful closed eyes until his eyelids fluttered open, beneath the stunning vista of an immense open view screen on his flagship, oceans of stars twirling above their vast bed.

His broad smile flashed open at her, his voice groggy as he licked his lips.

She licked them, too. Soon they were kissing.

They pulled apart briefly, all but breathless; the huge chamber dark, shaded, and serene.

"What time is it, my lovely one?" Ellis asked her.

"I think…it's time for you to love me again, my sweet prince."

"Most gladly, my heart." Ellis smirked rakishly. "But you do know, full well of course, that it is 'emperor now?' And by the powers, did you not tear me to tatters enough last night? Again? It's a wonder I'm still alive."

Naero laughed and kissed his face slowly, teasingly avoiding his lips, no matter how he sought hers.

"Whatever happens, you will always be my sweet prince." She poked at his broad chest. "And your black heart cannot burst until I am finished with you." She played with his long hair with her free hand.

He stretched back among the pillows and sighed, one hand rose to caress her face.

"Naero, you are a fusion fire that I love being incinerated by."

She kissed his fingers, one by one.

Unfortunately, their time together neared its end.

She would desperately miss the comfort and joy she had found with him. Intensely so.

He looked up at her sadly, sensing her thoughts.

She stopped him when he was about to speak.

"It's quite all right, my prince. These past few weeks have been incredibly sweet."

"For both of us, my heart."

"But we both knew from the outset, going into this, that it could never last. We both understood that. But both of us are strong. We'll be fine."

Ellis turned away, his countenance darkened. He blew out a breath. "The fools at court are already lining up rows of mewling, scheming wives, concubines, and mistresses for me to choose from, like boring political appointments."

Naero giggled. "Good, eager Matayan girls of excellent breeding. More than happy to keep their young, virile emperor happy and content. Even if it does take a herd of them to take my place."

"Impossible. None can do so. A thousand could not."

"Very gratifying." Naero grinned, turned his face to her, and kissed him on the forehead. "Oh, don't be sullen about it. Pick some you like. Find the ones who can truly love and help you and your people. You will try to have some fun with your new harem, won't you, my sweet prince?"

Ellis smiled. "I do love it when you call me that. I will miss it. Whatever shall I do? There won't be anyone like you at court, N. Who'll be there to kick my bloody ass when it damn well needs it?"

She climbed on top of him, arching her brows.

"Just send word. I'll come rushing in for a sparring match. It's going to be all right, Ellis. Things are changing rapidly, but we both know your people aren't quite prepared for you to have a spack empress, or even a spack mistress just yet."

"How I despise that vile word," he said. "I wish it had never been made."

"But we both know I'm right. We've had our fun, and it's been grand. But we both have important things to do. You have a new republic to run." Naero sighed.

"Whereas I have to face the music and pay off my Clan debts to Aunt Sleak, before I can even hope to start my own life. You know she still blames me for the loss of her ships?"

"How is that even possible? It wasn't your fault. It was Triax–and in any case, your lost brother betrayed you all."

"Please, don't remind me," Naero said. "No one can find Jan or the outcast–not even Baeven. But that doesn't erase my debts. And Spacer Intel still blames me for Baeven escaping from them."

"Well, you did help him get away, right?" Ellis pointed out.

"Yes, of course, but that's all beside the point."

"Look, this is silly. You know I can give you all the credits you need. Why won't you take them?"

"Very kind of you, and sweet," she told him. "But no. This is a matter of Spacer honor. Among Spacers, it doesn't mean anything if I don't do it on my own, by my own wits and abilities."

"Is there anything I can do, my heart?"

Naero grinned wickedly and kissed his mouth long and deep.

They broke for air.

"If you don't mind, my sweet prince. I don't want to waste our last hours together...merely gabbing."

His eyes and his broad smile widened.

"Granted."

57

Naero clung to the edges of her tiny bunk panel, let out a long deep sigh, and stared down at the floor of her small, spartan quarters. She recalled sweeter days.

Haisha. Time to get started.

A mist shower and a new set of flight togs didn't change her disposition.

Even she wasn't prepared for the storm of anger and dismay unleashed her way upon her abrupt return, just as sudden as her disappearance.

Spacer Intel was still in panic mode, with Klyne freaked out completely–especially when she finally revealed that she now controlled the *entire* Kexxian Data Matrix.

On top of that, Aunt Sleak was ready to shoot her for desertion and avoiding her debts to Sleak and Clan Maeris.

Plus, Naero felt pretty sure that Aunt Sleak somehow guessed how and to where she'd managed to drop out of sight for so many days.

Naero's new punishment duty beckoned; best get to it.

She'd been busted all the way back down to being a just a regular Spacer once more. But in a way, she didn't mind one bit.

She would miss *The Shinai,* the fleet–miss her Clan and all her friends.

Nobody saw her off. It was just after four bells and everyone understood she was being punished. They were all still sleeping.

She walked through the quiet Joshua Tech starport, the night sky ribbons of stars, muted dark washes of pink and purple. The smell of starships wafted from every bay. The hum of various engines rumbled all around her.

She could tell what makes and models they were just by listening to them.

A lumbering mining freighter groaned starward.

Back to being a civilian, the new merchant ship she'd be serving on was called *The Bolabba.* An independent with a non-Spacer crew. They owed Aunt Sleak a lot of creds, and like Naero, they were working off their debt.

How bad could it be?

She reached the location and just stared.

Aunt Sleak had out done herself.

Naero wasn't even sure *The Bolabba* was a starship.

It was an ancient, black bulbous nightmare of some unknown origin. It looked like a bloated, gigantic Frenarian toad with its head cut off, and that was being way generous.

It had staggered in with the Shadow Fleets and then been left behind, still shot full of holes from repeated fighter attacks. But it looked as if it had been falling apart well before that, to the point of being salvage for scrap.

Could the damn thing even fly?

Let alone jump?

Even salvagers on Boon-3 would pass the wreck by. It was hardly worth melting down or sending fixers in to collect components.

Aunt Sleak and Zalvano appeared around one side, both of their faces set. Naero snapped to attention and saluted crisply. They had resumed their civilian roles as merchant fleet captains of Fleet Maeris–minus a few ships.

Stripped down from all her own rank bands, Naero returned to being just a regular Spacer. And that was fine with her.

"I promised Klyne I'd find the worst duty I could cook up to keep you in line," Aunt Sleak told her. "This is it."

Naero nodded. "I'd say you've outdone yourself, sir."

"I have." Sleak smiled, clearly pleased with herself. "First you have to help get this heap up and running again. Second, I hear the captain's a major son of a bitch, and this crew will not cut you any slack whatsoever. Let's get on board, shall we? Time to join your merry band."

They squeezed onto the ancient scrap heap. No sign of any crew. Junk and debris were all over the place. Bare wiring. Missing floor, wall, and ceiling panels everywhere. Weird musty odors.

They'd be stuck for months just getting her flying again.

Zalvano forced a cabin panel open. By hand. It got stuck half-way. "I think these are your new quarters. You can stow your gear in there."

Naero had a hard time seeing where. The filthy, greasy little storage cabin was stuffed full of panels from top to bottom. She kept waiting for rats or bugs or some kind of vermin to scurry out.

Naero clung to her small duffle. "I'll do that later, sir."

Zalvano called forward on his com. "Be advised, Captain Maeris is on board. We're making our way to the bridge."

Naero hung her head. She just had to get through the next three years. Serve out her time.

Despite Zalvano's warning, the bridge was dark when they walked in. It sounded like a gang of thugs fought and cursed further in out of sight, smashing and trashing everything with clubs.

Zalvano actually drew his blaster and fired into the celling to interrupt the chaotic madness.

"All right, you scum. Fall to attention. Get some lights on, damn it. Captain Maeris is here to inspect this hole."

Aunt Sleak strode forward. Naero trudged in behind, hesitant to even look up.

Pale yellow work lights flickered on.

Naero lifted her eyes.

Her friends stood there to either side.

All of them saluted her.

Chaela and Saemar, Tyber and Zhen, even Tarim.

All five of them shouted, "Welcome aboard, Captain."

Naero's mouth fell open. She turned to her aunt and Zalvano.

They just grinned.

Aunt Sleak knelt and activated the glowing, golden vertical rank bands that shot back up both her arms. "You've got your work cut out for you, but I think you can handle it, Captain Maeris."

"But you said the captain was a–"

Aunt Sleak smirked again and rested a hand on her shoulder. "You come from a long proud line of them. Serve your crew, your fleet, and your Clan well. Good fortune to you, Captain. Safe journey. Launch when you're ready. Sign the contracts and pay me a cred when you get the chance."

"But I thought I was being punished?"

"Who says you're not? I still get fifty-percent off the top for the next three years. Can you live with that?"

Naero grimaced; that was a lot of creds. "I guess I'll have to."

"Good. Now get your asses to work."

Her friends clapped and cheered. Naero hugged Aunt Sleak, then Zalvano.

Tarim spoke up, once the brass had left.

"Orders, Captain?"

Naero thought her face might pop, she grinned so hard.

"Hop to it, crew. Get this crate in the air."

Chaela became first mate and pilot; Saemar co-pilot and navigator; Tyber her tek and engineer; Zhen her medical officer; and Tarim, her gunner and security.

The Bolabba barely ran two hundred and fifty tons, with one main cargo bay and loading hatches fore and aft. Ship's boats consisted of one transport and one sloop. For defense it had one top pulse turret, and one bottom missile turret.

In her absence, her friends had doctored the ship to make it look worse than it was, all for dramatic effect.

Now they put her back to rights.

First, they re-attached the missing front nose section of the ship. The missing head of the toad, housing all of their com, nav, and sensor arrays packed into its streamlined length. After that, their ship looked much improved.

Once they and their fixers put things in order, Tyber proudly boasted, "Now she'll manage Jump-7."

Naero gaped again. "Jump-7 on an old junker like this? How is that possible, even with the fixers?"

Baeven stepped out of the engineering room, wiping his hands. "I've taken the liberty of installing a few modifications of my own here and there, with the help of your crew, of course." He winked at Tyber.

Naero ran to Baeven and hugged him.

"Consider it your birthday present, Naero. You've more than earned it. Tomorrow you come of age. Your mother would have been so extremely proud. Your father too." Naero kissed him on both cheeks.

"Thank you, Uncle Kean." His face grew very grave.

"I have not earned the right to that name again yet."

Naero took both his hands and looked him in the eyes.

"To me you have."

He looked down for a moment and smiled sadly, shaking his head. "Perhaps one day. Let's stick to 'Baeven' for now, shall we?"

"Sure."

"Your ship should be ready to launch by morning. You'll be needing this." Baeven placed a large crystal bottle of expensive champagne in her hands.

"Goody. The crew and I will have fun sucking this down."

Baeven chuckled. "No, it's not for imbibing, Naero. As captain, you must name your ship, and christen it with this by smashing the bottle against the nose of your vessel as your declare her new name."

"Seems like a waste."

"Just do it. It's an old custom." His tone grew serious. "What of your new abilities? Have any of them returned?"

Naero shook her head. "Not yet. Nothing. I'm beginning to wonder if I burned them all out completely somehow."

"It is possible, but I doubt it. Such abilities are unpredictable and dangerous to everyone around you. If any of those powers do return, you'll need to be tested by the Spacer Mystics. Perhaps they can help determine exactly what they are."

"I thought the Mystics wanted you dead?"

Baeven smiled. "It's a growing club. They'll need to wait their turn. Yet, perhaps they can help you with your problem. Are you still having the strange dreams?"

Naero nodded. "Every night."

"Contact the Spacer Mystics through Klyne; I'm guessing they'll be more than intrigued by your case. Well, I do happen to be a wanted man still, so I'd better be on my way. This is your time, Captain Maeris. Use it well."

"Of course. Will we see you again, Uncle?"

"Most certainly. If you're anything like the rest of the blasted family, you're bound to get yourself into some dire peril and require my assistance at some point in the future."

Naero laughed, hugged him again. Baeven departed.

Early the next morning, Naero signed the contracts and changed the codes of her ship's registry. Just before they departed, she went out with her crew.

"I name you, *The Flying Dagger!*" She smashed the big bottle against the nose cone, in a splash of delicious-smelling liquor and sparkling shards.

"First ship in the merchant fleet of Naero Amashin Maeris and friends. May you always speed true!"

They climbed aboard, sealed up, took their flight positions and prepared to launch. Naero lounged in her green captain's gel chair, behind her two pilots.

"Plot a course, Captain?" Chaela asked. "Our hold's full of trade goods your aunt sent over. Where to?"

Naero smiled. "Wherever the deals take us, my friends. Take her up, Chae. Just get us up there."

The Flying Dagger launched into a clear blue sky from the Yalana-6 starport, as the sun rose over that continent.

Naero drew her energy cutlass and saluted the heavens.

"To my parents and Gallan, in their memory and to their honor," Naero shouted.

As one, her crew raised their fists and echoed her tribute. They belonged to the stars, and the stars belonged to everyone.

That's what Spacers know.

THE END

Call for Book Reviews

Please Post a Book Review Right Now

Please post a review of this book if you enjoyed it. Twenty little words are all that is required. Twenty words that say what you liked about this book while it is still fresh in your heart, mind, and soul. Please do so now before something else makes you forget.

Here is the link for Naero's Run, if you purchased it on Amazon:

http://amzn.to/1eRKCOb

Please click on the link and post your review now.

Done? The author would personally like to thank you very much.

In this busy world, everyone is pressed for time. Our time is so important, no doubt. It has reached the point now where authors of nearly every stripe compete not only for sales, but to garner reviews from their readers. Some authors even stoop to "purchasing" reviews in social media that some services now offer in bulk.

In the publish or perish work of competitive fiction, book reviews from readers are golden, they have now become a commodity even.

Many in the business even consider book reviews as important, or even more important than book sales in some ways. As crazy as that sounds.

So therefore, trust us in this. If you have authors whom you adore, and you want to read more of their books in the future, please post as many reviews for them as you can in all of the forms of social media that you use.

Doing so will help your favorite authors in numerous ways that you cannot even possibly imagine. Never forget that fact. Book reviews matter a great deal.

And if by chance, if you find that there is something about this book that you don't like, and you really do want to help authors, before you slam them with bad reviews, try briefly contacting them instead with your concerns through their contact info that is always readily provided, or through their publisher. Most authors, especially new ones, are usually happy to get constructive criticism that will make their books better. Only hating, online trolls slam authors with bad reviews without giving them a chance. Real pros and fen contact authors directly with any valid concerns. That is the current, accepted etiquette. Please don't be a troll.

Amazon Kindle Review Link for Naero's Run:

http://amzn.to/1eRKCOb

Barnes & Noble Review Link for Naero's Run:

http://bit.ly/M9nRur

Smashwords Review Link for Naero's Run:

http://bit.ly/1gqHB6e

<u>Other Review Sites</u>

Good Reads

Google

Pinterest

Reddit

Delicious

Stumble Upon It!

Please post one or more reviews for Mason for each of his books, everywhere that you can.

Thank you once again.

Cheers,

Mason Elliott

<u>Please Join my New Releases Mailing List</u>

Please use either of these two links:

http://bit.ly/1L2QpUL

or,

http://eepurl.com/FgQzv

Be first to learn about my new releases. I promise that I will not share your info or spam you. I will use the list only to inform you about my publishing projects.

<u>About the Author</u>

Mason Elliott grew up loving Science Fiction and Fantasy in all of their myriad forms. That love has transferred into his dedicated writing. Like most writers, he lives a spartan lifestyle and yearns to devote his life even more to his writing, and someday retire on the Pacific coast. So be a fan, buy his stuff, and enjoy!

Like and follow Mason on Facebook where he does most of his blogging at:
https://www.facebook.com/masonelliott731

or,

http://on.fb.me/1lx7XXc

And on Twitter at:

http://bit.ly/1nsqOSs

Visit Mason Elliott's website at

http://masonelliott.authorcontacts.com

And for even more information on Mason Elliott and his works, visit High Mark Publishing online at: www.HighMarkPublishing.com

ACKNOWLEDGEMENTS

First I would like to dedicate this book to my own Spacer clan: my family.

Next, I would like to thank the kind folks at High Mark Publishing for supporting and believing in this series. Special gratitude to managing editor Jennifer Cummings, the publishing board, and publicist Josh Marten. Without their kind and attentive help, this project might not have become a reality. And finally, I would like to thank my online writing group, my fellow toilers in the salt mines, who always have my back.

Mergeworld

Book One

Mergeworld 1 Amazon Link: http://amzn.to/1uboBDC

by Mason Elliott & Garan R. R. Faraday

David Pritchard woke up gasping from one nightmare and went straight into another. A terrible agony tore through him as if the universe twisted him inside out.

Then he snapped back again.

What in damnation had just happened? Something…was very wrong.

Startled, groggy, it only took an instant for his bleary mind to figure it out.

Flames engulfed the front of his college apartment building. The stench of smoke, and the sounds of screams and breaking glass outside, only confirmed it.

He felt dazed, and blinked his scratchy eyes. The first thing he instinctively reached out for was the framed picture of his dead parents.

That was the last picture he had of them, taken a few years back, right after he started college in South Bend.

They hugged and smiled at each other in medieval garb at the Bristol Renaissance Faire up in Wisconsin. The picture froze both of them happily in time, retired in their forties. Unlike many parents that age, they weren't divorced and they still loved one another. One of their Ren-Faire pals had taken that picture for them on their digital camera.

The same camera retrieved from the car accident on the Illinois highway on their way back home from Bristol. A tractor-trailer jackknifed in the heavy rain and took them away.

The same weekend David begged off going with them.

He had blown that picture up in Photoshop, printed out an 8 x 10, and bought a nice oak frame for it. He kept it with him wherever he went. He'd die before he'd part with it, fire or no.

All that history and pain flashed through David as he clutched their picture close to him in the dark. He didn't even have to see it, just cling to it in his hands. That picture always sat prominently behind his small alarm clock on his night stand with his smart phone and wallet while he slept. That was how he found it, even in the semi-dark. He also grabbed his phone and wallet.

His clock normally flashed bright green. Power outage, probably from the fire. And the backup battery must have gone dead. Light switches? Nothing, of course, due to the fire.

The growing reek of smoke triggered his desire for self-preservation. Once he got out, he could call his friend Mason Tyler, who lived in a duplex over on Allen Street. His buddy Mace would help him.

Somewhat more awake now, David struggled not to panic. He staggered out of his room like a robot. His lanky, five-eleven frame stumbled down the hall toward his front door. He stubbed his little toe hard in the darkness. A second later, he grunted and cursed the sudden blinding spread of pain, but kept moving.

Oh, hell. No way out the front.

Dangerous ribbons of smoke curled violently through the metal front door frame and snaked up across the ceiling like an upside-down waterfall. The paint of the metal fire door already bubbled and blistered. David choked and swallowed hard.

If that door had been wood, his entire apartment might have already been completely engulfed. He might not have even come to. He saw no sense in touching the steaming door knob.

The apartment building stairs acted like a natural chimney, funneling the fire and heat straight up.

A window–climb out a window. He was only on the second floor.

His three richer roomies were already off on spring break for the next week, to the Bahamas or some such. Their parents could afford such junkets. David could not.

He suddenly realized two very important things. First, the fire hadn't spread to the back part of the apartment building yet.

Next, he was only wearing navy boxers and a gray T-shirt over his shaking frame.

Early April in South Bend, Indiana, could be any weather from sun and sixties to a flippin' blizzard.

Clothes. Only seconds to throw some on. Even in the dim, flickering orange light spilling out of the thick curtains, he spotted his laundry basket on the couch.

The smoke in the living room grew thicker. He put his precious picture, smartphone, and wallet down for only a few moments.

Jeans. On. Socks. On. He snatched up his thick blue, gold, and green hoodie from the back of the old couch where he usually left it, and pulled into its soft, warm comfort. Stocking cap. Popped on his head. Wool scarf.

Around the neck. He sat down and jammed on his old gray Nike running shoes, feeling a pair of thin gloves and keys in his hoodie pockets still when he bent over.

Ready to ride, or, at least, climb out the back window to escape burning to death.

He stuffed his folks' picture, wallet, and smartphone into his dark green Jansport backpack with his pad, gel pens, and a few books. He zipped it all up.

To the back window. He pulled the curtains aside and yanked the big panel open.

He jumped slightly at the sight of some guy who had already climbed down the back of the building from the third floor. Their eyes locked, only a window screen between them in the dim, pre-dawn light and the cold morning air.

The guy looked utterly terrified.

"Watch out!" he warned, trying to keep his voice low. "Those things are killing people. They're everywhere!"

"What things?" What was this guy freaking out about?

The guy jolted, wide-eyed, and then choked.

A bloody iron arrowhead jutted out the front of his throat. In the time it took them both to blink, another arrow punched through the front of his chest, out his T-shirt. The poor guy's mouth gaped and worked. Then his eyes rolled up white. He fell backwards, head down.

David grabbed for him but missed, his hands blocked by the barrier of the screen. He tore it away and stuck his head out the window.

He spotted strange movement down in the darkness.

Two dark, twisted, hunched-over figures loped in on bandy legs and clawed feet wrapped in fur and rags. They were smaller than humans, about four to five feet tall, and very skinny and wiry.

Whatever they were, they were definitely not human.

One of them slit the dead guy's throat from ear to ear with a long, wicked-looking rusty knife.

Blood spurted bright black in the night.

The other creature sniffed the air and snarled up at David with a greenish-black, twisted, inhuman face. Long pointed ears stuck out of holes in its ragged hood. It had a big warty nose, and gleaming green eyes. It gave full draw to the same kind of short, black bow of jagged horn that the other one carried.

The creature took dead aim at David.

And fired.

Mergeworld 1 Amazon Link: http://amzn.to/1uboBDC

Mergeworld

Book Two

Amazon Link for *Mergeworld: Book Two*: http://amzn.to/1neuq0x

by Mason Elliott and Garan R. R Faraday

"Several of the enemy mage prisoners have escaped," a runner came to warn them. The young trooper looked terrified.

Mason drew his Spillers. They would have to be enough. After the bath, he didn't have all of his other guns. And there wasn't time to go after them.

It also worried him that he still felt–off his game, somehow. Something was still very wrong with him, but he couldn't figure out what. Perhaps that was merely what sorrow and depression felt like.

Blondie shook the terrified runner. "Calm down. Tell me what you know. Which prisoners? How many of them?"

"S-six, six, I think. They tried to free the rest, but the guards on the scene shot two down. Then the enemy mages fled this way, and started killing everyone they could find with magic."

Troops screamed, and close by to the west, magic blasts went off, and the sounds of battle and further bursts of magical rapidly sped their way.

The runner continued to stammer, "The tall n-n-necromancer is leading them. Five others. I don't know their names. As soon as they broke out, the duty officer sent me after you two and the Thul woman."

Blondie let the runner go. "Try to find the Thul. Go. Keep spreading the alarm."

"Yes, s-sir!" The young runner looked only too happy to keep running.

"They're coming for us, aren't they, Blondie?" Mason asked, hefting his Spillers.

Blondie clenched both fists, and violet magefire flared up to his elbows. "Yep. Just like I said they would. How do you want to do this, Mace?"

"Hmmm…too many to hit them head on. Let's go at them from the flanks. I'll hit them on the left."

His blond friend nodded. "Then I'll take them on the right. The necromancer's going to be the toughest of the lot. Let's peel off the other five, if we can, and then take him on together."

"Sounds good, Blondie. Let's ride."

They skirted around to either side, trying to stick to cover and stay out of sight. Mason quickly lost sight of his friend.

It did briefly occur to him that this would be an excellent time for Blondie to turn on them all, and help the mages make good their escape. But at this point, Mason had no choice but to keep trusting his good friend.

Blondie said that his abilities were returning.

He could tell them anything he wanted. How would they know if it was the truth or not?

From the sounds of things, the militia troops were putting up a pretty good fight and delaying the enemy at least somewhat. Each precious second they could hold them back, more troops would pour in.

Yet even as Mason got into position to attack, the enemy mages continued to push through, causing death and destruction all around them, and leaving many casualties in their wake.

Startled troops could slow the enemy down, but they would be hard pressed to stop six enemy mages bent on a rampage of devastation.

They were lucky that it wasn't all thirteen of the mage captives on the loose.

At Blondie's urging, Major Bill had spread several of the captive mages out to other nearby, secret locations–beyond the limited range of their prisoners' telepathy.

Mason spotted the enemy. The necromancer strode out in front with another sorcerer. A pair of enemy wizards marched slightly behind them on either side, guarding their flanks and watching the rear.

Blondie stepped up and raked the enemy left and the middle with violet lightning that knocked four of the six off their feet, and stunned the two flankers.

The first flanker on the other side turned to attack Blondie. The second one raised his hands and his eyes got big when he saw the Pistolero step out and aim both of his pistols.

Click! Click!

Nothing. Mason's guns wouldn't fire. He cocked and pulled the triggers again.

Nothing.

By then the one mage was charging Blondie, exploding anything that was made of wood around him. He sent the shards and splinters and whirling debris at Blondie, while the necromancer and the other sorcerer still looked dazed and tried to regain their feet. And the mage facing Mason shot greenish-yellow flames out of his hands at all before him.

Mason dove out of the way, tucked and rolled out of sight, and then crouched and ran. The enemy wizard would be on him in seconds.

Finally he came to a building and ducked inside. He scrambled out of sight into an adjoining back storage room and ducked down. He tried his guns again. Still nothing. Why was this happening,? Now of all times?

Blondie needed him out there.

Maybe if he reloaded. Yeah, that would do it.

Slowing his breathing, doing his best to stay calm, he broke out his spare cylinders for his guns and swapped them out. He was fast at it, but every second counted.

He went back out into the fight. As he expected, the fighting quickly turned Blondie's way, and blasts of magic nearby showed where the foes were pursuing Blondie hard and blasting everything around him. Blondie fought back as best he could, but from what Mason could tell, his friend was outnumbered four to one.

He raced that way, not even trying to stay under cover this time. He had to catch up quickly, and take them from behind, if possible.

Mason sped around a building and almost slammed into the same enemy mage as before. This one seemed to be holding back and protecting the rear of the other three while they stalked Blondie.

Mason had intended to shoot them on sight, but he clobbered the mage from behind now that he was right on top of him. The mage grunted and dropped, unconscious.

Pistol-whipping worked better in this instance. Mason dragged the mage back out of sight and quickly gagged him, and bound his hands and ankles behind him.

At this distance, Mason would not have any trouble taking out the other three with one or two shots, once he spotted them again. And their spells gave them away when they fired. Hopefully, Blondie was staying ahead of them.

Mason rushed forward once more, spotted several troops closing in with bows and crossbows, and motioned for them to go around and close in from one side or the other.

Finally he spotted the necromancer and the one wizard, crouched down and making plans of some kind.

Mason took aim at them with both barrels.

Click. Click.

Crap, not again. What the hell was going on?

Even worse, the necromancer turned and locked eyes with him.

"There's the other one. Let's get him!" All of their hands glowed with magefire.

Mason turned and ran for it. Dark lightning and exploding ice covered the area he had just been in.

His foes were right after him. Archers tried to fire upon the mages, but they swept the troops away from their positions with blasts of power.

A stone or outcropping of brick caught the toe of Mason's boot. He hurtled down upon his face, and tried to roll back up to his feet.

The third enemy mage stepped out right in front of Mason.

Now, the three of them had him fairly trapped.

"Kill him!" the necromancer roared.

The wizard still hesitated an instant. Then he prepared a spell, his hands beginning to glow brighter and brighter.

They were only a dozen or so feet away. Mason hurled his useless pistols at the wizard.

One missed as the fellow dodged to one side.

The other smacked him squarely in the face and dazed and bloodied him.

Mason expected to be cut down from behind by the other two enemies any second.

He glanced back just as the two stood ready to unleash their spells.

Amazon Link for *Mergeworld: Book Two*: http://amzn.to/1neuq0x

Please enjoy the following teaser from The Citation Series, Book 1, *Naero's War:*
The Annexation War

THE CITATION SERIES, BOOK 1, NAERO'S WAR:

THE ANNEXATION WAR

Annexation War Amazon Link: *http://amzn.to/1gmxGQk*

by Mason Elliott

Naero's flagship, *The Hippolyta,* was one of the latest, Dromon Class dreadnaughts. These warships were fashioned out of dense, iron-nickel planetoids, not less than half a kilometer in diameter. Incredibly tough and rugged on their own.

It took the most powerful mining plasma-borers–working in precise conjunction with construction fixers and an army of teks–months to hollow out armored crew quarters, lift and transport tubes, launching and loading bays. Next came space for power cores, sublight engines, jump drives, backups, gravitics, life support, sensor arrays, communications, navigation, weapons, main bridge and backup bridge.

Set in the exact heart of *The Hippolyta* were its signature big guns. A quad of the largest production guns ever constructed on any ship of war: Four, *16 meter*, rapid-fire, particle beam cannons.

Cannons any larger than that exploded, melted, or otherwise were not feasible within the limits of current tek and materials. Thirty-six secondary batteries, assorted specialized weapons and gun emplacements, and forty-five advanced fighters.

Seven hundred and forty able crew, including a full Rifle Company of two hundred and forty Spacer Marines, and all of their equipment, vehicles, and gear for ship's security and rapid response deployment. Strike Fleet Six's Marines came from the 3rd Spacer Marine Division– known as *The Death Eyes*–because of their superb snipers and their overall, excellent marksmanship ratings. Marines made up a third of the warship's complement.

Their motto: *If We Can See It…We Can Kill It!*

The main bridge was a massive armored dome constructed on top of the dreadnaught's big metal, rough-hewn orb, protected by heavy blast doors, and the latest, most advanced shielding in the fleet. Within, the circular bridge was laid out in four levels under the huge dome, a dome sixty meters high.

Each bridge tier was separated by the height of a few steps from one to the next. The inner three levels could rotate in any direction, independent of the others.

The fleet captain's command nanochair and station occupied the highest tier. Each bridge station had its own secondary shielding, in case enemy fire penetrated the shields, the blast screens, and the hull.

In combat, bridges were routinely targeted, for obvious reasons.

From that primary vantage point, the strike fleet captain could direct battles in three hundred and sixty degrees, through an advanced, battleholo display surrounding her, full zoom data-feeds, constantly updated by battle AIs. Naero could manipulate the displays by nanosensors programmed into the fingertips of her nanosuit gloves.

The battle display system also recognized her voice pattern, and would respond to voice commands, or commands punched in manually through pads on her command chair, or via other backups.

The next bridge level down from hers held the secondary bridge stations: Helm, Weapons, Communications, Navigation, and Scanning, spaced out equally along their ring.

The third ring held all of the twelve tertiary bridge stations, that monitored, controlled, and coordinated all of the ship's other important functions:

Engineering
Gravitics
Life Support
Power Supply
Security
Shields
Medical
Jump and Sub-light Drives
Damage Control
Alliance Fleet and Intel Communications
Main Computer
Launching Bays

The fourth ring went to the two powerlifts, leading from the bridge to the other movers, decks, and levels of the ship. All lift and access points throughout the ship were constantly guarded by two battle-ready Marines, stationed on either side.

If a warship was boarded by enemy assault craft during a battle, invaders could be cut off and eliminated between decks, before they could reach a vital area.

Today, Strike Fleet Six had a mission–a simple one.

Captain Naero Maeris and her fifty warships proceeded to probe the next system on the outer, port arcwall of the Alliance advance at Beleron-4.

A routine run. Current intel assured them to expect little or no Triaxian presence or resistance.

By any stretch of the imagination, Beleron-4 was a nothing world, in the middle of nowhere, with zero, nacha–absolutely no strategic or tactical value whatsoever.

Checking it off the list on the pacified worlds of the Alliance system-hopping schedule was more-or-less just a formality.

But it still had to be done. And Naero and her lot drew the duty at random.

So why did Naero's sense of warning go bonkers?

After they jumped in, simple three-stack, Delta-India-3 formation, the reasons for alarm grew perfectly clear.

They came in right on top of twenty Triaxian fleets of the enemy's latest warships.

And a gigantic new flagship–as huge as *The Hippolyta*–the advanced design of which did not even register as existing.

It had never been seen before.

Naero shot to her feet, kicked her command nanochair back out the way and sent it down into the nanofloor of her top-tier bridge control station.

She instantly called her battle display holos up in spinning, horizontal glowing ribbons and rings all around her.

Data relays went wild. Her fingers flashed among the highlighted screen arcs, taking control of them and their parameters.

Multiple warnings sounded, and with excellent reason.

Nothing about this was good in any way.

Haisha! Twenty enemy fleets could chop them into confetti–well before any other Alliance forces could even jump in to help.

No strategy, no formation could possibly save them against superior numbers such as these.

"All ships, full withdraw. Emergency retreat on this vector, in Charlie-Romeo-7, cone-ring formation. Shields and all weapons full front and hot. Maximize all targeting profiles on the lead attacking enemy elements–they'll be on us in seconds. Whatever happens–we fight until our carriers and some of our ships can break free and jump out behind us. Get the carriers out first!"

For a split second, everyone braced for the sheets of flame that would quickly overtake and overwhelm them.

The Annexation War Amazon Link: *http://amzn.to/1gmxGQk*

Please enjoy the following teaser, from the next Spacer Clans Adventure, Book 2:

NAERO'S GAMBIT

A SPACER CLANS ADVENTURE

NAERO'S GAMBIT

MASON ELLIOTT

NAERO'S GAMBIT

by Mason Elliott

Klyne set the huge Mystic testing room on board *The Kathmandu* to muted gray. Smartwalls, floor, and ceiling, Naero saw no equipment, no padding.

The lights were set low.

From experience, Naero knew that in a training room, just about anything could pop up out of anywhere.

She wore nothing but her black Nytex flight togs.

To her surprise, Klyne and his two adepts wore dark gray Nytex togs also, but with hoods and masks pulled up over their heads. Only their keen eyes showed.

All three of the Mystics appeared to be in top physical condition, including Klyne.

One of the adepts was female, with huge green eyes and light freckles across her nose. The other was male, with the black slanted eyes of the Lii-Kim Clans.

If black was the color of Spacers, the Mystics traditionally wore gray.

They all sat with their legs crossed in lotus fashion, focusing their abilities through meditation, and mental discipline. They formed a triangle, each side about three meters apart, with them at the points.

"Follow our instructions," Klyne said. "Take your place among us. Sit in the center; sit as we do. Face the instructor."

A circle of white light appeared at the center of the triangle. Naero walked over and sat down in it, facing Klyne. Her skin barely began to tingle.

A wider ring of similar light appeared, including the instructor and his two adepts.

Every hair on Naero's body went stiff with electric force.

"You have chosen to come before the circle of Spacer Mystics to be tested for Mystic training. Speak your name."

"Naero Amashin Maeris."

"You agree to be tested?"

"I do."

"I am Klyne, the instructor. My assistants are Adept Iselle, and Adept Makita. We shall refer to you as Adept Candidate Naero. Follow our instructions. Respond only if asked to respond. If you require any medical attention, it will be administered at the end of the testing. Until then, you are expected to endure and continue to do your best. If you understand, say yes."

"Yes."

"The training will begin. Defend yourself."

Without warning, Makita's attack smashed into her.

She blocked one or two out every four or five blows.

A snapwheel kick sent her flying twenty meters, nearly winding her.

The only things that saved her at all, once again, were the experience and knowledge she gained from her training sessions with Baeven.

Makita proved stronger and faster than her, but he still paled in comparison to the outcast's terrifying prowess.

Makita charged her.

Naero met him part way.

She took several punishing strikes, but flipped him hard to the ground.

He swept her legs.

They tangled on the ground, wrestling, slipping out of holds, twisting like snakes. They pummeled each other all the while.

They broke, crouched low, and launched themselves at each other again, like Telurian fighting blue cranes.

Naero landed a whipkick on the side of Makita's head.

He clipped her under the chin, grabbed her leg and ankle and swung her hard into the floor, stunning her.

She struggled to get up.

For a few dizzy moments, she couldn't.

She rose up and staggered back into her fighting stance.

She half-smiled.

"Come on."

Makita bowed his head, just slightly, and drew back.

"Defend yourself, "Klyne said again.

Naero whirled to face Iselle.

Too late.

An invisible force slammed into her arms and torso, flinging her back.

She rolled with the strike and came back up into her stance.

Iselle fought her from a distance, punching and striking with her hands in rapid combinations.

Naero struggled to advance, to close the distance between them, while heavy, unseen blows rained down on her from every direction, knocking her one way, and then the other.

"Telekinetic combat," Klyne called out. "Try to sense and block the blows. You cannot see them. Reach out with your battle senses, with your mind. Feel them coming. Counter and deflect them. True masters can fight thus, without even moving, simply by concentrating."

At least Iselle still had to physically move in order to project her attacks. That was some help.

Closer. Get closer.

Iselle thrust both hands forward violently.

A wall of force drove Naero slowly back. She pushed against it, slowing it even more.

"Resist. Focus on the energy before you," Klyne told her, "before it smashes you into the far wall. Fight back. Defeat it."

She rolled to one side and then the other. The barrier felt solid.

Naero leaped up four meters, felt the top, and flipped herself over it.

Iselle withdrew a step, cupping both hands loosely on the sides of her face.

Spinning orbs of pure telekinetic force shot out, rapid-fire.

Naero barely perceived them where they warped through the air; they made explosive popping sounds.

She tried to dodge them. One whirred past her head like an invisible ball at high speed.

The next clipped her left shoulder, spinning her aside.

Another knocked one leg out from under her.

She kept her feet and ducked, weaving to either side in turns.

Iselle directed her attack at Naero's feet.

Naero lost her footing, slipping and sliding on what felt like a bunch of invisible ball bearings cast beneath her.

She tried to roll back to her feet, but panes of force battered her from all sides, keeping her off balance.

It felt like being a rubber ball, bouncing around in a box that someone shook.

The sides of the box rapidly closed in.

They tightened all around her, threatening to crush her.

She couldn't breathe.

Iselle released her without warning.

Naero sprawled, gasping, face down on the floor.

"I'm somewhat surprised," Klyne noted. "Preliminary tests demonstrate no psyonic aptitude or innate talent to my trained senses whatsoever. That in itself is very rare. After your battle with the former

Danner entity, we simply assumed that you would exhibit some kind of psyonic ability."

"I burned myself out dealing with the entity. I burned both of us out. I'm a nud once more." She admitted it openly. "None of my former abilities have returned."

So she wasn't psyonic anymore. Not even a teknomancer. Disappointing, but not the end of the universe.

"Yet I sense something incredibly strange within you," Klyne said. "What could it be?"

Was it Om? He was still inside her somewhere. He had not emerged again either.

"Take your place at the center of us once more. Face me again."

Naero did so, resisting an urge to massage several bruises.

Klyne positioned himself directly in front of her, sitting lotus fashion just like her and the others.

"I'm going to attempt to merge directly with your mind telepathically, one of my gifts. I'm also an Auralcognitor. Once I link with your mind, I can sense any type of psyonic energy field you might have, active, passive, or latent. I might even be able to trigger or bring them out to the surface. There might be some discomfort. Shall we proceed?"

"Sure."

"Do as I do. I will show you how to place your hands to effect the mind merge."

Klyne cupped his left hand firmly behind the base of her skull.

Naero followed his lead.

He placed the fingers of his right hand on precise spots on her face.

Thumb on her forehead, directly between her eyes.

Index finger on her left temple.

The next two fingers curled slightly in front of her left ear. His smallest finger hooked at the point of her ear and jaw.

As soon as Naero placed her right hand the same way, she gasped slightly.

Thin hairs of what felt like burning hot energy threaded their way slowly through the layers of her awareness.

She could feel Klyne connecting with her thoughts, joining their two minds.

The dull ache continued to grow.

"You should be feeling the initial discomfort. Hold still. Keep focusing. Almost there. Almost..."

A spike of pure agony exploded within her skull.

Naero screamed, transfixed as if by lightning.

Through the torment, a voice awoke in her mind full-force.

Protocols unlocked and engaged. We...are.

Interface...partial.

Om awoke, reacting instinctively with fear and vast power.

Threat detected...Protect all access.

Neural net...INTRUSION. UNWARRANTED.

LEVEL 1.359 DEFENSIVE RESPONSE.

An intense blast wave of white-hot psyonic energy fanned out rapidly from the epicenter of her immolated mind.

Naero continued to scream.

As if far away in the distance, Klyne and his two adepts also shrieked.

Naero blinked, her eyes and mouth frozen open.

She lay with her head to one side, in a puddle of her own mixed blood and spittle.

More pain struck her when she attempted to move.

Blood continued to stream from her eyes, ears, nose, and mouth–a bloody mess.

It felt as if a fusion grenade had blown her head open.

She reached up with her hands, to make sure her skull was still intact.

Some kind of noise.

Warning alarms sounded.

A ship. Yes, they were on a ship. The Spacer Intel Ship *The Kathmandu*. She was...being tested, for the Mystics.

Something had gone terribly wrong.

Naero focused, getting to her hands and knees.

She heard other voices, groaning and whimpering.

Makita lay sprawled in a broken tangle, blasted across the room. His gray clothing had been shredded and scorched into tatters. He choked and coughed.

To the other side, Iselle fared little better. She lay convulsing, blasted, scorched, a yellow-white bone of her forearm sticking out of her wrenched flesh. One side of her face was blistered, her red hair burned, some of it still smoking. She trembled and shuddered in pain and terror.

Naero looked around for Klyne, and found the instructor in a burned, bloody heap, lying beneath a dark red smear on the far wall. His hands were charred black, and he was missing fingers.

Naero could not walk. She couldn't even stand. She crawled to Klyne as quickly as she could.

He still lived, just barely.

Then she noticed the intense effects of the blast, all around the room, less than a meter up.

A massive expanding ring of Cosmic force had sliced into the duranadium hull of the smartwalls, punching a deep crease right through them where they buckled, all along its full diameter.

The force of the strike disrupted all systems. The entire training room was compacted, crushed, and heavily damaged.

Rescuers struggled to force their way through the various ruined doors and access panels.

Naero's Gambit Amazon Link: *http://amzn.to/1lx5Tyy*

Please enjoy the following teaser from the next book in The Citation Series, Book Two:
The High Crusade

THE CITATION SERIES, BOOK TWO

NAERO'S WAR:

THE HIGH CRUSADE

Amazon Link to *The High Crusade*: http://amzn.to/1DbFD5F

by Mason Elliott

General Walker's Marines from Bravo Command maneuvered into position under the cover of darkness using their stealth gear.

Naero agreed to slip in ahead and bait the trap, in her battlefield role as Shettana–*The Dark Angel of Death.*

Get ready, Om. The show's about to start.

I will need some time to prepare, concentrate, and focus enough of our energies in reserve, before you deplete them all.

Just get ready and keep us ready. I'm going to set our game plan in motion.

I will do all that I can to assist. Call upon me when you require me. Good hunting, Naero.

Thanks, Om.

The invaders would do anything to have a chance to destroy or capture her.

She was–in fact–the actual, literal bait, and the trap was being set for an entire invasion force of Ejjai elite, ravaging the Corps border world of Tholos-4.

No local planetary army, military, or militia had been able to stand before the horrific onslaught of the alien invaders.

The Ejjai hammered the local landers into submission with advanced artillery, orbital bombardment from Ejjai fleets, and close assault gunships and gravtanks.

Then the terrifying collection process began, and all the living, wounded, and dead were hurled into the shrieking, whining processing blades of the robotic meatships.

The horrible sounds of the meatships warred with the screams of their countless victims.

Given time, Ejjai mass cloning factories and robotic ship and weapon-building factories would also be established onworld.

The murdering bastards had already wiped three major cities and their mixed populations off the surface of the hapless planet, before Naero and the Marines could even deploy on world.

The enemy left those lost cities little more than red, blackened, burning scars and stains that could be viewed from orbit.

Nothing left alive.

Ejjai hyaenanoids loved carrion.

Every man, woman, and child of any kind, species, or age that the enemy captured was routinely tortured, killed, and processed into rotting ration blocks in the horrific, robotic meatships of the invading aliens. That included any sentients, pets, livestock—anything and everything that was meat.

The meatblock rations were only frozen to keep them from breaking down, and decaying completely.

Hatred was too gentle a word for what most humans felt for the Ejjai invaders and their extreme methods. Spacers, landers, and each of the other known races that encountered the Ejjai quickly learned to feel the same way.

This vile, uplifted, intrusive and opportunistic species needed to be completely exterminated, wherever it was encountered.

The invaders proved that they were incapable of co-existing with any other living things.

The Ejjai could only dominate, torture, and destroy all life that they encountered, anything they could sink their teeth and claws into. Uplifting them, and giving them advanced weapons and starships had only turned them into a galactic abomination, an interstellar menace, a virulent plague.

An utter nightmare.

One that needed to end for the poor people of Tholos-4.

Naero and her Marine allies were here to see to that.

It was amusing that the Ejjai always saw themselves as invincible, the supreme warriors.

Shettana and Bravo Command quickly intended to disavow the foe of such jaded notions, time and time again.

The Marines of Bravo Commander were the textbook picture of professional warriors. A legend among all the known systems.

Naero loved serving with the elite of the elite. Together they made a fantastic team.

Even the Ejjai had learned grudgingly to fear them from their initial engagements, and the proof was there.

Every invader force that came up against Bravo Command had been completely wiped out–in record time. And then Bravo quietly packed up and headed on to the next world, ready to do it all over again.

The enemy struggled to halt the Spacer advance and throw it back.

They tried everything they could think of.

Increased enemy numbers.

Different tactics.

New weapons–traps and tricks of many different kinds.

The Ejjai generals turned themselves inside out trying to find a solution–way to achieve victory against the Spacer advance.

Bravo Command slipped in and ruined the invaders' sick, twisted party, every single time.

And Shettana, The Dark Angel of Death, used all of her amazing, Mystic powers and abilities to help the Marines keep up the pressure, and drive the enemy to terror, madness, and distraction.

General Walker worked closely with Spacer Intel, always making sure his leathernecks had the latest high-tek toys, weapons, and armor that came online.

As a result, they landed an entire Marine Division on Tholos-4 and slipped into position, without the enemy even knowing they were there yet.

By the time the Spacer Fleets swept in to destroy the enemy naval forces–Bravo Command would already be implementing their plan to put the foe down hard and fast on the ground.

Three Marine infantry regiments, one artillery regiment, plus specialized units of meks, armor, and air-to-ground support.

The ghosts of Bravo Command spread the impending Shadow of Vengeance and Death over their foes like an unseen net, without any knowledge or awareness among the invaders themselves.

Bravo and Shettana prepared for another stunning series of lightning attacks.

All became poised and ready, while the heedless enemy celebrated their vile victories and atrocities.

Naero struggled to remain silent as she slipped in among the foe. Death and damnation to any invader who thought they could invade the human sectors with impunity, death, and Cosmicide.

On every world, the invader needed to be taught that bloody lesson.

Naero strode right into the belly of the beast.

Alone.

Defiant.

Confident in her skills and abilities and all of her comrades depending on her and backing her up.

Her cloaked combat armor made her virtually invisible. The Ejjai could not even smell her.

She used her gravwing to slip into the most heavily guarded command and control bunker the enemy possessed. With her skill and her tek, she could crawl upside down on the ceilings like an unseen insect.

Her miniature vidcams and audio collectors fed data to Intel in real time, covering everything she saw.

Naero's small contingent of cloaked Intel fixers and microdrones stayed close, ready to disrupt key enemy systems and communications when ready, planting microbombs and detonation devices as they went.

The Invader High Command celebrated their latest triumph with what one might expect from them–a huge, decadent, disgusting feast–held within a shielded bunker.

They set up their victory celebration within a huge underground arena, probably used by the Tholosians for some kind of urban or regional sporting event.

Ejjai got drunk on stinking, fermented grog made from human blood. They shipped it in from the meatships by the tankerful.

Under the bright lights of the hi-tek arena, tens of thousands of Ejjai feasted and celebrated their latest victories. The enemy generals praised their troops and used the huge arena vidscreens to plot out their next attacks on the three nearest Tolosian cities.

On the center of the playing field, Ejjai transports and appropriated trucks had also hauled in and dumped huge piles of human corpses from the local population for their undefeated troops to feed on.

Piles of fresh and not so fresh meat, diverted from the enemy meatships to help sate the troops in large numbers.

One of the piles was all dead children and infants.

Even worse, to Naero's horror, some of the bodies in the various meat piles were somehow still alive. They twitched or cried out in pain and terror. Some weakly attempted to crawl away, despite broken or missing limbs.

The Ejjai quickly seized them and began tormenting them even further, laughing hysterically at the sport. They stabbed, cut, and skinned them alive—or otherwise got creative.

As Ejjai were wont to do.

Ejjai were among the vilest, most disgusting creatures Naero had even encountered.

She resisted the very strong impulse to cut loose on them right then and there.

But she couldn't–not yet.

These monsters needed to die. Every single one of them.

And very soon, she would have a direct hand in launching the attack that would accomplish just that.

The timing had to be just right, so she steeled herself.

The generals. Reach the generals and stay ready.

Six Ejjai generals held court like warlords at huge tables overflowing with comconsoles, sensor stations, map screens, and piles of loot. And the bloody remains of horrific, eviscerated meals.

All Ejjai clone troops were female. Smaller male Ejjai concubines were kept around on leashes for fun, for the leaders. They even dressed them in human clothing and poorly fitting human lingerie.

As an oddity, one of the generals even had a human male dressed up as a concubine. But the poor guy apparently had to be kept in a heavily guarded pen off to one side–to keep all of the other Ejjai from devouring and murdering him, most likely in that order.

Naero circled around the generals and studied the arena, trying to devise the best way to take them all down.

She listened intently to the plans the enemy generals were making, feeding it all to Intel.

"So, are all of the atomics and genocide devices in place yet?"

Another general pulled up a mapscreen displaying all of their installation of such devices planet wide.

Naero instantly transmitted all of that data directly to Spacer Intel as well–priority alert.

Intel and Bravo Command were most likely already neutralizing the most vital elements of the enemy plot. These genocide devices could be scanned and located from orbit. But it was always good to be sure, and to know their exact locations.

The Ejjai generals scoffed. "We will be ready for anything the enemy can throw at us in less than a day," one of the other Ejjai generals boasted.

"They won't know what's going to hit them until it's too late."

"Good, very good. Speed things up if you can. Get it all up and ready."

"Don't worry, sir. We will be more than ready to deal with their so-called Bravo Command—and their spack witch."

All of the Ejjai generals had a good laugh and congratulated each other.

The lead general stepped up to a waiting podium and addressed the crowd.

"Great news, sisters! We have it on good authority that the spacks are sending their precious Bravo Command and their spack witch Shettana against us."

Lots of cursing and booing about that roared up.

Their lead general continued. "This time, we are more than ready for them!"

Huge rounds of applause to that.

"Let me just say that we have some heavy duty surprises of our own ready and waiting and in store for our enemies. We can't wait for them to get here—and have them all for dinner!"

That brought an even bigger round of cheering, cursing, and applause.

"We will engage the spacks in a matter of days, and with our increased numbers and new weapons—I say we're going to kick their asses and stomp them bloody. We will gut them! I want all my girls out there to feast on spack Marine flesh until you puke!"

Further rounds of cheering and vile responses.

"We will ferment their blood in our huge vats and get drunk on it!"

More horrendous rounds of cheering and applause.

"And once we have captured their filthy spack witch, all of you will watch as I personally cut her up and rape her with red-hot knives, and torture her to death over the course of an entire week. She'll sing to all of us with her screams. Then I myself will feast upon her guts, and eat her heart while the light in her eyes fades. I'll crack her skull open and eat her brains!"

The Ejjai went crazy.

"Wait until we post *that* on the webnets for the spacks and the skinners to watch! I promise you victory. We cannot be defeated. And we will sweep the human skinners and all the other inferior races into our meatships and out of all existence. They are our prey! Yet another galaxy that shall fall to us and our mighty masters!"

More about their mysterious masters. Interesting.

Furious cheering continued in waves.

"So my warriors. Feast on meat until you vomit, and then feast some more. Then prepare for battle as we crush our foes and ravage the rest of this world. We shall drown it all in blood and swim in it! Prepare for our ultimate victory! Our time has come. None can stand against us!"

They erupted in an orgy of celebration and vile gluttony.

Fights broke out among the meat piles, and the Ejjai fought with and murdered each other in their frenzy.

The lead general returned to the others, rubbing her claws together eagerly in the midst of the chaos.

"My sisters, I have a special treat that I've saved just for us, at this exact moment. Please, enjoy my precious gifts to you all." She motioned to a large knot of troops off to one side among some gravtanks.

A full squad of Ejjai in heavy battle armor led out six terrified human women, all of them naked, and extremely pregnant.

None of them had a mark on them. Yet.

But from the looks on their pale faces, they all knew very well what the enemy generals intended to do with them. Each of them was heavy with child in the later stages of pregnancy.

That they had remained unspoiled and unharmed up until now would quickly change for the worse–the worst fate imaginable.

Although they were unbound, there was no chance for any of these captives to break free or escape on their own against so many foes.

The generals each glared at them and gloated. The Ejjai generals slavered and drooled, snapping jaws and smacking lips.

Each general had a set of rusty, bloodstained butchering tools that they began to place out in front of them in heady, eager anticipation of their coming feast.

Then the squad of Ejjai troops guarding the six women suddenly staggered a few feet away as if drunk.

Some melted into slag where they stood.

Other Ejjai troops exploded.

The six human captives looked around in confusion.

The next instant, they all vanished.

The six Ejjai generals shot to their feet in stunned surprise.

They couldn't even speak, but a few flung cleavers and knives at the spot where the captives had stood.

Their weapons fell harmlessly to the ground.

All of this was captured and displayed on the big arena screens, and slowly attracted the attention of the astonished crowds.

Then Shettana appeared as if by magic, right before the lead Ejjai general, resplendent in her full Angel of Death mode. She was all dressed in black, shining black hair flowing in the wind, violet eyes burning above her mask.

Twin blood-red katanas crackled and hissed in the damp air, at the ready in either hand.

413

Every eye fixed on her—while the mini-gravpods from her fixers whisked the six cloaked, female captives away to safety.

Naero only had to buy few more seconds for them to make it out. Fierce Marines waited nearby to take charge of them and keep them safe.

With the six captives out of the way, at last Shettana could go to work.

"I have come for you, filthy Ejjai cowards. I am Shettana!" she cried.

She rammed both of her swords through the lead general's eyes and out the back of the Ejjai's scorched skull.

Two of the generals tried to run.

The other three tried to attack her.

It did not matter.

Bolts of scarlet lighting tore forth from both her blades, ripping and blasting the other five into charred pieces of meat and bone.

Naero cloaked and shot away, as the area around the tables was engulfed in torrents of enemy weapon fire the very next instant.

Then the gravtanks, gunships, transports and other vehicles lined up nearby began to explode.

Naero projected multiple holos of herself all over the arena and in the in the air, drawing fire in all directions.

She used *the voice*, her words booming and echoing from several directions.

"EJJAI FILTH. PREPARE TO MEET DEATH. FOR SHETTANA IS THE DARK ANGEL OF DEATH, AND HAS NO FEAR OF MURDERING COWARDS."

The Ejjai fired in panic from so many angles that they cut down each other by the hundreds—just as Naero planned.

Fear began to infect them.

Gouts of red lightning lashed into the arena stands from several directions like gigantic whips of destruction. The devastation flung dead and dying Ejjai everywhere in a cyclone of slaughter, adding to the total chaos and confusion.

"NO MERCY, EJJAI SCUM. NO ESCAPE. FEAR IS MY MOTHER, DEATH MY SIRE, AND I THEIR DAUGHTER! YOU CANNOT HARM ME. THERE IS NO ESCAPE FOR YOU!"

Just as the enemy started to figure out they were shooting at holos and murdering each other wholesale, Naero merged with one in her mirror images in the midst of hundreds of Ejjai in the arena stands.

Multiple thin rods of red Chaos energy shot out from her, fanning in a diameter of thirty meters.

First she impaled hundreds of the shocked invaders.

When she spun, the red blades chopped them all into smaller gory chunks and pieces.

Torrents of unleashed Ejjai blood suddenly gathered and swept down the arena, carrying others away in a sudden red rushing tide of gore.

Naero cloaked and flashed away again.

More enemy fire stormed and tore at her former position.

She took the place of another holo, and sent forth a sweeping hurricane of of Chaos bubbles and orbs of every shape and size into another section of the stands.

The explosions collapsed that entire section. Wreckage toppled inward.

Next she appeared on the field before the horrendous meat piles, in the midst of hundreds of more frantic enemies.

Half of them flung their weapons away and ran in terror before her as she raced toward them. So much for the valiant Ejjai.

"STAND AND FIGHT, SCUM!"

Naero surged and fought with the mob of foes, sweeping one way and then the other, cutting them down by dozens, by scores.

She moved among them so fast they could not focus their attacks.

Then she would abruptly change direction and sweep another way before they could hem her in.

She unleashed more scarlet lightening strikes.

She sent random Chaos blasts into packed pockets of foes.

At times she just whirled and passed through them with her swords fully extended, mowing them down in lines and bunches.

Once she had shattered them completely, she merely turned her back on them and began walking away quickly and with determination, toward the nearest exit.

Naero set her shield pod full on.

Three enemy tanks roared at her, cannons blazing.

Naero dodged and deflected their blasts into the stands.

Two gravtanks she exploded with Chaos bombs.

The last she sliced the last in half with her swords and kept walking calmly, straight through the burning wreckage as the gravtank exploded directly behind her to either side.

She ignored all enemy fire directed at her, kept walking, and cut down anything stupid enough to attempt to stand before her.

She crackled with destroying red lightning as she passed into one of the exit tunnels, laying waste to anything before her.

The enemy regrouped and poured into the tunnel in hot pursuit.

Just as Naero hoped they would.

Another kill zone. How convenient of them to all bunch up for her.

She turned at bay, just before exiting, and focused all of her energies in an intense Chaos blast cone.

The massive detonation tore the tunnel apart and blasted shredded pieces of the packed invaders out the other end, right before a massive fireball that followed hard thereafter.

Naero cloaked, and called out over her secure link.

"You guys ready? I've got them primed, but I'm also almost out of juice."

"We're in place and ready to join the show, Shettana. You okay? Do you need us to extract you?"

"Negative. I can finish my part. It just takes a lot of energy to sustain attacks at this level. You guys know that. Did Intel take care of those genocide devices?"

"Almost all accounted for."

"All right, I'm setting up for my final show. They'll take the bait, all right. You guys hit them hard when they do."

"Hard as we can, Shettana. You know us."

"I sure do, and I can't wait to watch it all go down–right from the front row. Copy that. Make the legends proud, Bravo."

She took up her position in the center of the fallen city nearby, just outside of the shattered arena.

She formed a Chaos construct around her that duplicated her and her every move.

Her construct became a scarlet, giant version of herself, semi-transparent and fifteen meters tall, red and glowing with huge blazing swords.

She stomped on a meat ship and slashed at it until it exploded.

Then she attacked the clone ship factory next to it.

"FACE ME, COWARDS. SHETTANA SHOWS YOU HER MIGHT. SHOW ME YOURS. FACE ME AND PERISH!"

Yet in actuality, her energies waned with each passing second.

It wasn't like being back on Janosha where there was limitless Cosmic energy to tap into. Away from the Mystic Homeworlds, Naero's energy levels and her abilities were not infinite or limitless. She made a good show of it, but even she could not sustain these levels of attacks for very long.

The entire enemy invasion roared to life , and locked on, bunching and sweeping her way, to engage her from all directions.

The Ejjai went insane with fury.

Up in the skies above and beyond Tholos-4, the Spacer navy sent the invader fleets spinning down in flames.

Thousands of Spacer Marines suddenly materialized out of the black at key points and positions.

Phantoms who owned the night.

The black was their domain, their element, and they surrendered it to no one.

Bravo Command unleashed a torrent of concentrated, interlocking fire against the bunched up invaders. Veils of destroying fire, artillery, and ordnance–a deluge of precisely timed destruction that no living thing could possibly survive.

Within a matter of minutes, a quarter of a million Ejjai invaders flashed and flared into a sweeping typhoon of white-hot death that overtook them.

Naero had done her job.

Completely drained of all her mystic energies for the moment, she could barely stand.

Even as she staggered away, a full platoon of gigantic Sterodans in phaze armor appeared all around her.

They piled on and overwhelmed her with their greater mass, and several shock charges that hit and rippled through both them and her. The shock charges rattled Naero's teeth in her skull.

The Ejjai and their mysterious masters still wanted her and the KDM alive and intact, apparently.

Naero grinned.

Yet another trap, and she had stumbled right into it.

This time, the enemy thought they had her at last.

Yet Naero knew something they did not, and called out into her own mind.

Om–you're up. They've got me.

Take these bastards down hard and fast!

Amazon Link for *The High Crusade*: http://amzn.to/1DbFD5F

Please enjoy the following teaser from the next Spacer Clans Adventure, Book 3:
NAERO'S FURY

NAERO'S
FURY

by Mason Elliott

Naero still hadn't done it much, but going into a direct trance to enter the Astral Plane shouldn't be all that difficult. Master Vane had shown her how once. And she had gone there lots of times in her sleep, in her mind, to speak with Khai, using their astral crystals.

Before her friend Khai had vanished without a trace.

Yet she had never been completely trained in astral travel, and didn't know that much about exploring or moving around. Master Vane had taken her there once, just to teach her the basics and give her his marker. Many other times later to spar with her.

If nothing else, she could probably focus on his marker and locate him.

Zhen had roused Naero and reminded her it was time. And that she and Shalaen would monitor her while she was in the astral trance.

Naero focused her mind and abilities, controlling her breathing. Remembering the little she had recently learned.

Within several minutes of focused meditation, she open her eyes and found herself floating in the Astral Miasma, the nebulae of energy. She hugged her knees to her chest in her astral form.

Om spoke to her, even more easily here than in her own mind before.

I have accessed some of the Kexxian Matrix's data files on The Astral Plane. Like everything else, they explored it quite extensively.

Om, I'm naked here. I'm not complaining–but just tell me–how do I put astral clothing on again?

You control everything here by imagination, and force of will. Concentrate on your favorite clothing and they'll appear.

That's easy.

She looked down and saw her favorite Nytex flight togs, programmed just the way she liked them.

Naero blinked, spinning and twirling in one spot, turning upside down.

Why can't I move more than a meter at a time in front of us?

You're not used to this reality. So it's not clear to you.

The air around her looked opaque. Not mist. Not smoke or vapor. And it glowed slightly with its own bluish-gray light.

In the twilight she glowed softly blue-white with her own light. From within.

"I once heard rumors that the Mystics could travel and send messages this way, but I thought it was all just a myth."

Since the other planes are entire universes within themselves, it is said, they are all nearly infinite. Thus, it is difficult to pin point any kind of location or person unless you already know them.

Naero instinctively tried to stand up, but there was nothing to stand on.

Then she recalled Master Vane's Marker, and it appeared right before her. Where she found him, she would find the other High Masters.

At least she deserved a chance to be heard by them all. To try to explain herself and her actions. What happened with the obelisk was clearly not her fault.

But they would still blame her for it–especially Mater Vane, who seemed to blame her for everything since Hashiko's death.

Naero could not simply stand by and let the High Masters decide her fate without herself being present at her trial, in some way at least.

She focused on the crimson and black star more and swept forward, seemingly at great speed.

She came to an abrupt halt, like a starship coming out of jump at its destination.

The opacity around her partially melted away. She proceeded forward, opening her visual field far wider. She made out the area around her as the miasma peeled back.

Slightly below her, she saw spheres within glowing spheres, all spinning within greater spheres.

Her own sphere, glowing white-blue, suddenly surrounded her like a glittering soap bubble.

Yet it did not pop when she poked at it.

One sphere in particular, the largest, glowed and pulsed blood red, containing a withered old man with a long beard, pacing impatiently.

Burning eyes vanished and re-appeared at random all over his bald head. The red sphere absorbed Master Vane's marker.

Was this his true form? What he really looked like?

His scarlet sphere was also flanked by two smaller spheres with figures inside them.

Om made a calculated guess.

His current guardian adepts, no doubt. The ones you rescued from the enemy Darkforce generators on Janosha.

I think so, Om.

At most times, every High Master had at least two champion adepts protecting him or her, each of them very close to mastery themselves. Just as Hashiko had been.

Naero studied Vane's new guardians for the very first time, and tried to see into their spheres.

Something about each of them did seem strangely familiar.

One of Vane's adepts, the male, appeared to be so deep dark black, he could be a singularity. This adept's sphere was flat black on the surface and barely transparent.

If Naero had been able to breathe, she would have gasped.

Instead she simply raised her hand to her mouth.

She recalled that she had seen many of these adepts long before.

In her dreams, nightmares, and crazed visions. Perhaps even on the Astral Plane somehow.

Vane's other adept was the white female, the exact opposite of the other. So brilliant and blindingly radiant, she could be a pulsar. Her orb was like a high intensity bulb, blinding and almost completely crystal clear.

It occurred to Naero that during her initial testing, Klyne had male and female assistants as well.

She couldn't guess what the significance of that pattern was all about. Perhaps just some weird Mystic, egalitarian tradition.

Then why weren't any of the High Masters female?

Everyone seemed to ignore her where she floated.

The next larger sphere, farther away, glowed silver-blue.

If she focused intently on it, she discovered she could zoom in with her third eye–her mind's eye.

Within that silver-blue sphere, a silver man sat serenely, neither young nor old. Master Tree, in his purest form of order.

Two smaller guardian spheres flanked him.

Master Tree's female adept glowed with intense blue energy in a deep blue sphere.

The male likewise glowed with vibrant green force within a green sphere, a shining sword sheathed down his broad, athletic back. He seemed very familiar somehow.

Naero did a double-take. Long blond hair. Green skin. Big glowing sword.

Yep. In the flesh—or—astral form at least.

It was Khai! She was sure of it. He was alive.

Had he actually succeeded in his great task of forging his mystic sword in the heart of a gigantic pulsar? Was that it on his back?

Naero gasped again. Now that she knew what he looked like, Khai was also the dreamy green hunk from many past, pent up nightmares. The one who kept sticking his astral sword through her head.

What did it all mean? She wasn't nuts enough yet?

Now she knew for certain she needed serious help.

And to do some serious dating at some point, once-and-for-all.

If the Mystics continued to let her live.

Khai must have sensed her inner turmoil, or thoughts, or maybe just her concentration on him.

Mr. Green-god even glanced her way for a second, looking just as confused and puzzled by her sudden appearance.

Neither of them had ever met the other in person.

Naero covered her face with one hand and looked aside, withdrawing her sphere suddenly further away.

How fricking embarrassing.

She crept forward again. Slowly.

The third and final sphere glowed golden, and contained an equally golden child within, energetic and bristling with lightning. He bounced back and forth inside like a gigantic electron.

Master Jo of course.

Two flanking spheres.

One of his adepts had no clear form, eyes gleaming within a shifting, flickering miasma like the Astral Plane itself. His female counterpart shifted shape from one fantastic creature to another.

When she suddenly made out their voices, she could sense that an intense debate had been doing on. One that still continued.

"We cannot be certain in this matter," the golden child insisted. "We do not dare act in any rash way."

"Agreed, High Master Jo," the serene silver man added. "She might yet be another Trickster from what I can tell."

"Yes. Quite possible, High Master Tree."

The old man in the blood red sphere blustered impatiently. "Fools! Always conspiring against me. Taking positions opposite of mine for no reason but to anger me. I've been telling you all along, this child is clearly the Great Destroyer—long foretold. Our duty is clear. She is a threat to all existence. To multiple dimensions. She must be eliminated, at once, before she can grow even more powerful."

"High Master Vane," Tree said. "None of us can be sure of that fact. Including you."

"I am."

"You are always certain when it comes to destroying someone," Jo added. "Your pure Chaos answer to everything. Destruction or Creation."

"It works."

"No. It doesn't. It only delays and worsens the inevitable," Tree said. "The Universe shall have its way. We all know this. You were mistaken with the last savant when he appeared, and now he remains at large–a renegade beyond even our control."

Baeven? We're they referring to her uncle?

Vane rolled his eyes. "Idiots! The Renegade is the Trickster, I say. This child must in fact be the Great Destroyer. Just look at the powers roiling within her. They will surely corrupt and overwhelm her entirely and drive her mad in the end. She will go berserk on a scale that makes her recent outbursts feeble and puny by comparison. She must perish now, while we have a chance to put an end to her. While the only crimes she has committed include destroying an entire planet, and another of the vital obelisks!"

"We still don't understand the purpose of the ancient obelisks. And we've studied the mysterious disappearance of Janosha, and we still cannot be certain in any conclusive way, that she had anything to do with it."

"Really? Who else could it be then? Planets like Janosha aren't in the habit of just obliterating themselves suddenly for no reason at all. Everywhere she goes, destruction follows!"

I cannot allow this.

Quiet, Om. Don't do anything. I'm trying to listen.

Naero…they're discussing our destruction. The Chaos Master means to destroy us.

Master Jo continued to protest. "You can't just kill off every entity that manifests Cosmic Abilities such as these. Our universe is peppered with them. We must continue to locate and guide them–not find excuses to execute them. Like the Others have told us, Tricksters often appear to oppose Great Destroyers. Without the former, final victory is never possible. "

"High Masters," Tree said. "This young woman also possesses the Kexxian Data Matrix. We cannot destroy her without destroying it. Intel and The Spacer Council of Elders value our wisdom, but even they would not agree to such action."

"Regrettable," Vane said. "Yet I cannot take the risk. I have decided this matter on my own."

"You have no such authority on your own," Tree insisted.

"Idiots! I cannot stand by and allow our galaxy–perhaps our entire universe to be destroyed–just to satisfy your foolish, philosophical, and theoretical whims."

Master Vane turned to his adepts. "My finest students, obey me. Delay these fools. Keep them occupied whilst I act for the good of all existence."

More rapid than thought, the male dark ensnared the blue sphere and its satellites in coils and tendrils of darkness. While the bright female enveloped the golden sphere and its companions in waves of of pure light.

Naero tried to pull away, but in her panic she did not know where to go.

High Master Vane sped straight at her with impossible speed.

I must act, Naero.

No, Om. Please, this is already bad enough. Don't do anything.

I cannot comply. I must defend us!

Naero went down on her hands and knees before Master Vane. She called out, using *the voice* to project her words.

"Please, Master Vane. Do not attack me. I only wish to be trained to control my abilities. I have struggled hard to do so. I still don't understand what happened with the obelisk."

Vane bore down on her, arcs of pure scarlet energy bristling around him.

"Far too late for that, monster. Nothing is ever your fault, is it? Now, you must perish for the good of all. I told you this hour would come."

Instinctively, Naero drew back again, trying to evade his attack. She rose within her receding sphere.

Vane closed in once more, gathering his powers.

"Don't do this," Naero begged. "Please. Help me. I know I can't fully control all of my abilities yet. I'm trying as hard as I can. I can't be responsible for what will happen if you attack me. I can't control myself."

"Yes, and look at the results? Countless lives crushed and eradicated. Janosha vaporized–an entire planet. You must never be allowed to reach your full potential. Now–monster–hold still and embrace your fate."

Naero put her hands out before her, holding her palms out defensively. Pleading.

"No. Don't. I can't–"

"I know, Maeris. You can't help yourself. That is why you are *an abomination!*"

Vane smashed into her, piercing all of her defenses as if they were shattering glass.

In the distance, she sensed that Master Jo and Master Tree finally broke free.

Too late.

Master Vane attacked, trying to overwhelm her with raw power.

He pummeled her with impossible blows.

In the end, he beat her up badly, but only succeeded in knocking her around once more.

Om roared in their mind.

Kexxian defense protocols unlocked and on line.

An energized, glowing armor of some advanced origin formed around Naero like a hi-tek battle suit.

Naero saw out of her third eye as it awoke and burst into radiance like a blue-white star.

Master Vane came at her once more, all of his powers focused through his primary scarlet, burning eye, centered in his forehead.

All of his other flaming eyes closed as he concentrated, his skull wreathed in weird cosmic flames like a mane of cosmic fire.

"See how powerful you have already become? No adept could have withstood those lethal attacks. We must finish this now, before the others can interfere."

"Please, Master Vane. Please–I'm begging you–please, don't do this."

"Maeris, just as I foretold–you shall fall before the greatest of all Cosmic attack techniques. And I am one of the few who have ever learned to master it: The Eye of Annihilation!"

The same Chaos technique that had destroyed Hashiko–even she couldn't control it properly.

A massive blood red beam of destroying Cosmic force shot straight at her.

It all happened so fast. Naero heard Om screaming.

Reflection defense. Analyze incoming cosmic assault. Duplicate and reflect attack tenfold!

Just before the incoming blast vaporized her, a blue-white beam shot out of her own third eye to war against Master Vane's powers.

The Cosmic flows flared intensely.

Naero screamed as if her body and soul were being sucked through the eye of a black hole's needle.

The wide blue beam quickly drove the red beam back to its source.

At the last instant, High Master Vane cried out in terror.

"Impossible! There can be no such–"

The destroying energy ignited on contact.

A massive detonation on the Astral Plane blinded the area within a few light years.

High Masters Jo and Tree barely managed to withdraw and shield the others. All of their spheres shattered.

Pure cosmic energy punched into High Master Vane right before Naero's eyes.

It drove him back like a white-hot comet.

He struggled against it with all his might.

To no avail.

The reflected attack obliterated High Master Vane to glowing ash and dust, screaming in the wake of his own annihilation.

Vane's dying force of will echoed off into the universe.

Naero would have caught her breath if she had any.

The outcome left her completely stunned for a shuddering instant.

Om…what did we just do?

We had no choice, Naero. My sole purpose is to defend our current form.

Naero stared down at her hands in terror. Tendrils of Cosmic energy rippled and still curled off of her body and her sphere like smoke.

Om…*Haisha!* We just killed a High Master of the Spacer Mystics!

Please enjoy this teaser for The Citation Series, Book 3:

Naero's Trial Amazon Link : http://amzn.to/1oaMNE3

NAERO'S WAR:

NAERO'S TRIAL

Naero's Trial Amazon Link: http://amzn.to/1oaMNE3

by Mason Elliott

On the third day of Naero's trial, the Prosecution and the Defense made their final, closing statements.

Master Jo spoke first, for the Defense.

"In the final analysis, I would both conclude and insist that Naero Amashin Maeris has proven herself time and time again to be an honorable Spacer, and that her word is without question. She is also vital to the survival of her people in many important ways. Naero Amashin Maeris is a noble, invaluable warrior and a proven leader who has served the Clans and the Alliance well, in both peacetime and war. A Mystic Champion who is now part of the great and mysterious Cosmic Prophecy, long foretold. There is still so little that we do not know about those prophecies; who can say what her role will be in the end?"

Master Jo paced a bit. "And on a very basic level, she is a Spacer. As such, she has the right of all Spacers and all sentients to defend herself, to the death, against anyone who attempts to kill her. Reluctantly, she only resorted to lethal force when High Master Vane attacked her with the intent to destroy her, and take her life. Even after she had tried to get away from him, and begged him repeatedly not to attack her.

"She cannot not be convicted of murder for defending her own life against someone trying to kill her. Those are all many good reasons why you must see fit to exonerate her of these erroneous charges. We cannot take the life of this hero."

The Defense finally rested.

Master Tree was given the final word in the trial for the prosecution.

"Hero? First, let me also revisit the reckless side of this renegade, outlaw Spacer, who fled from justice and had to be brought back by force to face her crimes in shackles, in order to keep her from getting away once again. On several occasions, Naero Amashin Maeris has proven herself to be dangerous, unpredictable, and out of control. By her own words, she has more than once declared that if she ever lost control and became a threat to any of her people, that she herself agreed that she should be put down–and destroyed.

"The cold blooded murder of a High Mystic Master has not demonstrated this fact readily enough? Beyond all doubt? If she can slay a High Master of the Mystics so easily, how much more is she a danger to all? And she even admits that she cannot control her abilities. Her very existence has become such a clear and present threat that it cannot be ignored and must be dealt with. I repeat, she has admitted on several occasions that her powers can go out of control and be very dangerous.

"Next, she also clearly admits that she killed Master Vane. Now, of her own accord, she claims that she killed him in self defense. But she has thus far presented no single shred of proof of that. She claims that Master Vane attacked her, attempted to kill her, and that she killed him, as she now conveniently claims–in so-called self defense. And I remind everyone in this court, once again. It does not matter who she is, what she is, or whatever else she has done. No one is above Spacer Law.

"Not even the infamous, Naero Amashin Maeris."

Tree took in a breath and clasped his hands behind his back. "What are the facts, therefore? A High Mystic Master lies dead, murdered by his own student, who openly stated that she could not stand him. Who openly admitted that she killed him. Nothing else can be proven, beyond those facts. Nothing else exists as fact. And this case must only be decided, based solely upon the facts. Nothing else.

"A Spacer on trial for her life could readily claim and say anything. Merely stating something does not make it true. That does not prove it to be fact. According to the facts of what is known, Naero Amashin Maeris is clearly guilty of murder, and will undoubtedly say and do anything possible in order to get away with her crime. As anyone logically would, in order to escape punishment, justice, and execution."

Naero fumed. Haisha! What the hell did they expect her to say? Yes, I offed the asshole, I loved it, and I'm a fricking monster. Go ahead and kill me?

I wish that weren't so painfully funny, Naero.

Me too, Om.

Master Tree went on to demand that the jury uphold one of the key tenets of Spacer Law and Spacer society:

"Spacers do not murder other Spacers and take their lives! Naero Amashin Maeris is not above that law. Naero Amashin Maeris broke that solemn law. And like it or not, the law demands justice. There is no way around that law and no way to escape it. That law demands that she face the ultimate punishment for her being guilty of committing the ultimate crime!"

Tree emphasized his final point with a single, upraised index finger. "That punishment is immediate Death, by execution. To be carried out by beheading, at the hands and the blade of the Mystic Enforcer!"

The Prosecution rested its case.

Admiral Klyne looked slightly pale as he instructed the jury of Mystic Elders to decide the case and announce their decision after their period of deliberation.

Naero went back to her cell in silence feeling sick, unable to meet Khai's utterly heartbroken glance. She felt stunned and numb. She didn't know what to think. All that she could do was await the jury's decision, along with everyone else.

Yet it was her fate alone that was being decided.

But when she thought about it further it wasn't just her fate.

Everyone waited for eight long hours.

Naero could neither rest nor sleep.

Then everyone was summoned back to the court room.

A decision had been made. The jury had arrived at a verdict in her case.

Admiral Klyne announced, "All rise for the verdict to be read."

They did so.

The jury leader stood up and read their decision.

"According to Spacer Law, and based upon all of the facts and evidence presented, we the jury find the defendant, Naero Amashin Maeris, of Clan Maeris…guilty of murder in the death of another Spacer."

Naero gasped, nailed to the bedrock of the planet itself in almost complete shock.

Guilty meant…

Master Tree rose up. "This Mystic trial has ended; it is over. A verdict has been reached. Without question, this grim crime is punishable among our people by death. Under the circumstances, the sentence is to be carried out immediately and without delay."

Naero, I can–

Shut up, Om.

Naero gasped and covered her mouth with both hands as she sobbed and went down on one knee.

Then she dropped her hands to her abdomen and her eyes met Khai's in explosive waves of desperate horror and regret.

Their child from their love within that distant star barely grew within her. Now, no time remained to tell Khai all that she needed to before he performed his duty as the Mystic Enforcer.

Before he took her head…ended her life, and the lives of his own family.

Naero Amashin Maeris clenched her fists, and rose up with her head held high to meet her fate with her eyes clear and wide open, if that was what must be.

Amazon Link for *Naero's Trial*: http://amzn.to/1oaMNE3

Edition Notes

If you do not see this edition note here in this spot on the copyright page and on the very last page of your ebook or print version of this title, then you are not getting the final, polished version of this novel that the publisher, editors, and author intended for you to receive. Please contact either the publisher or the author via their emails or websites if you do not see the following update code:

High Mark Publishing Update Code K2428E

www.ingramcontent.com/pod-product-compliance
Lightning Source LLC
Chambersburg PA
CBHW071638260626
47170CB00001B/149